JACK OF
SPIES

JACK OF SPIES

DAVID DOWNING

SOHO CRIME

Published in the United States by

Soho Press, Inc.
853 Broadway
New York, NY 10003

Library of Congress Cataloging-in-Publication Data

Downing, David, 1946–
Jack of spies / David Downing.
p. cm
ISBN 978-1-61695-268-6
eISBN: 978-1-61695-269-3
1. Scots—Fiction. 2. Sales personnel—Fiction. 3.
Selling—Automobiles—Fiction. 4. Espionage, British—Fiction.
5. Man-woman relationships—Fiction. I. Title.
PR6054.O868J33 2014
823'.914—dc23   2013038342

Interior design by Janine Agro, Soho Press, Inc.

Printed in the United States of America

10 9 8 7 6 5 4 3 2 1

To Nancy

JACK OF
SPIES

The Blue Dragon

♠

At the foot of the hill, Tsingtau's Government House stood alone on a slight mound, its gabled upper-floor windows and elegant corner tower looking out across the rest of the town. Substantial German houses with red-tiled roofs peppered the slope leading down to the Pacific beach and pier; beyond them the even grander buildings of the commercial district fronted the bay and its harbors. Away to the right, the native township of Taipautau offered little in the way of variety—the houses were smaller, perhaps a bit closer together, but more European than classically Chinese. In less than two decades, the Germans had come, organized, and recast this tiny piece of Asia in their own image. Give them half a chance, Jack McColl mused, and they would do the same for the rest of the world.

He remembered the Welsh mining engineer leaning over the *Moldavia*'s rail in mid–Indian Ocean and spoiling a beautiful day with tales of the atrocities the Germans had committed in South-West Africa over the last few years. At least a hundred thousand Africans had perished. Many of the native men had died in battle; most of the remainder, along with the women and children, had been driven into the desert, where some thoughtful German had already poisoned the water holes. A few lucky ones had ended up in concentration camps, where a doctor named Fischer had used them for a series of involuntary medical experiments. Children had been injected with small-pox, typhus, tuberculosis.

The white man's burden, as conceived in Berlin.

McColl had passed two descending Germans on his way up the hill, but the well-kept viewing area had been empty, and there was no sign of other sightseers below. To the east the hills rose into a jagged horizon, and the earthworks surrounding the 28-centimeter guns on Bismarck Hill were barely visible against the mountains beyond. Some magnification would have helped, but an Englishman training binoculars on foreign defenses was likely to arouse suspicion, and from what he'd seen so far, the guns were where the Admiralty had thought they would be. There was some building work going on near the battery that covered Auguste-Victoria Bay, but not on a scale that seemed significant. He might risk a closer look early one morning, when the army was still drilling.

The East Asia Squadron was where it had been the day before—*Scharnhorst* and *Emden* sharing the long jetty, *Gneisenau* and *Nürnberg* anchored in the bay beyond. *Leipzig* had been gone a week now—to the Marianas, if his Chinese informer was correct. Several coalers were lined up farther out, and one was unloading by the onshore wharves, sending occasional clouds of black dust up into the clear, cold air.

These ships were the reason for his brief visit, these ships and what they might do if war broke out. Their presence was no secret, of course—the local British consul probably played golf with the admiral in command. The same consul could have kept the Admiralty informed about Tsingtau's defenses and done his best to pump his German counterpart for military secrets, but of course he hadn't. Such work was considered ungentle-manly by the fools who ran the Foreign Office and staffed its embassies—not that long ago a British military attaché had refused to tell his employers in London what he'd witnessed at his host country's military maneuvers, on the grounds that he'd be breaking a confidence.

It was left to part-time spies to do the dirty work. Over the last few years, McColl—and, he presumed, other British businessmen who traveled the world—had been approached and asked to ferret out those secrets the empire's enemies wanted kept. The man who employed them on this part-time basis was an old naval officer named Cumming, who worked from an office in Whitehall and answered, at least in theory, to the Admiralty and its political masters.

When it came to Tsingtau, the secret that mattered most was what orders the East Asia Squadron had for the day that a European war broke out. Any hard evidence as to their intentions, as Cumming had told McColl on their farewell stroll down the Embankment, would be "really appreciated."

His insistence on how vital all this was to the empire's continued well-being had been somewhat undermined by his allocation of a paltry three hundred pounds for global expenses, but the trip as a whole had been slightly more lucrative than McColl had expected. The luxury Maia automobile that he was hawking around the world—the one now back in Shanghai, he hoped, with his brother Jed and colleague Mac—had caught the fancy of several rulers hungry for initiation into the seductive world of motorized speed, and the resultant orders had at least paid the trio's traveling bills.

This was gratifying, but probably more of a swan song than a sign of things to come. The automobile business was not what it had been even two years before, not for the small independents—nowadays you needed capital, and lots of it. Spying, on the other hand, seemed an occupation with a promising future. Over the last few years, even the British had realized the need for an espionage service, and once the men holding the purse strings finally got past the shame of it all, they would realize that only a truly professional body would do. One that paid a commensurate salary.

A war would probably help, but until Europe's governments were stupid enough to start one, McColl would have to make do with piecework. Before McColl's departure from England the previous autumn, Cumming had taken note of his planned itinerary and returned with a list of "little jobs" that McColl could do in the various ports of call—a wealthy renegade to assess in Cairo, a fellow Brit to investigate in Bombay, the Germans here in Tsingtau. Their next stop with the Maia was San Francisco, where a ragtag bunch of Indian exiles were apparently planning the empire's demise.

A lot of it seemed pretty inconsequential to McColl. There were no doubt plenty of would-be picadors intent on goading the imperial bull, but it didn't seem noticeably weaker. And where was the matador to finish it off? The Kaiser probably practiced sword strokes in his bedroom mirror, but it would be a long time before Germany acquired the necessary global reach.

He lit a German cigarette and stared out across the town. The sun was dropping toward the distant horizon, the harbor lighthouse glowing brighter by the minute. The lines of lamps in the warship rigging reminded him of Christmas trees.

He would be back in Shanghai for the Chinese New Year, he realized.

Caitlin Hanley, the young American woman he'd met in Peking, was probably there already.

The sun was an orange orb, almost touching the distant hills. He ground out the cigarette and started back down the uneven path while he could still see his way. Two hopeful coolies were waiting with their rickshaws at the bottom, but he waved them both away and walked briskly down Bismarckstrasse toward the beach. There were lights burning in the British consulate, but no other sign of life within.

His hotel was at the western end of the waterfront, beyond the deserted pleasure pier. The desk clerk still had his hair in a pigtail—an increasingly rare sight in Shanghai but common enough in Tsingtau, where German rule offered little encouragement to China's zealous modernizers. The room key changed hands with the usual bow and blank expression, and McColl climbed the stairs to his second-floor room overlooking the ocean.

A quick check revealed that someone had been though his possessions, which was only to be expected—Tsingtau might be a popular summer destination with all sorts of foreigners, but an Englishman turning up in January was bound to provoke some suspicion. Whoever it was had found nothing to undermine his oft-repeated story, that he was here in China on business and seeing as much of the country as money and time would allow.

He went back downstairs to the restaurant. Most of the clientele were German businessmen in stiff collars and spats, either eager to grab their slice of China or boasting of claims already staked. There were also a handful of officers, including one in a uniform McColl didn't recognize. He was enthusiastically outlining plans for establishing an aviation unit in Tsingtau when he noticed McColl's arrival and abruptly stopped to ask the man beside him something.

"Don't worry, Pluschow, he doesn't speak German," was the audible answer, which allowed the exposition to continue.

Since his arrival in Tsingtau, McColl had taken pains to stress his sad lack of linguistic skills, and this was not the first time the lie had worked to his advantage. Apparently absorbed in his month-old *Times,* he listened with interest to the aviation enthusiast. He couldn't see much strategic relevance in the news—what could a few German planes hope to achieve so far from home?—but the Japanese might well be interested. And any little nugget of intelligence should be worth a few of Cumming's precious pounds.

The conversation took a less interesting tack, and eventually the party broke up. McColl sipped his Russian tea and idly wondered where he would dine later that evening. He glanced through the paper for the umpteenth time and reminded himself that he needed fresh reading for the Pacific crossing. There was a small shop he knew on Shanghai's Nanking Road where novels jettisoned by foreigners mysteriously ended up.

More people came in—two older Germans in naval uniform, who ignored him, and a stout married couple, who returned his smile of acknowledgment with almost risible Prussian hauteur.

He was getting up to leave when Rainer von Schön appeared. McColl had met the young German soon after arriving in Tsing-tau—they were both staying at this hotel—and taken an instant liking to him. The fact that von Schön spoke near-perfect English made conversation easy, and the man himself was likable and intelligent. A water engineer by trade, he had admitted to a bout of homesickness and delved into his wallet for an explanatory photo of his pretty wife and daughter.

That evening he had an English edition of William Le Queux's *Invasion of 1910* under his arm.

"What do you think of it?" McColl asked him once the waiter had taken the German's order.

"Well, several things. It's so badly written, for one. The plot's ridiculous, and the tone is hysterical."

"But otherwise you like it?"

Von Schön smiled. "It is strangely entertaining. And the fact that so many English people bought it makes it fascinating to a German. And a little scary, I have to say."

"Don't you have any ranters in Germany?"

Von Schön leaned slightly forward, a mischievous expression on his face. "With the Kaiser at the helm, we don't need them."

McColl laughed. "So what have you been doing today?"

"Finishing up, actually. I'll be leaving in a couple of days."

"Homeward bound?"

"Eventually. I have work in Tokyo first. But after that . . ."

"Well, if I don't see you before you go, have a safe journey."

"You, too." Von Schön drained the last of his schnapps and got to his feet. "And now I have someone I need to see."

Once the German was gone, McColl consulted his watch. It was time he visited the Blue Dragon, before the evening rush began. He left a generous tip, recovered his winter coat from the downstairs cloakroom, and walked out to the waiting line of rickshaws. The temperature had already dropped appreciably, and he was hugging himself as the coolie turned left onto the well-lit Friedrichstrasse and started up the hill. The shops were closed by this time, the restaurants readying themselves for their evening trade. The architecture, the faces, the cooking smells, all were European—apart from his coolie, the only Chinese person in sight was a man collecting horse dung.

It was quiet, too—so quiet that the sudden blast of a locomotive whistle from the nearby railway station made him jump.

The coolie reached the brow of the low hill and started down the opposite slope into Taipautau. The township was almost as neat and widely spaced as the German districts, and in the cold air even the smells seemed more muted than they had in Shanghai. They were halfway down Shantung Strasse before McColl could hear the beginnings of evening revelry in the sailors' bars at the bottom.

The Blue Dragon was open for business but not yet really awake. The usual old man sat beneath the candlelit lanterns on the rickety veranda, beside the screened-off entrance. He grinned when he recognized McColl and cheerfully spat on the floor to his right, adding one more glistening glob to an impressive mosaic.

McColl was barely through the doorway when an old woman hurried down the hall toward him. "This way, please!" she insisted in pidgin German. "All type girls!"

"I'm here to see Hsu Ch'ing-lan," he told her in Mandarin, but she just looked blank. "Hsu Ch'ing-lan," he repeated.

The name seemed to percolate. She gestured for him to follow and led him through to the reception area, where "all type girls" were waiting in an assortment of tawdry traditional costumes on long red-velvet sofas. Some were barely out of puberty, others close to menopause. One seemed amazingly large for a Chinese woman, causing McColl to wonder whether she'd been fattened up to satisfy some particular Prussian yearning.

The old woman led him down the corridor beyond, put her head around the final door, and told Madame that a *laowai* wanted to see her. Assent forthcoming, she ushered McColl inside.

Hsu Ch'ing-lan was sitting at her desk, apparently doing her accounts. Some kind of incense was burning in a large dragon holder beyond, sending up coils of smoke.

"Herr McColl," she said with an ironic smile. "Please. Take a seat."

She was wearing the usual dress, blue silk embroidered in silver and gold, ankle-length but slit to the hip. Her hair was piled up in curls, secured by what looked like an ornamental chopstick. She was in her thirties, he guessed, and much more desirable than any of the girls in reception. When they'd first met, she'd told him that she was a retired prostitute, as if that were a major achievement. It probably was.

He had chosen this brothel for two reasons. It offered a two-tier service—those girls in reception who catered to ordinary sailors and the occasional NCO, and another, more exclusive, group who did house calls at officers' clubs and businessmen's hotels. The latter were no younger, no more beautiful, and no more sexually inventive than the former, but as Jane Austen might have put it, they offered more in the way of accomplishments. They sang, they danced, they made a ritual out of making tea. They provided, in Ch'ing-lan's vivid phrase, "local-color fuck."

She was his second reason for choosing the place. She came

from Shanghai and, unlike any other madam in Tsingtau, spoke the Chinese dialect that McColl knew best.

She pulled a bell cord, ordered tea from the small girl who came running, and asked him, rather surprisingly, what he knew of the latest political developments.

"In China?" he asked.

She looked at him as if he were mad. "What could matter here?" she asked.

"Sun Yat-sen could win and start modernizing the country," he suggested. "Or Yuan Shih-kai could become the new emperor and keep the country locked in the past."

"Pah. You foreign devils have decided we must modernize, so Yuan cannot win. And you control our trade, so Sun could win only as your puppet."

"Yuan bought one of my cars."

"He thinks it will make him look modern, but it won't. It doesn't matter what he or Sun does. In today's China everything depends on what the foreign devils do. Is there going to be a war between you? And if there is, what will happen here in Tsingtau?"

"If there's a war, the Japanese will take over. The Germans might dig themselves in—who knows? If they do, the town will be shelled. If I were you, I'd take the boat back home to Shanghai before the fighting starts."

"Mmm." Her eyes wandered around the room, as if she were deciding what to take with her.

The tea arrived and was poured.

"So what do you have for me?" McColl asked.

"Not very much, I'm afraid." The East Asia Squadron was going to sea at the end of February, for a six-week cruise. The *Scharnhorst* had a new vice captain, and there'd been a serious accident on the *Emden*—several sailors had been killed in an explosion. The recent gunnery trials had been won by the *Gneisenau,* but all five ships had shown a marked improvement, and the Kaiser had sent a congratulatory telegram to Vice Admiral von Spee. And a new officer had arrived from Germany to set up a unit of flying machines.

"I know about him," McColl said.

"He likes to be spanked," Ch'ing-lan revealed.

McColl wondered out loud whether verbal abuse might sting the Germans into indiscretions. Maybe the girls could deride their German clients, make fun of their puny fleet. What hope did they have against the mighty Royal Navy?

As she noted this down, a swelling sequence of ecstatic moans resounded through the building. Ch'ing-lan shook her head. "I'll have to talk to her," she said. "The others do the same because they think their tips will be smaller if they don't, and after a while none of us can hear ourselves think. It's ridiculous."

McColl laughed.

"But I do have some good news for you. I have a new girl, a cousin from Shanghai. She speaks a little English, and now she's learning a little German—she knows that a lot of the men like someone they can talk to."

"That sounds promising."

"And more expensive."

"Of course—I have no problem paying good money for good information." He thought for a moment. "She could be worried that her officer might be killed in a war. The British are so much more powerful, yes? She could ask for reassurance, ask him how he thinks his fleet can win."

She nodded.

"And the flying-machine man. I'd like to know how many machines, what type, and how he intends to use them. Between spanks, of course."

She nodded again. "Is that all?"

"I think so. I'll come back on Friday, yes?"

"Okay. You want girl tonight? Half price?"

He hesitated and saw Caitlin Hanley's face in his mind's eye. "No, not tonight." He smiled at her. "You're still retired, right?"

"You couldn't afford me."

"Probably not." He gave her a bow, shut the door after him, and walked back down the corridor. Bedsprings were squeaking behind several curtained doorways, and several girls seemed intent on winning the prize for most voluble pleasure. Out on the veranda, the old man gave him a leer and added another splash of phlegm to his iridescent patchwork.

It was enough to put a man off his dinner.

The following day was as clear and cold as its predecessor. McColl rose early and took breakfast in the almost empty hotel restaurant, conscious that half a dozen Chinese waiters were hovering at his beck and call. Once outside, he made straight for the beach. A westerly wind was picking up, and he could smell the brewery the Germans had built beyond the town. The ocean was studded with whitecaps.

As he'd calculated, the tide was out, and he walked briskly along the hard sand toward the promontory guarding the entrance to the bay. The field-artillery barracks he'd noticed on the map were set quite a distance back from the shore and, as he had hoped, only the roofs and tower were visible from the beach. He was soon beyond them, threading his way down a narrowing beach between headland and ocean.

Another half a mile and he found his path barred by a barbed-wire fence. It ran down slope and beach and some twenty yards out into the water, to what was probably the low-tide mark. He had first seen barbed wire corralling Boer women and children in South Africa, and finding it stretched across a Chinese beach was somewhat depressing, if rather predictable. There was no EINTRITT VERBOTEN sign, but there didn't really need to be. Only an idiot would think the fence was there to pen sheep.

McColl decided to be one. A quick look about him failed to detect any possible witnesses, so he took off his shoes and socks, rolled up his trousers, and waded out and around the end of the fence. The water was deeper and colder than he had expected. After drying his feet as best he could with a handkerchief, he wrung out his trouser bottoms, inserted his sand-encrusted feet into the dry footwear, and ventured on down the forbidden beach. I went paddling in the Yellow Sea, he thought. Something to tell his grandchildren, should he ever have any.

As he approached the end of the headland, the stern of a passenger ship loomed into view. It had obviously just left the harbor and was already turning southward, probably bound for Shanghai. McColl found himself wishing he were on it, rather than seeking out German guns with a pair of cold, wet trousers clinging to his thighs. He'd already earned the pittance that Cumming was paying him. What did the man expect from a brief visit like this one? A serious spying mission to Tsingtau would need a lot more time—and a lot better cover—than McColl had at his disposal. Cumming's favorite agent, Sidney Reilly, had lived in Port Arthur for several months before he succeeded in stealing the Russian harbor-defense plans.

McColl stopped and scrutinized the view to his right. The guns were up there somewhere, and this looked as good a spot as any to clamber up the slope. If he ran into officialdom, he would play the lost tourist, afraid of being cut off by the incoming tide.

Five minutes later he reached the crest and got a shock. The gun emplacements were up there all right, just as the Admiralty had thought they would be, but so were watching eyes. McColl was still scrambling up onto the plateau when the first shout sounded, and it didn't take him long to work out that dropping back out of sight was unlikely to win him anything more than a bullet in the spine. They'd seen him, and that was that.

Two soldiers in pickelhaube helmets were running across the grass. He walked toward them, mind working furiously. The lost-tourist act already seemed redundant—an Englishman this close to German guns was surely too much of a coincidence. But what was the alternative?

One of their guns went off, and for a single dreadful moment he thought they were shooting at him. But it quickly became obvious that one of them had pulled his trigger by accident. Seizing what seemed like an opportunity, McColl lengthened his stride, shook his fist, and angrily asked in German what the hell they thought they were doing.

"No civilians are allowed up here," the older of the soldiers insisted. He looked a little shamefaced but had not lowered his rifle. "Who are you? Where have you come from?"

"My name is Pluschow," McColl told him impulsively. There were two thousand soldiers in the garrison, and it seemed unlikely that these two would have run into the aviation enthusiast. "Lieutenant Pluschow," he added, taking a guess at the man's rank. "I am sorry—I did not realize I had strayed onto army territory. But I can't believe your orders are to shoot first and ask questions later."

"That was an accident," the younger man blurted out. He couldn't have been much more than eighteen.

"And no harm done," his partner insisted. "But you still haven't explained what you're doing here."

"I'm surveying the area. Tsingtau needs an aerodrome, and I'm getting a feeling for the local air currents." He reached for his packet of cigarettes and held it out to the soldiers.

There was a moment of hesitation before the older one extended a hand and took one. His partner happily followed his lead.

"If I need to come up here again, I will get permission from army command," McColl promised. "Now, is there a supply road back to town?"

There was, and they were happy to show him where it started, on the other side of the emplacements. Walking past the latter, he took in the ferroconcrete installations, heavy steel cupolas, and lift-mounted searchlights. And the guns were new-looking 28-centimeter pieces, not the old 15-centimeter cannons on the

Admiralty list. "Our base seems well protected," he said appreciatively.

He thanked the soldiers, promised he wouldn't mention the accidental discharge, and left them happily puffing on his cigarettes. He managed to cover a hundred yards or so before the urge to burst out laughing overcame him. Moments like that made life worth living.

Fifteen minutes later he was skirting the wall of the barracks and entering the town. In the square in front of the station, a bunch of coolies were huddled over some sort of game, their rickshaws lined up in waiting for the next train. McColl walked the few blocks to Friedrichstrasse and wondered what to do with the rest of the day. Tsingtau in winter was worth a couple of days, and he'd been there for more than a week. Like an idiot he'd forgotten to bring any reading, and the two bookshops on Friedrichstrasse had nothing in English. A German book on his bedside table would rather give the game away.

It occurred to him that the British consulate might have books to lend, and indeed they did. Just the one—a copy of *Great Expectations* some careless English tourist had left on the beach the previous summer. But the consul was out playing golf, and the English-speaking Chinese girl left in charge of His Majesty's business was unwilling to let the salt-stained volume out of the building without his say-so. It took McColl fifteen minutes and no small measure of charm to change her mind. And all this, he thought bitterly, for a book he already knew the ending to.

Still, Pip's early travails kept him entertained for the rest of the morning and half the afternoon. He then ambled around the German and Chinese towns before dropping anchor in the bar of the Sailors' Home down by the harbor. Through the window he could see the huge gray ships straining at their chains in the restless water.

What would this fleet do if war were declared? It could hardly stay put, not with England's ally Japan so close at hand, with ships that outmatched and outnumbered the Germans'. No, if the East Asia Squadron weren't already at sea when war broke out, then it soon would be. But sailing in which direction? For its home half the world away? If this was the intention, then whichever direction it took—west via the Cape of Good Hope or east around Cape Horn—there would be ten thousand miles and more to sail, with uncertain coal supplies and the knowledge that the whole British fleet would be waiting at the end of its journey, barring its passage across the North Sea. And what would be the point? More than five cruisers would be needed to tip the balance in home waters.

If McColl were in charge, he knew what he'd do. He'd send the five ships off in five directions, set them loose on the seven oceans to mess with British trade. That, he knew, was the Admiralty's nightmare. Each German ship could keep a British squadron busy for months, maybe even years, and that *might* tip the balance closer to home.

Whether or not the Imperial Navy had such suicide missions in mind, neither he nor the Admiralty knew, and he doubted whether any of his current drinking companions did either. He bought beers for a couple of new arrivals, traded toasts in pidgin English to Kaiser and King, and eavesdropped on the conversations swirling around him. But no secrets were divulged, unless Franz's fear that he had the French disease counted as such. Most of the seamen had their minds on home, on babies yet unseen, on wives and lovers sorely missed. No one mentioned the dread possibility that none of them would ever see Germany again.

McColl stayed until the sun was almost down, then walked back through the town as the lamplighters went about their business. Guessing that von Schön had not yet departed, he looked in on the hotel bar and found the young German sharing a circle of armchairs with several fellow-countrymen. Seeing McColl, von Schön smiled and gestured him over. "Please, join us," he said in English, "we need your point of view."

He introduced McColl to the others, explaining in German that the Englishman was also a businessman. They raised their hands in greeting.

"What are you all talking about?" McColl asked von Schön.

"Whether a war will benefit Germany," the other replied.

"And what's the general opinion?"

"I don't think there is one. I'll try to translate for you."

McColl sat back, careful to keep a look of noncomprehension on his face. One middle-aged man with a bristling mustache was making the argument that only a war could open the world to German business.

"If we win," another man added dryly.

"Of course, but we haven't lost one yet, and our chances must be good, even against England."

Several heads were nodding as von Schön translated this with an apologetic smile, but one of the younger Germans was shaking his head. "Why take the risk," he asked, "when we only have to wait a few years? The biggest and fastest-growing economies are ours and America's, and the rules of trade will change to reflect that fact. It's inevitable. The barriers will come down, including those around the British Empire, and their businesses will struggle to survive. In fact, if anyone needs a war, it's the British. It's the only way they could halt their decline." He turned to von Schön. "Ask your English friend what he thinks. Would British businessmen favor a war with Germany?"

Von Schön explained what the man had said and repeated his question.

McColl smiled at them all. "I don't think so. For one thing, most businessmen have sons, and they don't want to lose them. For another, it's only the biggest companies that make most of their profits abroad and that benefit most from the empire. If the rules change, they'll find some way to survive—big companies always do." He paused. "But let me ask you something. After all, it's governments that declare war, not businessmen. How

much notice do the Kaiser and his ministers take of what German businessmen think?"

It seemed like a good question, if the wry response to von
Schön's translation was anything to go by. "This is the problem,"
one youngish German responded. "The old Kaiser understood
how to rule. Like your Queen Victoria," he added, looking at
McColl. "A symbol, yes? And an important one, but above politics.
It didn't matter what his opinions were. But this Kaiser . . . We Germans have the best welfare system, the best schools. We have given
the world Beethoven and Bach and Goethe and so much else. Our
businesses are successful all over the world. We have much to be
proud of, much to look forward to, but none of that interests this
Kaiser. He grew up playing soldiers, and he can't seem to stop. In
any other country, this would not matter a great deal, but because
of our history and our place at the heart of Europe the army has
always occupied a powerful position. I agree with Hans that we
can get what we want without war, but when the crucial moment
comes—as we all know it will—I think the Kaiser and his government will follow the army's lead, not listen to people like us."

It was a sadly convincing analysis, McColl thought, and as von
Schön translated the gist of it, he listened to the others mut-
tering their broad agreement. These German businessmen had
no desire for war, but they realized that their opinions counted
for little with their rulers. The one named Hans might be right
in thinking that Britain was in decline, but only in an abstract,
relative sense. And while it might be in a few traders' interests
to fight a war of imperial preservation, it wasn't in anyone else's.
As far as most British businessmen were concerned, peace was
delivering the goods. McColl himself was thirty-two years old,
and he'd been born into a world without automobiles or flying
machines, phonographs or telephones, the wireless or moving
pictures. Everything was changing so fast, and mostly for the better. Who in his right mind would exchange this thrilling new
world for battlefields soaked in blood? It felt so medieval.

War would be a catastrophe, for business, for everyone. Particularly those who had to fight it. He was probably too old to be called up, but you never knew—with the weapons they had now, the ranks of the young might be decimated in a matter of months. Whatever happened, he had no intention of renewing his acquaintance with Britain's military machine and finding himself once more at the mercy of some idiot general.

It rained that evening and for most of the next two days, a freezing rain that rendered the pavements and quaysides treacherous and obstinately refused to turn to snow. McColl divided his time among cafés, the hotel lounge, and his room, following Pip on his voyage of discovery and engaging all those he could in conversation.

On two occasions he slipped and slithered his way to the edge of the new harbor, drawn by some pointless urge to confirm that the fleet was still there. It was. The occasional sailor hurried along the rain-swept decks, but no tenders were moving, and the bars on the quayside were shuttered and closed.

On Friday morning a note arrived from the consulate reminding him to return the book, which seemed somewhat gratuitous. The beautiful mission-taught writing was clearly the work of the Chinese girl, the overwrought concern for property more likely the golf-playing consul's. He decided to have the note framed when he got home.

The weather changed that afternoon, the clouds moving out across the ocean like a sliding roof. He went for a long walk down the Pacific shoreline, ate dinner alone, and, once darkness had taken its grip, rode a rickshaw across town to the Blue Dragon. The old man was still hawking up phlegm, but the girl who'd rushed to greet him in the lobby was busy in the reception area, hovering over a young and nervous *Kriegsmarine* lieutenant. He was having trouble choosing and, seeing McColl, politely suggested he jump the line. "If you know which girl you want."

"English," McColl explained, shaking his head and gesturing that the other should proceed. The German threw up his hands, sighed, and turned back to the line of waiting females. "This one," he said eventually, pointing at a child of around fifteen. McColl could almost hear the eeny, meeny, miney, mo.

The child took the German's much larger hand in hers and led him away like a horse.

The other females all sat back down in unison, reminding McColl of church. "You want see Hsu Ch'ing-lan?" the girl asked McColl.

"Yes." After making sure that the German was behind a curtain, he walked down to the madam's room.

Hsu Ch'ing-lan was just the way he'd left her, sitting at her desk, holding a cigarette between two raised fingers, wearing the same blue silk. But this time she was reading an ancient copy of *Life* magazine—he recognized the cartoon of Woodrow Wilson.

She smiled when she saw him, which seemed promising.

They went through the usual ritual, exchanging small talk until the tea arrived, before getting down to business. "The girl I told you about," she began, "my cousin from Shanghai. She is very intelligent. She has been with an officer on the flagship and persuaded him to talk about their plans."

"How?" was McColl's immediate reaction.

"How do you think? There are many men—most of them, I think—who like to talk about themselves after sex. They feel good, and they want the woman to know how important they are."

"But . . ."

"Let her tell you herself." Ch'ing-lan rang her bell and told the answering girl to bring Hsu Mei-lien. "You will see how intelligent she is," she told McColl while they waited.

The girl who arrived was still a child, but every bit as bright as her cousin had said she was. She began in halting English, then switched to rapid-fire Shanghainese when Ch'ing-lan told her that McColl spoke that language. Her officer's name was Burchert, and they'd been together the last three nights. If she had understood him correctly, he was an *Oberleutnant* on the *Gneisenau*. Once he was in the mood, she had started by saying how she'd seen the big English battleships in Shanghai and how brave she thought the Germans in Tsingtau were, to think of fighting them. But surely just sailing out to meet them would be foolhardy. They must have a better plan than that.

And that was all she'd had to say—after that, nothing could stop him talking. As far as he was concerned, it was entirely about coal. They could keep their ships together if there was enough coal, while the English who were hunting them would have to split their fleet to search an ocean as wide as the Pacific. And that would give the Germans their chance, to destroy them a piece at a time. But only if they had the coal.

"And where will they find it?" McColl wondered. "Did you ask him?"

She gave him a derisive look. "I don't ask questions," she said. "I just let him talk. If I ask a question like that, he will suspect something."

"Yes. He probably would." McColl smiled at her—she really was quite remarkable. But had she told him anything new and useful? The East Asia Squadron's dependence on limited coal supplies seemed obvious enough, even for the British Admiralty. Where could the Germans find coal in the Pacific? If Japan entered a war against them, then not from the home islands or Formosa. Supplies from Australia and New Zealand would be cut off once war was declared. And the Germans would know that any colliers loading up in a time of deepening crisis would be followed. So they would have to build up stocks on various islands while peace continued—stocks that the Royal Navy would have to seek out and burn if and when a war broke out. "Anything else?" he asked her.

"He says their gunners are better than the English."

"I wouldn't be surprised." He smiled at the young girl. "Thank you."

Hsu Ch'ing-lan dismissed her. "Clever, yes?"

"Very," McColl agreed. Too clever to be working in a Tsingtau brothel. But then millions of Chinese people seemed to be short-changing themselves, biding their time. "How about the man with the flying machines? Has he booked another spanking?"

"Pao-yu is seeing him tonight," Hsu Ch'ing-lan told him.

"Then I'll be back tomorrow."

As it happened, he saw her sooner than that. It was still dark on the following morning when a hand shook his shoulder and he woke to the smell of her perfume.

She said something in a dialect he didn't understand, and the gaslight flared to life. More words, and a familiar-looking member of the Chinese hotel staff slipped out the door and closed it behind him.

"This is a nice surprise," McColl said, hauling himself up onto his elbows. She was wearing a long black coat over the usual dress.

"I don't think so," she said, coldly. "Pao-yu—the girl who spanks the flying-machine man—has been arrested."

"When? Who by?" He swung himself out of bed and reached for his trousers.

"The Germans, of course. Her questions must have made the man suspicious, and they took her to their police building. Last night."

"But they haven't come to the Blue Dragon? I wonder why."

"Because the girl hasn't told them anything. Not yet. A friend came to let me know they have her. She knows not to say anything, but she's not as clever as my cousin—they'll trick it out of her. So you must leave. There's a train in an hour."

"Oh. Yes, I suppose I should." He found himself wondering why she had come to warn him. "What about you?" he asked. "Will they arrest you?"

She shrugged. "I shall say I know nothing. If you are gone, then all they have is guesses."

"I see." And he did. She was afraid he would be caught, would implicate her, and that once the white folks had patched things up between them, she would be left as the scapegoat. Given the history of the last century, it was a reasonable enough assumption for a Chinese person to make. "Well, thank you. But what about the girl?"

"I can probably buy her back, but I will need money."

"Ah." He reached for his wallet on the bedside table, checked the contents, and handed her a wad of notes, thinking that he had now given her more than Cumming had given him. Some businessman.

"This won't be enough," she said.

"I'll need the rest to pay my bill and reach Shanghai."

"All right," she agreed reluctantly, stuffing the notes into a coat pocket and walking toward the door. When she turned with her hand on the knob, he half expected her to wish him luck, but all she said was, "Don't miss the train."

He hurriedly crammed his few belongings into the battered suitcase, happily realized that there wasn't time to return *Great Expectations,* and went to the door. It was only when he opened it that he heard the commotion downstairs. One voice—male, German, and coldly insistent—was demanding a room number; the other—Hsu Ch'ing-lan's—was angrily protesting a client's right to discretion. She was almost shouting, presumably for McColl's benefit.

He hesitated for a second, wondering whether he should just walk down and bluff it out. He decided against it. If he were arrested, the Germans could probably make a case against him, and some sort of punishment would doubtless follow. Best not to give them the chance.

When he'd checked in a fortnight earlier, he had taken the precaution of exploring the hotel for possible exit routes. This had felt a touch histrionic at the time but now seemed pleasingly professional. Walking as quietly as he could, he headed down the long corridor toward the back staircase.

He met no one in the corridor or on the stairs, but one of the Chinese staff was lounging in the kitchen doorway, a hint of a smile in his eyes. McColl fished some coins from his tip pocket, raised a finger to his lips for silence, and opened the door leading out into the backyard. He didn't expect to find anyone stationed outside and wasn't disappointed—the German authorities had obviously assumed that they would find him asleep in his bed.

Hurrying across the yard and down the alley, he emerged onto Prinz Heinrich Strasse and into a bitter wind. The sky was lightening, and a Chinese man was working his way down the street, dousing the ornate gas lamps. The side of the station building was visible up ahead, but no smoke was rising above it—if Hsu Ch'ing-lan was right about the time of departure, he'd have at least forty-five minutes to wait.

Which was obviously out of the question. He might as well give himself up as sit in the station for that long.

Perhaps he could hide somewhere close by and then surreptitiously board the train at the moment of departure.

This possibility sustained him until he reached the corner across from the station and leaned his head around for a view of the forecourt. There were several uniformed Germans in evidence, and one was looking straight at him. "Halt!" the man shouted.

McColl's first instinct, which he regretted a moment later, was to turn and run. Better a few months in jail than a bullet in the back, he thought as Prinz Heinrich Strasse stretched out before him, looking too much like a shooting range for comfort. But it was a bit late now to take a chance on his pursuers' levelheadedness. He swerved off between two buildings and down the dark alley that divided them. He reckoned he had a fifty-meter start and must have run almost that far when a crossroads presented itself. Sparing a second to look back, he found the alley behind him still empty. But as he swung right, he heard shouts in the distance, which seemed to come from up ahead.

Staying put seemed the better of two poor options. A doorway offered a few inches of shelter, enough to conceal his body if not his valise. Hearing German voices nearby rendered this problem more acute, and the notion of perching the suitcase on his head occurred to him just in time. As the Germans drew nearer, he stood there holding his breath, feeling more than a little ridiculous.

He heard the feet stop some ten yards off, imagined the eyes looking this way and that.

"Hanke probably imagined it," one man said.

"He *is* getting fond of the pipe," a second man suggested.

The first man laughed.

"But we might as well go down to the end," his companion decided. "Then work our way back around the block."

"Beats just standing here," the first voice agreed. "Christ, it's cold this morning. And no fucking breakfast."

His voice was fading, and McColl gingerly lowered his suitcase to the ground. He decided he would give them ten minutes to abandon this particular search and then make a run for it before the wider search got under way. But how? The train was out of the question, and God only knew how he'd get on a ship.

He felt real anxiety for the first time. But it was not the prospect of captivity and consequent physical hardship that worried him so much as the personal failure it would represent. Getting caught now would likely destroy any future he might have had in Cumming's organization.

Was there any way he could go to ground in Tsingtau? Could he persuade Hsu Ch'ing-lan that finding him a bolt-hole was in her own best interests?

Considering her circumstances, she was more likely to give him up.

Still, the Chinese town seemed a better bet than the German, and once his ten minutes were up, he cautiously worked his way northward through the slowly waking streets. There were more people about now, but all of them were Chinese—the German police had vanished, their civilian counterparts still in bed.

Once in the Chinese town, he bent his knees to disguise his height and let habit draw him toward the Blue Dragon. There was no sign of the usual doorkeeper, but there was a coal cart standing outside, its horse pawing absentmindedly at the cobbles with a front hoof.

On its way into Tsingtau, McColl remembered, the train had stopped at a small station in the outskirts. Which couldn't be more than three miles from here. Or four at the most.

He was still weighing the pros and cons of theft and hire when the coal coolie emerged, a bowlegged Chinese man with a queue that reached down to his buttocks. McColl managed, with some difficulty, to explain what he wanted and then showed his incredulous audience the wad of German notes that should have paid his hotel bill. All doubts vanished from the coal-encrusted visage. Offered more money than he'd make in five years, the man bared his teeth in a grin of compliance and hustled McColl up onto the cart. After clambering up himself, he jerked the horse into motion with a tug of the woven-string reins.

A real stroke of luck, McColl thought as they clattered down the slope toward the railway line and harbor. Directly ahead, the four funnels of either *Scharnhorst* or *Gneisenau* loomed above the long line of storehouses; away to the right, a few desultory puffs of smoke were rising from the vicinity of the rail station. Just a shunter, he hoped—surely his train couldn't be leaving.

As they approached the railway tracks, the coal coolie turned onto the parallel maintenance road the Germans had laid on the landward side and cajoled the horse to increase its pace. Soon they were almost flying along. Looking back, McColl could see no telltale smoke behind them. Perhaps he really would escape.

One step at a time, he told himself—sooner or later the Germans were bound to pick up his trail. And if he were caught . . . well, truth be told, it probably wouldn't be all that bad. He would be questioned at length and most likely put on trial. And then they would likely deport him, with as much publicity as they could manage. He might even serve a few months in prison. Which would be unpleasant, but he'd survive it. Jed and Mac would have to get the Maia back to London. And he would miss the chance to renew his acquaintance with Caitlin Hanley.

Which was something he really wanted to do.

She was still uppermost in his thoughts when the road abruptly degenerated, smooth asphalt giving way to ridged and rutted frozen mud. McColl clung to his seat, only too aware of the creaking axles, and prayed that neither would snap. His driver showed no inclination to slacken their pace—either the promise of riches had rendered him oblivious to everything else or the cart was a good deal stronger than it sounded. As the minutes went by and nothing more serious occurred than the loss of several coal sacks, McColl allowed himself to hope it was the latter.

It felt as if they'd been traveling for hours, but his watch told him twenty-five minutes. If he hadn't underestimated the distance to the next station, they should reach it in time—the prospect of the train steaming past them didn't bear thinking about. What in heaven's name would he do then? Start walking toward Shanghai?

About ten minutes later, their track veered inland, away from the rails, but his chauffeur shrugged off his anxious questions. And sure enough, a few minutes more and they were back by the rails. By this time most of Tsingtau seemed behind them—they had to be nearly there.

They were. The stop he remembered came into view as they rounded a bend, its single platform facing out across the bay. The station building wouldn't have looked out of place in the Black Forest and had no need of the imperial flag that fluttered from its roof. European-style houses were clustered behind it, and beyond them was the famous brewery.

The station was still two hundred yards ahead, but McColl ordered a halt—he had no desire to show up on a coal cart. The driver pulled on the reins, brought them to a stop, and anxiously held out a hand for payment. He seemed almost surprised to receive it, but McColl could hardly blame him—with his face still wreathed in coal dust, he didn't seem a man accustomed to good fortune.

McColl wished him good-bye and started walking. The station ahead, he now realized, looked worryingly deserted. He hoped to God that the morning train was scheduled to stop there, because he didn't much fancy trying to flag the thing down.

But he needn't have worried. Several Chinese would-be travelers were sheltering from the wind on the far side of the building, and the German stationmaster was in his office, warming himself in front of a blazing coal fire. The man was consulting his pocket-watch when McColl appeared in his doorway, and as he snapped it shut, a whistle blew in the distance—the train was approaching.

His face flushed with alarm when he saw McColl, who thought for a moment that the game was up. But it was only the usual German annoyance at lateness and the wrecking of schedules that might ensue. Concealing his relief, McColl asked if the train's imminent arrival meant he should pay the guard, but that of course was against regulations, and the locomotive was hissing to a halt by the time the flustered official had written his ticket. "You'll reach Tsinan at five," the stationmaster told him. "And the connection to Pukow is at six."

Steeling himself, McColl walked out onto the platform, half expecting a posse of policemen to erupt from the two carriages. But there were none, only fifty or more Chinese men staring out of the open wagons hitched to the back of the coaches.

He entered an almost empty saloon. There were no other foreigners and only two Chinese men, both in Western suits. They stood up to bow and smile but offered no conversation, and McColl was happy to follow their lead. He took a window seat at the other end of the car and barely had time to place his luggage on the rack before the train slipped into motion.

If his memory of the local geography was accurate, they would be outside the Tsingtau concession in ten minutes or so and, the-oretically at least, beyond German jurisdiction. Of course they owned and ran the railway and probably considered it part of their writ. The local Chinese population might argue the point, but he wouldn't like to bet on it. There was a British consulate in Tsinan, but also another German concession. This was much smaller than the one around Tsingtau but would still have some soldiers on hand.

He wouldn't feel safe until he was on the train to Pukow and Nanking, which was eleven long hours away.

The line was still following the shore of the bay, the train advancing at a satisfying pace. It occurred to him that cutting the telegraph wires that ran alongside the tracks would increase his chances by leaps and bounds, but even if granted an opportunity, he lacked the requisite tools.

And maybe there was no need. The train rattled past the concession's border post without even stopping, and there were no police or army officers waiting on the platform at Kiautschou, the first town in Chinese territory. It looked like he could relax until they reached Tsinan.

He got off for a stroll at Kiautschou and took a small clay pot of tea back to his seat. As the train got under way, the conductor sat down beside him with a pot of his own, clearly intent on conversation.

Over the next twenty minutes, McColl learned a lot about the man and his family. The wife who loved living in Tsingtau, who taught in the school there—the best school in China, according to some. The children liked it, too, though he sometimes thought they were missing much of their German heritage. But they could never have afforded servants in Germany.

It was clear that he loved his train and the pretty German stations, so out of place against the Chinese backdrop. He told McColl about the line's short history and how flat it was, with several hundred bridges and not a single tunnel. He pointed out kilns by the side of the line, where bricks had been baked and then broken for ballast, because Shantung province was devoid of suitable stones.

McColl responded with a wholly fictional life, which he located in Alsace to mask any linguistic mistakes. It was a relief to be speaking openly again, after a fortnight of pretending not to speak German, and he found himself liking the conductor. It was a strange place for a German to end up, but this one seemed at peace with himself and the world.

The man left after an hour or so, and McColl sat there watching the barely changing scene through his window—a wide valley dotted by small villages, an occasional row of planters in the winter fields, the distant line of brown mountains under a gray sky. He eventually woke with a jolt of alarm, but it was only a coal train rumbling past in the opposite direction, bound for Tsingtau and von Spee's ships. He imagined the colliers steaming out into the wide Pacific, dropping their loads on a hundred scattered islands for the future use of a fugitive fleet.

He thought about the girl the Germans had arrested. What would they do to her? If it had been Hsu Ch'ing-lan's cousin, then Ch'ing-lan would have moved heaven and earth to save her—that was the Chinese way. But Pao-yu wasn't family—at least not as far as McColl knew—and if not she'd probably just be abandoned. Which was also the Chinese way.

There was nothing he could do for her now.

After Wei, the mountains grew higher and the valley seemed less populated. It was almost a shock when a mining complex suddenly appeared in the window, complete with winding gear and mountains of glistening coal. Black-faced Chinese coolies were doing all the work, dragging carts of coal up ramps and tipping them into the railway wagons. Three German overseers were standing to one side, comparing notes about something or other.

The train soon stopped at a station, and two more Germans got on. They ignored the Chinese people who had bowed to McColl and then ignored him, too, as if intent on proving that race had no part in their arrogance. Which suited him well enough—if word of his escape were clicking along the telegraph wires, it clearly hadn't reached them.

But it had been clicking—he was almost certain of that. Failing to find him in Tsingtau, the Germans were bound to spread the net wider. They might not know he was headed their way, but the German authorities in Tsinan would certainly be on the lookout.

The last major stop was Tschou-tsun. After the train pulled out, the conductor stopped for another chat, and there was no change in his manner to suggest fresh intelligence, causing McColl to wonder whether he himself was in flight from a phantom. Maybe the girl was still refusing to speak or didn't know his name—that was something he should have asked Hsu Ch'ing-lan about. This wasn't his finest hour, he realized. His report to Cumming would need some glossing.

And he still had Tsinan to cope with. His best bet, he decided, was a variation on his departure from Tsingtau. On the journey down from Peking ten days earlier, he had noticed that Tsinan had two stations, one where travelers on the Peking–Pukow line changed for the Shantung Railway and another, closer to the town, that was served only by the latter. Any pursuers would assume he had a through ticket and would be waiting at the junction. If he got off at the town station and took a rickshaw across town, there was a reasonable chance he could sneak aboard the Pukow train without being seen.

The last stage of the journey seemed eternal, but the straggling outskirts of Tsinan finally appeared in his window, and almost immediately the train began to slow. He grabbed his suitcase and made for the vestibule farthest from the luggage car and the conductor.

The line was running along a slight embankment between a series of small lakes, the town visible beyond those to the south. The moment the train stopped, the Chinese passengers in the open wagons were dropping the sides, leaping down to the ground, and hurrying away. Cautiously inching an eye around the corner of his carriage, McColl saw the conductor sharing a convivial word with another German stationmaster. There were no other uniforms on display.

On the other side of the train, a team of coolies was transferring sacks of rice from a boxcar to a line of waiting carts. When the whistle blew and the train began to move, McColl stepped nimbly down and watched it steam away. It couldn't be much more than a mile to the other station, and for a moment he considered simply walking down the track. But the land on both sides was open, and there was still too much light in the sky—he would stick to his plan.

Which proved harder than expected. The rickshaw coolie he tried to engage spoke no dialect that McColl could understand and needed more than a little convincing from a better-traveled colleague that this foreigner wanted transport to the town's other station—a station he could have reached much more simply and cheaply by staying on his train. Once persuaded that his prospective passenger wasn't simply deranged—or at least not dangerously so—he allowed McColl into the seat, picked up the bamboo shafts, and set off at a steady jog for the city gate some two hundred yards distant.

Passing through this, the rickshaw swayed along a narrow street that ran parallel to the town's crumbling wall. This was the old China, seemingly untouched by progress, its buildings dirty and decaying, its children half naked and clearly malnourished. Stares followed McColl, and one beggar ran after the rickshaw, stretching out a hand until he tripped on the uneven road.

The coolie crossed a stinking canal, turned through another gate behind a scurrying rat, and emerged onto a slightly more prosperous street. Several artisans were working outside their shops, making the most of the remaining light, and a brazier was burning in front of a small hardware emporium, the hanging copper pots reflecting the fire. The smell of food from a couple of cafés reminded McColl that he'd hardly eaten that day and started his stomach rumbling. Two more coolies ran by with a sedan chair, and he caught a glimpse of an old woman's face within.

They skirted a small lake and headed up a long, straight street toward what looked like a railway station. A column of smoke, dyed red by the sinking sun, rose up behind the German roof, confirming the fact. McColl waited until they were a short walk away, then shouted to the coolie to stop. The man did so with obvious reluctance but conjured up a toothless smile when the foreign devil overpaid him.

McColl walked toward the station, keeping to the rapidly deepening shadows on one side of the street. There was an automobile and at least a dozen rickshaws in the forecourt, all waiting, no doubt, for the train from the north. He ignored the gaslit booking hall, cautiously worked his way around the building, and found an area of shadow from which he could safely scan the platform. The first thing he noticed was a group of uniformed Germans, who seemed to be interrogating his friend the conductor. The train that had brought him from Tsingtau was sitting in the bay platform, lazily oozing steam.

So he hadn't been overreacting—they really were after him.

He took in the rest of the tableau. The platform lamps were glowing in the gloom, and there were several dozen Chinese people waiting for his train, many with several items of luggage. At the other end of the platform, four coolies were waiting with shovels beside a coal wagon, ready to refuel the incoming engine. One of the uniformed officers seemed to be staring straight at McColl, which gave him a moment of acute anxiety. But he soon looked away. The darkness was apparently enough of a cloak.

There was nothing to do but wait and take whatever chance was offered to get aboard the train. The minutes turned into an hour, and the temperature steadily dropped, but at least the darkness deepened.

There were several blows on the whistle before the headlight swam into view and the train steamed in alongside the low continental platform. It was more prepossessing than the one from Tsingtau, with five European-built carriages and no open wagons. The moment it clanked to a halt, scrimmages developed at all the vestibule doors as Chinese passengers trying to alight collided with those seeking entry. Above their heads the peaked caps of the German police were turning this way and that, looking for a British spy.

Up ahead the pipe from the water tank was being slewed across the tender, and beyond it the coolies were presumably shoveling coal. He had at least ten minutes, but there was no way he could cross the wide platform without being seen.

Two of the policemen were boarding the train, but the others were still keeping watch outside. He should have crossed the tracks out of sight of the platform and waited on the other side, but it was too late for that now.

He suddenly had an idea. He walked quickly back to the forecourt and up to the last rickshaw in line. "Hat," he said in Shanghainese, pointing it out for greater clarity and waving a note worth twenty times as much under the man's eyes. The coolie gave him an *Is this really Christmas?* look and slowly removed his conical headgear. McColl handed him the note, grabbed the hat, and walked back toward the platform. The police were still there, and the train seemed almost set to leave—there was nothing else for it. He put on the hat, arranged his suitcase so that it would be shielded by his body, and started the long, semicircular walk that would take him around the back of the train. He was too tall and the suitcase too big, but out where the light barely reached, he was hoping they'd see only the hat.

And it worked. Thirty nerve-racking seconds and he was behind the train, looking up at the dimly lit carriages. As he reached the inner end of the last carriage, the whistle sounded, and almost instantly the wheels began to turn. He stepped aboard and climbed up onto the vestibule platform. The temptation to stand and wave his coolie hat at the Germans was enormous, but discretion triumphed. He ducked inside what was clearly a third-class carriage and strode up the aisle in search of less crowded accommodation.

The Chinese passengers, noticing his bizarre souvenir, seemed relieved to see him pass. They were doubtless thinking that he would be more at home in first, with all the other inscrutable foreign devils.

The House Off Bubbling Well Road

♠

Most of those traveling first class were European, and the only two Chinese occupants of the carriage were dressed in Western attire. McColl exchanged smiles with a couple of fellow Englishmen whom he recognized from his time in Peking and, after placing his suitcase in the luggage rack, gratefully sank into the forward-facing seat of the last unoccupied booth. The train was already out in open country and rapidly gathering speed.

The carriage had modern electric lights, both along the ceiling and above the seats. He took time to scan the other passengers, taking care not to arouse suspicion, and saw none who looked obviously German. Seeking to untangle the low murmur of voices, he could pick out only English, French, and Chinese.

Surely he was safe for now. There might be Germans waiting in Nanking or Shanghai, but they had no jurisdiction in either. He just had to reach a telegraph office and send off the information he'd gathered, and they would have to accept that further pursuit was meaningless.

He closed his eyes and realized how easy it would be to fall asleep. But first there was work to do—summarizing his findings as briefly as possible and then encrypting them for dispatch. He pulled out his notebook and pen, ordered a whiskey from the hovering steward, and put his mind to work.

It took about two hours, and the resulting page and a half of cipher seemed a somewhat derisory return on his investment of time and money, not to mention the risk to life and limb. But the aviation unit and bigger harbor guns were new information, and he thought that Cumming would be pleased. Not enough to give him a bonus, but perhaps enough to offer more work.

He yawned, switched off the light above his seat, and turned his mind to Caitlin Hanley. It was a long time since he'd felt so attracted to a woman. The name, like the dark brown hair and green eyes, suggested Irish descent, and the New York accent had seemed softer than most he remembered, even when berating the local American consul at a diplomatic reception. "Women deserve the vote more than men do," was the first thing he heard her say, and the patronizing chuckles that followed from the consul and his minions had been enough to make McColl intervene on her behalf. He had no strong opinions on the matter of suffrage, but he knew a bunch of reactionaries when he saw one. It was hard to imagine, he told the other men, that women would do a worse job of running the world.

She had given him a suspicious look, as if uncertain of his motives, and soon walked away to join a Western-dressed Chinese couple.

McColl wasn't sure he had liked her, but there was something there that intrigued him, and he'd casually asked one of the junior diplomats who she was. The young man had confided her name and the fact that she was a journalist, but he hadn't known where she was staying. Next morning McColl had left Jed and Mac to sort out the automobile's return shipment to Shanghai and tried, unsuccessfully, to track her down. He had come up empty at all the hotels favored by foreigners, and then, remembering the Chinese couple, started on the better establishments catering to Europeans. She was staying at the third but had just left on an overnight motorcoach excursion to the Great Wall. A small payment to one of the busboys secured the information that she was leaving in a week and had already purchased her ticket back to Shanghai.

McColl had seen her once more. He was on his way to the railway station, his rickshaw passing her hotel at the exact moment her excursion returned. Which, he thought, had to be some sort of an omen. She had even offered a smile in response to his wave.

He stared out at the Chinese night. The sky had cleared, and an orange moon was rising above a wide plain. A few minutes later, the train crossed a wide braided river, moonlight rippling on the different channels as it rumbled loudly across the iron structure. When the river disappeared and the noise of their passage abruptly lessened, he finally closed his eyes, a smile on his face.

Sleep, however, was still not in the cards. The train was already slowing and soon pulled in to a surprisingly well-lit station. JENCHOU, the signs announced. A few minutes later, a bulky American approaching old age squeezed himself into the seat facing McColl's, offered a hand to shake, and introduced himself as Ezekiel Channing III. He was, it transpired, the missionary who ran the local orphanage, on his way to Shanghai to collect a shipment of American school books.

McColl listened, offering little in return. The American seemed a decent enough sort, and if he needed to interrupt each thought to insert a quote from the Good Book, then what was the harm? He was doubtless doing valuable work, and he did, eventually, notice that his audience was struggling to stay awake.

"I didn't get much sleep last night," McColl said apologetically.

"Well, don't let me stop you now," Ezekiel said affably, opening up his leather-bound Bible.

It was still in his lap when McColl jerked awake seven hours later, but the missionary was asleep, gently snoring, with an almost beatific look on his fleshy face. McColl wondered how many years the man had been in China and whether he would ever go home again.

The golden light of the just-risen sun was streaming in through their window, the train running along a high embankment. Dry paddy fields stretched toward the distant horizon, with only an occasional cluster of houses and trees to break the monotony. At the foot of the embankment, two women and a water buffalo raised their heads to watch the train go by.

They were an hour from their destination according to the conductor, and McColl, seeing no reason to wake Ezekiel, stared out through the window at the Chinese landscape until the outskirts of Pukow came into view. The missionary woke with a start as the train rattled though points and entered the terminus, and he gave McColl a lovely smile.

On the platform, rickshaw drivers and porters were jostling for position, intent on providing at least one European passenger and his luggage with transport to the river. Beyond them some modern-looking railway workshops nestled incongruously in the shadow of ancient city walls.

McColl took his time, alighting almost last and waving away frantic offers of assistance. It was warmer than in Tsingtau, particularly out in the sun, but winter was winter, even this far south. He joined the Chinese crowd marching down toward the quay in the wake of the conquerors' rickshaws, keeping a wary eye out for anyone looking suspicious. But he saw nobody, either on the road or down by the mile-wide Yangtze, where a shiny, white steam yacht was waiting among the sampans to ferry them all across. He pushed through the beggars' outstretched arms to the sloping gangplank and climbed back into the bosom of his fellow Europeans.

Once aboard it seemed an age before they cast off, but the crossing itself was quick, the launch ploughing through the ponderous brown current toward the far shore and the high city walls of Nanking that lay just beyond. The only interruption was provided by a floating body, which surprised and distressed the American woman who noticed it. She would be well advised to avoid the Whangpo in Shanghai, McColl thought. Some days there seemed to be more bodies than boats in that river.

As he knew from the original journey to Peking, the walk from boat to station was fairly short on both sides of the Yangtze, but was he going straight on to Shanghai? The seven-hour journey was probably safe enough in daylight, but he felt eager to pass his information on, and the British consulate in Nanking was only a short ride away. If he missed the connecting train, there would always be another, and they weren't expecting him in Shanghai for another couple of days. On the other hand . . .

The two men on the quayside decided him. They were Chinese, not German, but there was something in the way they scanned the disembarking passengers that put him on alert. True, one looked straight at him with apparent disinterest, but a watcher with evil intent would hardly attack him there and then, when he was surrounded by other Europeans.

McColl swung himself up onto a rickshaw and let the man pull him fifty yards toward the station before ordering a change of course, onto the road that ran toward the nearest city gate. "The house of the British," McColl told him. "And the faster you get me there, the more I'll pay you."

The speed increased, and as they swung through the huge gateway, McColl leaned out to look back. There was no sign of pursuit, either then or when he looked again, half a mile or so down the long avenue that led to the consulate. The men he had feared had probably been waiting for a relative.

The Union Jack came into view, hanging limply above a traditional Chinese building. He paid off the rickshaw owner and thumped on the heavy wooden door, ignoring the sign in English and its highly inconvenient opening hours. A Chinese woman eventually opened it and seemed too surprised by his fluency in Shanghainese to protest his walking past her. The official offices at the front of the house were empty, but a young Englishman was eating scrambled eggs in the kitchen at the back, still without a collar on his shirt.

"I have a signal for London," McColl said as the young man swallowed. "Who are you?"

"Tompkins, Neil. First secretary. Only one, come to that. Nanking's not exactly on the map these days."

"My name's McColl. I work for a man called Cumming in London. Connected to the Admiralty," he added, with appropriate imprecision. He passed across the encrypted report. "It's important this gets home as soon as possible."

"Ah," Tompkins said, staring blankly at the apparently meaningless jumble.

"It's in code," McColl pointed out.

"Ah," he said again.

McColl had visions of the young man taking it down to the Chinese post office. "You can send it from here, I presume?"

"Of course. We have our own connection to Shanghai. But what is it?" he asked. "Or shouldn't I know?"

"It's naval intelligence. From Tsingtau."

"Ah."

"The sooner it's sent, the better."

"Our operator will be here at nine."

"Chinese?"

"Yes, but utterly loyal."

"Good," McColl said. A pity, was what he thought—the sooner the Germans knew the information had been sent, the safer he would be. "I don't suppose you know what time the morning train to Shanghai leaves?"

"Ten o'clock." Tompkins consulted his pocketwatch. "You've still got time."

It had been dark for an hour when McColl's train pulled in to Shanghai's main station. He walked out across the wide forecourt to the tram stop on Boundary Road, where a huge crowd of Chinese people were willing a tram to appear around the corner of Cunningham Road. Three or four trams would be required to carry so many, and even then oxygen would be in short supply. And he felt impatient after so much sitting on trains. Deciding to cut his losses, he checked the change in his pocket. The meal on the train had cost him his taxi fare, but a rickshaw was still within reach. He hailed one of the hovering coolies and called out "the Palace Hotel" as he stepped up into the seat.

They set off, the coolie jogging along beside the new tram tracks for a few hundred yards before veering south onto North Honan Road. The smell of horse dung was strong in the air, the piles of manure awaiting collection by the night-soil teams. All the shops and cafés were still open, lit by the yellow glow of their paraffin lamps, and despite the evening chill many owners were sitting outside, blankly watching the world go by.

The coolie turned off the main road and hurried down an alley, the rickshaw bumping on the uneven surface, causing McColl to grip the sides. They were still in the International Settlement, but these back streets were Chinese territory in all but name, lined with vegetable and fruit sellers, cobblers and barbers and letter writers, fortune-tellers and tea traders. A succession of aromas teased McColl's appetite—clove-scented rice, roasting chestnuts, egg foo yong. Every now and then, a beggar's arm reached hopefully out and just as swiftly disappeared.

There were people everywhere, and at first sight all of them seemed to be arguing, haranguing one another in that barking tone some Europeans found so offensive. But look a little closer and there were smiles on many faces, especially the children's. Family life often seemed a happier affair here than it did in London or Glasgow, and even the dogs seemed less aggressive.

The rickshaw emerged from the maze of allies, turning onto North Szechuan Road just up from the General Hospital and crossing the Soochow Creek with its myriad sampans and dreadful smell. The coolie was panting a little now, sending yellow gusts of breath out into the cold air, but his pace showed no sign of slackening, and soon they were passing the Chinese post office. Another two blocks and they took the last turn onto Nanking Road. Here, outside the big stores, the faces on the sidewalk were mostly European, and the Chinese people packed in the passing trams looked like tourists in a foreign town.

The coolie stopped as close to the hotel's front door as the line of automobiles would let him and carefully counted the coins McColl handed over. "*Cumshaw*," he demanded, holding out an upturned palm.

McColl had included a tip but added another. Why argue over a farthing?

Inside, the Chinese desk clerk informed him that Jed and Mac had taken Room 501 but were currently out. Despite a careful perusal of McColl's passport, he refused to relinquish the room key until the English night manager had been summoned from wherever it was he lurked. The latter accompanied McColl up in the brand-new elevator and opened the door on what turned out to be a suite—the others had somewhat exceeded their instructions. It was at the back of the hotel, which McColl hoped had lowered the cost.

Once the manager had left, he took a look around. A Chinese variant on the British army's camp bed had been erected in the lounge, and Mac's belongings were neatly stacked alongside it. Jed's were liberally scattered on either side of the double bed in the adjoining room, which the two of them would presumably be sharing. Well, it wouldn't be the first time.

The bathroom contained a large iron bath, and the hot-water tap was actually that. For Shanghai this was luxury. He started the water running in earnest, and by the time he'd come up with a fresh towel and a change of clothes, the bath was almost full. Stretched out in the water, he watched two tjiktjak lizards chasing each other across the steam-blurred ceiling and thought about Caitlin Hanley.

Toweled and dressed, he went back down to the bar for a drink. They had Tsingtao Tsingtau beer, for which he had acquired a definite taste and which seemed the appropriate brew for toasting his recent escape. He took it over to an empty table, where someone had abandoned a copy of the *North China Daily News*. The local news was uninteresting, but one short piece caught his eye. Mohandas Gandhi had been arrested in South Africa.

McColl had met Gandhi, and under somewhat unusual circumstances. Their paths had crossed more than fourteen years earlier, when he himself was a nineteen-year-old soldier in the British Army. During the Battle of Spion Kop, his regiment had been one of those ordered to a supposed summit only to find itself surrounded by higher-placed Boers and subject to a withering crossfire. McColl had been badly wounded early on, then trapped underneath a dying comrade's body for the rest of the night. The first face he'd seen when the corpse was lifted off him belonged to a smiling Indian medic.

They had talked a lot on the long stretcher trip down. The Indian was sure that McColl would recover—his faith in the body's self-healing properties was matched only by a parallel faith in humanity's. McColl hadn't recognized his savior's name at the time but had later discovered that Mohandas Gandhi was already a national celebrity. He had followed the Indian's political exploits in the British press ever since and knew he'd recently been leading a series of nonviolent protests in Transvaal against the forced registration and fingerprinting of his fellow Asians. His arrest suggested he'd been too successful for his own good.

McColl sat back with his beer, remembering their walk down the mountain. It felt strange, even to him, but ever since that day he had drawn comfort from knowing that the Indian was out there somewhere, offering up his beatific smile and bringing hope to those without it. The only person McColl had ever told this to was his mother, and her only reply had been a tearful hug.

"Fancy meeting you here," a familiar voice said, interrupting his reverie. His younger brother was two inches taller than he was but not much more than half his age. He bore a striking physical resemblance to their father but lacked the latter's less forgivable traits. Jed might be willful, obstinate, and full of himself, but he had inherited his mother's kindness.

Although she had wondered out loud if the boy was old enough to go gallivanting around the world, she had made no real objection to the trip, provided his older brother promised to take care of him. And so far there'd been no cause to worry.

Mac was with Jed. "It's good to see you, too," McColl said, smiling up at the pair of them. Was he imagining it, or was Jed looking a little shamefaced? And Mac a little nervous?

"I'll get the beers," his younger brother said with a conspiratorial glance at Mac.

"So how was Tsingtau?" Mac asked as he took a seat.

"Cold. But useful." Mac and his brother knew that he'd been making inquiries for someone back in London but had probably assumed it was all about commercial matters. McColl had done nothing to disabuse them of the notion. "Is the Maia in one piece?"

"It's fine. The railway did us proud—there was even a special boat waiting to take it across the Yangtze. It's in the hotel basement for now, but we have to drive it over to Woosun on the twenty-eighth. The freighter doesn't come upriver."

"Good." It sounded as if Mac had been his usual efficient self. He had worked for Athelbury's firm for almost six years now, after answering an advertisement for a mechanic. Fifteen men had come to interview, but the skinny, shock-haired seventeen-year-old with the pleasant, puglike face had known more about automobiles and their engines than the rest of them put together.

Jed returned with three beers. He seemed to be growing by

the day, McColl thought—their mother would hardly recognize him when they got home. "So where have you been this evening?" he asked them.

They exchanged glances, almost involuntarily, McColl thought. He knew where they'd been.

"Don't blame Mac," Jed said. "I would have gone on my own if he hadn't come with me."

"I hope you went somewhere decent. Somewhere clean?"

"We went to the Lotus Flower—it's in the French Concession. It's famous—the navy goes there."

"So diseases from all seven seas. I—"

"Come on, Jack. Don't tell me you've never been to a place like that."

No, he couldn't. And "Not for a while" would hardly help.

"So how old were you the first time?" Jed demanded.

McColl laughed. "The same age you are now. Satisfied?"

Jed laughed, too. "Yes, I think so."

"Just don't let Mum find out."

"I wasn't planning to!"

"All right. So did you enjoy it?"

"Yeah. It was kind of quick, though."

"It gets slower."

"I was thinking—we only have a few days left . . ."

"And you'd like another go?"

"No, no. Mac and I were talking about trying some opium—"

"Christ, first a sex fiend, then a drug addict. I'm supposed to be looking after you."

"You're supposed to be showing me the world. And everyone says you can't get addicted on one pipe. I'd just like to try it, see what it's like. What harm could it do?"

"You, too?" McColl asked Mac.

"I've always been curious," Mac confessed.

"You've had it, haven't you?" Jed challenged his brother.

"Only once, when I was here before. But I met a lot of

Europeans who liked to indulge, and some of them were addicted." He caught their expressions. "Oh, all right—I don't suppose one visit will do us any harm. But I'll be busy for the next few days. How about celebrating the Chinese New Year in a stupor?"

"Sounds good to me," Jed said.

"What are you busy with?" Mac asked.

"This and that. Somebody I said I'd look up for a friend. I don't suppose either of you has run into Caitlin Hanley?"

"Who?"

"The American journalist from Peking. You thought she was too clever for her own good."

"Oh, her. No, I haven't."

Mac shook his head. "Nor me."

"I think he's smitten," Jed suggested to Mac.

"She is a looker," Mac responded, like the dimmer half of a comedy team.

McColl drained his glass. "Let's get some fresh air."

They walked out onto the pavement, zigzagged their way through the traffic still filling the Bund, and leaned in a line against the parapet above the river. The moon was rising downstream, the sampans shifting in the dark waters below. Some firecrackers exploded somewhere behind them, outriders of the coming New Year, and what looked like a giant firefly was rising up above the opposite bank. "It's a burning kite," McColl explained. "Someone just died, and a relation is sending their goods on behind them."

They watched it climb and disappear.

"I like it here," Jed said.

McColl smiled to himself and cast a glance at his brother. He could smell the Chinese perfume on him, sense the liberation that his evening had been. And then a darker thought, how young and full of life Jed looked and how coldly that group of German businessmen had discussed the prospect of war on that afternoon in Tsingtau.

➝ ➝ ➝

Jed and Mac seemed reluctant to rise the following morning, and McColl breakfasted alone in the huge Victorian dining
room before venturing out into the cold, crisp air. Cumming had
asked him to look into the recent visit of an Indian revolutionary named Mathra Singh while he was in Shanghai, and there
seemed no time like the present.

The Central Police Station was only a five-minute walk away,
on the corner of Foochow and Honan, and he was soon presenting himself at the duty desk. Superintendent Brabrook was the
contact name McColl had been given in London, but he was on
compassionate leave. His deputy was a Chief Inspector Johnston.

McColl was escorted up several flights of stairs and along a
corridor whose only concession to Chinese culture was a series
of cuspidors. Johnston's room was similarly English, with just an
electric ceiling fan to distinguish it from a Scotland Yard office.
The man himself was bald, red-faced, and seemed less than
pleased by McColl's arrival. "Yes, we heard you might drop in,"
he said after offering a moist hand. "But what Mathra Singh has
to do with London, I've no idea. Anything related to the Indian
community here, we report to the DCI. In Delhi," he added, in
case McColl had forgotten where the Department of Criminal
Intelligence had its headquarters.

"London is keeping a close eye on Singh's allies in San Francisco," McColl explained calmly. "So they're naturally keen to
know what messages Singh brought across the Pacific."

"The usual gibberish, I suppose," Johnston said contemp-
tuously. "But one of our own Sikhs, Constable Singh, has the
details. Mathra Singh was his assignment."

"Was?"

"Oh, yes. He's gone. Back to India, I think. Singh will know.
I'll find out if he's in the building."

McColl was left to examine the paintings on the walls—all of hunting expeditions—and the photograph on the desk of an angry-looking wife and bored-looking children. "The usual gibberish," he murmured to himself.

Perhaps. Indian would-be revolutionaries had been giving the British some considerable headaches over the last decade. Groups of exiles, first in London and then in New York City, had talked, published pamphlets, sought support, and raised money in pursuit of liberation from British rule. They had been continually monitored, arrested, and deported whenever sufficient cause could be found, and sometimes when not. But they kept popping up. The latest manifestations were in Berlin and San Francisco, where anti-English feelings were strong enough to grant the Indians significant political latitude. A young man named Har Dayal had arrived on the American West Coast in the summer of 1911 and over the last two years had managed to imbue Indian students and migrant workers with his brand of revolutionary fervor. The previous November he had launched a party and a newspaper, both called *Ghadar,* the Punjabi word for "revolt." Neither was likely to topple the empire, but rather more worryingly for Cumming and company, Har Dayal had cultivated links with other enemies of the Crown resident in San Francisco, most notably the Irish and the Germans. If a European war did come, it wouldn't be confined to Europe.

Johnston returned with a uniformed man in a turban. "This is Constable Singh," he told McColl.

They shook hands.

"Tell him about your namesake," Johnston instructed the young man.

"There's not much to tell, sahib," he began. "Mathra Singh arrived on September thirteenth and left on the Monday of last week. He stayed at a hostel in the Chinese city and attended several meetings of the Indian community here. He was very outspoken, as you would expect. His views are not commonly held in my homeland, but they are not without supporters.

Those who expressed agreement at the meetings here were noted, and an eye has been kept on their activities. The *Ghadar* newspapers that Mathra said were on their way from the United States have been intercepted and burned, and I forwarded a full report of his visit to Delhi. I think that is all, sahib. Unless you have questions?"

McColl couldn't think of any. "No. Thank you, Constable."

Singh bowed slightly, exchanged glances with Johnston, and left.

"And thank you, Chief Inspector," McColl added, shaking the moist hand again. "Your cooperation is appreciated."

So that was that, he thought once back outside—there was no need to think about *Ghadar* again until he reached San Francisco. He wasn't sure whether he felt relieved at ducking a chore or annoyed that a possible payday had eluded him. A bit of both probably. At least he could concentrate on looking after his brother and finding Caitlin Hanley.

But first there was the matter of his wardrobe. He walked back up past Trinity Cathedral to Nanking Road and took a tram heading west. The tailor's shop he'd used on his last visit was at the eastern end of Bubbling Well Road, across from the Race Club, and seemed unchanged from five years earlier. Li Ch'ün was still standing over his cutting table, scissors in hand, pins lined up between his lips. He not only recognized McColl but even remembered his name.

"I don't think I'm any fatter," McColl said as Li took his measurements with a tape labeled MADE IN BIRMINGHAM.

"Half inch maybe," Li Ch'ün decided. "Look fabrics," he ordered.

McColl chose two and saw no point in haggling over a few pennies. He arranged to pick up the suits in a couple of days and told Li Ch'ün to expect a visit from his younger brother, Jed.

"I give good deal," the Chinese man promised, helping McColl into his coat.

A tram clanged to a halt as he reached the stop, and he climbed aboard, running the usual gauntlet of Chinese stares. The racing grounds slipped past on the right, and soon they were passing the town hall and back among the European shops on Nanking Road, where a posse of businessmen's wives were window-shopping for jewelry. Where would she be staying? In one of the better Chinese hotels, as she had in Peking? There were so many more of them in Shanghai.

He decided he would try the European establishments first, if only because their number was limited. The Kalee, the Burlington, and Bickerton's were all within an easy walk, and then there was Astor House, the city's most exclusive hotel, on the other side of Soochow Creek. Surely no self-respecting suffragette would stay there?

There was also the Hotel des Colonies in the French concession, and probably others he hadn't heard of. It might make more sense to hang around the Shanghai Club and ask any fellow Americans that he ran into.

Four hotels and two hours later, he passed between the two Sikh doormen and entered the club, intent on lunch. The food was disappointing, and expensive by Shanghai standards; more to the point, no one had news of his quarry. Two of the Americans he approached were certain she was still in Peking, while one was convinced she'd already gone home.

He left, walked south down the Bund, then turned inland along the canal that marked the border between the French and International concessions. The Hotel des Colonies was on the Rue du Consulat, but she wasn't staying there either. He was back on the pavement, wondering where to start with the Chinese hotels, when he saw her across the street, in animated discussion with a rickshaw coolie.

Though "discussion," as McColl soon discovered, was something of a misnomer. She wanted a ride to an authentic Chinese teahouse, and either the man couldn't understand her or he was simply refusing to comply, on the not-unreasonable grounds that single European women did not visit such places.

It turned out to be the former.

"I didn't know you spoke Chinese," she said, almost indignantly.

He seized his chance. "I know a teahouse not far from here. Will you let me buy you tea?"

"A real one? One that the Chinese use?"

"I promise," he said. "If there are any other Europeans, we'll leave immediately."

She smiled at that and allowed him to help her into the rickshaw. She was wearing a long, black coat over a crimson blouse and an ankle-length gray skirt, but no hat. Her hair was tied back in a loose bun, stray wisps hanging over her ears.

McColl told the bemused coolie where they were going—a teahouse he knew just inside the nearest Chinese city gate—and climbed up beside her.

"Thank you," she said, giving him another smile.

Like most of the buildings that surrounded it, the teahouse looked shabby from the outside, but the carved wooden screen beyond the door was truly beautiful. "To keep out the bad spirits," she murmured to herself, as if she were remembering a line of homework.

Inside, numerous round tables were scattered across a huge room, and upwards of a hundred people were talking, shouting, laughing, eating, or playing mah-jongg. None of the faces were white, and if the stares the two of them received were anything to go by, European patronage was far from a common occurrence. Once they were seated, she showed no hesitation in staring back, her eyes aglow with excitement. When McColl asked her what tea she wanted, she just waved an arm and told him to order for both of them.

He did so.

"There's no deference," she noted with satisfaction. "They're just being who they are."

He had never thought of it that way, but she was right. "This is their city," was all he said.

"Yes," she murmured.

"I hear you're a journalist," he said.

"Yes, yes I am."

"On which paper?"

She reluctantly turned her face to his. "It varies. I'm here for the *New York Tribune*. Supposedly to report on the revolution." She smiled wryly. "But it seems to have been postponed."

"Yes."

Their tea arrived, a green brew with floating jasmine blossoms.

She sipped at her cup and grimaced slightly. "You must know China well?"

"No, not all . . ."

"But you speak the language."

"I speak quite a few. They just come easily, I'm afraid."

She looked at him with what he hoped was interest. "How lucky. I wish they came easily to me."

"I suspect you have other talents."

"Perhaps, but not speaking the local language is such a handicap. I feel more than a little lost here, to be honest. I came to stay with a college friend—her name's Soong Ch'ing-ling—but when Yuan Shih-kai attacked Sun Yat-sen, her family all fled to Japan. Ch'ing-ling made sure I had somewhere to stay, but it's not the same as having a friend who knows her way around." A thought occurred to her. "How long are you here for?"

"Oh, quite a while." He felt absurdly reluctant to put any limit on his availability.

"Well, if you have any spare time for chaperoning, I'd love to see the Chinese city—the rest of it, I mean. And eat some real Chinese food. And maybe see some of the countryside . . ."

"I'd be delighted."

"Oh, that's wonderful. Thank you." She pulled a watch from

her purse and consulted it. "I'm afraid I have to go in the next few minutes—there's someone else I'm meeting. And I have an engagement tomorrow. But can we do something on Friday? I could come to your hotel if that's easiest."

McColl felt faintly shocked by the suggestion. "No, I can pick you up. Just tell me where and when."

She gave him the address. "It's just off Bubbling Well Road."

"Ten o'clock?" he suggested.

"I'll be waiting."

He called for the bill, which arrived almost immediately.

She leaned across to look at it, and he felt the warmth of her breath. "Look," she said, "I almost dragged you here. Let me pay my half."

"No, of course not," he said, again feeling slightly shocked.

"All right, but on Friday we must share. Or I won't come."

He couldn't help smiling. "If you insist."

Thursday passed slowly. McColl wandered idly around the European city in the morning, in the vain hope that he might run into her. He was behaving like a schoolboy with a crush, he realized, and reminded himself that he knew next to nothing about the woman. Merely that she had modern ideas— and lips he dearly wanted to kiss.

Passing a shop with postcards on display, he went in and bought two—a photograph of a rickshaw and coolie for his mother and one of the Bund for Tim Athelbury, his boss back in London. The nearby British post office supplied him with the necessary stamps, and he walked down Peking Road to the public gardens overlooking the confluence of Soochow Creek and the Whangpo River.

It was another sparkling winter day, and he found himself remembering the house in Morar with its view of the sea, where he'd spent his early childhood. They'd moved to Fort William when he was seven and then to Glasgow five years later, as his father worked his way up the union hierarchy. He wondered how his mother was coping now that there was no child at home to act as a buffer.

He could picture her picking the postcard up off the hall carpet and carrying it through to her chair in the parlor, but he couldn't think of much to say. He told her he and Jed were safe and well, that the food was interesting but not a patch on hers, that all Chinese porridge was made with rice. Which was probably untrue, he realized—the best Shanghai hotels probably imported oats for their homesick Western guests. "Love to you and Dad," he concluded, preserving the form for her sake. He would have to go and see them when he returned—it had been almost two years since his last visit.

After scribbling a few trite lines to his boss—Tim was already receiving cabled reports of their sales—McColl walked back up the riverbank to their hotel, where he dropped off the cards in the guests' mailbox.

He spent the afternoon sightseeing with Jed, Mac having excused himself to write some letters of his own. As they traipsed around the Chinese city, McColl twice caught glimpses of the same Chinese man some twenty yards behind them. He could think of no reason anyone would be following him—the Germans would certainly know by now that he had unburdened himself of his Tsingtau observations—so it was probably a coincidence. Either that or a thief hoping to catch one of them alone in some dark alley. If so, he was out of luck.

But then, out on the Bund a couple of hours later, he thought he saw the man again. He and Jed were standing at the parapet across from their hotel, watching the never-ending show that was the river, when McColl caught a glimpse of the familiar silhouette only to have it instantly obscured by a tram grinding its way around the bend into Nanking Road.

"It makes me feel like an old hand," Jed was saying, and McColl followed his gaze to where a party of Europeans was disembarking from a steam tender and taking what for many was a first wide-eyed look at the Orient. Seeing the expression on his brother's face, he felt really glad he had persuaded their parents to let the boy tag along.

When he glanced back across the street, his shadow was nowhere to be seen. A phantom, most likely. He remembered being told on his first visit that Europeans often imagined they were being followed—all empires, it seemed, were haunted by their subjects.

Friday morning he was up with the light. The carriage and ponies he had hired for the day would be at the hotel entrance by nine-thirty, which gave him time to attend to some business. After strolling down the Bund to the telegraph office, he had a five-minute wait for the doors to open, but the replies he was expecting had indeed arrived and the three automobiles ordered earlier that month were awaiting shipment at the London Docks. Another two days and he could inform the Shanghai buyers that their vehicles were at sea.

He walked back to the hotel, pleased that the weather hadn't deteriorated overnight. It was certainly cold, but the sun was out, the sky mostly blue. The countryside around Shanghai could be depressing at the best of times, particularly for those with a social conscience. And that, he suspected, was something Caitlin Hanley had in abundance.

The carriage was already outside the hotel, the smartly liveried Chinese handler chatting to one of the uniformed Sikh doormen, the ponies idly pawing the ground. McColl introduced himself to the handler and received the usual graduated reaction to his fluency in Shanghainese, the surprise shifting into annoyance—this foreign devil would be harder to bamboozle. After he had taken a quick trip back inside to check his appearance and collect a bottle of Hirano drinking water, they started down Nanking Road, where both ponies chose to empty their bowels.

They found the house without difficulty, a suburban villa that wouldn't have looked out of place in Hampstead. A Chinese amah opened the door, but Caitlin was right behind her, ready to go. She looked approvingly at the ponies and carriage and allowed him to help her up. "So where are we going?" she asked.

He joined her. "I thought we could drive out into the country for a few miles, turn south, and visit the Longhua Pagoda—I'm told it's quite something. We can have lunch there and then head back along the river to explore the Chinese city on foot. How does that sound?"

"Wonderful," she said with a smile.

The handler jerked the Mongolian ponies into motion and directed them back to Bubbling Well Road. The road wound its way west for a couple of miles through European-style housing, passed the sentry box marking the border of the International concession, and headed out into increasingly open country. The land was flat, crisscrossed by irrigation ditches and larger channels, and there seemed to be a lot of people working the fields for the time of year. McColl would have liked to explain what they were doing, but he didn't have a clue. When was rice planted? And were those mulberry trees?

Fortunately for him, she appeared happy just to drink it all in. They sat in companionable silence for what seemed a long time—long enough, he decided eventually. "Where's home?" he asked her. "Where in the States, I mean."

"New York City. Brooklyn, if you know where that is."

"I do. Did you grow up there?"

"Yes." She smiled, apparently at the memory, and hitched her riding skirt up an inch or so. "In a brownstone near Prospect Park."

"Brothers and sisters?"

"Two brothers, one sister."

"And what does your father do?"

"He's sort of retired," she said vaguely.

"And did you always want to be a journalist?"

"No. But I always wanted to be something. I went to Wesleyan College," she added, as if that explained something.

"That's in Connecticut, isn't it?"

"No, that's Wesleyan University. Wesleyan College is in Georgia. It's the oldest college for women in America. That's where I met my Chinese friend Ch'ing-ling. She's Sun Yat-sen's secretary now—that's why she's in Japan."

"You do move in exalted circles."

She laughed at that. "We were both outsiders at Wesleyan—which is probably why we became so close. She for being Chinese, me for . . . well, I didn't come from a wealthy Protestant family like all the others. My aunt paid for me—she wanted me to have chances in life that she never had. She would have paid for my sister Finola as well, but Finola wasn't the slightest bit interested in going to college. I love her dearly, but green eyes are about the only thing we two girls have in common."

They were entering a cluster of houses that, with their attendant trees, felt like a small island in the sea of paddies. There were men sitting outside most of the doorways, their eyes firmly fixed on the intruders, even when talking to one another.

"I'd love to see inside one of the houses," Caitlin said hopefully.

McColl told the handler to stop and tried to think up an acceptable reason to snoop around in someone else's home. There wasn't one. "I'll give you a mace for a look inside your house," he told the nearest resident. A mace was worth about threepence, probably quite a sum in a place like this.

The man quickly conquered his surprise and extended a hand toward his door. McColl took the lead, holding the door open to let in light. There was not much to see, just a few pots, a makeshift bed, and a stub of candle. It would be cold in winter, wet and mosquito-infested in summer. And they were less than ten miles from the Shanghai Club.

Caitlin was trying, and failing, to say thank you in Mandarin.

McColl handed the man the coin he had promised, helped her back aboard, and gave the driver the nod to proceed.

"Did you notice?" she said. "They were all men. The women are in the fields."

"It's the same the world over. In poor countries the women work the land."

"I know. But why is that? And how do you square that with the situation back home, where women who want a career are frowned upon? Talk about having your cake and eating it!"

He knew better than to smile at her outrage. "Did you find it hard getting into journalism? There can't be that many women writing for newspapers."

She looked slightly sheepish. "I had help. A friend of the family. But once I was in, I had no trouble proving I could do the job. And well. I've been doing it for six years now."

"What area are you in?" he asked. He found it hard to imagine her writing about fashion or cooking recipes.

"Politics, mostly. I was on the city desk for the first three years, and then I persuaded the editor to send me to England to do pieces on the suffragettes and the situation in Ireland. Two years ago I covered the strike in Lawrence—did you hear about that?"

"I did." Twenty thousand textile workers in the New England town—most of them poorly paid recent immigrants—had come out in protest when their pay was inexcusably cut and eventually won a famous victory. "Being there in the thick of it must have been something."

"It was at the time, but go there now and it's hard to believe they won. When last year's strike in Paterson was lost, it all felt very depressing, as if nothing would ever really change."

"You were there as well?"

"Oh, yes. And I met some wonderful people."

"You love your work, don't you?"

She glanced across at him, as if to check that he wasn't pulling her leg. "I do," she said simply.

They traveled for several minutes in renewed silence, the ponies picking their way down the rutted road. In the fields on either side, rows of plantings stretched toward the flat horizon. Winter wheat, he thought, but he wouldn't have put money on it.

She asked what sort of business he was in.

"Automobiles."

"Oh. There can't be much of a market in China."

"Just a few rich Europeans, a few rich Chinese. But my boss in England likes the idea of having our cars on every continent, even if it's only a handful of them. He says it's an investment, but I think it just makes him feel important."

"He might be right about this country. Ch'ing-ling thinks that once things really begin to change, there'll be no stopping China."

"But she's had to flee to Japan."

She grimaced. "True."

"The world never changes as fast as we want it to."

She turned her face to his, challenge in her eyes. "Yes, but do you want it to? Do you want women to have the vote? Your empire to end? Everyone to get a fair share of the wealth?"

He held her gaze. "Yes," he said, "I do. And what's more, I'm pretty sure all those things will happen, whether *I* want them to or not. Women should have the vote, and they will—it's just a matter of time. And all empires come to a sticky end sooner or later, even those that do some good. As to sharing out the wealth . . . well, I can't see it happening anytime soon. But state pensions and unemployment benefits have been introduced in the last few years, at least in England and Germany. Things *are* changing . . ."

"Just not as fast as I want them to," she quoted him.

"Exactly."

"Maybe. On bad days I think like you do. When I was in Lawrence, covering the strike, I saw how terrible the workers' conditions were—it was heartbreaking. And the other day one of Ch'ing-ling's Chinese friends told me that girls in the silk factories here are forced to spin the silk over pans of boiling water so that the steam elasticizes the threads, and their hands are completely crippled within a few years. And then the owners fire them and throw them into the street. How can people like that live with themselves?"

"I don't know." It was, he realized, one of those questions he'd given up trying to answer.

"Neither do I," she murmured, and it felt as if they'd come to some sort of basic agreement.

They reached the Longhua Pagoda early in the afternoon. The site was mostly ruins, the pagoda itself chipped and faded but impressive in a cold sort of way. Like most classical Chinese architecture, it appeared designed to awe rather than lift the spirit. The restaurant nearby seemed reasonably clean, and McColl ordered rice and vegetables for them both. She struggled with the chopsticks, but when he offered to ask if they had a fork, she quickly refused. "It'll help me get slim," she said.

When he raised an eyebrow at that, she gave him a look he couldn't decipher.

They followed the line of the Whangpo back to Shanghai and arrived at one of the southern entrances to the walled Chinese city. McColl arranged for the carriage to collect them up at the northern gate in a couple of hours and led the way into the maze of narrow roads and alleys. They explored for an hour or more, stopping to look at temples, gardens, and the hundreds of small shops. She bought only one thing—a small brass dragon. "A memento," she said as the shopkeeper wrapped it in cloth. "I could have gotten it for a tenth as much, right?"

"Probably."

She shrugged happily, and he liked her for that.

They visited the famous Willow Pattern teahouse, heading upstairs for the view across the tiled rooftops. But McColl had other ideas for tea—a new establishment he'd visited a month earlier where the Chinese people brought their caged songbirds and sipped while they sang.

On the way to the gate, they were forced to wait while a line of prisoners yoked in cangues filed past under guard.

"They look like condemned men," she observed.

"That space outside the first temple we saw is the execution ground," he explained, without stopping to think.

"Oh," she said, more interested than upset, turning to watch the receding column.

He half expected a plea to witness the executions, but she just shuddered slightly and walked on toward the looming gateway.

The carriage was outside, the handler feeding one of the ponies from a canvas bag. As they drove north across the French concession, she said, "I don't want to presume, but I have some shopping to do—presents for the family—and I wonder if you would come with me, as an interpreter. It would make things so much easier."

"Of course," he said.

"Tomorrow afternoon," she suggested. "I'll meet you in the Whiteaway Laidlaw department store. In the tearoom."

"All right."

Perhaps he sounded offended, because she quickly added that she also wanted his company as a friend and placed her hand on his to emphasize the fact. He felt something like an electric shock at the contact and hid his confusion behind an idiotic smile. He had read about such reactions in novels but had never believed they were real.

She was punctual, too, as he discovered the following day. Over tea she asked him what he was doing for Chinese New Year, and he told her he'd be spending it with his brother and Mac. "We'll probably eat too much and drink too much," he said, neglecting to mention their date with three opium pipes.

"I'm spending the day with friends of Ch'ing-ling," she told him. "Seeing how the Chinese do it."

They passed a couple of hours hopping from shop to shop on Nanking Road and its cheaper side streets, sifting through bronzes and brasses, cloisonné vases and Chinese jewelry, then moved on to Honan Street, famous for its silk and furs. By the time darkness had fallen, she had presents for everyone—jade earrings for her sister, a beautiful shawl for her aunt, and dragon cuff links for her father and older brother. She had already bought an antique map for her younger brother, who apparently loved such things.

When he offered to see her home in a rickshaw, she suggested they take the tram instead. "Rickshaws make me feel guilty," she said. "I feel like jumping out and walking alongside to lessen the weight. I know it's silly, I know I'm taking work away from them, but . . ."

They rode the tram and walked through the European houses to that of her absent friends. He carried the presents into the hall and turned to find her shutting the door. She walked up to him, placed a hand either side of his waist, and told him she would like to be kissed.

He put his lips gently on hers, then matched her more passionate response, his momentary shock at her brazen behavior swiftly subsumed by desire.

Their bodies pressed together with predictable results.

She pulled back slightly and looked him in the eyes. "Jack," she said calmly, using his name for the first time, "would you like to take me to bed?"

He just stared at her.

"A yes or no will do."

"Yes, yes, of course. But I have no . . ."

"I do. Let's go up to my room." Taking his hand, she led him up the wide staircase and along the landing to the farthest door. His brain dimly registered the large iron bed facing the screened-off window, the low tables on either side bearing tall brass candleholders.

He might have dreamed a moment like this.

"Light the candles," she told him. "I'll be a few minutes."

He did as he was told, turned out the lights, and took off his shoes and socks. He could hardly believe what was happening. There were so many reasons he should have said no, so many reasons she shouldn't have asked, but all he felt was longing.

"You're still dressed," she said, coming back into the room. She was wearing a Japanese dressing gown, and unbound hair now framed her face. With a smile she discarded the kimono, offering a glimpse of nipples and the dark bush between her legs as she slipped under the blankets.

He removed the rest of his clothes, climbed in himself, and reached to take her in his arms. She held him back with a hand on his shoulder, looking into his eyes, as if for reassurance. Whatever she saw there seemed to satisfy her, and she snuggled up against him, her tongue looking for his, their bodies squirming this way and that with the rapture of embrace.

After he had come, he lay back in wonder at what had just happened. Some whores pretended to enjoy it, but his wife had not even done that—admitting on their honeymoon that she found the whole business disgusting, she had offered herself up with firmly closed eyes and unnerving rigidity. Never in his thirty-two years had he encountered a woman with Caitlin's sexual passion. For the first time in his life, he knew why they called it making love.

It was wonderful, yet still he felt disconcerted, a ludicrous sense that this was not how it was supposed to be.

She asked him for a cigarette, deepening that sense.

He leaned over, pulled a packet from his coat pocket, and turned back to find her sitting up against the wooden headrest, displaying her beautiful breasts.

She must have caught something in his expression. "In case

you're wondering," she said, "I don't sleep with every man who takes me shopping. I'm not a virgin, as you now know, but I haven't slept with hundreds of men. Or even ten. And you've probably slept with more women than that."

"Probably."

"So?"

"It's different for women," he said, almost reluctantly.

"Why?"

"Men can't get pregnant."

"These days women don't have to, as long as they're careful. And I am." She put out the cigarette and got up from the bed. He thought she reached for the kimono, then decided against it. "I'll be back," she said over her shoulder.

A few minutes later, she was, and seeing her walk toward him across the candlelit room almost took his breath away.

She climbed back into bed, and while her lips sought his, her hand found his rapidly hardening penis. "I think we're ready again," she whispered.

"I don't think you should stay the night," she said after they'd both listened to the clock strike eleven. "You know how people are, and I wouldn't want anyone talking about scandalous goings-on in this house. My Chinese friends have enough problems to deal with at the moment."

"Of course," he agreed. "But when can I see you again?"

"I don't know. I'm staying at my friend's friends' for the next two days, but after that . . ." She smiled wickedly. "I'm sure we can find time to do this again before my ship sails on Friday."

"Which ship?" he asked.

"The *Manchuria*—why?"

"I'm booked on the *Manchuria*."

"You are?" There was confusion in her eyes, perhaps even a touch of panic. But nothing that looked like delight. "I assumed you were going back to England," she said, as much to herself as to him.

"I am—via the States."

"Oh. Well, I expect we'll see each other on the ship, then."

"And before that? Can I call you? I saw the telephone downstairs."

"Yes, why don't you? I'll be back here late on Monday—I don't know when."

Her smile seemed forced, and he felt a sharp pang of disappointment.

She put on the kimono to accompany him downstairs, watched as he wrote the telephone's number, and kissed him good night with what almost felt like anger. Walking away down the dark, silent avenue, McColl tried to make sense of what had just happened. And he could find only one interpretation that fit the facts. She had seduced him, and enjoyed the experience, safe in the mistaken assumption that they would be parted by thousands of miles. Once aware of her error, and the impossibility of a brief and finite affair, she had not known what to do with him. Or, more precisely, not known how to tell him good-bye.

It was all for the best, he told himself. He liked to think himself a willing part of a fast-changing world, but perhaps there were some things he just wasn't ready for.

Which was easier to think than to feel, while all his senses were still dancing to her tune.

When McColl left their hotel late in the morning on Chinese New Year's Eve, the change in the weather mirrored his mood, and the cold fog hanging over river and city reminded him of the summer's Fu Manchu stories. Sax Rohmer's Chinese villain had spun his webs in London's Limehouse, not Shanghai, but today the cities seemed eerily alike, from the yellow-lit trams to the mournful horns of invisible ships.

Mac and Jed had decided to ignore the fog and drive the automobile to Woosun. He hoped they wouldn't run over any peasants or end up in some stagnant canal. The two of them would be coming back by boat and had left a note suggesting they all meet at the Carlton Hotel on Ningpo Road. The circled newspaper advertisement accompanying the note claimed that the Carlton was "the one place where you can get a meal that reminds you of home." And in case anyone conjured up a mental picture of cockroaches clinging to sausages, the kitchen was declared "open to inspection at any time." McColl could hardly wait.

In the meantime he had an anxious client to placate. After coffee at a Nanking Road café, he reluctantly made his way up to Hongkew for his appointment with Hsi Lun, one of the wealthy Chinese entrepreneurs who had ordered a Maia. The man had asked his son, Chu, to be there—a young man of around twenty who had returned from three years of college in America armed with enough alien habits, quirks, and idiosyncrasies to put anyone's teeth on edge. Chu's insistence on checking through every detail of the purchase agreement seemed tantamount to calling the buyer an idiot and the seller a thief, but his father looked admiringly on, and McColl just smiled and bore it. The deal was already signed and delivered, and it always paid to keep a customer sweet, even when you felt like slapping his son.

After this encounter McColl reckoned that a decent lunch and several stiff drinks at the Shanghai Club was the least he deserved. Emerging a couple of hours later, he thought he saw the possible shadow from several days before, but the air was still heavy with mist and he couldn't be sure. After hiring a rickshaw, he spent much of the journey glancing back over his shoulder, but no one was following. He was imagining it—he had to be—if anyone were following him, where had whoever it was been the last few days? After alighting at the cable office, he stood in the doorway for more than a minute, scanning the street they'd come down, but no one loomed out of the mist.

Inside, he received his first good news of the day—Cumming

not only praised him for his work in Tsingtau but had also wired extra funds to cover his "unexpected costs."

He went back to the hotel, spent the rest of the afternoon reading a collection of Sherlock Holmes stories he found in Mac's suitcase, then set out for the promised feast. The boys were there when he arrived, and they greeted him with stories of getting lost in the fog and almost driving into the sea—they had obviously had a good time. The meal proved as bad as expected, an impersonation of the British fry-up that tasted completely wrong but looked sufficiently familiar to make you cruelly aware of what you were missing. It didn't remind them of home so much as of how far away it was.

Chinese New Year's Eve in Shanghai, he thought sourly, and wondered where in the city she was.

New Year's Day was at least sunnier, the bitter north wind having driven the clouds away. The three of them lunched rather too well at the Shanghai Club, took a walk down along the Bund for exercise, and enjoyed a late-afternoon siesta ahead of their meeting with China's bane. McColl had gotten the address of a respectable opium den in the French concession, and soon after dark their two rickshaws were pulling up outside a decrepit-looking building in a side street behind the Chinese Theater. The golden characters above the doorway claimed that it was Heaven's Gate, which seemed somewhat optimistic. The interior, however, was as rich as the exterior was squalid, a symphony in sculptured wood, embroidered silk, and exquisite watercolors. There was very little noise for a Chinese establishment, and most of those at the dark wooden tables sat alone with their thoughts and their tea.

"Blimey," was Jed's first reaction.

"They're on their way out," McColl told him. "Getting themselves ready for the outside world. Are you sure you want to go through with this?"

"Of course," his brother declared, a sliver of doubt in his eyes.

McColl spoke to one of the staff, who led them upstairs and into a small, paneled room. There was a wooden couch against each wall and a large scroll painting of misty mountains on the one facing the door. The pillows were made of porcelain—and felt like it. In the center of the room, a low Chinese table with upturned ends held a small oil lamp and a joss-stick holder. The latter was already burning, infusing the room with its odor, but McColl could also smell the opium, heavier, sweeter, like bait in a trap.

They laid themselves out on the couches, the other two looking slightly self-conscious, and watched as a young girl lit the oil lamp and heated the sticky balls on wicked-looking needles. The look on her face was intensely serious and reminded McColl of Jed as a small boy, trying to write his own name for the first time.

He took a few deep drags on the offered pipe and lay back. "It's not instantaneous," he warned the others, but it felt quicker than the last time he had taken it. The lines of wall and ceiling seemed to soften, curling like a burning piece of paper, only so much slower. He looked across at Jed, who smiled back at him, and the smile itself seemed to stretch, like something out of Lewis Carroll. He looked again and, for once, saw his mother's face in his brother's. He remembered skipping down the street with her, hand in hand, jumping over those paving stones with cracks and laughing fit to burst. He could feel his own smile stretching, and such pleasure in the memory.

Time loosened its hold. When the girl returned with the pipe, he couldn't have said whether hours had passed or only moments. Both Jed and Mac had beatific smiles on their faces, and the flame of the oil lamp was dancing shadows on the ceiling. The smoke from the joss stick coiled like Caitlin's hair, and when he closed his eyes, he saw the green of hers. He felt no anger, no anxiety, no disappointment. And if there was sadness, it was oh, so sweet. Everything was as it should be.

When the girl eventually led them downstairs, his watch said they'd been there for three hours. Tea was provided, and they sat in silence for a while, giving each other *Can you believe it?* smiles and sipping from the patterned porcelain cups. As the drug began to wear off, McColl felt his sense of serenity slowly start to fracture, and he almost cried out in resentment.

The city itself was still wide awake, and while he settled their bill, his companions decided on a second visit to the Lotus Flower. They tried to persuade him to join them, but Jed seemed more than a little relieved when he refused. "I have a call to make," McColl explained, without divulging whom it was to or his fear that no one would answer. Back at the hotel, he asked the operator to get him the number, had a moment of hope when the phone was picked up, then listened to the *amah* intone, after a suspiciously long interval, that "missee not home." Much to his distress, he could picture Caitlin at the top of the stairs, silently shaking her head.

He thanked the clerk, walked back outside, and worked his way through the traffic on the Bund to the parapet above the river. He just had to accept it, he told himself—it had been wonderful, strange, and for only one night. It might be awkward at first on the ship, but they would soon get over it. She, it seemed, already had.

The sound of running feet pulled his eyes from the river, and he barely had time to shift his body before the man was upon him. A knife glittered in the yellow light as it arced toward him, and his outthrust fist smashed across the side of his assailant's head at exactly the moment the blade cut agonizingly into his abdomen. McColl was briefly aware of the man falling, picking himself up, and running away, and of shouts from several directions. He was, he realized, on his knees, the knife still buried in his body, the blood seeping through his questing fingers. He resisted the temptation to pull the knife out, and his last thought was self-congratulatory, that he had at least learned something from Gandhi and his fellow medics on the long slog down from Spion Kop.

Stateroom 302

♠

McColl could feel and just about hear the low throb of the engines—the ship was under way. Jed and Mac would be leaning over the rail and waving China good-bye, but he was flat on his back in an upper-deck cabin, and all he could see of the outside world was a circle of gray sky.

He had spent a good portion of the last few days either asleep or deep in drug-induced unconsciousness, so that much of what he knew of recent events was hearsay. He did remember the jolting rickshaw ride to the General Hospital, but all he could recall of his arrival there was a bewildering kaleidoscope of anxious faces. The next thing he knew, he was coming to in a private room, with an anxious brother looking on. As Jed had later admitted, he hadn't relished telling their mother where he'd been while his brother was getting murdered.

McColl was, it seemed, out of danger but confined to bed for at least a week. The knife had pierced his liver, which was better news than it sounded—apparently, as organs went, this one healed quicker than most. He had spent the first day staring at the ceiling, occasionally dozing off despite the pain. Whenever the door to his private room opened, he hoped it would be her, but it never was. Perhaps she hadn't heard, though that was hard to believe—the story of the Englishman almost killed by a Chinese person had made the front page of the *North China Daily News*. There was a small, extremely blurred picture of him, along with a bigger and clearer one of the Maia, which had to be good for business.

Even Cumming had heard the news from someone and sent a get-well cable.

The hospital doctor had reluctantly agreed to his joining the *Manchuria* and that morning a horse-drawn ambulance had transported him down to the steam-tender quay. He had been looking forward to the trip downriver, but all he saw from his stretcher were chimney tops, upper masts, and an occasional seagull. And after that there was the final indignity of being winched ashore by one of the liner's derricks.

McColl and his brother had planned to share a cabin, but Jed and Mac had decided to bunk together while he convalesced. Which was something of a relief—Jed was exhausting at the best of times, and he felt utterly drained of energy.

He couldn't even summon up what seemed an appropriate level of anger. His assailant had not been caught, and the man's motives remained a mystery. Perhaps he'd seen McColl in the street and taken an instant dislike to his face. Perhaps he hated all foreign devils and had picked him out at random. Or maybe the man was off his head. The only other possibility was that someone had hired him to kill McColl, which seemed ludicrous. Who would want him dead? His only current enemies were the Germans, and they would know that the intelligence gleaned in Tsingtau had already been dispatched. As far as McColl was aware, spying in peacetime was not considered a capital crime by any of the great powers.

Over the next two days, the *Manchuria* steamed slowly eastward across the East China Sea toward its next port of call, the Japanese city of Nagasaki. After working his way through Mac's

Sherlock Holmes stories and Jed's *Riders of the Purple Sage* he was forced back on the sundry newspapers the two of them had collected for him in an hour's scouring of the ship. Some were several months old, but most of the stories were still news to him. There were the usual disasters—an early-November storm over the American Great Lakes had killed more than 250 people—but also a cheering series of debuts. A ship had traversed the Panama Canal; the first transcontinental US highway had been dedicated; the Ford Motor Company had introduced something called an assembly line, which put automobiles together in a fifth of the time and would of course make them cheaper. More welcome still, peace had been declared in the Balkans, and the prospect of a wider war seemed to have receded. There was even good news for suffragettes everywhere—Norway was the latest country to give women the vote, following New Zealand, Australia, and Finland. Caitlin would be pleased.

He knew she was on board. Jed and Mac came by at regular intervals to regale him with news—the sighting of a whale, the consistency of the plum pudding, a rundown of their fellow passengers. She turned up in the last of these, among the women they considered attractive. McColl had said nothing about meeting her in Shanghai, but the two of them had recognized her from Peking. "Remember that American journalist you fancied?" Jed asked. "She keeps staring at us, and I've no idea why. She smokes in public, and I think she's one of those radical women. She is a looker, though."

His brother and Mac were having the time of their lives, McColl thought. Jed had a job waiting for him at home—his school career had been less than distinguished, and college had never been an option—and McColl wondered how small the boy would find a Glasgow insurance office after having circled the globe.

The ship's physician and surgeon both came to see him, the one to check his general state, the other to admire his Shanghai colleague's stitchwork. Neither had anything other

than rest to suggest—time, it seemed, would work a cure. And
by the time they docked in Nagasaki, McColl was making trips
to the toilet and able to dispense with the bedpan. That morning, after Jed and Mac had gone ashore in search of a samurai
sword, his steward arrived with a short note from her—she
hoped he was feeling better and would soon be up and about.
Her handwriting seemed wholly in character, somehow both
bold and controlled, but he found the whole thing strange.
There was obviously no way she could come to his cabin, but
why had she waited three days to send the message? He wondered whether to send a reply, and what he would say if he did.
"Thank you for your note" seemed somewhat ludicrous after
those hours in the candlelit room.

Soon after dark the ship weighed anchor and headed
north and east up the Kyushu coastline; by midmorning it had
passed through the narrow Kanmon Straits and was beginning
its two-day passage of the Inland Sea. On the second of these,
the weather changed for the better and McColl finally felt well
enough to sit outside on the promenade deck. He had been
enjoying the play of sun on sea for almost an hour when her
silhouette loomed above him.

"You must be better," she said.

"Yes, I am."

"Can I join you for a minute?"

"Of course." She was wearing the same black coat, with a rose-
colored hat and matching scarf.

She settled herself in the adjoining chair. "It was terrible, what
happened to you in Shanghai."

"I've had better days." He smiled. "It was the shock more than
anything else—one moment I'm standing there looking at the
river, the next I'm on my knees with a knife in my gut. It happened so fast."

"And you've no idea why the man attacked you?"

"None at all. I hadn't made any enemies in Shanghai, or at least none I was aware of."

"I only found out the morning we left—I saw a copy of the day before's paper. I would have come to the hospital if I'd known."

There was a hint of appeal in her eyes, but he didn't know what for.

"So what's in the *Times*?" she asked eventually, nodding toward the paper in his lap. "I've been shutting the world out since we boarded."

"Oh, it's all old news."

"Anything new on Irish Home Rule?"

"Nothing, but there wouldn't be. The bill doesn't get its third reading until the spring, but it'll pass. And the Ulstermen will opt out if the Nationalists let them, fight them if they don't."

"How do you feel about that?" she asked, looking him straight in the eye.

"Home Rule? I'm all for it." The cheer from farther down the deck was for an accurate punt on the shuffleboard court, not his political opinion.

"And Ulster opting out?" she pressed him.

He considered. "Well, I suppose if the Irish are justified in throwing off English rule, then they can hardly insist on ruling Ulster from Dublin."

She bridled at that. "You could say that we've put up with minority status for eight hundred years and now it's Ulster's turn."

"You could," he conceded. "So are you one of those Irish-Americans who give money for fighting the English?"

"I agree the English should leave," she retorted. "But there are other battles that interest me more."

"Women's battles?"

"Yes, but not only. Working people's battles. The poverty's better hidden at home, but it's still there. And there's so much less excuse."

He said nothing. Inside the ship the Filipino band had started serenading those enjoying an early lunch. "Don't you agree?" she asked.

"I agree that it's there. How quickly anything can be done about it is another matter."

She shook her head slightly, loosing a few stray locks. "We have to try."

"I suppose so. But how?" He wondered if she wanted to kiss him as much as he wanted to kiss her.

"Well, by writing and by organizing. Writing so that people know what the situation is, then organizing them politically, so that the bosses have to listen to them."

"You think people don't already know? All those Europeans back in Shanghai know perfectly well what sort of life the Chinese have."

"Perhaps. Look, I don't know enough about China to argue with you—if my friend Ch'ing-ling were here . . . but she isn't. So let's talk about the States or England. I don't think most people in our countries have any idea what their rulers are up to, either at home or abroad. For instance, I don't think many English people would be happy if they knew how Indians are treated by the authorities there."

McColl was unconvinced. "I don't think many would care if you presented them with the facts."

"You have a very low opinion of people."

"No, I think you overestimate the power of the written word. Just knowing that people are badly treated isn't enough." McColl smiled to himself. "A couple of years ago a friend of mine was in New York, waiting for the ship that was supposed to take him home. It was the *Titanic.* When the news reached his hotel that the ship had sunk, other residents booked on the return voyage held a meeting in the lounge. And spent the whole time complaining about how hard it would be to make fresh arrangements."

"So people are just rotten through and through."

"Not at all. I'm sure most of those people are kind to their children and servants and pets. But they weren't actually on the ship, and unless they were close to someone who went down with it . . . well, it wasn't real enough for them to actually feel any empathy. For most people, just knowing isn't enough."

"Of course. That's why the best writers are the ones who stir the heart as well as feed the mind."

"Touché. And are you one of those?"

"Not yet." She smiled and stood up. "Will you be here again tomorrow?"

"If I'm not racing round the deck." He couldn't read her expression. He had, he realized, no clue at all as to what she was feeling.

Jed was sitting with him the following day but quickly gave up his seat when she appeared. McColl introduced them and noticed a new ease in his brother's manner with the opposite sex. Whatever else the Lotus Flower had given him, it seemed to have cured his chronic shyness with women.

"Is he your only sibling?" she asked once Jed had left.

"Yes," he said, offering her a cigarette.

"And your parents are still alive?" she asked after they'd both lit up.

"Oh, yes. My father's an official in the NUR—that's the main railway union. A dyed-in-the-wool socialist. You and he would find a lot to agree about. Though you'd find his attitude to women something of a problem."

"And your mother?" she asked, not rising to the bait.

"She used to work part-time. Since they moved to Glasgow, she's been keeping house for my father and Jed, but sooner or later Jed will move out."

"What will she do?"

McColl shrugged. "She has friends."

"That helps."

"Tell me about your family."

"Okay. My mother died when I was small, and my Aunt Orla—my father's sister—more or less took her place. My older brother, Fergus, is a lawyer—he's very conventional but very kind. My younger brother, Colm, is not much older than yours, and he's a bit of a rebel. My sister, Finola—she's two years older than me—she got married last year, and I expect there's a baby on the way by now. All she's ever wanted is a family of her own."

Unlike you, McColl thought. "And your father?"

"He owns a construction business, but other people run it now. They do a lot of work for the city—Brooklyn, that is."

Her face clouded, and McColl had a glimpse of the girl she'd been.

"He's . . . from the old school, I suppose. He likes the old songs, the old ways. The old attitudes to women. If he'd made the family decisions, I'd never have finished high school, let alone gone to Wesleyan. But being from the old school, he went out to earn the money and left Aunt Orla in charge of the home."

"She never married?"

"Oh, yes. But he died young, younger even than my mother. He left her a little money, and I sometimes wonder what Orla would have done if my mother hadn't died a few weeks later. The world would have been her oyster, and she was only thirty. But my father asked her to care for his children, and she couldn't refuse. I don't think she's had a bad life—my father made a lot of money, too, and we children all love her. But sometimes I see a particular look in her eyes, and I know she's wondering what could have been." She regarded McColl. "I don't ever want to have that feeling," she said. And she said it with such quiet force that he bit back the obvious retort, that regrets for roads not taken were the fate of anyone with the least imagination.

By the time the ship left Kobe, he was able to complete a circuit of the deck, albeit with some pain and difficulty. Caitlin had been using most of her waking hours to write up her impressions of China for several magazines back home, but that afternoon she announced herself almost finished and suggested an evening drink in the oak-paneled smoking room and bar.

The two of them never seemed short of subjects for conversation—or indeed subjects for good-natured argument—and the first time he looked at his watch, he was surprised to find it was almost midnight. They had, he realized, been drinking for several hours.

She had never brought up their evening in Shanghai, which seemed strange only until he realized that he hadn't either. Perhaps it had been unimportant to her, a brief fling soon forgotten, but he couldn't really believe that. The more he knew her, the more conflicted she seemed, but he had no idea why. Had she been hurt by someone?

Studying her face through the bar's haze of smoke, he didn't think he could stand another three weeks of holding back his feelings, and now seemed as good a time as any for crashing through the ice. "That evening we spent in Shanghai," he began. "At your friend's house. I . . ." He was going to say "enjoyed it," but that was ridiculous. "It meant something to me," he managed, which sounded every bit as feeble.

She lowered her eyes for a moment, as if in search of inspiration, and the silence seemed almost tangible. "I like you," she said eventually. "And I . . . I liked having sex with you."

He wanted to ask if that was all, and it must have shown in his face.

"If that were all, I would be wanting more. But I don't want to fall in love with you. Or with anyone."

"Why not?" he asked, his heart beating faster at the possibility.

She smiled ruefully. "Where would it go? You'll be returning to England, or traveling the world selling automobiles. I'll be in New York City trying to tell people what's happening to their fellow citizens. We lead such different lives, but even if we didn't . . . I don't want a marriage and a home and a family, not for a long while, if ever."

She was right, he thought. For herself, she was right.

"Or we could live for the moment," she murmured. "Enjoy the time we have."

"We could do that."

"And when the time comes, part like friends. With no regrets."

"We could do that, too," he said, although it was much harder to imagine.

"Are you . . . ?" She searched for the word.

"Firing on all cylinders?"

She laughed. "Something like that. My stateroom's on this deck. So . . ."

They walked there arm in arm, stopping to kiss several times on the way. After putting out the Do Not Disturb sign, she helped him undress and winced at the sight of his wound. "I'll be gentle," she promised, letting loose her hair.

They spent most of the next two days in her stateroom, emerging only for fresh air and meals. Jed and Mac seemed shocked, envious, and happy for him, and they treated Caitlin with the exaggerated courtesy of characters in a Victorian romance. What they actually thought of her, McColl dreaded to imagine.

Eight days after leaving Shanghai, they docked at Yokohama for a thirty-six-hour layover. Caitlin was staying the night with the exiled Ch'ing-ling, so McColl explored the imperial capital with Jed and Mac, returning early to the ship when he grew tired. They intended to visit the red-light district and sample whatever was to be had.

Next day the ship was due to leave at noon, and McColl was leaning over the rail, keeping an eye out for her, when an official-looking automobile drew up on the quay below and discharged another familiar figure—Rainer von Schön. Ascending the gangplank, the German engineer noticed McColl and waved an acknowledgment. A few moments later, they were shaking hands.

"I heard you had some trouble in Shanghai."

"You are well informed."

"It was in the English paper here."

"Ah, well. Yes, I was attacked with a knife. But as you see, I survived."

"Who was it?"

"A Chinese. They hadn't caught him when I left, and I don't suppose they will. I couldn't give them much of a description."

"I see. Well, look, I have to make sure my luggage is aboard. We'll have plenty of time to talk."

He hurried away, and McColl turned to see Caitlin ascending the gangplank. Her eyes were scanning the ship, and he realized with a thump of the heart that she was looking for him. Parting as friends would not be easy.

He didn't see von Schön again until the following morning, when he caught the German's eye across the crowded dining room. Once Jed and Mac had left for their usual twenty circuits of the promenade deck, von Schön came to claim a vacated seat, just as Caitlin claimed the other.

McColl introduced them.

"So what are you doing in Asia?" Caitlin asked the German.

"I'm a businessman, like my friend Jack here."

"Are you selling automobiles as well?"

"Nothing as beautiful. Or as substantial. I sell only expertise. I'm an engineer—water filtration—all very boring. I've been in Tokyo for ten days, talking with government contractors."

"Did they buy what you had to sell?" she asked.

"Oh, yes." He gave McColl a quick glance, as if to ask, *Who is this forward female?*

"Any news from Europe?" McColl asked him.

Von Schön's face dropped. "The only thing the people at my embassy were talking about was the Saverne Affair."

"The what?" Caitlin asked.

"Saverne is in Alsace, which was part of France before 1870," McColl told her. "A few months ago, a young German officer insulted the locals—I can't remember how exactly. But I thought the business was over."

"Unfortunately not," von Schön told them. "When the officer had his wrist slapped, the locals mounted protests and his superiors compounded the mistake by overreacting. They arrested hundreds of people, most of them completely innocent. Progressive Germans were enraged, by both the army's actions and the Kaiser's refusal to censure the officers concerned." He brushed a speck off his trouser leg as the Chinese waiter removed some cups from the table. "Things would probably have died down eventually, but then the officer who started it all used his saber on a shoemaker who laughed at him, and the whole thing took off again. There were protests by the left all across Germany, and the Reichstag passed a vote of no confidence in the government, the first time it had ever done so."

Von Schön shook his head and looked hopefully out at the ocean, as if its size might dwarf his concerns. "And there we have the rub," he went on, "as your Shakespeare would say. Because nothing happened. The Kaiser and the army just carried on as if the Reichstag were completely irrelevant. The young officer's superiors, the ones who overreacted so stupidly at the start, are up in court next week, and everyone knows that they'll be exonerated. The military have come out of this stronger than ever, the Reichstag considerably weaker. All of which is bad news for Germany."

"And for the world," McColl muttered.

"You remember our discussion in Tsingtau, I see. You are right. For the world as well."

For the next nine days, the *Manchuria* plowed south and east across the Pacific, heaving gray seas slowly giving way to a calmer blue as the ship crossed into the tropics. Jed and Mac made the most of the entertainment on offer, swimming in the saltwater tanks, tossing quoits and paddling pucks on deck, dancing to the Filipino band. Mac inveigled his way into one of the ship's illicit poker games, and, left to his own devices, Jed trailed hopelessly after the golden-haired daughter of an American missionary, whose innocent eyes seemed so worthy of rescue.

By this time McColl was able to walk the ten circuits that made up a mile without too much discomfort, but the steps and staircases still hindered his movement between decks, and he spent many hours sitting in the communal areas, either alone or with von Schön. The German seemed happier with him than with his few fellow nationals, all of whom were older and probably more conservative. The two of them shared their enthusiasm for automobiles and airplanes and other wonders of the modern world, and talked about their pasts. Von Schön often spoke of his wife and two young children back in Stuttgart, whom he hadn't seen for almost six months. He liked his work, he said, but he didn't know how long he could cope with all the traveling. McColl, he assumed, was not married.

No, McColl lied. Not because he minded von Schön's knowing, but because he feared that Caitlin might find out. He and Evelyn had been divorced for years, but he feared how it would look, particularly as he still worked for Evelyn's brother.

Most of his time was spent with Caitlin. When they weren't eating three-course meals in the ship restaurant, sleeping, or making love, they were talking—on deck, over drinks, lying replete in each other's arms. They talked about the other passengers: the English couple who couldn't stop apologizing to each other, the elderly American husband whose every attempt to placate his wife seemed to enrage her more, the spinster from Oregon who had a kind word for everyone despite her obvious sufferings from old age and arthritis. They talked about politics, with him doing most of the listening. She had a long list of heroines, and he found to his surprise—and not a little shame—that he recognized few of the names. Sylvia Pankhurst he knew of, but Alice Paul, Charlotte Perkins Gilman, Elizabeth Gurley Flynn, Margaret Sanger? They were all American "feminists"— even the word was new to him—but each in a different field. Paul was a suffragette leader, Gilman a writer and reformer, Gurley Flynn one of the labor leaders in the Lawrence and Paterson strikes. Margaret Sanger worked in the New York slums Caitlin had written about, defying the law and convention by handing out advice on female contraception. As he listened to Caitlin talk about these women, he felt a bewildering mixture of emotions— envy of her certainties, shared excitement, fear of the distance between them.

But that needn't be true, he told himself. The people he admired might all be men, but they weren't the ones refusing women the vote or sex education, or the ones exploiting workers or glorying in war. They were the engineers and scientists who were turning the world upside down and bringing it out of the darkness. There was no incompatibility there, no reason his heroes and hers couldn't change the world together.

A European war, of course, would set everything back. They talked about the prospect—as, it sometimes seemed, did everyone else on the ship. Most were determined to be optimistic. There hadn't been a major war in Europe since Prussia's demolition of France almost half a century before, and peace had become a habit. Maybe too much of one, an aged veteran of the American Civil War told his dining table—there were too few people left who remembered how ghastly a war could be.

"You won't have to go, will you?" Caitlin asked during one such conversation.

"I doubt it. But Jed and Mac—who knows? God help them if they do," he added bitterly.

She gave him a look.

"I was in the last one," he told her. "The South African War."

"You never said."

"It never came up. And I guess I'd rather forget the whole business."

"You must have been terribly young."

"I was eighteen when I shipped out." He grimaced. "And all through my own stupidity. I thought Oxford had turned me down, and I couldn't wait to get away from home. So I joined up, thinking at least I'd see the world. When the letter finally arrived confirming I had a university place, my father pulled every string he could find to get my enlistment reversed, and at any other time he'd probably have succeeded. But the war in South Africa was just getting started, and the army wasn't about to let anyone go. As it happened, I was badly wounded and back home in a few months. But that's another story." He felt, as ever, reluctant to relive the night on Spion Kop, but he needn't have worried—she had different questions.

"So did you get to Oxford in the end?"

"For my sins."

"I always thought Oxford was for the rich, the sons of the establishment. No offense, but how did you get in?"

"There are scholarships for the gifted poor. Not many, but I have this ridiculous knack with languages—"

"I'm so jealous," she interrupted. "What others do you speak?"

"Apart from Shanghainese? My Mandarin's not bad. French and German, of course, Spanish, Russian, and Urdu—I think that's the lot. Oh, Scottish Gaelic—I grew up with that."

"I'm impressed," she said with a smile.

"It's just a gift," he replied, but listing them for her he felt a rare sense of pride in his linguistic abilities. There was obviously a first time for everything.

"So they gave you a scholarship . . ."

"They did. It felt like an honor, being the first person in the family to go to university, but I struggled from the start. Not with the work—that was easy—but with fitting in. I lost my Scottish accent, tried to wear the right clothes and have the right opinions, but it was no use. No one was convinced, least of all me." He had a sudden memory of a particularly obnoxious boy mocking the way he spoke, the flush of shame he'd felt.

"You must have made some friends."

"Not that many. After trying—and failing—to fit in, I eventually realized that I didn't much like most of my fellow students. After what I'd been through in South Africa, most of them seemed like spoiled children, and I couldn't take them seriously. The few friends I did make were fellow outsiders for one reason or another, and about the only thing we had in common was drinking too much. I left after a year when one of them offered me work as a salesman in his father's whiskey business. If nothing else, I told myself, I really would see the world. And I have, or at least large chunks of it."

"Your time at Oxford sounds a bit like mine at Wesleyan," Caitlin told him thoughtfully. "There, but not really part of it."

So they did have things in common, he thought later that night as she slept with her head in the crook of his arm. But they had reacted differently—she had taken on the world, while he . . . What had he done? What was he doing? Lurking in the shadows, in more ways than one.

On several occasions he had come close to divulging his other source of employment, but he had always drawn back. It would, he knew, be foolish to do so. For one thing it would be utterly unprofessional, for another it was unlikely to meet with her approval. She would see it, at best, as government work and, at worst, as serving the global needs of the English ruling class. She would not see him as he sometimes liked to see himself, as a player in a global game in which men from various nations tested their wits against one another.

It would be foolish to tell her, but he hated the deception. If they had been set on a future together, then living such a lie would have been impossible. But they were not. Indeed, their future was the one subject both avoided like the plague. And he could keep the secret for the few weeks they had, no matter how much it gnawed at him.

It was hot on deck now, even at night, and they slept to the whir of the stateroom's electric fan. The ship arrived at Honolulu for another thirty-six-hour stopover, and after exploring the town he and Caitlin hired swimming costumes on the famous Waikiki Beach and waded out into the water. She couldn't swim very well—"There was never room to move at Coney Island!"—and he helped keep her afloat while she learned the Australian crawl. Farther down toward Diamond Head, they walked off into the lush vegetation and found a place to make love beneath the swaying palm fronds. Walking back to the town, he had never felt happier. He had fallen in love, but he knew better than to say so.

There was news from China in the local press—Yuan Shih-kai had dispensed with the new parliament and seemed intent on restoring the empire. McColl's cynical response annoyed her more than seemed reasonable, and they had their first row on a Honolulu street corner. It simmered all the way back to the ship but then just blew itself out in the throes of passion.

Next morning at breakfast, McColl detected a change in von Schön. The German had also gone ashore, to "look around and buy some postcards," but something had happened to leave him less at ease with himself. When McColl asked if he'd had bad news, von Schön almost jumped. "No, no, I'm sorry," he said before mumbling something about the Saverne Affair turning out as badly as he'd expected.

McColl didn't see much of the German over the remaining days of the voyage—he and Caitlin hardly ever seemed to leave Stateroom 302—but von Schön sought him out on the crowded rails as the ship passed through the Golden Gate. They swapped hotel addresses, shook hands, and wished each other well.

Provided the freighter carrying the Maia had arrived on schedule, McColl would be in San Francisco for around ten days, time enough to win some orders and complete the task that Cumming had given him. Caitlin was staying with friends of her father but couldn't, or wouldn't, tell him for how long. They weren't yet saying good-bye, but as he left the ship, it felt like the end of more than a voyage.

The Shamrock Saloon

♠

McColl had never been to California, or indeed anywhere on the American West Coast, and had been looking forward to this part of their round-the-world trip. San Francisco showed no signs of disappointing him—the city's situation, on hills overlooking a gorgeous blue bay, could hardly have been more beautiful. And most of the damage done almost eight years earlier had apparently been put right—during the short taxi ride from dock to hotel he saw precious little evidence of 1906's devastating earthquake and fire.

The St. Francis Hotel was on the western side of Union Square. It was expensive, but a prosperous front usually encouraged buyers, and the rooms were large and well fitted out. On the assumption that Caitlin would be a frequent visitor, Jed and Mac announced that they would carry on sharing, and McColl accepted their gift, though more in hope than expectation.

There was a cable from Cumming waiting at the desk, and once ensconced in his room he tore open the envelope. It was long and encrypted, which didn't bode well. Deciding it would wait, he buried the flimsy in his suitcase and accompanied the others down Geary Street in search of a late lunch. They found a cheap and cheerful restaurant serving steak and potatoes but had to make do without tea—from the look of surprise on the waitress's face they might have been asking for champagne.

By the time they had finished, it was midafternoon, and all agreed that work could wait for morning. Mac and Jed were intent on an exploratory walk, but McColl declined, pleading tiredness. After watching the two of them stride off, he took a short stroll down Market Street, which seemed like the city's busiest thoroughfare. There were a lot of people on the sidewalks but only slightly more automobiles on the streets than there'd been in Shanghai. The big difference, he realized, was the smell, or the relative lack thereof. The wonders of underground drainage.

He walked back toward the hotel, wondering what Cumming had to say for himself. When they'd spoken in London, the Secret Service chief had known that McColl was spending only a week or so in San Francisco and had lowered his demands accordingly—all he wanted was a thorough update on the situation there, particularly as it pertained to German involvement. McColl's first point of contact would be Sir Reginald Fairholme, an old yachting friend of Cumming's who served as His Majesty's consul in the city. "The Department of Criminal Intelligence in Delhi have their own people in San Francisco," Cumming had added, "most of them undercover. But the only thing the DCI people care about is their precious Raj, and since they can't imagine the Germans turning up at the Khyber Pass, they tend to dismiss them. And to ignore our requests to be kept informed. But Fairholme will know whom you should talk to."

"So what do the Germans hope to get out of it?" McColl had mused out loud.

"Isn't that obvious?" Cumming had snapped back at him. "Trouble in India. Not enough to threaten the white man's rule—the Germans would hate that—but enough to make Delhi think about how many soldiers—English and Indian—it could safely send to Europe in the event of war. A couple of divisions might make all the difference on the Rhine."

Not a bad return on the odd illicit shipment of rifles, McColl thought as he climbed the stairs to his second-floor room. He could appreciate Cumming's concern.

After decoding the message, he felt less sympathetic. Cumming was asking him to prolong his stay in San Francisco, to take as long as he needed in order to make a thorough assessment of the situation. "Alarming reports" had reached London of deepening collusion between the German diplomatic service and those Indian and Irish groups sworn to oppose the Crown. And while contacts between these groups were occurring in Europe, Asia, and the eastern United States, the epicenter of their global conspiracy seemed to lie in San Francisco. What, Cumming wanted to know, were these people planning?

A grateful Crown would of course compensate McColl for any business losses sustained on its behalf. Once he'd filled in a dozen forms, visited a bewildering array of offices, and waited an eternity, McColl added sourly to himself.

It was highly inconvenient, but he could hardly afford to say no, not if he wanted an expanded role in the Service's future. And there was really no reason Mac and Jed couldn't handle their business in Chicago. His brother would probably learn from the experience, and Mac would be there to hold his hand. With any luck McColl would catch up to them in New York.

It was cooler in San Francisco than it had been in Honolulu, but still remarkably pleasant for late February. While Jed and Mac collected the bottle green Maia from the docks, McColl hired space in a Market Street showroom and placed advertisements in five newspapers explaining where and when the luxury automobile could be ogled and test-driven. When the other two finally arrived back at the hotel with the freshly cleaned vehicle, they all set off for the showroom, whose owner was waiting. He examined the Maia carefully, opined that an expensive English automobile would be a hard sell in San Francisco—"There's not enough money and too many Irish in this town"—and reluctantly settled for a 5 percent rake-off.

It was extortionate, but the location was excellent—a crowd was already gathered at the window—and McColl doubted they could do any better. He put a sign in the window repeating the hours in the advertisement and told the owner they'd be back first thing in the morning. When the other two suggested a walk around the city, he almost accepted, but a hunch that Caitlin would turn up at the hotel proved both irresistible and correct. He walked through the doors to find her writing him a note in the lobby.

"I've only got an hour or so," she said. "Do you want to eat or . . . ?"

"Or."

Afterward, sitting and smoking by the window that overlooked the square, she said she couldn't see him again until Saturday. "My father's friends have arranged a sightseeing and social schedule you wouldn't believe, and there's other people I have to see."

He was disappointed but managed not to show it. Was she trying to let him down gently? He had no way of knowing. Her physical passion seemed undiminished, and her kiss good-bye seemed even more loving than usual.

As he watched her walk across the square, she turned and flashed him a wonderful smile.

The British consulate had been housed in temporary offices since the earthquake, but Cumming's agents were, in any case, always expected to contact the local diplomats away from their official place of work. Sir Reginald Fairholme's personal address, as included in Cumming's cable, was a large house north of Laurel Hill Cemetery, close to the border of the Presidio Military Reservation. Judging by the height of the surrounding trees, it was one of the districts that had escaped the fire.

The consul was not surprised to see McColl and seemed

unperturbed at having his dinner interrupted. He ushered his guest up to a small study at the back of the house, drew the curtains over the last of the sunset, and gestured him into an armchair. Fairholme was probably about forty, with a single gray streak in his black hair and the sort of well-bred, well-meaning face McColl had often encountered at Oxford.

He was interested in McColl's trip, and particularly the Maia, but soon came back to the matter at hand. "So how well up are you on the situation here?"

"Assume I know next to nothing," McColl advised.

"All right. But you do know about Har Dayal?"

"I know the name, that he wants us out of India, and that he's started a newspaper here. But not much else."

The consul hitched up a trouser leg and folded his arms. "Both paper and movement go by the name of *Ghadar*. He's been here on the West Coast since the summer of 1911. He kept his head down at first, and Berkeley University—Berkeley's on the other side of the bay, by the way—hired him to lecture on Eastern philosophy. He was only there about six months, but it was enough." Fairholme looked suitably dismayed. "During that time he recruited several sponsors to fund scholarships for Indian students, and around forty arrived over the next year or so. Once they'd become his disciples, he sent them out to spread the word. There are several thousand Indians in California."

"Have you met him?"

"No, but people who have are impressed. He's made a lot of friends in the Bay area, and not just among the Indians. The *San Francisco Bulletin* is fond of quoting his anti-British statements— their writer John Barry thinks he's wonderful. The local IWW—the Industrial Workers of the World union people, I presume you've heard of them—well, they love his socialist rantings. He even corresponds with Sun Yat-sen. But his most important allies are the Irish. I don't know how well you know this city—"

"I've never been here before."

"Well, one in three San Franciscans is of Irish descent, and most of them hate us as much as Har Dayal does. From what I've been told, the Irish and Indians had close links in New York until recently, and now they're in each other's pockets out here. Have you heard of Larry de Lacey?"

"No. It's Kell's people in the Security Service that deal with the Irish," McColl explained, responding to Fairholme's look of surprise. "Not Cumming's bureau. And yes, I know it's ridiculous that we don't pool our information, but . . ." He shrugged.

Fairholme smiled. "I understand, but you really need to appreciate how important the Irish are in this."

"Tell me about de Lacey."

"He's the local republican leader. I doubt he's thirty yet, but he has influence in city hall and friends in the press, and most of the priests in the city seem willing to run errands for him. He and John Devoy—he's the daddy of Irish republicans in America, by the way—they're always corresponding, so de Lacey must be a member of Clan na Gael—that's the main Irish-republican organization on this side of the Atlantic. And they'll both be thick as thieves with the Irish Republican Brotherhood back in Ireland. De Lacey hates us with a passion."

"Which gives him and Har Dayal something in common, and no doubt they're willing to help each other. But what about the Germans? It's their involvement that worries Cumming."

"With good reason. We're pretty sure that de Lacey plays the go-between for the Indians and Germans—he and the German military attaché, von Brincken, have been seen together on more than one occasion. Both von Brincken and his boss the consul were at the big Ghadar meeting in Sacramento on New Year's Eve, when Har Dayal announced that Indian revolutionaries should make the most of an Anglo-German war."

"A sensible plan," McColl said, "but what are they doing to put it into practice? Other than talking and writing articles."

"I don't think we can discount the newspaper. I'll let you have some copies, and you'll see—it's well written, persuasive, just the sort of thing we don't want turning up all over the empire. And that's what it's doing already, before the Germans lend a hand with the distribution. Har Dayal's aim is pretty clear: He wants another Indian Mutiny. And what could help the Germans more?"

"Agreed, but he'll need more than propaganda. What about weapons?"

"We've heard rumors of a German arms shipment, but nothing definite. Har Dayal's students have been using Japanese friends to buy revolvers and rifles from a store in Berkeley, obviously with India in mind. We're not talking large numbers, but the ones we know about might be the tip of an iceberg."

McColl was unconvinced. "Even if it was, the threat seems pretty remote. And from everything you've said, I get the impression we're usually one step ahead of them. Our people are intercepting their mail, attending their meetings, probably hiding under their beds . . ."

"Ah, well. A few weeks ago, that was the case—the DCI had several men undercover in the Ghadar organization, and they'd persuaded several of Har Dayal's converts to turn informer. We'd been paying the Mundell and Pinkerton agencies a small fortune for surveillance and managed to convince the local branch of the BOI—that's the national Bureau of Investigation—that arresting and deporting Har Dayal would be in everyone's interests. And then one of the Mundell men got a tip-off, which looked like it might sew everything up: An Irishwoman on Eddy Street who was acting as a postbox for all of them—Irish, Indians, Germans. The BOI raided the house and arrested the woman, who did admit to sometimes receiving mail for friends. But the only thing they found in the house that was vaguely incriminating was a list of names and addresses. Not of her friends, but of all our people who were spying on them—DCI men, Mundell and Pinkerton detectives, even BOI agents. They knew them all. And next day one of the DCI's informers was found on the headland north of here. He'd been shot, executed. If the other informers are still alive, they're keeping their heads down. As things stand at the moment, we have to build a new network from the bottom up, which will take months. I only hope we have that long."

"They don't know me," McColl murmured, mostly to himself.

"I was hoping you'd say something like that." Fairholme opened a desk drawer and brought out a wad of photographs. "These are the pictures we have," he said, passing them across. "There are names and addresses—those we know, that is—on the backs. Jatish will fill you in on the wider picture—he's one of the DCI men we've had to reassign. He was undercover in Ghadar for almost a year and only got out by the skin of his teeth. He's on his way to Vancouver, but we asked him to delay his departure for a couple of days. He's staying at the Station Hotel in Oakland, under the name Chatterji. Here, I wrote down the hotel number for you."

McColl put the slip of paper in his pocket. He would talk to the DCI man and decide what, if anything, he should do himself. Fairholme obviously considered Har Dayal worthy of serious attention, but outwitting the local intelligence setup was not, in McColl's mind, proof of a far-reaching threat. Nor was killing some hapless informer. Molehills often looked like mountains from close up, and the prospect of risking his life on a mere bump in the imperial road held no attraction whatever.

As he waited on California Street for a cable car to take him back downtown, he forced himself to consider another unpalatable subject. Listening to the consul's strictures on the importance of the Irish dimension, he had realized just how worrying Cumming would find his involvement with Caitlin. The first thing his boss would want to know was how much McColl actually knew about her and her family and any possible links they might have to anti-British organizations. And when it turned out that McColl knew next to nothing, Cumming would probably hit the roof.

McColl was glad he had never succumbed to temptation and

told her about his clandestine work—with her family history, she would probably have run a mile in the opposite direction.

Of course, the notion of her as an enemy was ridiculous, but Cumming might fear he was blinded by lust or love. McColl could imagine the conversation—Cumming noting that his new girlfriend was Irish, a friend of Sun Yat-sen's secretary, an open sympathizer with the sort of revolutionary nonsense that people like Har Dayal spouted. Had it occurred to McColl, he would ask sarcastically, that someone like her might not have the best interests of the British Empire at heart? Might in fact be working against it? Might even have been planted on McColl as part of that work? If anyone knew the value of pillow talk when it came to gathering information, it had to be His Majesty's recent visitor to Tsingtau.

What did McColl have to offer in rebuttal? Only those things he had learned in their time together as lovers, things he could hardly define or express, let alone put in a cable.

He should have her and her family checked out, he thought—it was the professional thing to do. Cumming's man in New York could do it, and she need never know. If she came out clean, as McColl was certain she would, then no harm would be done. And there was no need to make a big deal of it—next time he cabled Cumming about more important matters, he could slip it in as an aside.

Back in his hotel room, he worked his way through the literature that Fairholme had given him. Har Dayal made no bones about his objectives or how he planned to achieve them. Assassinations, as the Russian secret societies had proved, were righteously effective—they put governments under pressure and forced them into mistakes. The price of one pamphlet, as trumpeted on the cover, was "the head of an Englishman."

And some Englishmen were fairer game than others. Har Dayal demanded constant vigilance when it came to spies—those "wolves" of the British government. "Fixing them" was Ghadar's highest priority.

⚊ ⚊ ⚊

Next morning McColl told Jed and Mac that they would have to do without him until the afternoon. Neither asked him why, which made McColl wonder how much they had guessed about his "government work." While he was in the Shanghai hospital, Mac had asked whether there was anything he and Jed needed to know and seemed somewhat relieved when told that there wasn't.

Once the two of them had left for the showroom, McColl asked the hotel desk clerk to connect him with the number in Oakland. A man with a booming voice told him Chatterji had just gone out but had promised to soon be back. He agreed to pass on the message that McColl would be there in a couple of hours, but he couldn't guarantee that the Indian would take much notice—"He looks like a man who might just skedaddle, if you take my drift."

So no time to waste, McColl thought. He walked down Geary and Market to the ferry piers and had time for a coffee before the next Oakland departure. The *Melrose* was a modern craft, its whole lower deck reserved for automobiles. He joined the other foot passengers upstairs, took a place by the port rail, and watched the shoresmen slip the ropes as the two giant wheels began to churn.

The trip across the sunlit bay took around twenty minutes, the walk to the Station Hotel less than five. The man with the booming voice was, as often seemed the case, not much larger than a midget, and McColl almost mistook him for a child. "Mr. Chatterji" had received the message and was waiting in his room, number 102.

McColl climbed the stairs and knocked.

"Who is it?" an Indian-accented voice asked.

"Consul Fairholme sent me."

The door opened slightly, and a single eye came into view. Apparently satisfied, its owner widened the gap and waved McColl in before offering a limp hand to shake. "Thank you for coming so promptly," he said. "My name is Narayan Jatish. And you are?"

"Edward Finney," McColl said, picking up a name at random.

"Thank you for waiting." The man had fair skin for an Indian and was smartly dressed in the European style. He looked like he came from a wealthy family, and McColl wondered why he was risking his life for someone else's country.

Jatish walked across to the window, drew back the curtain a few inches, and took a cautious look out at the street. "I'm not safe here," he said, somewhat unnecessarily.

"The consul said you were going north."

"Yes, I have just purchased a ticket for this evening's train." He pulled the curtains closed again, offered McColl the only seat, and sat himself down on the bed.

"The consul suggested you bring me up to date with what's been happening," McColl said. It wasn't strictly true, but he wanted to see whether Jatish's take on recent events was the same as Fairholme's.

In large part it was, but Jatish proved more willing—eager even—to apportion blame. According to the Indian, half the DCI operatives in San Francisco were incompetent fools and half the Americans were on the take. He named names and insisted that McColl write them down. "If you trust these men, Mr. Finney, you will know regret." He pushed both palms down on the bed, then abruptly leaped up and walked to the window for another peek outside.

"I just need some basic facts," McColl told him. "Like where is the Ghadar office? I assume they have one."

There were two offices, Jatish told him, though strictly speaking both belonged to the Yugantar Ashram. Ghadar was the name of the movement, but its leaders were all members of the ashram, which rented two properties—a house on Hill Street that doubled as a hostel for Indian visitors and a second-floor office on Valencia. They weren't that far apart, about two miles south of the downtown area. Har Dayal lived at the Hill Street address, but he was off to Washington in a couple of days to lobby against new congressional plans to limit Asian immigration. "Ramchandra Bharadwaj will be the new editor of the newspaper, but that is all.

Pandurang Khankhoje will be the party organizer, the one who must be watched. He has been Har Dayal's favorite lieutenant for many months now."

"I think I have a picture of him," McColl said, taking out the photographs Fairholme had given him.

"That is Khankhoje," Jatish said, jabbing a finger at one of the pictures as McColl leafed through them. "He often sleeps in the Valencia office."

"How about the others?" McColl asked. "Can you add anything to what's written on the backs?"

As they went through the photos together, Jatish offered lots of comments, some of which might well prove useful. In response to another question, he said that the Irish rarely turned up at the Ghadar addresses. The two groups had worked so closely together in New York City that a single informer had betrayed them both, and in San Francisco they were heeding the lesson.

"Do de Lacey's people have a meeting place?"

They had several, but the Shamrock Saloon was the one they used most. It was a bar in the Mission District where de Lacey held court, often in the company of the priests he used as couriers. Collins, Doyle, and O'Brien were the ones he used most, but Father Yorke was the one who mattered. He was among the city's most prominent figures, and he hated the English. He gave lectures and speeches about the Irish struggle and probably financed it, too. "He is a very rich man—he owns the building on Howard Street where the Irish print their newspaper."

"But de Lacey is the man who makes things happen."

"That is correct."

"And what about the Germans?"

"Their consulate is near Lafayette Park. The military attaché—"

"Von Brincken."

"Yes. He arranges matters with the Indians and Irish, but not in person. Other Germans go to the Shamrock Saloon, talking to de Lacey and his friends, and we think they are von Brincken's men."

"And do you know of any people on the other side—Irish or Indians—who might be willing to talk if enough money were on offer?"

Jatish shook his head. "Not now. The Ghadar people keep close watch for informers. You must have two party sponsors to join, and you are not told any secrets for first six months, so any informer must wait and wait. We had these people, but now they are gone, and most of them are probably dead. That is Ghadar punishment for telling secrets, and the Irish are same. It was Irishmen who killed the man found in the bay, and no one will want to be next."

McColl asked Jatish what he would do in his place.

The Indian shrugged. McColl would stand out "like a sore thumb" at a Ghadar meeting and learn nothing useful. He wouldn't be so noticeable at an Irish gathering, but the Indian found it hard to believe that anything illegal would be broached in a public forum. McColl's best hope lay in intercepting messages between the two, but that would require a great deal of groundwork, identifying sources and their lines of communication. "These things take many months," the Indian concluded. "More time than you have, I think?"

McColl asked him whether he actually considered the people he'd been watching a threat to the empire.

Jatish wouldn't or couldn't say. The Ghadar membership was already divided between those craving action and those who believed it wiser to wait, and if they lost Har Dayal—a likely development, if the BOI had its way—the movement might just splinter and collapse. On the other hand, if the Germans increased their support—if they backed someone like Khankhoje, with enough money and weapons to make a real splash—then Ghadar's influence could grow, particularly in India. A European war would make all the difference, Jatish thought. That was what Har Dayal and de Lacey were waiting for. That would be their chance.

McColl thanked him for the briefing and offered his hand.

Jatish took it, smiling for the first time. "The best of British luck," he said, without a hint of irony.

As he started back down the corridor, McColl heard the lock click behind him and hoped that the Indian was safer than he imagined. The elevator eventually arrived, and both passengers stepped out, leaving it free. The door was almost closed before he realized how Irish the faces had seemed, and his hand reached the button a second too late to abort the downward journey.

At the lobby desk, the day clerk was talking to a woman in a fur coat. McColl barged in front of her. "Those two men who just went up," he demanded, ignoring the woman's angry protests, "did they ask for Chatterji?"

"Yes, but—"

McColl strode back to the elevators, acutely aware of his lack of a weapon but knowing he had to do something.

He was still waiting when he heard the scream. It came from the street, and people were rushing out to see what had happened.

McColl followed, already knowing.

Jatish was lying in the road, a few feet from the sidewalk. The body shuddered once as McColl walked toward it and then fell still. Blood was trickling down the camber, pooling in the gutter.

A beat cop was approaching as fast as his girth would allow, and McColl hung back, one eye on the hotel doorway. What should he do if the two men came out? Follow them? Point them out to the dumb-looking cop? He'd probably just get the poor bastard killed.

In the end it was all academic—by the time more cops arrived with the mortuary wagon, it was obvious that the two men had made use of another, less public exit. McColl watched the corpse hauled aboard, one arm dangling loose. It was less than half an hour since he'd shaken that hand, felt the life in the Indian's grip.

Walking toward the ferry terminal, he remembered how close he had come to stopping the elevator. A little bit quicker and Jatish might still be alive.

Or both of them dead.

✦   ✦   ✦

As he watched the hills of San Francisco draw ever closer from the bow of the ferry, McColl tried to shake off the numbness that seemed in danger of immobilizing him. Jatish was dead, and that was that—he had no time to mourn a man he'd known for only an hour. But was he himself in danger?

He had been for the briefest of moments, but merely for being in the wrong place at the wrong time. Jatish's killers probably hadn't even noticed him, and if they had, there'd clearly been no recognition. The Indian had been punished for his undercover role in an operation that predated McColl's own arrival in the city.

He'd been shown how ruthless this enemy was, and he would have to be more vigilant. Disembarking, he scanned the waiting travelers with more concern than usual, double-checking several faces that instinct told him were innocent. In this job, he realized, paranoia could become second nature.

Keep moving, he told himself, take a tour of the enemy encampments. He would cast his eye over the ashram's two addresses and the Shamrock Saloon and check out the surveillance possibilities. If a serious operation looked feasible, he would need to hire some help, which might turn out to be expensive. He could apply to Fairholme, but it would probably be safer to cable Cumming, now that the enemy had the consul's number.

When it came to the Germans, perhaps he could make use of von Schön. The engineer had told McColl where he was planning to stay, and they had vaguely discussed meeting up for a meal. Von Schön might know someone in the consulate, perhaps even von Brincken.

Before getting started, McColl dropped in at the showroom. Mac was out with a possible buyer, Jed extolling the virtues of the vehicle to two more awaiting their turn. He sounded enthusiastic enough, but it had not, Jed told his brother in private, been a very good morning. A lot of people had turned up and duly admired their beautiful vehicle, but most had left when they heard the price. "They all trot out what Henry Ford is charging for the Model T," Jed said disgustedly, "as if it's in the same league." And those who hadn't left, he added darkly, just felt like a drive.

The motor business had been fun while it lasted, McColl thought as he walked back up Market to a bookstore he'd noticed earlier. Jed might be right in thinking that Ford and his Model T were no threat, but someone would start making luxury automobiles on a production line before too long.

The bookstore had a street map for sale, and the woman behind the counter was willing to let him use their telephone directory to look up addresses. It was hard to tell where the numbers fell on the long streets, but the ashram's two properties and the saloon were probably not that far from each other, a mile or more to the southwest. The German consulate was one of the official addresses listed on the back of the map; it was a mile to the north and west, facing Lafayette Park.

He thought for a moment about hiring an automobile but realized he had no idea how noticeable one might be in the districts he planned to visit. And the electric streetcars seemed frequent enough. He took one up Market, was pleased to find that it eventually veered south down Castro in the direction he required, and got off at the first stop beyond the junction with Hill Street.

The neighborhood looked less than prosperous, and Hill Street was badly enough in need of repair to deter any motorized traffic. There were not many more pedestrians, and the few residents sitting on their stoops seemed remarkably reluctant to return his smiles. The address in question was a three-story house with yellowed stucco walls and a yard full of rotting mattresses. There were no signs of any inhabitants and none that it served as a political headquarters. Walking past, McColl mentally compared it with the Admiralty building in London. He knew who he'd put his money on.

It was a ten-minute walk to Valencia, a busier, wider street with tramlines running down its center. The ashram office was another three-story building, but much more modern, with double doors onto the street. There was a large apartment building opposite, which might provide a window for surveillance and photography.

There was a convenient coffee shop on the far side of the block, and McColl found a booth with a view across the street. He'd been there about five minutes when an Indian in a turban walked out through the double doors and stood on the sidewalk, gazing up and down the street. McColl was wondering whether the man was on the lookout for watchers when a woman and a small boy followed him from the building, and the threesome walked happily off together, looking more like a family out for a treat than agents intent on sedition.

McColl was struck—not for the first time—by the inherent absurdity of it all. He paid for his coffee and started working his way north and west across the Mission District toward Twentieth Street. There were signs of Irishness everywhere, from green flags to bars that looked more like pubs, from Blessed Virgins carved in alabaster to the Kellys and O'Learys that proliferated on the store and workshop signs. The Shamrock Saloon was at the bottom of Potrero Hill, a large, well-kept building with green velvet curtains drawn halfway across the windows and a wide room inside striped by beams of sunlight. Few of the tables were occupied, and only one pair of eyes seemed to notice his arrival.

He was confident he could manage an Irish accent but changed his mind at the last moment and ordered a beer in the Scottish tones of his youth. He might have abandoned the idea of bringing Caitlin here, but there was no guarantee that she wouldn't walk through the door in the next few minutes—she was probably staying somewhere in the area.

The barman asked him what he was doing in San Francisco and expressed no further interest when told he was here to sell automobiles, leaving McColl with the distinct impression that all strangers were asked the same question. There was a copy of the *Irish Leader* on one of the tables, which he brought back to the bar and sat with, slowly drinking his beer and eavesdropping on the other patrons. There were framed drawings of Wolfe Tone and Edward FitzGerald behind the bar, but the two conversations he could hear concerned the coming weekend's horse racing and a woman named Niamh who had thrown out her drunk of a husband.

"Nice place you have here," he told the barman, who didn't bother to reply. "But a bit on the quiet side," McColl added. "Does it ever liven up?"

"There's a crowd on Saturdays," the barman conceded.

"Maybe I'll come back then."

Back on the street, he realized how much walking he'd done when his wound—which he'd hardly noticed since Honolulu— suddenly began to throb. A cab, he decided, and stood leaning against a convenient stop sign until one came along. The driver's license bore the name O'Leary, but the man himself had no trace of an accent and no apparent interest in his homeland's affairs. Instead, he spent the entire drive railing against the city's politicians and developers and the profits they had made from reconstruction. "At least *some* of the bastards are in jail," was his parting remark as he dropped McColl off at the corner of Lafayette Park.

The German consulate was easy to spot, the black, white, and red tricolor of the imperial flag floating above a tall mansion on the northern side. Any comings and goings could be observed from the comfort of a nearby park bench, but the observer would be visible to anyone watching from the consulate's windows, which wouldn't do at all. There were several automobiles parked on each side of the road, so another wouldn't look out of place, and a motorized watcher could follow anyone leaving.

At least McColl knew where everything was, where the various kingpins held their courts. Now he needed helpers, to follow the courtiers home and start the process of sifting through their lives for a point of weakness, a point of entry. Helpers who could take photographs and get all these people's faces on file, which was half the battle when it came to foiling their plots. Cumming liked photographs and didn't mind paying for them.

A light went on in one of the consulate's upstairs rooms, and a woman briefly appeared in silhouette as she pulled the curtains together. Night had fallen with almost tropical swiftness, McColl realized; he felt both hungry and tired, and unusually reluctant to spend the evening with Jed and Mac. But he needn't have worried—arriving back at the hotel, he was handed a note in Jed's childlike writing: The two of them had tired of waiting and gone out "gallivanting" without him.

Feeling relieved, he ate in the hotel restaurant, retired to his room with a pint of whiskey, and spent an hour encrypting a request for additional funds, which he planned to send off the following morning. After completing that task, he found himself revisiting the two issues of *Ghadar* that Fairholme had loaned him. One statement in particular attracted his attention: That Englishmen were never punished for killing Indian men or dishonoring Indian women. He remembered Caitlin angrily mentioning her recent discovery that Europeans enjoyed a similar immunity in China during their day trip out to Longhua.

It never paid to demonize an enemy, McColl thought. People like Har Dayal—people like Caitlin—had every right to demand change. It was the former's penchant for bombings that rendered him fair game.

McColl drained the last of the whiskey and tried not to feel sorry for himself. His side was still aching, and he really missed her. He was lonely, in a way that he hadn't been before she danced into his life.

A boisterous knock on the door snapped him out of his reverie and heralded the return of his companions. They had been to the nickelodeon, watched two comedies and a dramatic short called *The Mothering Heart*, and Jed had fallen in love with an actress called Lillian Gish. They had also imbibed a large quantity of alcohol and taken a walk through Chinatown. "It's not China," was Mac's considered opinion. His report on their workday was almost as succinct—after adding three hundred miles to the Maia's clock and suffering a badly scratched head lamp, they had added no new entries to the order book.

"How was your day?" Jed asked his brother.

"I walked up more hills than I could count," McColl told him. And I watched another man die, he thought.

Thursday morning McColl picked up a copy of the *Bulletin* on his way to the Chicago & North Western freight office and stopped to read it over a coffee. He was glancing through the pages in search of Har Dayal's friend John Barry when he noticed a more familiar name above a feature piece titled "The Changes in China"—one Caitlin Hanley. He had never doubted her journalistic credentials, but seeing her name in print was still a bit of a shock. So, to his shame, was the high quality of her writing, which somehow balanced an enthusiasm bordering on passion with a cool command of the facts. McColl was absurdly pleased to see that a couple of his own observations had been included and credited to "a friend with long experience of the Orient."

After arranging the Maia's shipment, he walked back to the hotel, borrowed the telephone directory from reception, and made a list of promising-looking detective agencies. Excluding Pinkerton's and Mundell's, there were seven in the downtown area.

Given the nature of his business, auditioning agents and explaining what he required would have to be done in person. And given a choice between walking for miles, relying on trams, and hiring an automobile, his shortness of funds seemed almost incidental. The hotel gave him the name of a reputable firm only a short walk away, and after several minutes spent in reassuring the nervous agent that some Englishmen did know how to drive, he was allowed behind the wheel of a brand-new Model T Touring Car. The vehicle was certainly lacking in frills but, as he quickly discovered, it ran and handled remarkably well.

He had three requirements when it came to choosing an agency: It shouldn't be run by Anglophobic Irish- or German-Americans, it should have enough operatives to run a two-person surveillance throughout the daylight hours, and at least one of those operatives had to be well acquainted with the most up-to-date photographic equipment. The first agency failed on the second and third counts, the owner a one-man band who could hardly hide his contempt for gimmicks like the Kodak Brownie. McColl wondered how he got any business, but then again, if the state of his office was anything to go by, he probably didn't.

The second and third agencies were too busy to take on the sort of work McColl required, the fourth was run by an Austrian Jew with an anglicized name. When the fifth turned out to be defunct, McColl began to lose heart, but salvation was soon at hand. The sixth address was on the eastern side of Nob Hill, the agency run by a hook-nosed Hispanic named Juan Palóu, who claimed that his great-great-grandfather had led the first Spanish expedition to reach the site of the present city overland. He worked with his two sons and was a photography enthusiast. "Though not like my older son," the detective added. "He has all the latest equipment. He calls each camera an investment, but if he doesn't stop spending money, there'll be nothing left to invest in."

When McColl explained what he wanted, Palóu's first reaction—that he needed to see the house on Valencia for himself—was exactly what McColl wanted to hear. They drove there together in the Model T, Palóu lamenting the fact that his younger son was demanding one of his own, and parked in a convenient side street. From the same booth in the coffee shop, McColl pointed out the windows of the Ghadar center. "Any white man seen in there, I'd like his picture, name, and address—or as many of them as you can get. I'm particularly interested in Catholic priests."

Palóu raised an eyebrow at that but only asked how long McColl wanted the surveillance to last.

"Let's say five days to begin with."

"That won't be cheap. I'm going to have to rent one of the rooms across the street, and none of them look empty—someone will need paying off."

"So how much?"

"Ten dollars a day, plus expenses."

It didn't seem extortionate to McColl, and Cumming would just have to pay up. "I'll have half for you on Monday," he promised, hoping he'd be able to deliver.

The detective shrugged his acceptance, as if money were the least of his worries. Perhaps, like Sherlock Holmes, he had a private income. "We'll start as soon as we can," he said. "Do you want a daily report?"

"No," McColl decided. "I'll come and see you on Monday. Say nine in the morning?"

"Okay. I don't suppose you want to tell me what this is all about."

"The office you'll be watching is the headquarters of an Indian political group—"

"Not Red Indians?"

"Indian Indians. And you should know that they're fond of violence, at least in theory. If you find you need to know more, then you'll just have to get in touch with me."

Palóu took that in his stride. "An Englishman watching Indians—I think I can guess most of the rest. We Spanish are experts when it comes to losing empires," he added. He seemed faintly amused by it all, a trait McColl had always considered a sure sign of sanity.

"One other thing," McColl said. "Can you recommend somewhere to buy a gun?"

"There's a gun store on Mason, between O'Farrell and Ellis."

"Thanks."

He drove Palóu back to his office and went in search of the

gun store. Being able to walk into a shop and buy a firearm seemed odd to McColl, but the proprietor obviously didn't find it so. He laid out a selection of small pistols and revolvers on the counter and listed the sterling qualities of each. McColl wavered between the Mauser Broomhandle, which he knew from the South African War, and the Browning M1900, which looked easier to conceal on his person. Opting for the latter, he was provided with a cardboard box containing enough ammunition to mount a small war of his own.

After a late lunch in a department store on Market, he walked on to the hotel where von Schön had said he would be staying. The desk clerk failed to recognize the name, and his search through the register proved unavailing. Nor was there any record of an advance booking. McColl decided he must have misheard—or perhaps the German had changed his mind. He asked the desk clerk for a list of San Francisco's better hotels and phoned them one by one from the booth in the lobby. Von Schön was not staying at any of them.

Which was annoying. Had the German run across friends and gone to stay with them? Or had a message arrived calling him home to Germany? McColl hoped that nothing had happened to the man's wife or daughter back home.

He worked his way through the second tier of hotels the following morning, driven as much by curiosity as by any real hope that von Schön could help him with his task. But there was no trace of the German. Stymied, he spent the afternoon at the showroom, where the owner was loudly regretting waiving a flat fee in favor of a percentage. His pretty blonde secretary was much friendlier, having persuaded Jed to take her out dancing that evening. She had already found a partner for Mac and offered, somewhat doubtfully, to seek one out for the ancient McColl. He let her off the hook, claiming he had paperwork to do.

Once they'd called it a day, he ate alone at an Italian restaurant, then read the evening edition in an almost empty bar on Geary. Stepping out into the night several beers later, he decided on impulse to visit the Shamrock and eavesdrop on plots against the empire. He hailed a cab and opened a window to sober himself up. It had rained on and off all day, and the lights of the city were reflected in myriad puddles as his taciturn driver motored south.

The Shamrock was much busier than on his previous visit, but the clientele was still overwhelmingly male. One table in the corner was empty, and he made a beeline for the stool at the bar that lay closest to it. An hour and two beers later, he was rewarded for his foresight—a group of men in suits threading their way through the tables with many a raised hand, rather in the manner of rulers acknowledging their subjects. McColl recognized Larry de Lacey from the photographs that Fairholme had given him. San Francisco's republican boss looked barely out of school, wiry, dark-haired and -eyed, with an almost impish face. As one of the barmen hurried over to take their order, de Lacey sat packing tobacco into his pipe, occasionally smiling at what seemed a private joke.

McColl ordered another drink and spent the next hour trying to disentangle that table's conversation from the others swirling noisily around him. Watching the speakers in the mirror behind the bar was some help and made him wish he'd added lipreading to his list of accomplishments.

They were talking, predictably enough, about the Dublin workers' lockout, which had been dominating the Irish situation since the previous summer, when McColl was still in England. Caitlin, of course, supported Jim Larkin and his followers—it was a scandal, she said, that workers should be denied the right to unionize in this day and age. But the last news she'd heard had been of families starving, and now it seemed that the lockout was over. The workers had been defeated.

The men at de Lacey's table were divided over this outcome. Some thought the lockout had been a dangerous distraction from the real business of Ireland's liberation and plainly distrusted what they considered Larkin's communistic leanings. Others were clearly in awe of the man and insisted that it was all part of the same battle. As one man put it, "The English don't just rule our country—they own it. An independent Ireland that leaves them still running our business . . . well, that would be worse than useless."

De Lacey smiled at that but offered little support for either side. The different points of view were obviously held seriously enough, but there was a lot of good-natured banter and laughter, and no one grew visibly angry. All in all, McColl thought, it was a thoroughly reasonable discussion and possible only because everyone involved agreed on one basic premise: that Ireland should cast itself free of its English overlord. As he listened to the conversation, McColl had to remind himself that the latest surveys showed that 90 percent of the Irish back home were happy with the Home Rule now on the table.

In the mirror he noticed another large group entering the saloon, this one half composed of women. Caitlin had told him she was going out to dinner with friends, but what if they turned up here afterward? The prospect both thrilled and worried him. How would he explain his presence here, not to mention his broad Scottish accent?

"I noticed you listening to our talk," a voice said at his shoulder. It was de Lacey himself, at the bar for a new box of matches. "So what does a Scotsman make of these things?" de Lacey asked as the barman dealt with his request.

"The lockout?" McColl asked, noting, as the American doubtless intended, that his identity had already been probed. "My father always told me that you shouldn't fight battles you couldn't win."

"And your father would be . . . ?"

"A union man."

"And you?"

"I wanted to see the world."

"A fine ambition," de Lacey agreed, taking the matches from

the barman. "As to the other business, if you only fight battles you can win, you'll probably die in your bed, but your children won't hear you remembered in song." He smiled briefly, then went back to his table.

It was time to leave, McColl decided—he was deep behind enemy lines and had already drunk more than was sensible for someone in that position.

Outside, it was raining again, and the world seemed devoid of cabs. He eventually caught a tram down Mission and then walked the rest of the way, cursing his lack of a hat.

There was a message waiting at reception, his name in her writing on a cream envelope. She wanted picking up outside the main post office at one o'clock on Saturday, in an automobile if that was at all possible. They had a lunch appointment with unnamed friends, but she was hoping that the two of them could go for an afternoon drive if the weather was fine.

She smiled as he pulled up in the Model T, arranged herself in the passenger seat, and gave him a big kiss. The friends, she told him, were Agnes and Ernest Brundin, and they were meeting at a Mexican restaurant that overlooked the bay. Agnes had said to follow Powell as far as it went, then turn left along the waterfront. The restaurant was called El Gran.

She had met Agnes a couple of years earlier—Agnes Smedley as she was then—and they had written to each other at fairly regular intervals ever since. "They're both socialists," she warned McColl, "but I think you'll like them anyway."

The Brundins were already there when McColl and Caitlin arrived, heads hunched over menus in a sparsely populated room. Agnes jumped up when she saw them and hugged Caitlin warmly. She was also tall for a woman, with hair that seemed barely under control and large, soulful eyes that gazed into McColl's as they were introduced. Her young husband was quiet, almost solemn, and clearly besotted with her.

After ordering, Agnes demanded to know about China and listened wide-eyed to Caitlin's impressions of her time there. Once she discovered that McColl was the "friend" in Caitlin's article, she included him more in the conversation, but he soon realized that any hint of cynicism was unwelcome and settled, like Ernest, for listening. Through the meal and after, the two women moved from the stalled Chinese Revolution to the growing ferment in India, then ventured back home for the latest news in birth control and the struggle over suffrage. Their enthusiasm was hard to resist, but as he listened, McColl had a growing sense of a whole other world, one not closed off only to men but to most of the rest of humanity. And yet people like Caitlin and Agnes, who created and lived in that closed-off world, were convinced they were serving the wider one. Wasn't that a fatal contradiction, or was he just being cynical? He told himself that these were intelligent, well-intentioned people, something the world badly needed.

It was raining again when they left, and once they'd dropped Agnes and Ernest off at the cable car terminus on Hyde, he and Caitlin abandoned the idea of a country ride in favor of his hotel bed. "What did you think of Agnes?" she asked after they'd made love for the first time.

"A force of nature," he said. "Like you."

She took that as a compliment. "And Ernest?"

"He's liable to get blown away."

She thought about that. "Perhaps," she conceded. "But you won't," she added with a smile.

No, he thought, he probably wouldn't. But was that a good thing?

"Let's get out of the city tomorrow," she said. "Even if it's raining. I want to see the giant sequoias in Muir Woods."

"Where's that?"

"Across the bay to the north. We can meet at the Sausalito ferry."

"Aren't you staying here tonight?"

"No, I won't. I . . ."

"Word might get back to your father," he guessed.

"I wouldn't care about that. But my aunt . . . She's old-fashioned in some ways, and I don't want to hurt her."

"Understood."

"But we've got hours yet."

When it was time, he insisted on driving her back. Her father's friends lived in a big house on Twentieth Street, about half a mile from the Shamrock Saloon, and McColl saw a curtain twitch as he pulled up outside. She probably did, too, because he got only the briefest of good-night kisses.

Back at his hotel, another envelope was waiting. This one had come courtesy of a consulate courier and was full of twenty-dollar bills.

Sunday started gray and wet, but by the time they reached Muir Woods, a pale yellow sun was filtering down through the magnificent trees. McColl knew that it was a cliché, but the place really did feel like a cathedral. Like most gods, these sequoias were bound to make humans feel small.

For most of the hour their driver had given them, he and Caitlin walked the well-laid paths in companionable silence, listening to the birds and the steady dripping of the night's rain from the branches above. And on the long buggy ride back to Sausalito, they gripped each other's hands with more than the usual intensity, as if they'd just shared some sort of spiritual experience.

One of the quayside restaurants was open for lunch, and it was warm enough to sit outside, with a gorgeous view of the bay and its surrounding hills and cities. "We have to get back soon," she announced once they'd eaten. "I have a meeting at five."

"Who with?" he asked, disappointed.

"No, it's a public meeting in a church hall. A friend of my father's friend is giving a talk."

"About what?"

She grimaced. "Oh, the usual stuff. Ireland's situation and what to do about it. I know it's important, but . . ."

"Hmm. Can I come?"

"You won't like what you hear." She grinned suddenly. "But why not? It might be good for your soul."

"Perhaps. I've already sampled the local Irish hospitality. Do you know the Shamrock Saloon?"

She gave him a surprised look. "What took you *there?*"

He shrugged. "I was out walking, wondering when my girl would deign to see me again. It's a nice enough bar."

"I suppose so. The church hall is just around the corner, and people tend to go there after a talk."

"Well, if that happens tonight, don't be surprised by my accent. In establishments like that, I like them to know I'm Scottish."

She was amused. "That says it all about the English in Ireland."

Not quite, he thought, but he let it go. At least she wouldn't get a shock if he had to exaggerate his accent.

A rain squall caught up with them as they crossed the bay, and their subsequent cab inched down a half-flooded Market Street at a swishing crawl, its windshield wipers utterly unequal to the scale of the downpour. The entrance to the church hall was full of people furling umbrellas and removing dripping coats, the hall itself almost packed. Caitlin led the way down the aisle and introduced McColl to her father's friend, a cadaverous man in his fifties with thick gray hair and black-rimmed glasses. "Liam, this is Jack McColl, the Scot I met in China. Jack, this is Liam Keane, an old friend of my family's. And this," she added, turning to the balding priest beside him, "is Father Meagher. A fellow guest at the Keanes'. And a fellow New Yorker."

Both men accepted the offer of a handshake, Meagher with a pursing of lips, Keane with what felt like a hostile smile. "I'm afraid we only saved the one seat," the latter said almost smugly, and McColl could feel Caitlin tensing beside him. "I'll see you afterward," he told her, and walked away before she had a chance to protest.

He found a seat nearer the back and had been in it just a few moments when Larry de Lacey walked past with two of the men who'd shared his table the day before. They had seats reserved at the front.

Several announcements were made before the scheduled address, one about a lost cat, another concerning the arrival of a new piano teacher, a third detailing someone's funeral arrangements. The collection cap doing the rounds was in aid of sending the local boys' club on a trip into the mountains, and McColl wondered whether Caitlin would contribute or slip in a note on behalf of overlooked girls.

The speaker, somewhat unsurprisingly, turned out to be a priest. His subject was what he—and his audience—considered England's long oppression of Ireland and how it should be brought to a speedy end. He began with a rambling account of the Gunpowder Plot, one of several events the English had used to justify anti-Catholic legislation. McColl had no way of knowing whether this was true and doubted whether anyone else in the audience had. The priest's next generalization, that every subsequent improvement in the lot of British Catholics came not from English benevolence but from English fear, seemed similarly suspect as historical truth but rang all the right political bells. Making the English fear them was what mattered, the priest said, and the Church should set an example "in the deeds of patriotism." Or to put it another way, as McColl did to himself, should do anything and everything in its power to support the struggle for independence. As the priest noted in another ringing phrase, "Faith and fatherland are one and indivisible." No wonder de Lacey could count on men of the cloth to serve as his couriers.

The audience members clapped in all the right places and were willing to fill another collection cap for the struggle, but there was no great passion in the response—they had heard it all before, and Ireland was a long way away. What most struck McColl was the absence of Christian spirit in a Christian place of worship, the lack of even a token attempt to see the situation from more than one perspective. But it didn't really surprise him. He knew from Caitlin that most priests in Dublin had sided with the employers during the lockout, even once their flocks began to starve. Those priests knew which side their bread was buttered on, and so did the man on this platform. Both seemed happy to let their positions dictate their politics, and their politics determine how they interpreted their faith.

He couldn't see Caitlin's face from where he sat, but he thought he knew which expression it would be wearing—one of dutiful boredom. These were her people, and she wouldn't fight them openly, but he knew that her view of humanity was more generous than this.

He waited for her outside and was pleased to see that she took his arm despite the presence of Liam Keane and Father Meagher. "We are going to the Shamrock," she said. "Are you coming?"

The walk was just long enough for McColl to express his general agreement with the speaker's point of view and to suggest that once Home Rule was a reality, any lingering English presence would soon disappear.

"And what of Ulster?" Keane asked.

"Oh, I expect there'll be some sort of compromise," McColl suggested airily, and received a contemptuous snort in reply.

"You did that deliberately," Caitlin said once they had their drinks and a table to themselves.

Keane and Father Meagher, McColl noticed, were talking to one of de Lacey's friends. And when de Lacey himself joined the group, he gave Keane an affectionate slap on the shoulder. What, McColl wondered, was Cumming's man in New York going to turn up on Caitlin's father? "I don't suppose you can come back to the hotel?" he asked her.

"No, I can't. I wish I could." She looked around the bar and wryly shook her head. "This is just a boys' club."

"But not the one they're sending up the mountain."

She laughed. "If only."

→ → →

McColl was at Juan Palóu's office first thing the next morning. He wasn't expecting instant proof of an Irish-Indian conspiracy, and he wasn't disappointed. It had taken the private detective twenty-four hours to set up the surveillance operation, and visitors to the ashram over the weekend had been few and far between. All had been photographed, but many of the pictures lacked clarity on account of the dreadful weather.

McColl looked through them. With one exception the male visitors were Indians, but none resembled Har Dayal or Khank-hoje. The odd man out was wearing what looked like a Catholic priest's robe, but his face was blurred by rain. If only the weather had been kinder . . .

The one woman pictured was also white, and heavily pregnant. Palóu couldn't be certain that she'd visited the ashram office, but his son Alfredo had seen what looked like waving arms in the window at the same time as he heard shouting, and when the woman emerged, she looked angry and tearful. His second son, Paco, had followed the woman to an apartment on Sanchez Street, and identified her as Alice Burrows. She was unmarried, with two young children.

It wasn't a bad start, McColl thought, and today the sun was shining. He paid Palóu for the last three days and told the detective to persist for another three. There was at least enough money for that.

Back at the hotel, he found Jed and Mac completing their packing. They had already driven the Maia to the city freight depot for ferrying across the bay and were now required to make their own way to the Oakland terminal. McColl went over on the ferry to see them off, and as he watched the Overland Limited rattle out across the points he felt both relieved and depressed at the prospect of spending so much time alone. "Beware knife-wielding Chinamen," had been Mac's farewell comment. Or knife-wielding Indians, McColl silently added. Or gun-toting Irishmen.

He decided to visit the pregnant woman and spent the ride back to San Francisco wondering how to approach her. If the most probable explanation of her visit—that one of Har Dayal's bright young men had gotten her pregnant and then abandoned her— were true, then anger might induce her to talk. But only if she'd given up hope of getting him back. And maybe not even then.

What did McColl have to offer in exchange? Nothing except money, which she might well need. Could he say he'd come from the ashram in the spirit of putting things right? No, because then he couldn't ask questions. His only hope was some sort of honesty—he wanted information on her boyfriend and his chums, and he was prepared to pay for it.

When the cab dropped him off on Sanchez, he realized that her apartment was just around the corner from the other ashram building on Hill Street. It was a poor area, and her building seemed poorer than most. And here I am, he thought sourly, an angel of deliverance.

Or not. The encounter didn't go well. She opened the door with a small boy in her arms, obviously swollen with his unborn sibling, and declined his suggestion that they talk inside. When he offered payment for information about the Yugantar Ashram, her only response was to coldly ask him who he was. A private detective, he lied, thinking he should have left all this to Palóu.

"And who's paying you?"

She was, he realized, far from stupid. "I'm afraid I can't tell you that."

She gave him a long, disdainful look, then shut the door in his face.

Next morning he walked to the top of Nob Hill and took in the view that Jed and Mac had raved about. Their train would be halfway across Nevada by now, still two days away from Chicago. He hoped Jed would realize his dream of seeing some authentic Red Indians.

Caitlin had said she would try to come over that afternoon, and the lack of a message when he returned was a hopeful sign. She arrived soon after two, and asked if she could have a bath—there'd been no hot water at the Keanes' since the previous morning. Half an hour later she emerged in a towel, which slipped away in mid-embrace. "Why are you still dressed?" she asked.

"We're getting good at this," she said half an hour later, with what sounded almost like sadness.

Because we love each other, McColl thought but didn't say.

"So what are Jed and Mac doing today?" she asked after a while.

"They're on the train to Chicago. They and the Maia left yesterday."

"Oh. So why are you still here?"

"Loose ends," he said vaguely, before realizing she might think he meant her.

If she did, she found no objection. "So when are you leaving?" she asked.

"I don't know yet."

"I'm taking the train on Monday. I've seen all the people I need to—I saw Agnes again yesterday—she liked you, by the way—and the Keanes are driving me mad. I was planning to go on Tuesday, but Liam took the liberty of reserving me a compartment for Monday, because Father Meagher was already booked on that train, and Liam—or my father—thinks I need a chaperone. For the last four days of a three-month trip!"

"Don't you like Father Meagher?"

"He's a horrible man. One of those priests who stares at your breasts while he gives out moral instruction. He probably spends as much time jerking himself off as he does praying."

McColl laughed.

"But I do have nice breasts," she said, looking down at them.

"You do indeed."

"Not too big and not too small."

"Just perfect," he agreed.

"I'm glad you like them," she said, reaching for the cigarettes on the bedside table.

"What sort of man is Liam Keane?" he asked, once they'd both lit up.

"Oh, he's not so bad. He's one of them—you know the type—a revolutionary where Ireland is concerned, reactionary in every other respect."

"I know the type."

She turned toward him, as if intent on gauging his response to what she was about to say. "I was wondering . . . Will your business be finished by Monday?"

"It should be. Why?"

"Well, I thought we could take the same train. Make passionate love under Father Meagher's nose . . ."

"Not literally, I hope."

"You know what I mean. It'll be fun on the train. And after that you'll be going back to England, and who knows what'll happen."

"To us?"

"To us."

"What would you like to happen?"

"I don't know," she admitted. "But at the moment I find it hard to imagine letting you go."

"Likewise," he murmured.

The Keanes had guests that evening, and Caitlin was expected back. After walking her to the tram stop, McColl ambled aimlessly down Market again toward the ferry terminals and bay, trying to make sense of the situation he'd gotten himself into. The thought of their sharing the journey to New York was irresistible, but then so was the opportunity of intercepting whatever seditious messages the good Father Meagher would probably be carrying from sea to shining sea. How could he do both? Wouldn't he, in one way or another, be using her, an avowed enemy of empires, to help him serve his own? He told himself that there was no real conflict of interest, that he would be investigating Father Meagher's probable role as a courier whether or not she was on the same train, but that wasn't how she would see it. She would feel betrayed, and he couldn't blame her. She would know that he had deceived her from the very beginning and would find it unforgivable.

But what else could he do? What else could he have done? If honesty had been the price of keeping her, he might have considered it, but she'd made it clear that their time together would be measured in weeks, not years. And like it or not, that still seemed the obvious outcome. At some point in the not-too-distant future, she would go back to her life and he would go back to his—something he could do only if his cover remained intact.

And nothing had really changed—his choices were as limited now as they had been in Shanghai. He knew he couldn't just walk away, either from her or from his work, so he *would* take the train with her and Father Meagher, and he *would* make the most of whatever opportunities happened to arise. Maybe things would work out in some way or other that he couldn't yet envisage.

He started back up Market, freshly intent on having an enjoyable evening. Over the next few hours, he found a pot roast to thrill his taste buds, moving pictures to tickle his funny bone, and whiskeys enough to prepare him for sleep. At the St. Francis, he was just getting into the elevator when the night clerk caught him with an envelope marked "Urgent." He read it on the way up, pressed the button to take him straight back down, and read it again in the empty hotel bar: "An assassin waits in your room."

A joke, he thought. Some delayed-action prank by his younger brother.

But it wasn't in Jed's writing. Or Mac's.

The Browning was still in his pocket, and touching it felt reassuring. What should he do?

He went back to the night clerk and asked him who had left the message.

"A boy."

"What sort of boy?"

"A Spanish boy, I think. A poor boy."

"And when was this?"

The night clerk shrugged. "Two hours ago. Maybe three."

McColl walked back toward the elevator, changed his mind, and went for the stairs. He climbed a few steps, then forced himself to stop—he really had to think this through. There was, apparently, an assassin in his room. Maybe one of the men who had killed Jatish. Armed, presumably, with a gun or a knife. If he took the man on, there seemed a fair chance one of them would get killed. It might be him, which would be most inconvenient. It should be the assassin—McColl did, after all, have the advantage of knowing that the man was there. But he would probably have to shoot him, which would be both noisy and distressing. Guests would be screaming, the police would be called, and he would be taken down to the local precinct house for questioning. The press would get hold of it, and his picture would adorn another front page, putting an end to his hopes of a new career.

And not only that. It felt vaguely ridiculous, but he found himself wondering what Caitlin would think. One attempt on his life might be written off to madness or greed, but two, on either side of a very wide ocean? She would guess that there was more to him than she had previously suspected and start asking awkward questions. Which would also finish them.

There had to be some other way. And he knew what it was.

He went back to the lobby and shut himself in the telephone booth. It took a long time for someone to pick up at the Fairholme residence and even longer to persuade whoever it was that Sir Reginald had to be woken. When Fairholme appeared, he sounded sprightly enough and grasped the situation with commendable alacrity.

"This can't get in the papers," McColl concluded.

"Of course not. Leave it to me."

McColl told the night clerk he was expecting visitors and that he'd wait in the bar. Once there, he poured himself three fingers and sat in the dark, watching the street outside and imagining the man waiting upstairs.

About forty minutes had gone by when an automobile pulled up close to the hotel entrance. Four men got out, none of them in uniform. A few moments later, two of them entered the bar.

"I'm Strawson," the older of the two introduced himself. "BOI. Is he still up there?"

"As far as I know. I haven't seen him, only this." He passed across the message. Now that the cavalry was here, he hoped to God it wasn't some kind of practical joke. "Shall I come up with you?"

"Nope. You stay right where you are. We'll take care of this."

McColl watched them go and spent the next ten minutes anticipating gunfire.

None came, and Strawson reappeared. "Your assassin was in the wardrobe," he said. "With this." It was a fearsome-looking kitchen knife, the blade long enough to run him through.

"Who is he?"

"He hasn't said. Local man, though, Caucasian. Just hired help, would be my guess."

"Ah," McColl said, wondering if that was good or bad.

"And he had this in his pocket," Strawson added, unfolding a piece of paper on which "Death to English spies" had been written in large letters. "For leaving on the body, no doubt."

McColl shivered despite himself. "Where is he?"

"He's being taken out."

"And what will you do with him?"

Strawson shrugged. "We'll question him, of course, but I doubt he'll even know who hired him. We can only charge him with attempted murder if we reveal his target, and I don't suppose you want that sort of publicity?"

"No."

"Well, we might be able to pin something else on him, but I can't guarantee it. Odds are he'll be back on the streets in a few weeks."

"Oh, I'll be long gone by then." McColl offered Strawson his hand. "Thanks."

"All part of the Service," the American told him.

Outside, three men were apparently helping another into the backseat of an automobile. As McColl watched from the window, Strawson claimed the seat beside the driver and the car moved slowly off, skirting three sides of the square before turning away down Geary.

He took the elevator up to his room, where the bedclothes lay in disarray from his afternoon tryst with Caitlin and the wardrobe door was still hanging open. Love and death, he thought.

He put the bed back together and lay down, wondering how Har Dayal's people had gotten onto him and who had sent the warning.

When he woke the next morning, the whole episode seemed like a dream, but the message of warning on his nightstand was real enough. His Shanghai wound was throbbing in protest, perhaps at the thought of another knife, more probably on account of the weather. Fog had rolled in overnight, and the buildings on the far side of Union Square were vague silhouettes.

He took breakfast in the hotel restaurant and anxiously checked the morning papers for any news of himself. There was none. Leafing through the pages, he came across a picture of Larry de Lacey surrounded by teenage boys, all smiling at the camera. The next generation, McColl thought.

He collected his coat and walked up an eerily fogbound Stockton Street to Juan Palóu's office. As far as he could tell, no one followed him.

"Better news this time," the detective told him, reaching for one of the folders on his desk. "We have a lot of pictures and quite a few addresses. Here."

McColl leafed through them, admiring the clarity of the images. The first six faces were Indian, the seventh the one he wanted to see.

Father Meagher featured in four of the photographs. He'd been caught twice through the window of the Ghadar office, once coming out through the door, and again crossing the street toward the camera. In the latter two pictures, he was carrying a large suitcase.

"Did he bring the suitcase with him?" McColl asked.

"It should say on the back of the picture."

According to the operative's notes, the priest had been empty-handed when he arrived.

McColl felt both vindicated and excited. If that suitcase turned up on the eastbound train, he was in business.

The sense of self-congratulation lasted less than a minute. Two more Indians were caught by the camera, and the second was clearly Pandurang Khankhoje. And then a white face, one much more familiar than he expected. Rainer von Schön had his head turned toward the street as he pushed against the building door, as if to check that no one was observing his entrance.

McColl stared at the picture for several moments, thoughts and questions tripping over one another.

How blind had he been? All that time he'd thought he was fooling the German, had von Schön been fooling him?

He thought back to Tsingtau. Who had made the first overture, himself or the German? He couldn't remember, but the latter now seemed more likely. If von Schön worked for German intelligence, he might well have initiated an acquaintance with a suspicious British visitor.

But if the German had seen through McColl, he would surely have arrested him there and then, not allowed him to escape and report his findings. No, von Schön had left Tsingtau still believing that McColl was the businessman he claimed to be and only later been told that this was not the case. He had then boarded the *Manchuria* intent on finishing the job that his Chinese hireling had bungled in Shanghai and been frustrated by the fact that his target was hardly ever alone.

McColl felt as if he'd been betrayed and knew that the feeling was ridiculous. His enemy had proved himself more adept at deception—it was as simple as that.

And the game was not over.

Dates and times were written on the backs of the photographs. Von Schön had visited the ashram the previous afternoon, only hours before the latest would-be assassin had climbed into McColl's hotel wardrobe. Which hardly seemed a coincidence. The one remaining mystery was the identity of his savior, the author of the warning message. One of the undercover Indians, he guessed— the note-writer's command of English had seemed a bit on the shaky side.

So where had von Schön been staying? And where was he now? "Did anyone follow this man?" he asked Palóu.

"My younger son tried, but the man jumped on a tram at the last moment."

Which came as no surprise. McColl went through the rest of the photographs, which were all of Indians. Most had names and addresses penciled in on the back—Palóu and his boys had done a wonderful job.

McColl said as much.

"The weather's against us today," the detective said with a gesture toward the fog-filled window.

"Yeah, well, I'm afraid I can't afford any more days anyway. Not for the moment at least. But I'm going to leave your name with . . . with my boss here and recommend that he use you if he decides to take matters any further."

"Thank you." Palóu smiled. "You're leaving San Francisco?"

"In a few days. But there is one last thing I need to know. Could you find out if a particular someone has booked a seat on a long-distance train in the past few days?"

"That shouldn't be too tough."

McColl pulled von Schön's photograph from the pile and handed it across.

"Ah. Without a name it might be."

"His name is Rainer von Schön. At least I think it is. Until I saw that photograph, I thought he was just a businessman, but it seems he works for the German government. And I'd like to know where he's headed."

Palóu nodded. "If he's made a booking in that name, I should be able to trace it."

Settling accounts with the detective left McColl's supply of dollars seriously diminished. Outside, the fog showed no sign of lifting, which seemed like a comment on his recent work. He paused to scan the surroundings, but there were no lurking shapes in the immediate vicinity.

Walking on, he told himself to look on the bright side—he had, after all, unmasked a German agent, even if the German agent had unmasked him first. The fact that von Schön's countrymen had tried so hard to prevent McColl from leaving their Chinese enclave suggested that, for all his blundering, he had managed to garner some useful information. And whether or not his work here in San Francisco would bear useful fruit was still an open question. A reborn intelligence setup was bound to find the photographs, names, and addresses useful, and Father Meagher might prove a thread worth unwinding. His misreading of von Schön hadn't proved fatal. Not quite.

But his vanity had taken a knock. He owed his shot at Father Meagher as much to knowing Caitlin as to anything else, and the odds on their getting together must have been infinitesimal. When it came to writing the next report for Cumming, he would need to be creative.

Farther down Powell he stopped off at the Chicago & North Western passenger office and booked himself onto Monday's Overland Limited. There were no single compartments left, which was just as well since he couldn't afford one. He prayed that Caitlin had reserved one in time, or their three-day journey would be less of an idyll than planned.

Next stop was the telegraph office and a cable to Jed and Mac announcing the date of his arrival in New York City. He would, he reckoned, be only a day or so behind them. His last task took him back to his hotel, where he watched the manager place the envelope of photographs in the cast-iron safe, clang the door shut, and twirl the combination wheel with a wholly spurious flourish.

With nothing left to do that day, and wary of secluding himself in his room, he went back out into the fog. The restaurants on Geary seemed like well-lit caves in shadowy cliffs, and after eating lunch in one he wandered down to the junction with Market and caught a tram heading west. By the time he got off at the northeastern corner of Golden Gate Park, visibility had begun to improve, and as he took the long walk west toward the ocean, it seemed as if a vast curtain were lifting in front of him. When he finally reached the shoreline, the sky behind him was a mass of gray, the heavens ahead the purest blue.

He stared out across the Pacific, remembering the weeks spent crossing it. Von Schön had certainly not been who McColl thought he was. Had Caitlin?

He took the tram back to the city center and walked up to Union Square. There was another message waiting for him, but it contained no warning of a second assassin. The consul wanted to see him and suggested they meet at eight that evening in a bar called the Schooner. McColl left a message of acceptance on the consulate phone and spent the next hour stretched out in a hot bath, getting his story straight.

The Schooner was close to the fishing wharves, with the low-beamed ceilings and wood paneling of many an English country pub. Maybe that was why Fairholme liked it, or maybe he'd taken a fancy to the buxom brunette behind the bar. The consul led the way to a booth in the corner and leafed through the envelope of photographs that McColl had brought along. "Excellent," was all he said, a judgment he perhaps regretted when McColl explained about von Schön. "You make interesting friends," he eventually murmured, removing a folded sheet of paper from his inside pocket. "You asked me to request a check on Caitlin Hanley and her family."

The good news was that Caitlin was exactly who she claimed to be, a working journalist with extremely radical views on a wide range of issues, most notably those concerning women's rights, workers' rights, and European behavior in the rest of the world. The bad news took longer to digest. Her father, Ronan, had, until recently, been secretary of the New York branch of Clan na Gael and was still a close confidant of its leader, John Devoy. Ronan Hanley was almost certainly a member of the Irish Republican Brotherhood and was suspected of helping to organize an arms shipment to India three years earlier. Caitlin's sister, Finola, was not involved—at least openly—in political activity, but her older brother, Fergus, was a lawyer who had represented known Clan na Gael members. Her younger brother, Colm, was a member of both the Irish Brotherhood and the homegrown Industrial Workers of the World. He had spent a month in Dublin the previous year, where his contacts had included extreme socialist friends of the rabble-rousing union leader Jim Larkin.

"They sound like a family to give London nightmares," Fairholme concluded. "If Finola's as innocent as she seems, she must be wondering what she's done to deserve the rest of them."

McColl bristled inwardly on Caitlin's behalf but managed a thin smile. He dreaded to think what Cumming had made of the report, assuming he'd already seen it.

"Look," Fairholme said, "I'll be blunt. I assume you realize that working for the Service and having a good time with this girl are not very compatible pastimes. And that anything more than a good time would be completely out of the question. The only thing you have to ask yourself—because this is what Cumming will ask you—is how willing you are to use this relationship to serve your country."

McColl could not smile at that. "To betray her, you mean."

"Don't be insulted," Fairholme said quickly, raising a hand. "I'm trying to help. If you don't feel you could do that, then drop her now, while you still can."

The last four days in San Francisco felt endless. On Thursday, Palóu sent him a final bill, along with the information that Rainer von Schön had taken the previous morning's train to Los Angeles. He had waited, it seemed, until he knew the result of his plotting.

Caitlin had promised to come by on Friday, but only a message arrived—she had a bad cold and was in "such a foul mood you wouldn't want to see me." She softened the blow by saying how much she looked forward to Monday.

He went nowhere near the Shamrock or the ashrams, and spent most of his time away from the hotel, in case another assassin had been primed. On Saturday he hired a Model T and explored the still-Spanish towns farther down the peninsula; on the wet Sunday he spent half a day playing eight ball in a bar on Geary and won enough money to leave a tip at his hotel. Those long-past evenings in Oxford billiard halls had not been completely wasted.

Compartment 4

♠

The train was stretched out on the Oakland quay, ready to leave. The weather had cleared again overnight, and the sunlight sparkling on the waters of the bay almost offset the chill of the wind. McColl's compartment was toward the rear, his three fellow sharers already in occupation. A dark-haired man with a long and bushy mustache introduced himself as William Pearson, and a younger replica as his son, Gabriel. "Pearson and Son," he added, as if to stress that business came before family. The third man was a young naval officer named Bragg, who offered McColl the choice of upper or lower bunk. Unsure of how much nocturnal rambling his trip would entail, McColl opted for the latter.

He had caught a glimpse of Caitlin on the railroad ferry, wearing her rose-colored scarf and hat, and had started walking toward her. She had noticed him and quickly shaken her head, adding a slight tilt of explanation in the direction of her companion. Father Meagher, resplendent in long black cassock and biretta, was too busy arguing with a railroad official to have noticed McColl, and she obviously liked it that way. He felt a pang at being spurned but knew he was being ridiculous. Doubtless she had her reasons.

Once his suitcase was safely wedged under the lower bunk, he moved back into the corridor to watch their departure. A shrill blast of the locomotive's whistle and the train clanked into motion, pulling away from the quay but keeping to the edge of the bay. Two battleships were anchored close to shore, reminding him of the morning he had fled Tsingtau.

He walked forward in search of the club car, found it still empty, and took possession of a leather armchair facing west across the bay. After ordering a beer from the steward, he noticed a fan of newspapers on a table at the end of the car and went to choose one. As McColl returned with an ancient, dog-eared copy of the London *Times*, the steward arrived with his drink and proudly pointed out the electric reading lights that hung above each chair.

McColl read through the paper, occasionally pausing to return a new arrival's greeting or admire the changing view of the bay. In recent months he had acquired the habit of scanning a newspaper for signs of change in the international weather, but on this occasion nothing leaped out at him—no reports of bloodthirsty speeches or frontier incidents or suspicious war games. The Kaiser obviously hadn't wedged his foot in his mouth in recent weeks, and the Balkans seemed quiet as Balkans could be. It might be the lull before the storm, but maybe the governments that mattered had finally begun to see some sense.

The one story that did draw his attention concerned fellow spies. A British husband and wife had been arrested in possession of "documents relating to the navy." Who they were spying for was not mentioned, but the woman had been caught heading for Brussels and a meeting with someone called Petersen. The police had discovered as much after laboriously reconstructing a note that she had torn to shreds in one of their vehicles. Why no one had stopped her was not explained.

The moral of the story, McColl decided, was burn or memorize.

By the time he'd finished the paper, the train had reached the Carquinez Strait and was being divided for loading aboard what the railroad company proudly proclaimed the "largest ferry boat in the world." The *Solano* was certainly enormous, with two towering chimneys flanking the paddle wheel and four tracks running the length of the vessel to hold the segmented train. The strait was about a mile wide, and the crossing itself took much less time than the maneuvers that preceded and followed it.

The train put together again, the journey resumed. McColl took lunch in the buffet car, then walked back down to the observation car at the rear. All the seats were occupied, but one opened up as he stood looking in, and he gratefully took possession. The upholstered armchairs, like their leather cousins in the club car, all faced inward, which seemed a strange decision, in that observation had to be conducted through the gaps between those sitting opposite. But the arrangement did have the advantage of preventing an approach from behind, which, in view of his recent experiences, McColl found somewhat comforting. As did the fact that all the babbling voices sounded distinctly American.

He wondered if the Germans would persist in their efforts to kill him. There seemed no reason they shouldn't; spies weren't like grouse—there was no official season for bumping them off. The Germans could just keep trying until they succeeded, which was rather a chilling thought.

Then again, there had to be some sort of limit—surely he wouldn't have to spend the rest of his life evading the Kaiser's minions. Perhaps Cumming could arrange some sort of deal, offer to abandon an ongoing British vendetta, if such an animal existed. Cumming would have to do something about McColl's predicament, if only to show he could protect his agents. In the meantime McColl would have to be careful.

It was still a nice day, the sun accentuating the rich colors of the Sacramento Valley. Soon after two they reached the state capital, where a second locomotive was added for the long climb ahead. As the line ascended the valley of the American, the river itself receded beneath them until only a silver ribbon was visible, at least a thousand feet below. A white blanket now covered the slopes, and as the light began to fade, the train drummed its way through a series of snowsheds and tunnels.

The novelty had clearly worn off, and the observation car had almost emptied out, leaving only McColl and two old women at the other end. He closed his eyes and let his thoughts turn, as they often had in the last couple of days, to what Fairholme had said about the perils inherent in continuing his romance with Caitlin.

The man had meant well. More to the point, he was probably right.

But so what? McColl had never known anyone like her—and very much doubted he ever would again. Given that, he had no intention of simply throwing in the towel. A love affair with an Irish radical and a career with the British Secret Service might not be compatible in the longer term, but for a few weeks more? If this turned out to be nothing more than a glorious interlude, then he didn't want to lose his career as well. And if by some miracle it lasted, then perhaps by another they might make it work. Because when all was said and done, there was no real conflict of interest. They didn't even disagree about Ireland, not in a fundamental way.

He knew that keeping his work a secret was a form of lying. But he thought the man she liked was the man he really was—he couldn't imagine her having this sort of affair with an ordinary automobile salesman. Deep down—unconsciously, as Freud would say—some part of her knew that he was more than he seemed.

He asked himself who he was kidding, and the answer was no one. But he still wouldn't choose between her and the Service.

It really was dark now, and time to show himself. Dinner was already being served, and after eating he lingered over coffee and liqueur in hope of seeing her. He'd almost given up when she finally appeared, with Father Meagher in close attendance. This time the priest did notice him and seemed visibly irritated when Caitlin stopped to wish him good evening. En route to the toilet a few minutes later, she contrived to slip him a piece of paper, which he read outside in the vestibule: "Car 4, Compartment 5, eleven o'clock. Knock ever so quietly."

Three hours later he was outside the door, rapping it softly as she had requested. She appeared with a finger across her lips, beckoned him into the compartment, and pointed toward the en suite dressing room. Once inside it, she closed the door behind them, put her arms around his neck, and gave him a passionate kiss. "He's in the suite next door. That way," she added, "on the other side of my stateroom—sorry, that's a nautical term, isn't it? But you know what I mean. And this room seems to be next door to my other neighbor's dressing room, so Father Meagher's bedroom must be next to mine. Either we drag the mattress in here or we'll have to make love in ghostly silence."

As he loosened the cord of her dressing gown, slid a hand inside, and kissed her again, the train roared its way through another short tunnel. "I think we can afford a few creaking bedsprings," he said.

They did creak, but not alarmingly so, and sometime after they'd spent their passion, McColl was surprised to hear other springs vibrating through the wall. "I told you so," she whispered gleefully.

He eventually put his clothes back on in the dressing room, and they stood hand in hand by the window, looking out at the moonlit fields of snow. "Father Meagher is taking me to breakfast at eight o'clock," she said. "Arrive a few minutes later and I'll invite you to join us. He won't refuse. As far as he knows,

I met you in China and you helped me out with some translation work, both there and on the ship. Tell him you've a wife and children at home and how much you're missing them."

"Okay."

"You don't have a wife and children you're missing?"

"No. I had a wife once, but we're long since divorced." He hoped he sounded as indifferent as he actually was.

Her hand loosened in his, but only for a second. "You never said."

"I hardly ever think about her. It was all a long time ago, and we were only together a couple of years."

"And you haven't seen her since?"

"Oh, I see her—she's my boss Tim's sister. But only to exchange the odd polite word. She's married again now."

"What's her name?"

"Evelyn. You're not upset, are you?"

"No. Surprised perhaps, which is absolutely ridiculous. For some strange reason, I just assumed you had always been single."

"To tell you the truth, I've never felt anything else. And never more so than when we were married. But I don't want to talk about her. Let's go back a bit—what made you dream up a fictitious family for me?"

"To deflect him, of course. If he thinks you're interested in me, he'll keep watching me like a hawk. So when we meet at breakfast, remember to hardly notice I'm there. There's nothing he'd like better than to tell my father that I've fallen from grace. He positively revels in other people's sins."

"Does he know your father?"

"They've met a few times, but they're not friends. Even my father has better taste than that."

"Okay," McColl said. "So I'll see you at breakfast."

"Quiet as you go," she reminded him.

He could hear the priest snoring as he let himself out, and back in his own compartment Pearson and Son were both hard at it. He lay on his bunk cursing the two of them but knew in his heart that they weren't the ones keeping him awake. His conversation with Caitlin had stirred up memories he normally left alone, and now he found himself thinking about Oxford and Evelyn and the man he had been then—a very square peg in a very round hole. Spies were outsiders, too, but usually of their own volition.

The sleep that finally took him was fitful and dream-filled, and he woke to the first hint of light feeling barely rested. Now father and son were both turned to the wall, and the officer above him was snoring.

He put on his trousers, shoes, and socks, made his way to the washroom at the end of the car, and doused his face with cold water. The car steward had already brewed coffee, and McColl carried a mugful down toward the observation car, stopping to admire the sunrise when the train was on a curve. Darkness still filled the rear windows when he reached the observation car, but over the next few minutes, with what seemed astonishing speed, light flamed on the ridgetops of the receding Sierras and began to conjure all manner of colors from the surrounding desert.

The coffee was strong, but he still found himself dozing off, and he finally woke with a start when the train jolted to a halt in what turned out to be Elko. The station was bathed in sunlight, but frost glistened on the ground, and as they pulled out, he noticed a porter's telltale plume of breath.

At eight o'clock he walked up the train, stopping only to check his appearance in one of the toilets. Not too bad for such a dissolute life, he told himself.

They were in the middle of the crowded dining car, the priest facing forward.

"Mr. McColl," she greeted him warmly. "Won't you join us? You've met Father Meagher."

"Father," McColl said, taking the seat next to him. The priest had a mouthful of toast and looked more surprised than annoyed. "How was your stay in California?" McColl asked him jovially once his order had been taken. "Were you on vacation?"

Father Meagher wiped his lips with a napkin while considering his answer. "I was on vacation, yes. Seeing old friends." He looked at McColl for the first time. "You're on a working trip, I understand. Miss Hanley tells me you're a salesman."

McColl managed to look a trifle aggrieved. "I represent a British automobile manufacturer," he conceded.

"And now you're on your way home?"

"On the way, yes. I have some business in New York, but then I take ship, I'm glad to say. I've already been away from my wife and children for far too long," he added, trying to look as if he meant it. "I miss them a great deal."

"As you should, sir."

"Indeed," McColl agreed, knife and fork poised above his omelet. "Though I have to say that on my travels I meet many men who seem to feel differently, who are only too ready—how should I say this?—to abuse the trust of those left at home." Caitlin, he noticed, was keeping a straight face with some difficulty, but Father Meagher was nodding his agreement. "As a man of the cloth," McColl went on, "you must be only too aware of human frailty."

The priest nodded some more. "Too much so, I sometimes think. But I suppose it's an occupational hazard. What man confesses his good deeds?"

McColl smiled sympathetically. "It must be dispiriting sometimes."

"Sometimes. Miss Hanley tells me you're from Scotland."

"From Glasgow. My father's parents came over from Donegal in 1851, so I'm half Irish really."

"So you're a Catholic, then?"

"I am," McColl declared, rather too glibly for his own good. He hoped he wouldn't be tested on doctrine.

"Well, I'm pleased to meet you," the priest said before drinking the last of his coffee. "Now, Caitlin, what are you doing today?"

"I have some writing to do. And you?"

"Well, I know I could do with a haircut. And then perhaps some reading. But I can meet you for lunch at one o'clock."

"That suits me," she said, "but this evening I think I'll take dinner in my compartment. The noise of the train kept me awake until dawn, and I'm sure I'll want to retire early tonight."

"That suits *me*." Father Meagher said. "I'm sure I can find a bridge game to while away the time. Now, Mr. McColl, if you'd just let me out . . ."

McColl watched the priest exit through the vestibule door. "So," he said, sitting back down, "am I included in the early night?"

"Of course," she said, taking his hand. "But I really do have a piece to finish this morning. Let's meet up this afternoon."

"In the observation car," he suggested. "I've more or less taken up residence there."

And that was where he spent the morning, watching the desert slide by and considering his next move. He needed to search through Father Meagher's compartment, but when would be the best time? Not when the priest was in it, obviously. Not when he might return at any moment. And not when someone else might witness the break-in. An ex-burglar on Cumming's payroll had taught him the art of picking locks—it was almost the only training he'd had—but it wasn't something one could manage in an instant.

There were more people walking up and down the train during the day, so there'd be less chance of his being seen at the door in question after dinner. So midevening, he decided, while the father was playing cards. And it would have to be today—he couldn't risk leaving it for the final night, when there might not be a similar opportunity.

Caitlin, though, was a potential problem. He would need an excuse for leaving her company and would have to make sure she didn't hear him moving around in Father Meagher's compartment. Tiredness, he decided, would do for the first, and it might well turn out to be true. The second he would just have to manage.

He made do with a snack in the club car for lunch and returned to his post in time to enjoy the twelve-mile crossing of the Great Salt Lake. The train had a lengthy stop in Ogden, the connection for Salt Lake City, and he took the opportunity for some exercise, walking the length of the platform as he smoked a cigarette. It was bitterly cold, and by the time he reached the locomotives, he was hugging and shaking himself to generate warmth.

When he got back to the observation car, she was there, talking to one of the few children on the train, a boy of ten or eleven. "Marty here tells me that we'll soon be seeing the Devil's Slide and the Thousand Mile Tree," she told McColl.

"And what are they?" he asked the boy.

"The Devil's Slide is like a huge playground slide," Marty explained. "On the side of a mountain. It's hundreds of feet long."

"And the tree?"

"That's a funny accent you've got," Marty decided.

"I'm Scottish. What about the tree?"

"It's just a pine tree, but it's exactly a thousand miles from Omaha. That's where they started building the line."

"Okay. And how long do we have to wait?"

"About half an hour after Ogden, the conductor told me."

It passed quickly, the valley narrowing as the train climbed away from the desert. Marty seemed starved of conversation—he was traveling with his mother—and eager to talk about almost anything. He told them his father was a soldier and currently in Europe attending a conference that he wasn't allowed to write home about, in case his letters were intercepted. The boy's father thought there would be a war in Europe, because the Europeans all distrusted each other. But the United States would keep out of it, because these days Europe didn't really matter to Americans. "I'm sorry about that," Marty apologized to McColl.

"Don't mention it," McColl told him.

The tree, when it appeared, was disappointingly small, the slide exactly as Marty had described it. He insisted on shaking their hands when he left—his mother, he said, would be wondering where he was.

"Will there be a war, do you think?" Caitlin asked McColl.

He shrugged. "Who knows?"

She wasn't to be put off. "I just can't believe it could happen. Not in today's world."

"Why not?"

"Oh, so many reasons. Who would hope to benefit, for God's sake? Businessmen would know that their profits would be slashed, and the workers would know they were risking their lives for someone else's profit. Why would they fight? Why would German workers agree to kill French workers?"

"They always have."

"In the past, yes, but now there are organizations like the Second International to put the case for peace and solidarity."

"I hope you're right."

"But you don't think I am."

"I don't know."

She was silent for a few moments. "You know what war's really like, don't you? You should be out there telling people."

He gave her a wry smile. "I know what mine was like. But no one would listen if I tried to tell them. Any more than I would have done. Old men desperate to leave their mark and young men lusting after glory—it's a marriage made in heaven."

"Or hell."

"Yes." He had a sudden mental picture of the Indian from Spion Kop. "Have you heard of an Indian named Mohandas Gandhi?"

"Of course—he's the leader of the protests in South Africa. Why?"

"I met him once, during the war there. He's famous these days, but back then he served in the Ambulance Corps. He was one of the men who helped carry me down off a mountain when I was injured. We talked for hours, or rather he did—I could hardly breathe, let alone talk. He seemed so positive about everything. I was still half convinced I was going to die, and he just took it for granted that I was going to live. I often think about him."

"As an inspiration?"

"Yes, I suppose so. It would be better if men like that were running the world." He shrugged. "But they're not."

"All right," she said. "But people do evolve. We *did* get rid of slavery, and women *will* get the vote. And men like Gandhi will win more support."

"Maybe. And one day organizations like the Second International might really make a difference. But it won't happen quickly and not, I fear, in time to prevent a major war."

"Well, I hope you're wrong."

"So do I."

She smiled. "Why don't we go back to my suite and order in some dinner?"

"All right, but will we have to eat in silence?"

"He won't be in his compartment, but no—inviting a man to dinner wouldn't upset my aunt. It's dessert that has to be discreet."

The food was excellent, the lovemaking even better—long

and languorous, with no distracting noises through the wall. Hating to leave, but knowing he must, McColl seized on a yawn as proof of her tiredness and insisted she have an early night.

She voiced her reluctance but was almost asleep by the time he got dressed. He kissed her lightly on the cheek, let himself out, and went in search of Father Meagher.

He found him in the club car, sharing an end booth with three other men. They were playing poker rather than bridge, and the priest's face reflected the pitiful pile of chips beside his hand. He was losing but with any luck might survive a few more hands. As far as McColl was concerned, it was now or never.

He swiftly retraced his steps to Caitlin's carriage. The car attendant was sitting in his tiny cubicle, reading the Zane Grey novel Jed had enjoyed so much, and only glanced up as McColl passed by. There was no one in the corridor and no reason to wait—he inserted the burglar's thin metal tool and twisted and turned it the way he'd been taught. The lock clicked open rather more loudly than he'd hoped, and he stepped inside, closing the door behind him with more control. For a moment he considered relocking the door, but what would be the point? He couldn't leave by the window while the train was moving at speed, and anyway there wouldn't be time.

He turned on the overhead light and looked around the compartment. There was a suitcase on the cradle, but it wasn't the large one in Palóu's picture—if that was on board, it must be in the baggage car. He quietly opened the connecting door, turned on another light, and examined the dressing room, where three identical cassocks were hanging on hooks. There were two pairs of shoes on the floor, the usual toiletry items around the basin, and nothing much else.

He went back to the suitcase, where socks and undergarments overlaid several books, a San Francisco newspaper, an illustrated New Testament for children, and a folder full of sheet music for traditional Irish songs. Underneath the music were two sealed envelopes bearing names but no addresses. One was for John Devoy, the head of Clan na Gael, the other for Erich Rieber, whoever he might be.

Success, he thought. And then he heard sounds through the wall, a clump on the floor as she got out of bed, and then footsteps. Had she heard him? She seemed to be pacing up and down, for heaven only knew what reason.

He forced himself to ignore her. What should he do now? He could tear the letters open and read them, but only at the cost of alerting Meagher, who might well suspect him of being responsible. That wouldn't matter in itself, but as Cumming was fond of saying, half the value of knowing something lay in the other side's not knowing you knew. If there were plans in either letter, then disclosure would lead to their being changed, and nothing would be achieved.

He had to steam them open, and he couldn't do that where he was. He would have to take the letters with him and hope that their temporary absence was not noticed. The chances had to be good—Father Meagher didn't strike him as the compulsive sort, someone who needed to check where everything was at regular intervals. The man was too sure of himself at the best of times and, judging by the amount he was drinking tonight, seemed likely to collapse at the sight of his bed. And when he woke up, the priest would be too busy nursing a hangover to think of checking through his belongings. If McColl could put the letters back in the suitcase while Meagher was having breakfast, then he should get away with it.

A sudden creak next door, which he hoped was her climbing back into bed, gave way to what seemed a lasting silence. He took a deep breath and cracked the door open, half expecting to find the priest outside. There was no one there, but he could hear footsteps. Inching an eye around the jamb, he saw the car attendant briskly walking away—a few seconds earlier and there would have been some explaining to do.

Once the man had disappeared into the vestibule, McColl slipped out, clicked the door shut, and set about relocking it. For what seemed an age, the latch wouldn't take, and by the time it did, sweat was beading on his brow. Again the click sounded terribly loud, and he almost ran to the sanctuary of the following car.

In the club car, Father Meagher was still playing poker and looked to have recovered some of his losses. There was now a whiskey chaser by the side of the beer, and the priest seemed redder in the face. McColl hoped he didn't have a heart attack, or the letters would never be delivered.

Walking on, he considered ways of steaming the envelopes open. He would go to one of the kitchens, he decided—tell them he felt congested and ask for some boiling water to give his sinuses a face bath in one of the washrooms. It sounded a good idea, but not for very long. The envelopes were bound to look different after such treatment, and how would he ever restick them?

As he passed the stenographer's office a simpler idea occurred to him. Office hours were long since over, but the door was open, the typewriter waiting for anyone wanting to use it. McColl went through the bureau drawers and found what he was looking for—a selection of plain envelopes. Reasoning that he might need more than one attempt to copy the names on the originals, he took six of similar size and walked on toward the observation car, expecting to find it empty.

It wasn't, but the young couple at the far end were too bound up in each other to care what he was doing. With a keen sense of anticipation, he used his pocketknife to slit the envelopes open.

The letters within did not disappoint.

The one to the Clan na Gael leader was from Larry de

Lacey and ran to four pages. The letter *looked* dangerously high-spirited—de Lacey was fond of exclamation marks and found it hard to write in a straight line—but the content was sober enough. He began with some social news—one mutual acquaintance had gotten married, another had sired twins—before saying how glad he was that Devoy's health had improved.

The niceties dealt with, de Lacey turned to the news from Ireland. He saw the workers' defeat in Dublin as "an opportunity for the Brotherhood to reassert its own truly Irish agenda." The ejection of the British was what mattered, and the Irish people must not let "utopian social goals" distract them from this task, particularly at this juncture, when other events seemed to be moving in their favor. De Lacey was pleased that the Brotherhood had secured control of the recently formed Volunteers and adamant that they should resist any attempt by Redmond's Nationalists to usurp them.

So much, so predictable, McColl thought.

A report on funding followed. The California chapter of Clan na Gael had raised $1,704 for the struggle back home, a figure that de Lacey seemed more than pleased with, and several additional events were planned for St. Patrick's Day.

Relations with "our Indian friends" were said to be good. "The British and BOI are making every effort to get HD declared persona non grata, and will probably succeed. But whether or not they shut the stable door, I think this horse has bolted! The organisation HD built up is strong enough to do without him, or at least without his presence here in the US. The focus of their efforts is already shifting home from exile, partly thanks to our joint efforts. The first shipment left here on the 26th of last month, and is expected in Singapore around the 15th of March. The second shipment is currently being organised by our other friends."

Which could only be the Germans, McColl assumed.

"I had quite a long talk with vB the other evening, and he more or less admitted that they weren't expecting very much but would be grateful for whatever we can give them. Which seemed realistic to me, and I told him it did. When the moment of opportunity comes, of course things will be different. They will give us the guns we need, not because they love us but because it will be in their interests to do so. And we will give our all in return, not because we love them but for the cause of a free and independent Ireland.

"I also talked to GF, who says he saw you a few months ago. He let slip that a joint operation on enemy soil is under consideration but proved remarkably coy when I pressed him on names and what was intended. Have you heard anything about this?"

Having asked this rather plaintive question, de Lacey asked to be remembered "to all at the *Gaelic American* office" and brought the letter to a close.

Who was GF? McColl wondered. He would have to cable Fairholme and ask if any known official at the German consulate had those initials.

He turned to the letter for Erich Rieber. This was much shorter, comprising less than two whole sheets of neatly written German, headed *San Francisco, March 8* and signed *Ernst Reischach.*

The first half of the letter dealt with the Indians. Reischach spoke highly of Har Dayal and stressed the need to make good the material assistance "we previously discussed," a reference, presumably, to the shipment de Lacey had mentioned. He added that the Ghadar organization had been subjected to a British-inspired campaign of harassment by the American authorities, but that this had been thwarted, at least in the short term, by the unmasking and punishment of several informers.

The remaining paragraphs of the letter were a revelation,

and a shocking one at that. Their subject was "the English spy Jack McColl" and the German attempts to kill him. "As you know," Reischach wrote, "our agent was unsuccessful in Shanghai, and I regret to report a second failure here in San Francisco."

The sentences seemed to leap out at McColl, as if intent on finishing the job. He took a deep breath and continued reading. According to Reischach, his attempted murder had proved "both frustrating and divisive." The Indians had apologized most profusely for their lack of success and guaranteed the silence of the failed assassin, who "knew nothing of his employers. They are adamant that none of their people sent the rumored warning and refused to make a second attempt until whoever it was is discovered. I suspect that only their fear of forfeiting our assistance in the other matter prevents them from openly accusing us."

And it seemed that the Germans were divided. "Some of our people here were far from happy at the decision to make an example of the Englishman. RvS in particular was highly put out and has appealed for a change of heart in Berlin. Some of our people here agreed with him, while others did not, and feelings ran quite high for a while. RvS is now on his way to Mexico, so things have had a chance to settle down. By the time you read this, the whole business should have been settled—if Berlin has rejected RvS's appeal, then our people in New York will have taken steps to greet Herr McColl on his arrival and taken the appropriate action."

McColl put the letter down, wondering why he still felt relatively calm. It wasn't over—another knife, or something equally unpleasant, might be waiting for him in New York. He would need to steer clear of crowds and be careful not to put Caitlin in danger. He had intended to ask Jed to meet them, but he didn't want to put his brother at risk either. Perhaps Cumming would be able to help.

It could have been worse. Meagher obviously knew nothing of the Reischach letter's contents—his attitude toward McColl, and the fact that it was sealed, seemed to prove as much. If the priest ever did read the letter, he would discover who and what McColl was and doubtless share the news with Caitlin. But if he hadn't yet broken the seal, there seemed no reason he should.

And it was clear to McColl that he had, at least partly, misjudged von Schön. The fact that the young German had argued against his death sentence was gratifying, not least because it showed that McColl's original judgment of the man's character had not been so wide of the mark. He might not have realized that von Schön was a spy, but he had correctly identified him as a decent fellow.

And it also occurred to McColl—as it obviously hadn't to Reischach—that von Schön could have sent McColl the warning. If so, he owed the German his life.

So much for the personal side.

Who were Rieber and Reischach? If they were diplomats, why weren't they using the safer channels open to them? If they weren't, then why were they discussing their government's policies and illicit activities in the United States? And if they were government officials making use of unofficial channels, then who they were trying to bypass—their enemies or their friends? The more McColl thought about it, the more convinced he became that these were two intelligence agents operating outside the diplomatic cocoon.

In the end he didn't suppose it mattered much. Whatever positions they held, they held them for the enemy.

What had he learned from the two letters?

First, that the Germans had supplied Har Dayal with two arms shipments, one of which was reaching Singapore in five or six weeks' time. The DCI might know all about that already, but if they didn't, then Cumming would be more than pleased.

Second, that the Germans were also sending arms to the
IRB but were not expecting an immediate return. Their guns
to the republicans would match those already smuggled into
Ulster and might indeed see use in an Irish civil war. But if
war broke out in Europe, they could be used to wrest independence from a fully engaged Great Britain.

Third, and most worrying, was the news that "joint action
on enemy soil" was "under consideration." By whom? And
what exactly were they considering? It couldn't be conventional military action; it had to be some sort of terror attack.
A strike at Britain's morale, like blowing up the King or Parliament. Or was he getting carried away?

If Cumming were to make a judgment, he would need a
full copy of de Lacey's letter. But did he need the full text
of Reischach's? Because it occurred to McColl that Cumming
might balk at offering full-time employment to an agent the
Germans had already unmasked.

On reflection he decided that was overly pessimistic. The
empire had other enemies beside the Germans, and he could,
in any case, change his name and appearance. Cumming's
favorite agent, Sidney Reilly, was always turning up in the society columns, and it didn't seem to make him any less effective.

He would copy out the second letter as well. Once Cumming saw the German admission in writing, he might arrange
help in New York.

Needing paper and a table to write on, he walked back up
the train. The poker game in the club car had run its course,
and Father Meagher had disappeared, presumably to bed,
hopefully without checking his suitcase. McColl continued
on to the stenographer's office and shut himself in with the
sun blind down on the door. Copying the letters took him
almost an hour, the envelopes another fifteen minutes. He
had used up the six he'd taken and most of those left in the
desk before he was satisfied with his copies. He was probably

being overzealous—people weren't that observant when it came to other people's handwriting—but there was no point in stinting on effort.

It was almost one-thirty by the time he was finished, and the only remaining occupant of the adjoining club car was asleep in his chair. The snow swirling outside the windows reminded McColl that they were spending the whole night traversing the Rockies and most of the next day crossing the plains.

The other men in his compartment were all asleep, and more quietly so than on the previous night. He laid himself out without much hope and thought that only minutes had passed when a yell from outside woke him up. His pocket watch said ten past six, and a look around the end of the curtain told him the train had reached Laramie. After twenty minutes of trying, he gave up on getting back to sleep and repeated his trick of the previous morning, carrying coffee back to an empty observation car. This time there was no sunrise to color the land, only snow-draped valleys and tracks receding into mist.

At a quarter to eight, he made his way forward to the end of the dining car and, after checking that neither Caitlin nor Father Meagher had yet arrived, walked quickly through to the next carriage, where he ensconced himself in a convenient toilet. He gave them twenty minutes, then walked back to the dining car's doorway for a quick look inside. They were in the same seats—Caitlin with her back to him, staring out the window, Father Meagher looking down at his plate with a decidedly hungover expression.

McColl strode swiftly back to their car, where the corridor was empty and the metal shim worked its magic on the lock. The suitcase was still on its cradle, and there was no discernible rearrangement of the contents below the clothing. He put the two letters back in the same order and slipped out through the door into the still-empty corridor.

And then things began to go wrong. Try as he did, he

couldn't get the shim to relock the door, and after what seemed a couple of minutes he began to consider leaving it as it was. If Father Meagher found it so, he would doubtless go straight to the letters, but once he'd found them where they should be, there would be no reason to open them. And he was more likely to blame a lax car attendant for the unlocked door than a British agent. Being suspected himself would still be a damn sight better than being caught in the act.

But then Pao-yu, the girl from the Blue Dragon, wormed her way to the front of his mind. She was enough for his conscience to carry without adding a sacked car attendant.

He was trying again when a middle-aged couple suddenly entered the corridor. Pushing himself up against the door, as if making space for them to pass, he managed to conceal the shim, and they walked on through to the next car without ever looking back. But it was too risky. He gave the shim one last twist for luck and almost burst out laughing when the lock clicked shut.

Now all he needed was a second sojourn in a toilet, so as not to meet Caitlin and Meagher on their way back from breakfast. Even this proved a close-run thing—suddenly hearing her voice, he ducked through a convenient doorway with only seconds to spare. He supposed he could have found some explanation for being at this end of the train, but he was tired of lying to her. Not that hiding in a toilet felt much better.

The train was pulling in to a snow-covered Cheyenne, and he went to get some breakfast. He'd done it, he told himself. He should be feeling triumphant, but he wasn't.

After a shave at the barber's, he walked back to the observation car, where he found Caitlin scribbling in what looked like a diary. As he sat down beside her, she packed it away in her bag.

"It only just occurred to me," she said, pushing back a stray lock of brown hair, "but I never asked whether you were booked through to New York."

"I am."

"On the 20th Century."

"Of course."

"Thank God. Do you have a sleeping compartment?"

"Just a seat, I'm afraid. San Francisco was more expensive than I expected."

"It doesn't matter, I have one. And here's the good news— Father Meagher is spending a few days in Chicago, so we won't have him for company."

"That *is* good news. How long are we in Chicago? Do you know?"

"An hour and forty-five minutes, if we arrive on time. I know because I'm meeting an editor who might be interested in hiring me."

"A job in Chicago?" he asked, thinking how far away from England that would place her.

"Yes. It's a great city."

"I've never been."

"And I've been thinking it's time I left the family nest."

"You could come to England."

She smiled at that. "One day, maybe. But this is my home. I understand how things work here."

"I know what you mean," he admitted. Through the rear window, the Rockies still straddled the horizon and the receding line of telegraph poles stood stark against the snow and clouds.

They talked for most of the morning, about everything from suffragettes to the Catholic priesthood. "They're not all like Father Meagher," she insisted. "Our priest when I was growing up was a wonderful man—kind, wise, committed to helping the poor, the sort of man who gives the Church a good name." She told McColl how she had wanted to be a nun when she grew up and seemed mildly offended when he looked surprised.

They moved on to their younger brothers and the concern

each of them seemed to feel. She worried that Colm had poor taste in friends and was too easily led astray. "And sometimes I feel responsible," she said. "Aunt Orla was so bound up in Finola and me that she didn't have time for Colm. She left him to my father, who was hardly ever there. When he was, he just laid down rules, which no one else ever enforced. Colm . . . well, he's a good boy, but he has no judgment. He never knows when to stop."

McColl saw a little of Jed in her characterization of Colm, but only a little. His brother had grown up quite a lot on this trip, and not just in ways involving whorehouses and opium dens. What worried McColl was what came next. "If war comes," he pondered out loud, "then Jed will be first in line at the recruiting office. And even if I could persuade him other-wise—and I'll try my damnedest to do so—the boys in his age group will be the first ones conscripted."

A steward brought the latest batch of newspapers, which had come aboard at Cheyenne, and each of them found one item of real interest. The Saverne Affair had reached its conclusion, with the guilty officers escaping punishment. And, almost mir-roring that story, the American radical Joe Hill was still behind bars, despite a growing campaign to secure his release. He had been arrested in January for a murder that Caitlin was certain he hadn't committed. "I've met him," she said. "He's not that sort of man. If he hasn't been framed, I'll eat Father Meagher's biretta."

She told McColl about meeting Hill in a Brooklyn labor club and how during his second set he'd dedicated a song to her. "It's called 'The Rebel Girl.' He wrote it for Elizabeth Gurley Flynn, but he said it was mine for that evening. I know the last lines off by heart: 'And the grafters in terror are trem-bling / When her spite and defiance she'll hurl. / For the only and thoroughbred lady / Is the rebel girl.'" She laughed. "Who wouldn't want to hear herself described like that?"

Most women, McColl thought, but then she wasn't most women.

"I have to meet the father for lunch," she said without enthusiasm. "I don't suppose you'd consider joining us?"

"Why not?" McColl said. He didn't want to lose her company and was anxious to evaluate the priest's disposition—if Meagher had read the letters or noticed their temporary absence, surely it would show on his face. The priest didn't strike him as a born dissembler. He needn't have worried. Meagher looked like someone who had lost a lot of money at the poker table and was quietly obsessing about winning it back. He picked at his lunch, spoke to Caitlin in monosyllables, and hardly seemed to notice that McColl was even there.

After lunch Caitlin and McColl agreed to meet at seven and went their separate ways. She had work to do, and he had a cable to compose. Lacking the time to encrypt the two letters in full, he settled for a summary of the salient points and a promise to forward the copies on the first available ship. He was en route to hand it in for dispatch at the next available stop when the view through the corridor window changed his mind. A blizzard was raging outside, and some telegraph poles seemed to be swaying rather too violently. He would wait for Chicago.

In his compartment the Pearsons were asleep in their seats, and as no one had taken the place of the departed officer, he laid himself out on the opposite seat and followed their example. He awoke feeling groggy about three hours later, to find the Pearsons gone and the blizzard still blowing outside. As he passed the car attendant's booth on his way to the washroom, the man leaped out and handed him two cables. "I didn't want to wake you, sir."

McColl tipped him and read them, one from Jed boasting that they'd sold six cars during their week's sojourn in Chicago and one from Cumming that wasn't in code and advised him to contact "an interested party" at a New York address.

Once a hot shower had restored him to life, he went to

meet Caitlin in the buffet car. She arrived a few minutes later, with the news that Father Meagher was already back at the card table.

"Can he afford it?" McColl wondered out loud. He rather hoped the priest was losing Clan na Gael's money.

"I neither know nor care," was Caitlin's assessment. "Let's have dinner."

After sharing their first public meal on the train, they went back to her bed and made love, once with the fierceness that seemed their natural meeting place and then with a tenderness that seemed to surprise them both. He had no idea how long they'd been lying entwined in the narrow bed when they both heard the key in next door's lock.

"I'll go when we hear him get into bed," McColl said quietly.

"If he's lost again, he may throw himself out the window," she whispered back.

A few minutes later, they heard the springs creak as the priest lay down, and McColl levered himself onto the edge of the bed to get dressed. He felt nostalgic for the long nights they had spent together on the *Manchuria* and unreasonably annoyed with Father Meagher for unknowingly sending him back to the Pearsons. Once he and Caitlin had kissed good night and he had slipped quietly out through the door, the sense of resentment led him, through several mental twists and turns, to the matter of the priest's other suitcase, the one he'd carried away with him from the Ghadar office on Valencia.

It had to be in the baggage car, which McColl remembered was at the front of the train. The car was probably locked or guarded, but there was no harm in taking a look.

As it turned out, the only disincentive to entry was a solid-looking door, which opened when he pushed on the handle. McColl closed it behind him and turned on the overhead lights, which revealed two rows of floor-to-ceiling racks filled with luggage. Since each item was labeled and stored in alphabetical order, he had no trouble finding Father Meagher's suitcase and was about to pull it down when the recklessness of what he was doing finally stopped him short.

He went back to the door, cracked it open, and listened for a few moments. Reassured, he pulled down the suitcase, and applied his metal shim to the lock. It opened easily, to reveal more of the priest's wardrobe and about two hundred copies of the *Ghadar* newspaper.

It was tempting to throw them overboard—the good people of Nebraska, or whichever state they were crossing at this moment, would doubtless be thrilled by Har Dayal's politics—but Father Meagher would notice they were missing and perhaps start wondering about the letters.

McColl relocked the suitcase, put it back in its place, and let himself out.

Ten minutes later he was lying in his bunk, listening to the Pearson chorus and rebuking himself for running such a risk. He knew only too well it wasn't a game, and if he wanted Cumming to take him seriously, he should stop acting as though it were. If he'd been discovered in the baggage car, all his good work with the letters might well have been for nothing and the chance to foil the Germans lost.

And that seemed to matter more than it had before. Like most people, McColl felt attached to his homeland—in his case London as much as the Highlands or Glasgow—but that didn't mean he trusted its government. If he were to relish involvement in the struggle between England and Germany, he needed to believe that a German-run world would be worse than the one he already lived in. And he was pretty sure that he did. Becoming a target for the Kaiser's hired assassins was one thing—he could accept the Germans' anger with him, if not their extreme reaction—but the Saverne Affair, so fortuitously served up by von Schön, was something else again.

It confirmed McColl in all his prejudices against the Kaiser's Germany. There might be liberals and socialists in the Reichstag, and there might be decent young businessmen in Tsingtau, but Saverne showed only too clearly that the horrors of South-West Africa had not been an aberration. And a Germany grounded in arrogance and contempt for everyone else really was worth resisting.

He was woken by the clanging of wheels on an iron bridge, and a lift of the curtain revealed an impressive river. The Mississippi, he guessed—another picture put to a name. He spent the morning in the observation car, staring out at the snow-covered fields of Iowa and Illinois. Caitlin appeared as the train entered the outskirts of Chicago, to tell him she'd find him on the 20th Century.

He didn't see her at the Chicago terminus. After checking his suitcase, he found the cable office and sent off his message to Cumming, then consulted his watch and walked outside in search of a taxi. "Can you get me to the lake and back in an hour?" he asked.

"In twenty minutes, bub."

"Then show me some sights on the way."

They drove down through a canyon of skyscrapers to the ice-fringed lake, where he got out and stared for a few moments, feeling faintly ridiculous. On the return trip, the taxi stopped at lights underneath elevated tracks, and the thunder of a passing train was such that he feared it might fall through. He was back at Union Station in plenty of time and enjoyed walking down the long red carpet laid out for passengers on the famous express.

The train was still in the suburbs when she found him in his seat, took his hand, and led him to her compartment. For the next twelve hours, they talked, ate, made love and slept—it was like being back on the boat, except that now the whole journey was ending. It seemed to McColl that the only subject they had deliberately avoided, on both this train and the last, had been their future, or the lack thereof.

They could avoid it no longer.

"How long are you staying in New York?" she asked, with a brittleness in her voice that seemed completely out of character.

"I don't know. A week, maybe two. Maybe even longer."

She was silent for a moment. "What are we going to do?" she asked, and before he could reply, she supplied the answer. "We will go our own ways, as we said we would. We'll make the most of each other until the day we have to part, and when that day comes, we'll wish each other well and try not to cry."

The Giant Racer

♠

The train drew to a shuddering halt beside one of Grand Central's subterranean platforms at precisely nine-thirty in the morning, and McColl lingered in his seat for a few moments, wondering how best to make his exit, in the midst of a sheltering swarm or out in the open where a prospective assailant would find it harder to surprise him. Deciding it was six of one, half a dozen of the other, he joined those squeezing out through the vestibule and stepped down onto the platform.

At least he didn't have Caitlin to worry about. Unspecified family members were waiting to welcome her home, and McColl had gladly gone along with her wish to introduce him at some later date. It was bad enough being British—putting her loved ones in the line of German fire was unlikely to win him much kudos as a potential suitor. If that was what he was.

He walked slowly up the platform, scanning the moving crowd for signs of hostile intent. With the grip of his suitcase in one hand and the butt of his pocketed gun in the other, he was approaching the ticket barrier when a familiar smile came into view.

It was Jed, wearing a smart new fedora with the suit he had bought from Li Ch'ün.

McColl smiled back but didn't relax his guard. Once through the barrier, he urged his brother across the cathedral-like concourse until they both had their backs to the wall of the baggage-checking room. "I don't want to sound too dramatic, but there may be another killer waiting for me," McColl said quietly in explanation.

Jed's instinctive laugh lasted a few split seconds. "You're kidding! But . . ."

"Unfortunately not. And yes, there are things I have to tell you. But let's get out of here first. A cab, I think. And keep your eyes open. Shout if you see anyone coming toward us."

"Jesus!"

"Anyone but him."

Jed shook his head—in wonder, not refusal. "The cabs are that way," he said, pointing out two flights of steps on the far side of the concourse.

As they walked across, it seemed to McColl that the cavernous grandeur of the place was designed for drama. An assassination here would certainly make the front pages.

But no one came at them with knife, gun, or bomb as they wove their way through the thinning crowd. Outside, the sky was gray, the cabs queuing up for fares. With one look back, McColl clambered into the first in line and breathed a little easier.

"Thirty-sixth and Fifth," Jed told the cabbie, who looked Italian. "I thought you'd like to see the showroom and then go on to the hotel. But . . ."

McColl was staring back over his shoulder as they pulled out onto Forty-Second Street. As far as he could see, there was no other cab in pursuit. "I'll explain it all to you and Mac," he told his brother. "Tonight, when we're alone," he added quietly, with a nod toward their apparently oblivious driver.

Jed laughed and shook his head again. "What have you got yourself into?"

It was clearly a rhetorical question. McColl sat back and

reacquainted himself with New York City, which he'd last seen almost five years earlier. There were many more automobiles competing for road space with the streetcars, buses, and traditional horse-drawn traffic, and the sidewalks seemed even more choked with pedestrians than he remembered. The noise was tremendous—those not shouting were pressing on their car horns. America's premier city combined London's modernity with almost Oriental bustle.

The buildings seemed taller, though that might just be his memory playing tricks.

They drove past the impressive public library, which had still been under construction on his last visit and which Caitlin had told him she often used for research. Two stone lions stood guard outside the entrance.

The showroom in which Jed and Mac had rented space was a few blocks farther south on Fifth Avenue. It was twice the size of the one in San Francisco, and McColl couldn't fault the location. He could just make out the bottle green Maia through the left-hand window, cloaked as it was by a line of admiring spectators.

Mac was busy giving a young and rich-looking couple a guided tour of the automobile, which still appeared in gleaming good shape, considering the time spent in freighter holds and boxcars. "We're showing her off until two and using the rest of the afternoon for trial drives," Jed explained. "This is only our third day, and we're full up till Wednesday."

"Wonderful," McColl said. He was pleasantly surprised. Maybe the market in one-of-a-kind luxury automobiles would last longer than he thought.

After booking the young couple an appointment, Mac came over to shake his hand. "Good trip?"

"He's still got people trying to kill him," Jed said in a low voice. He was trying to sound flippant, but McColl could hear the anxiety.

"I'll talk to you both tonight," he promised. "But right now I need a bath. Where's our hotel?" Jed had cabled him the name—the Aberdeen—but not the address.

"It's four blocks south, on Thirty-Second Street. They're expecting you."

"Great. I'll see you both back there."

He could have walked or taken a streetcar, but another cab seemed the prudent option and took only a couple of minutes. The hotel looked fairly new, the lobby laid out and furnished in the modern style. He collected his key from reception and followed the bellboy into the elevator for the ride to the fourth floor. His room was at the front and came with a spotless bathroom. He decided not to worry about how much it was costing.

He'd been soaking in the bath for about twenty minutes when a rap on the outer door had him reaching for the gun that he'd left on the washstand. He sat there in the water, ears straining for any indication that someone was trying to get in, but all he could hear was the traffic outside.

Somewhat belatedly he realized that he hadn't checked the wardrobe.

He was really working himself up, he thought. He climbed out, wrapped himself in a towel, and went to investigate.

The wardrobe was empty, but someone had pushed an envelope under his outer door. Presumably a bellboy had rapped on the door, hoping for a tip.

"The coffee shop downstairs," the note inside the envelope read. "The old man couldn't make it."

It was the first half of the password that he'd received by cable. McColl dressed, put the letter copies in his inside pocket, and went down in the elevator. The coffee shop had a line of wooden booths with leather cushions arranged along one wall, beneath a mural depicting an Arcadian wilderness. There were people in most of the booths, but only one hand was beckoning him over.

"Jack!" the man said. "I'm afraid the old man couldn't make it." The accent was American enough, but it wasn't from New York City.

"I'll be seeing him at the weekend," McColl replied, completing the exchange of passwords and sliding into the opposite seat. The man across the table was about his own age, wiry, with dark bushy hair and a dark mustache that failed to conceal a slightly crooked mouth. He still had his winter coat on, but his hat was on the seat beside him.

"Coffee?" he asked, and raised a hand to call the waitress over. She looked about sixteen but took their order with the air of someone who'd been there forever.

Once she'd gone, McColl's contact offered a cigarette and introduced himself. "I'm Kensley, Nathan Kensley." He took a quick look over his shoulder, presumably to make sure that no one else was in earshot. "I'm in charge of the network here, such as it is."

"And you report directly to Cumming?" McColl asked. The way the various intelligence organizations had evolved over the last few years, it was often hard to identify a chain of command.

"And no one else," Kensley confirmed, as if he understood only too well why the question had been asked. The coffee arrived, along with the napoleon that Kensley had ordered for himself. He took a large bite, then wiped the cream from his lips and mustache with a napkin. "So no problem at Grand Central."

"You were there?"

"I was keeping an eye. Cumming has had a word with a German friend of his, an old contact from his navy days who still has some clout in Berlin. He asked him to use his influence to get the dogs called off." Kensley shook his head in apparent wonder. "Cumming seems to think that this is just a few rogue operatives exceeding their authority, that their superiors are still willing to play the game the way gentlemen should."

"But you don't?"

"Oh, he may be right, if only because the Germans know that their operatives are as vulnerable as ours in a free-for-all. But I doubt it. I'd say they're beginning to pursue intelligence work with the seriousness it deserves—and we should do the same."

"So I shouldn't stop looking over my shoulder?"

"No. Or not yet, anyway. Now, where are these letters?"

McColl handed the copies over and sipped at his coffee while the other man skimmed through them.

"Interesting," Kensley said reflectively once he'd finished. "I'll send these off to Cumming this afternoon. How, exactly, did you get hold of them?"

McColl went through the circumstances, from the young Palóu's camera catching Father Meagher outside the Ghadar office to his own nefarious activities on the Overland Limited.

"Okay," Kensley said when he was finished. "And I got the message about the priest staying over in Chicago. But you didn't say how many days."

"He never said, and asking might have made him suspicious. He's that kind of man."

"Not to worry—I'll have someone check with the railroad. But I'll want you with me at Grand Central when he does get in—he may be the only priest on the train, but if there's a whole convention, I'll need you to finger him."

"Fine," McColl agreed. "Just let me know when."

"Will do. Now, one other question—what's left of your cover? The Germans obviously know you work for us, but who else?"

McColl thought about it for a moment. "I had no actual contact with any of Har Dayal's people in San Francisco, and I used a false name when I hired the private detective to keep watch on them, so I've no reason to believe that the Indians would recognize me or even my name. And the same goes for the

Irish. There was no mention of me in de Lacey's letter to Devoy, and Father Meagher obviously didn't know who I was or he'd have watched me like a hawk. So it's just a matter of whom the Germans have told. And since they don't seem to have shared their knowledge with their allies on the West Coast, we can only hope that they're equally tight-lipped here."

Kensley asked if they had access to a photograph.

"Not that I know of. There was one in the Shanghai paper, but it was dark and blurred—my mother would have had trouble recognizing me."

The American looked relieved. "Okay. So how long are you staying? Do you have your passage home booked yet?"

"No. My boss in London is expecting me back by the end of the month, but a few days here or there won't make much difference."

Kensley raised an eyebrow. "Business must be good, to stay in a place like this."

McColl sighed. "Not that good. My colleagues made some sales in Chicago without me, and they got a bit carried away."

"Still . . ."

"Oh, I'm not complaining. Or moving. How long have you been in New York?"

Kensley hesitated, as if weighing up whether to answer. "About five years. I came down from Toronto in 1909. I was a policeman there."

"A Mountie?"

Kensley grimaced. "A detective."

"Of course. So how do we keep in touch?"

Kensley took a card from his pocket and passed it over. "If you ever need to speak to me, ring that consulate number and leave a message for me. Say that Jack called. I'll leave messages for you at the hotel reception. Or I may simply turn up in the lobby. If you see me, just walk on by and meet me here in the coffee shop a few minutes later. Okay?"

"Okay."

Kensley slid himself out of the booth, stood up, and raised a hand in farewell as he turned to leave. As the Canadian pressed his hat down over his bushy hair, McColl was reminded of someone trying to close the lid of an overfull suitcase.

But the man seemed intelligent, which boded well.

McColl went back up his room and had almost finished unpacking when someone else rapped on his door. He took his gun from the suitcase, stood to one side, and asked, "Who is it?"

"Your brother," Jed said loudly.

McColl put the gun back under a pillow and opened the door. "How did it go?"

"Not bad. One definite and three probables, I'd say."

"Great."

"So Mac and I thought we could all celebrate with dinner and a show. If you don't have anything else planned?"

"Sounds wonderful. When are we leaving?"

"Soon as you're ready."

It proved an enjoyable evening once the elephant in the room had been wheeled out and discussed. McColl knew that Cumming would disapprove—to put it mildly—of his revealing anything of his Service activities, but as long as Jed and Mac were also in the line of fire, they deserved some sort of explanation. He didn't tell them everything by any means, but he did admit to working, on a part-time basis over several years, for a government organization.

"It started when I went to Russia in 1909," he went on once they'd secured a table in a Broadway restaurant and ordered roast turkey with all the trimmings. "An old acquaintance from Oxford looked me up a few weeks beforehand and said that a friend of his had a proposition that might interest me. So I went to see this friend, who knew more about my upcoming Russian trip than I did. He had a short list of Russians whom he wanted me to get in touch with—men he and his superiors thought they could count on to support England in an international crisis." The spoken appeal had been to his patriotism, but he had eventually come to realize that Cumming had deliberately seduced him with the unspoken promise of adventure.

"I won't go into details," he continued. "You get the general idea. This man—the one who sent me—was willing to pay me a small amount for doing this, to cover expenses and supply a little profit on the side, but he was very insistent that I should see such work primarily as a means of serving my country. And I did. I do. I went to Tsingtau for him—I'm sure you can guess what for—and I ended up having to make a run for it. The man with the knife in Shanghai was almost certainly hired by the Germans to make an example of me. There was another attempt in San Francisco that you don't know about—another man with a knife waiting in my wardrobe—"

"What?" Jed exclaimed.

"Yes, I know. But I was luckier second time around—someone warned me there was an intruder in my room, and the British consul called in the federal police to deal with him. The reason I'm telling you both all this is that the Germans may have another go, and it's possible—not likely, but possible—that they'll try again when the three of us are together. So keep your eyes open whenever you're with me."

"But there was no one waiting at the station when you arrived," Mac said hopefully.

"No, and there's a chance a deal has been done between London and Berlin—a sort of gentlemen's agreement to let each other be. But we can't count on it, so be careful."

"And I don't suppose you're taking questions?" Jed asked perceptively.

"I'd rather not."

"Okay, but surely you can tell us what happened with Caitlin."

McColl looked at the two of them. "Why, have you got bets on the outcome?"

"No!"

"We traveled on the same train. But she hasn't seen her family for months, so I don't suppose I'll see her for a few days."

"And then?" Jed asked, with the bluntness of youth.

"And then what?"

"Will you be staying on here or will she be coming to England?"

So that was how they saw it, McColl thought. He could hardly blame them. "Neither for now, but we'll see," was all he could think to say, and he was saved from further questions by the arrival of their food.

The dinner was excellent, and so was the only show they could find with empty seats. A two-hour roller coaster of music and comedy put them in high spirits, which they soon found they shared with most of the city, if the Friday-night revelers thronging Broadway were anything to go by. With work the following morning, they restricted themselves to a couple of drinks and walked happily back to the hotel. As far as McColl could tell, his earlier revelations had not made his two companions overly nervous. Should he be pleased that he hadn't spoiled their fun or alarmed that they hadn't taken the situation seriously enough?

Mac's insistence that they all check McColl's wardrobe eased his mind somewhat, and while the two of them were doing so, he pocketed the latest note the staff had slipped under his door.

Once the wardrobe had been declared safe and his companions had disappeared, he tore the envelope open and read the message. "Meagher arrives Grand Central at ten on Sunday morning," Kensley had scrawled. "See you at nine-thirty outside the barbershop."

They all spent Saturday morning in the showroom, either talking to prospective buyers or, in Jed's case, passing comment on each New York princess that walked past their window. After lunch McColl left the two of them to handle trial drives and walked back to the hotel, hoping to find a message from Caitlin. There was none. He reminded himself that she would be fully engaged catching up with family and friends, but he couldn't quite quiet the mean little voice in the back of his mind telling him it was over and that a cold but beautifully written note would soon arrive laying out all the reasons they couldn't go on.

There was nothing he could do about it, other than turn up unannounced at the family house in Brooklyn, loudly declare his undying love, and insist that she do the same. Something he had no intention of doing. Not yet, anyway.

He found a lunchroom serving meat loaf, mashed potatoes, and two veg for fifteen cents, then took a long walk, heading east into a world of dirty streets and yellow-brick tenement buildings whose only decoration was a latticework of fire escapes. As good as lost, he was accosted by an enterprising urchin who offered to sell him the way back to "safety." The neighborhood reminded McColl of Glasgow, and he half suspected he was safer here among the tenements than he ever would be on Fifth Avenue, but he handed over his dime in exchange for some very basic directions—"See that tall building? That's the Woolworth Building. It's the tallest building in the world. Just walk toward it and you'll end up on Broadway."

That evening he went out again with the others, and this time they drank rather more, so much so that they ended up chorusing Al Jolson's recent hit, "You Made Me Love You," with sufficient volume to warrant an in situ lecture from one of New York's finest.

McColl felt distinctly hungover next morning but managed to reach Grand Central Station on time. Kensley seemed in little better shape, and the two of them smoked their cigarettes in silence until a third man arrived. "Jack, Andrew," was the extent of Kensley's introduction. Andrew was probably around McColl's age, as thin as Kensley but with fairer hair and mustache.

At nine forty-five the three of them took up position within sight of the platform egress, and only seconds later the first passengers from the 20th Century Limited were streaming past. Three priests appeared before Father Meagher, who eventually emerged, resplendent in cassock and biretta, trailing a porter and a trolley piled with the familiar suitcases.

"That's him," McColl told the others.

They watched the priest lead his porter across the concourse and into the waiting room opposite, then followed as far as the entrance. Kensley turned to McColl. "He knows you, so keep your face turned away. Andrew, what's he doing?"

"He's telling the porter where he wants the suitcases. Now he's paying him. And now he's sitting down, with his back to the door."

McColl risked a look over his shoulder, just in time to see a man approach the priest.

"He's talking to someone," Andrew said. "An Indian, by the look of it. And the Indian's picking up one of the suitcases."

"The newspapers," McColl guessed.

"You'd better follow him," Kensley told Andrew.

The latter watched for a few seconds more, then walked swiftly after his quarry.

"Meagher's not moving," Kensley murmured.

"More business?" McColl wondered.

They didn't have long to wait. According to Kensley, the priest's second visitor was older, clean-shaven, wearing a slate gray suit and hat.

"They're talking," Kensley told McColl. "And Meagher's handing over an envelope. One of your letters. Okay," he said reluctantly, "since Meagher knows you by sight, you'd better take this guy. But for God's sake don't lose him."

"Can I turn around?" McColl asked.

"You don't need to. He's coming our way."

The man passed within a few feet of them, and McColl slipped into his wake. The courier—if that's what he was— still had the envelope in his hand, but he stowed it away in an inside pocket as he started down the ramp to the subway platforms. A train was thundering in, and McColl's sudden realization that he might not have the nickel required induced a few moments of panic, but a frantic scramble through his pockets proved successful, and he made it through the barrier in time to step aboard. The man in the gray suit was at the other end of the car, examining the subway map.

Which might be good news, McColl thought. It suggested a local knowledge no better than his own.

He hung on to the strap as the train stormed and clattered its way through the tunnel. Thirty-Third Street, Twenty-Eighth, Twenty-Third, Fourteenth, and soon they were into the names—Astor Place, then Bleecker. It was a fairly shoddy suit that the man was wearing, McColl thought; there were clear signs of wear at the cuffs and elbows. It was the sort of suit an aging errand boy might wear.

Like a lot of others, he got off at Fulton, and McColl followed him up and out. They emerged onto Broadway, two blocks down from the towering Woolworth Building. His quarry crossed at the light and walked in that direction, turning left down Barclay Street toward the Hudson. McColl kept some forty yards behind him but had the feeling he was being overly cautious. The man hadn't looked back since leaving Grand Central, another indication that he was just hired help.

Beyond West Street a long line of piers jutted out into the river. The one opposite Barclay was host to the Hoboken Ferry, and this, it transpired, was the man's objective. McColl followed him on board and took a seat a few rows behind him. The ferry was soon under way, and as it plowed a diagonal course across the mile-wide river, McColl stared back at

Manhattan and the low clouds brushing the peak of the Wool-worth Building.

All the big British shipping lines used Manhattan piers, but their German equivalents were here on the New Jersey shore. McColl and his unwitting guide had already walked past the North German Lloyd terminal when the man turned in through the gates of its Hamburg America rival. He ignored the passenger terminal building, headed around the side of the enormous quayside warehouse, and walked into what looked like an accompanying suite of offices. McColl hesitated and decided against following him inside. If the man didn't come out in a few minutes, then perhaps . . .

Five minutes later he did come out, counting out green dollar bills with his thumb. His fee, McColl assumed, but he supposed he ought to make sure—Hamburg America wouldn't be going anywhere.

It didn't take him long. Rather than return to the ferry, the man walked away from the river and into Hoboken. A bar, McColl guessed, and sure enough, after zigzagging through several blocks, the man pushed his way through the doors of the Lorelei Beerhouse. Considering the time of day, it could only just have opened, a deduction soon confirmed within by the absence of other patrons. His quarry gave McColl a quick glance and went back to admiring the golden schnapps flowing from bottle to glass.

McColl ordered a cup of the ready-brewed coffee and settled down to eavesdrop. "I did a job for Johann," the man was telling the barman. "He knows I'm reliable, and he gives me work when he can."

The barman managed an "uh-huh" or two, but only from politeness. McColl sat with the coffee for a few minutes, then walked back to the Hamburg America pier. It seemed obvious that the letter had changed hands in the warehouse offices. Did Herr Rieber work there? McColl could hardly just walk in and ask.

Then again—why not? The sign by the door said this was the freight-handling office, so why not invent some freight to handle? Automobiles, he told himself, stick to what you know. He worked for a small firm in the old country, which was interested in starting an export business. And since he was over here looking at premises, he thought he'd investigate rates and timings. He'd already been to North German Lloyd.

He explained all this to the woman at reception, who told him he needed to see Mr. Fromm.

Five minutes later he was offering the same spiel to a middle-aged, balding German-American. Tables for weight–cost ratios were produced and studied, along with the additional costs of rail transportation in Germany. The Hamburg America Line had already acquired considerable experience in the shipping of automobiles, and Mr. Fromm was ready to guarantee delivery in New Jersey within a fortnight of collection. At what he swore was a highly competitive price.

McColl agreed that it was. He would recommend Hamburg America to his partners, and Mr. Fromm would almost certainly be hearing from them shortly. In the meantime, "I believe my old friend Rieber works here. Can you point me in the direction of his office?"

Fromm looked surprised, but not suspicious. "Erich Rieber?"

"That's him."

"He's on the second floor. I'll get someone to show you the way."

"No, don't worry. I'll find him." He offered Fromm his hand. "Until next time."

He climbed the stairs and walked down the passage, checking names on doors. Rieber's was the fourth he came to. McColl stared at the sign for a few seconds, considering his next move. Was seeing Rieber's face worth letting the German see his own?

Deciding it was, he abruptly turned the knob and stepped across the threshold.

The man looking up from his desk was still in his twenties. He was clean-shaven, with a handsome, chiseled face and striking blue eyes. McColl was probably being fanciful, but his first impression was one of cruelty.

The single sheet of Reischach's letter lay on one side of the desk, as if saved for future rereading.

"Gee, I'm sorry, wrong room," McColl drawled, backing out into the corridor and clicking the door shut behind him. He wouldn't forget that face, he thought, as he walked down the stairs and out onto the quay. And he had the feeling that Rieber would remember his. But at least he could now point him out to the others, and if Kensley wanted to know where the German lived, one of them could follow him home.

It started to rain as he walked to the terminal, and it was falling in sheets by the time the ferry reached midstream, blurring both Manhattan and Jersey shorelines. Matters hadn't improved when they docked, so he lunched at a café in the Barclay Street terminal and sat watching a Cunard liner inch up the river until the sky began to brighten. As he headed for Broadway to catch a trolley home, the upper quarter of the Woolworth Building slowly dropped out of the clouds.

When he reached the Aberdeen, Kensley was sitting in the lobby, ostensibly reading the *New York Times*. McColl continued on up to his room, thinking to change his damp trousers before joining the Canadian in the coffee shop, and found that yet another note had been pushed under his door. It was from reception: A Miss Hanley had rung and would do so again at 5:00 P.M.

He felt his heart lift, and almost danced down the corridor to the elevator.

Kensley was in the same booth and might have been stirring the same cup of coffee. He sat with interlinked fingers in front of his mouth as McColl delivered his report, then offered a brief "Good work" when he was finished. "I'll get someone onto Rieber," he decided. "It's interesting that he has an office at Hamburg America. All the Germans we've dealt with until now have worked out of their embassy. The controllers, I mean. They use local German-Americans for the small jobs, like your man in the gray suit. Tell them it's their patriotic duty."

"Maybe the Germans are making more use of people like me," McColl guessed.

"Maybe. Or maybe someone's decided to set up a whole new organization outside official channels."

"How did you get on?" McColl asked.

"Oh, Meagher went straight to Devoy's house, where he doubtless delivered the letter. He only stayed a few minutes, though, and Devoy was in. Which suggests that the letter was more important than anything Father Meagher might have to say. I'd lay odds he's just a courier."

"So we're left with the arms shipment and the action on enemy soil."

"Yes. And I'm waiting to hear how Cumming wants to proceed." He looked up at McColl. "He might ask you to help out here for a few weeks. Could you do that?"

"Maybe. I'd like to know what he has in mind." A plan to foil Irish-German plots that didn't involve the destruction of his relationship with Caitlin would be a good start.

Kensley went off to meet Andrew and to find out where the copies of *Ghadar* had ended up. McColl asked reception where he could find a bookstore, walked to the one recommended, and purchased Conan Doyle's latest story, *The Poison Belt*. He started reading in the hotel lounge and by ten to five was wondering how the creator of Sherlock Holmes could have sunk so low.

He took her call in a booth behind the lobby. "How are you?" she asked. "How's the hotel?"

"Fine. And your family?"

"Oh, they're all fine."

"Did they like their presents?"

"I think so. Colm liked his map, and Orla hasn't taken the shawl off since I gave it to her, but, Jack, I can't *really* talk for long, and I can't talk, if you know what I mean."

He pictured her in the hall of the family home, surrounded by open doors. "I understand. When can we meet?"

"Not tomorrow, I'm afraid. I have so many people to see and an interview out in Queens. But Tuesday—are you free for dinner? I could meet you downtown."

"Why don't you come to the hotel?"

"For hors d'oeuvres?"

"Something like that."

"I'll be there at six."

"I can't wait."

"Neither can I."

The next forty-eight hours were uneventful. He took one man for a trial drive and wished he hadn't—the potential customer could hardly drive, and McColl had to commandeer the steering wheel on several occasions to avert collisions with pedestrians and other vehicles. When the man announced that he was ordering a Maia, McColl felt like posting a city-wide warning.

He heard nothing from Kensley and suffered no apparent attention from Rieber or his friends. Perhaps Cumming's entreaty to play the game had struck a chord with his Prussian counterparts. Or perhaps McColl was low on their list of priorities.

It was a minute past six when Caitlin rapped on his door. "This is a refreshingly progressive hotel," she said, taking off her coat. "They had no objection to my coming straight up, especially when I let slip that I was a journalist."

"The power of the press."

"Indeed. And speaking of that, I have something to show you." She started to unbutton her blouse. "Remember I told you I had someone to interview this afternoon. Her name's Mary Phelps Jacob. She's younger than I am, and look what she's invented."

Caitlin's breasts were covered by the lightest of garments, with no sign of metal stays or stiff lacing.

"Mary calls it a brassiere. It's basically two silk handkerchiefs and a few lengths of ribbon. And you wouldn't believe how much nicer it is to wear. I feel like I've been set free. And so will millions of other women."

"That's wonderful," McColl said.

"And it's so much easier to take off," she added, releasing a knot in the ribbon and snuggling into his arms.

Their lovemaking showed no sign of growing stale; their physical passion for each other seemed, if anything, even more intense than before. Afterward they lay entwined in joyous exhaustion until his rumbling stomach forced them to contemplate dinner. As they went past the reception desk, McColl made sure to mention how much he'd enjoyed the interview.

They walked to an Italian restaurant she liked, ordered olives, bread, and wine, and caught up on each other's last few days. Hers had been full, and she'd loved every minute. Her various employers had nothing but praise for her pieces on China and seemed to be falling over themselves to commission more. The brassiere girl had been a delight, and Caitlin had just discovered that during her absence a woman had been appointed commissioner of the New York City Department of Correction. "The first woman to *ever* head a municipal agency," Caitlin insisted. "That's another wall down."

Her eyes positively shone, and McColl found himself thinking how lucky he was to have met her.

"You know, sometimes I despair for my country," she said. "When I see children virtually starving not five miles from Fifth

Avenue. And when I see how desperate people are to turn a blind eye. Ch'ing-ling and I once hired a man in Macon to drive us out into the countryside. We both cried for days over what we had seen, and the other girls just laughed at us." She shook her head. "But sometimes, like this week, I feel almost drunk on the possibilities. And I have to keep reminding myself that most people think I'm crazy. Even those who love me."

He asked how her family was treating her.

"Like a homecoming queen. But what have you been doing?"

"Not much, compared to you. Jed and Mac had arranged everything by the time I got here, and they seem so proud of how professional they've both become that I've more or less left them to it. I've been doing a lot of walking—I even got lost the other day."

"In Manhattan?"

"Well, I expect I'd have found my way home, but a six-year-old sold me directions for a dime."

She laughed. "Have you taken the Staten Island Ferry? That only costs a nickel, and it's a lovely ride. When I go away, it's usually the first thing I do when I come back. Like I'm saying hello to the city."

"I'll do it tomorrow."

"Oh, and Central Park. You have to walk from one end to the other—it's close to three miles. But pick a nice day."

"Maybe we could do that together."

"I'd love to, when I have some time to spare. Now I have something to ask you. My aunt invites you to lunch next Sunday—will you come?"

"Oh. Of course. I'd love to," he added, though his emotions were actually mixed. He welcomed what the invitation implied about her feelings, but couldn't help worrying over how Cumming and Kensley might seek to exploit it.

"Didn't you think you'd be meeting my family?" she asked.

"I wasn't sure how you'd feel about that."

She took his hand. "Much as I like being ravished in luxury hotel rooms and train compartments, I think it's time we brought our romance into the open."

"You're not going to announce that we've been enjoying intimate relations since Shanghai?" he asked, more than slightly alarmed.

She laughed. "At the dinner table, you mean? No, I don't think so. But I'd like you to meet my family, and I'd like them to know that you and I are . . . are fond of each other."

"Have you told them anything about me? About us?"

"Just my Aunt Orla. What you do, where you come from, how we met. That we like each other."

"Will they all be there? At dinner, I mean."

"Maybe not Fergus, but everyone else. And there's a young man from Ireland who's staying with us for a few weeks."

"Will I have need of the Scottish accent?"

"Just a touch, perhaps."

McColl had cause to visit Central Park earlier than he expected. The note on his carpet the following morning was brief and to the point: "59th and Fifth at 10:00 A.M., NK." He saw the others off to the showroom, lingered over a second coffee in the hotel restaurant, and took the elevated on Sixth up to the Fifty-Eighth Street terminus. It was a fine spring day; above the soaring buildings the sun was playing hide-and-seek in a forest of white clouds.

Kensley was waiting on the specified corner, wearing the usual clothes and smoking the usual cigarette.

"Why the change of venue?" McColl asked as they dodged across the busy street toward the park entrance.

"It always pays to keep them guessing," Kensley said. "And my girlfriend tells me I need the exercise."

They walked down a wide pathway, a small expanse of water

off to their left. McColl had recently read a newspaper article lamenting the state of the park, but it didn't look too neglected.

Kensley stopped to light a new cigarette from the butt of the old. "Cumming has a proposition for you," he announced.

"Yes?"

"A full-time job with the Service."

"I see." It was what he had wanted, but what would Cumming want in return? "And how would that work?" he asked warily.

"What do you mean?"

He wasn't going to do Kensley's work for him. "Well, I'd need a new cover story for a start."

The Canadian grunted. "Well, you wouldn't be much use with an automobile permanently in tow. So yes, you would. But I've no idea what Cumming has in mind—something diplomatic perhaps."

"Not a permanent posting somewhere?"

"I doubt that very much. He tells me you speak nine languages, and I expect he intends to make use of them all."

They were on a bridge across a transverse road, and Kensley stopped to watch a bright red Ford pass underneath. "I had a look at your Maia the other day. How much would that cost me?"

"Almost three thousand dollars."

"Pity I don't have a grandmother to sell," was the Canadian's reply. He tossed the cigarette over the parapet and set off again. "Your first job would be here," he went on, almost too casually. "And you're not a fool—I'm sure you can guess what Cumming wants from you."

"Why don't you spell it out?"

"Okay. He wants you to use your relationship with Caitlin Hanley to infiltrate republican circles here in New York. To find out how and when they plan to ship the arms and what de Lacey's 'joint operation' is, assuming it even exists."

They walked awhile in silence, McColl wondering if Kensley

had checked that he and Caitlin were still seeing each other or had simply taken it for granted. The former, most likely.

"We're assuming she doesn't know that you've been working for the Service?"

"No, of course not." Though he'd been tempted to tell her more than once.

"Well, in that case . . ."

It was McColl's turn to stop. "So since I'm already lying to her, I might as well betray her completely?"

Kensley ignored the anger. "There's no suggestion that she has any part in any of this. Or her father, come to that. From what we can gather, his activist days are over."

"And her brother Colm?"

"Not even him," Kensley insisted, setting them in motion once more. "You wouldn't be targeting the Hanleys, just making use of their contacts."

They were passing a statue of Columbus, which seemed strangely appropriate—the Italian explorer had never had more than the foggiest idea of where he was actually going. McColl knew he shouldn't blame Cumming, who could hardly ignore such an obvious opportunity.

"And Cumming asked me to tell you this," Kensley went on. "That your country is facing its greatest challenge for a century and that this business you've uncovered could make a huge difference to whether or not it survives."

"The stakes are high, then," McColl murmured sardonically. He sighed. "I find it hard to believe that a few Irish exiles in New York City could do any serious damage to the British Empire."

"The world's a much smaller place than it used to be," Kensley retorted. "And trouble tends to spread more quickly."

"Maybe," McColl conceded. Rather than swap more bland assertions, he changed the subject. "Where I come from, a job offer usually comes with a figure attached."

"I suspect you can more or less name your own."

"Which means Cumming hasn't?"

"No, but I do know that the Admiralty has increased his budget. Their lordships are worried, too."

McColl put up a hand. "Look, I'll have to think about it. I'd love a full-time position, but this particular business . . . I don't know." How could he justify spying on her?

"This business doesn't exactly suit serious relationships."

McColl looked at him. "That sounded heartfelt."

"When I moved to New York, my wife stayed in Toronto. The job had already done us in."

"Ah."

"Have you met her family yet?"

"No." He almost told Kensley he was meeting them on Sunday, but something held him back.

"Okay. You think it over. In the meantime we'll be tackling the German end. We've confirmed that Rieber works for Hamburg America, but what position he holds is far from clear. It's probably a shell job. He doesn't seem connected to their embassy in any way, and Cumming thinks it's possible that the Germans have set up a Secret Service like ours, one even more independent of the military than we are. Rieber lives in a very nice apartment uptown on the West Side, so someone's plying him with funds. He might lead us straight to his Irish contacts here, but they're probably using a cutout, and it might be easier to make the connection from the Irish side."

And perhaps through the Hanleys, McColl thought. "And the GF in the letter," Kensley was saying. "There's a Geli Furtwangler who works in the San Francisco consulate, but she's only nineteen and seems an unlikely prospect. Of course GF could be Irish . . ."

"If I run into a Gerry Flynn, I'll let you know."

After leaving Kensley at the park entrance, McColl took the subway south to the end of the line and sought out the ferry to Staten Island. He needed a place to sort through his options, and the rail of a ship crisscrossing New York Harbor seemed as good as any.

The day was getting even nicer, and as the ferry struck out for the distant shoreline, he spent a few minutes just enjoying the view. A sudden awareness of movement to his rear had him twisting around, but it was only a boy in pursuit of a rubber ball. The mother gave McColl a *What's the matter with you?* look and walked on toward the stern.

Was he getting careless? He found it hard to imagine the Germans sanctioning his murder in such a public place, particularly one that offered the killer no hope of escape.

He could see the Statue of Liberty now and away to the right the huge immigration building on Ellis Island, which looked from a distance like a cross between the Tower of London and a railway terminus. The Ellis Island wharves were lined with small boats, which had presumably ferried would-be immigrants from their transatlantic ships. Most would be welcomed, but some, after all that hope and effort, would be sent back to Europe. Compared to theirs, his problems were small.

But real enough. Why did he want to work for the Service? Because until Caitlin had appeared, working for Cumming had been the one thing in his life that had allowed him to feel good about himself. Speaking a multitude of tongues had always made him feel a bit of a freak, more like a performing animal than the master of a real craft, and learning that he had a talent for something else had pleased him immensely. It was dangerous work, but he rather enjoyed danger, as long as he had some measure of control over the situation. It wasn't like being in the army, where you could end up buried in a trench on the say-so of some moronic general you had never met. And if worse came to worst, a full-time post in the Service would presumably exempt him from ever being at that sort of idiot's mercy again.

If Caitlin had never appeared, he would have jumped at the offer.

But she had, and as he was willing to admit to himself, he had come to love her. Had, in fact, loved her almost from the day they met. So how could he justify spying on her family and deceiving her in order to do so? Loving someone should involve some sort of honesty.

This felt like the moment he had to choose, but was it that simple? Given a choice between life with her and life with Cumming, he wouldn't have needed to think about it. But if a few more hours of hotel passion and a sad good-bye were all that she was offering, then the scales began to tip. Whatever they'd had certainly bowled him over, but that didn't mean it was built to last. Once they brought everything out in the open, would it all just crumble away? People said that sexual passion always cooled eventually, and how did he know the two of them had anything more? If it turned out they didn't, he would have given up the life he wanted for a few weeks of romanticized lust.

What would happen if he refused Cumming's request? Someone else would be found to investigate the Hanleys, someone much less sympathetic. And if her father or her brother ended up in prison, his own role in the chain of events would probably be revealed and his refusal would count for nothing.

What if he said yes? He had bristled at Kensley's unspoken suggestion that a betrayal had already occurred, but only because it contained more than a few grains of truth. He had certainly deceived her, and although he didn't believe he had betrayed her in any real sense, he knew that she would think he had. In this regard he had nothing left to lose.

If Kensley was right, and not just sugarcoating the pill when he said that the Hanleys were not really implicated, then perhaps there was a way. If they were only stepping-stones, could he not step lightly across and leave them none the wiser? If it turned out that they were implicated, then the question would be—in what? If father and sons were up to their necks in plots against the empire, then he would just have to play God and decide for himself how big a threat they posed. A German alliance, a bombing campaign in London, a plot to kill the King—any of those and he would have to give them up and no doubt lose her in the process. But despite de Lacey's letter, he found anything that ambitious hard to imagine. Irish-Americans had been making anti-English noises for decades, but what had they actually done? They were still celebrating the Fenian triumph of 1867, which as far as McColl could make out had been a catastrophic failure.

And if all that the Hanleys were involved in was running a few guns to Ireland, then good luck to them. Everyone on God's earth seemed hell-bent on arming themselves, so why not the Irish Catholics? He would simply tell Kensley and Cumming that he hadn't found anything out.

Whatever dark secrets the Hanleys had, he would be the one to uncover them and the one who decided which to pass on. He would not betray her if he could possibly avoid it, and maybe, at some point in the future, the moment would come when he could tell her the truth and perhaps even earn her forgiveness. It didn't sound the likeliest outcome, but stranger things had happened, and what other hope did he have?

As the ferry steamed back toward Manhattan, his relief at reaching some sort of decision was tempered by a sudden flash of memory—his mother in the kitchen at Fort William, talking to his grandmother about his father and saying, with a striking blend of bitterness and awe, "That man could forgive himself for anything."

He spent most of the next three days with Jed and Mac, working by day and making the most of New York's entertainment industries by night. A couple of hours on the Friday afternoon were all he spent with Caitlin, and there was no fresh word from Kensley or Cumming. They had probably decided that further persuasion would be counterproductive, and McColl, for his part, was in no hurry to announce acceptance of the proffered job.

At noon on Sunday, he found himself standing across the street from the Hanley family's four-story Brooklyn brownstone. A twitch of the front parlor's curtains told him he had been spotted, and he started across the street. He hardly had time to let go of the iron knocker when the door swung open to reveal a thin young girl wearing a maid's cap and a plain working shift. Behind her in the hall, a small, elderly woman was waiting to greet him, Caitlin at her shoulder.

"I'm Orla McDonnell," the woman said, offering a hand. She seemed older than McColl had imagined, well into her sixties. Stern features were softened by warm brown eyes, and her long gray hair was coiled in a loose bun. Her short, slim figure was encased in a wine red dress of heavy fabric with a high, military-style collar.

"Jack McColl," he replied, presenting the bouquet of daffodils he had bought on Prospect Avenue.

"They're lovely," she said, with more than a trace of Irish accent. "Thank you kindly. Mary, find a vase and put these in water. Mr. McColl, please come through."

"Jack, please." He followed her into the front parlor, giving Caitlin's hand a brief squeeze as he went past her.

The man within was probably seventy. He put aside his newspaper, rose from his chair with less than perfect ease, and advanced to shake McColl's hand. "This is Caitlin's father," Orla announced, "my brother, Ronan."

Ronan Hanley was several inches taller than his sister and stocky without being fat. His gray hair was slicked back from his forehead above—and there was no other word for it—twinkling green eyes. After everything Caitlin had told him about her father—and much that she hadn't—McColl had been expecting a man to dislike, but his first impression was quite the opposite. He reminded himself how amazed acquaintances of his own family had been whenever they heard him criticize *his* father.

There were two others in the room. Caitlin's sister, Finola, had neatly curled light brown hair and big green eyes; she was the prettier of the two, but not, in McColl's estimation, the more beautiful. Her husband, Patrick, was dark and almost insultingly handsome, but he seemed friendly enough.

They all sat down. Caitlin's father asked McColl a couple of questions about automobiles and their possible future and then seemed content to let his sister dictate the conversation. She was more interested in McColl's gift for languages and ticked all nine off with her fingers. "What do you do—learn a new one each year?"

"Nothing so deliberate. I've traveled a lot, and I just seem to pick them up." On the wall behind Orla, there was a painting of a woman who looked remarkably like Caitlin and was presumably her mother.

"I understand that your elder son is a lawyer," McColl said to Caitlin's father after Orla and Caitlin had excused themselves to check on lunch.

"Yes, he's at his wife's parents' today. I have two children with sense, Mr. McColl—Fergus and Finola here. And then there's Caitlin and Colm—I expect the boy'll be down when the mood takes him. Orla tells me I shouldn't complain—that once upon a time I was a bit of a rebel myself—but these days the young don't seem to know when to stop." He looked at McColl. "But then I suppose you're of a mind with Caitlin and her radical friends or you wouldn't be taking up with her."

"I agree with a lot of her ideas," McColl said cautiously. "Though I sometimes think she expects too much too quickly."

The sound of feet racing downstairs had them turning toward the doorway. Two young men came in, followed by Caitlin, who introduced them. "This is my younger brother,

Colm," she said, introducing the taller of the two. He was almost lanky and seemed slightly uncoordinated, as if he hadn't quite learned how to work his limbs. He had a shock of floppy brown hair, the same green eyes as his sisters, and the sort of face that better suited smiling than the frown it was wearing now.

"And this is Seán Tiernan," Caitlin said. "He's visiting from the old country."

Tiernan was equally thin, with a pale, sharp-featured face. His black hair was brushed straight back from a high forehead and worn slightly long at the nape and sides. The brown eyes were slightly hooded and brimming with intelligence.

Both men shook hands with McColl, but not with any friendliness. There was something close to resentment in Colm's eyes and a colder watchfulness in Tiernan's. The Irishman was probably in his late twenties, wearing a suit a couple of sizes too large for him. They would all have gone to Mass that morning, McColl guessed, and Tiernan would have borrowed the suit from Colm.

"Lunch is served," Orla announced from the doorway.

The dining room was at the back of the house, its table set for eight. There was a tree visible through the window and two landscapes on one wall. McColl recognized the Cliffs of Moher, but not the town nestling by the sea. "It's Lahinch," Caitlin said, following his eyes. "My father's family came here from Clare."

She put him between herself and Patrick, sitting opposite Finola, Colm, and Tiernan. A plate of carved roast chicken and several vegetable dishes were passed around, and, rather to McColl's surprise, Caitlin's father produced a bottle of Bordeaux for the men to share. The women were offered only lemonade.

They ate in silence, resuming conversation between courses. "Where is your home, Jack?" Orla asked him as the first plates were taken away.

"I rent a flat—an apartment—in London at the moment, but I'm hardly ever there. My mother and father live in Glasgow now, but we came from the West Highlands originally. A place called Fort William." There were more questions about his family, which he answered as briefly as politeness allowed. From what Caitlin had told him, Ronan Hanley had little sympathy for his own father's socialist views.

The talk turned to China and the warm reception accorded Caitlin's newspaper pieces. Orla was clearly immensely proud of her niece and annoyed that the male members of the family hadn't even read most of her articles. "She'll be a famous journalist, you mind my words. Just so long as she follows her star."

She was looking at Caitlin as she spoke, but McColl had the distinct feeling that the words were also aimed at him.

"And when are you returning to England?" Orla asked, as if to confirm his suspicions.

"I'm not sure," he told her.

"But you are going back?"

"Eventually. And when are you returning to Ireland?" he asked Tiernan, intent on changing the subject.

"In a few weeks. I'm not certain."

"And where in Ireland are you from?"

"I'm from Cork, but I live in Dublin now."

"Oh, what part?"

"Do you know Dublin?"

"Not that well," McColl acknowledged.

Tiernan allowed himself a smile. "Well, fitting as it sounds, I live on Cork Street." He allowed himself a slight smile. "The district has the name of Dolphin's Barn, and it's not so bad."

"Colm fell in love with Dublin when he came to stay with you," Caitlin said, smiling at her brother.

"As much as you can love an occupied city," Colm said without smiling back.

He was a deeply angry young man, McColl thought. And anger allied to a righteous cause, as someone had said, made for a dangerous combination.

The Irish issue had been broached, and once the women had left the table, Ronan Hanley took it up in earnest. "So, Jack, how are you seeing the future of Ireland?"

McColl felt four pairs of eyes swinging his way. "The next step is Home Rule," he replied. "After that . . ." He shrugged.

"They've promised Home Rule before," Ronan said. "So what makes you think they mean it this time?"

"It's as good as done. I can't see anything stopping it."

"A European war," Tiernan suggested in his soft and almost menacing brogue.

"That might delay things, but . . ."

"Ah, we've waited long enough," Ronan said, almost wistfully.

"And what about Ulster?" Colm asked with more than a trace of belligerence.

"That may take a bit longer," McColl conceded. "The last I heard, there were plans to let the Ulstermen opt out for five or six years, until they got used to the idea."

Tiernan was having none of that. "They never will get used to it, and they're bringing in guns. And if your government in London orders your army to coerce them, then our information is that the army will refuse."

"A mutiny?"

"It won't be called that. I doubt it'll see the light of day. The politicians will just bring their promises back into line with what they can deliver, which won't include Home Rule for the whole island."

"And that's the least we could accept," Ronan added with a sigh. "And that only as a stepping-stone to full independence." He seemed almost resigned to missing his dream's fulfillment.

"Then maybe I'm being overoptimistic," McColl said. He was wondering who Tiernan's "our" was, but risking a direct question felt unwise. "How did people here feel about the Dublin lockout?" he asked Caitlin's father, hoping that the question would draw out the others.

Ronan grunted. "A sideshow. Ireland needs rid of the English, not a socialist revolution."

"Ireland needs rid of English capitalism," Colm disagreed, looking to Tiernan for support, "or nothing will really change."

Ronan shook his head. "Now, don't give me any of that IWW drivel, not in my own house."

Tiernan looked down at the table, a slight smirk on his lips, but said nothing. Colm opened his mouth but closed it again when Caitlin reappeared.

"Before you get trapped in a century-long discussion about Ireland's future," she told McColl, "I'm taking you to see Coney Island."

He got to his feet, pleased at the chance for time alone with her, a tad frustrated that the conversation had been cut short. He thanked her father for his hospitality, shook hands with the other men, and went to say good-bye to Orla and Finola. Caitlin's aunt seemed genuinely pleased to have met him, but perhaps she'd been reassured by confirmation of his eventual departure.

He and Caitlin walked down to West Street and joined those waiting for a Culver Line streetcar. "So what did you think of my family?" she asked, the look in her eyes belying the lightness of tone.

"I liked them," he said simply. Which was mostly true. They had certainly seemed a far cry from Reginald Fairholme's "family to give London nightmares." "Your aunt's lovely, and your father was less frightening than I expected."

"He was on his best behavior."

"Patrick doesn't say much, but he and Finola seem nice enough."

"They are. And Colm?"

"He's incredibly angry."

"About the state of the world? He has cause."

"I'm sure he does." McColl paused, choosing his words with care. "But that's not where the anger comes from. Or not all of it."

He half expected her to bite his head off, but she didn't. "I don't like Seán Tiernan," she said, as if he were the cause of her brother's ire. "He's been the perfect guest, and I've nothing against the IWW—quite the contrary—but there's something about him."

"I know what you mean."

"Do you? I'm glad. And here comes our streetcar."

The journey took about twenty minutes, and continuing their conversation proved impossible amid the hubbub of excited children. It felt as if half the residents of Brooklyn were heading for the beach, and some for the first time. "But what does the ocean *look* like?" one small child kept asking her mother.

Some of the families looked desperately poor to McColl, the children sallow and very thin, wearing clothes and shoes that bore signs of repeated repair, their parents tired-eyed and looking older than their children suggested they should be.

When the car reached Coney Island, the beach was less crowded than McColl expected and only a few brave souls had taken to the water. Caitlin led him eastward along the line of sideshows and rides, many still closed for the winter. The spider boy and the four-legged girl were pulling them in at Dreamland Circus, but Caitlin had something else in mind.

"We've only just had lunch," McColl protested, staring up at the Giant Racer roller coaster.

"That was hours ago," Caitlin insisted, pulling him toward the ticket line.

Ten minutes later they were sharing the front seat of a car slowly ratchetting its way up an extremely steep pair of rails. As they neared the summit, McColl heard the Italian-American

girl behind him lauding the view of the Long Island coastline, then her partner's sardonic response. "I wouldn't get too
attached to the view, sweetheart," he drawled, concluding this
warning, with wonderful comic timing, at the moment the
world dropped away beneath them.

Several long minutes and heart-stopping plummets later,
their car grated to a blissfully permanent halt on planet
Earth. McColl climbed gingerly out and wondered if kissing
the ground was in order. Caitlin took one look at him and
laughed. "Wasn't that wonderful!" she exclaimed.

"Let's walk along the beach," McColl suggested before she
demanded a second ride.

"All right," she agreed, her eyes still full of laughter.

They wove their way through sand-castle builders and soft-
ball games to where the Atlantic waves were gently rippling
ashore. The sea was warm to the touch and, considering its
urban neighbor, looked surprisingly clean. They walked hand
in hand along the water's edge, in silence for quite a while,
until Caitlin announced, out of the blue, that Tiernan was in
New York to find recruits.

"Recruits for what?" McColl asked, almost in spite of himself. She was doing Cumming's work for him, and if she ever
found out, he doubted she would forgive him for her own
naïveté.

"I don't know," she replied. "I just overheard him and Colm
talking. The Republican movement, I suppose. Or some part
of it."

"Has he recruited Colm?"

"I hope not, but I wouldn't be at all surprised."

"What does Colm do?" he asked her. "Does he have a job?"

"Oh, yes. When he decided he didn't want to go to college, Father told him that was fine but he shouldn't expect to
sponge off the family. And he hasn't. He's working in a bar at
the moment, but he's had lots of different jobs."

"He and your father don't seem to get on."

"No. They used to, when Colm was still a child. But these days . . ." She sighed. "It seems worse than it was before I went to China. I think Colm will move out soon and find a room somewhere. It'll be better for both of them." She looked at McColl. "He's not a bad boy. Really."

A sister's intuition, he wondered, or wishful thinking? "He's young," was all he said. In the distance a large liner was heading out into the Atlantic, gray smoke pumping from all three funnels.

"When Aunt Orla asked when you were leaving—" she began.

"After warning me not to derail your career," he wryly interjected.

"Oh, you noticed that . . ."

"It was hard to miss. Not that I blame her."

"She wants what's best for me. But was it true? Do you still not know when you're going?"

"Yes, it was. And no, I don't. Jed and Mac are sailing on Tuesday, but I've still got some business to wrap up." Being with her, he thought, and spying on her family.

"So not long, then?"

"A couple of weeks, I expect. Are you keen to see the back of me?"

"No," she said, taking the question more seriously than he'd intended. "But I have so much work this coming week, and I'm off to Paterson on Saturday morning."

"Why? And where exactly is it, come to that?"

"It's in New Jersey, about an hour's ride on the train. I told you about the strike there last year—most of the silk workers were out for more than six months. I interviewed a lot of the wives in the first few weeks, and the paper I was working for then wants me to go back and do a catch-up piece. There's a rally planned for next Sunday, so it seemed a good time to go."

"Could I come with you?"

She looked surprised, then grinned. "Why not? You should find it interesting. But I've arranged to stay with one of the strikers' families on Thursday night, so you'll be alone in your hotel."

"And Friday night?"

"I think that might be possible. Ah. But I should tell you— Colm and Tiernan are both coming along."

"Why?"

"It's an IWW event. The IWW more or less ran the strike last year."

"Well, I'm happy to spend a couple of days with the two of them. Unless your brother has a violent objection to my sleeping with his sister."

"I suppose he might. But if he does, he'll have me to deal with."

That night McColl telephoned the number Kensley had given him and left a message requesting a meeting the following morning. On his way back from Brooklyn, he had decided that the Hanleys had little to fear from his professional attentions and that he could take Cumming's job with a reasonably clear conscience. Ronan Hanley was obviously past it, and Caitlin, while quite possibly a threat to patriarchy, was only a passive foe of the British Empire. Colm and his friend Seán Tiernan were actively involved in something with an Irish dimension, but whatever it was seemed much more likely to involve international socialism than German intelligence.

He told Kensley as much when they met next day. "No one mentioned the Germans or the fact that a European war might provide the Irish republicans with an opportunity. All the Hanleys want an Irish republic that includes Ulster, but Colm and his friend Seán Tiernan want a socialist revolution as well, and I can't see them regarding the Kaiser as a suitable ally."

"People take guns wherever they can get them," Kensley observed. He had suggested the two of them talk as they walked, and they were now zigzagging their way uptown. "I take it you're accepting Cumming's offer of permanent employment?"

"I suppose I am."

"Without knowing the salary?" Kensley asked, sounding amused.

"I can always demand a raise when I get back to London." Riches were all very well, but lately an interesting life seemed more important.

"Fair enough," Kensley said. "So where were we?"

"People needing guns not caring where they come from," McColl reminded him.

"Oh, yes. Well, if the Germans offer Seán Tiernan and Colm Hanley guns to fight Ulster," Kensley continued, "I can't see them refusing."

"Mmm, maybe."

"We do know that some of these Irish bastards are in bed with the Germans."

"If de Lacey's rumor wasn't just that. I take it you've had no luck with Rieber."

"Not yet," Kensley admitted, "and it is possible that de Lacey was imagining things. But I still don't think so." He paused as they crossed a road. "Seán Tiernan is a new name to me," he said when they reached the other side. "I'll ask Cumming to check him out with Kell—that's his opposite number in the Security Service. If Kell's people don't know the man, then they'll go looking. Ireland's their responsibility."

"He normally lives in Dublin, on Cork Street," McColl offered.

"Good. Do you know when he's going back?"

"He said a few weeks when I asked him, but I wouldn't

count on it. He'll be in Paterson this weekend, him and Colm
Hanley. There's an IWW rally, something to do with last year's
strike. Caitlin will be there, too, interviewing wives."

"And you?"

"Yes, I'm going. What can you tell me about the IWW? It's
just another union, isn't it?"

Kensley shook his head. "It's more than that. Their idea
is a giant union that includes all the workers and is powerful
enough to see off any employer. With no one allowed to make
profits, we'll all live happily ever after."

"You're not a believer, then." They were walking past the
entrance to a luxury apartment building, where a black man
in a brass-buttoned suit was helping a resident with her latest
shopping.

"They have some decent people—Eugene Debs is a man
who's hard to dislike—and they've won a few battles, but
there's no way they're going to overthrow the whole goddamn
system, and I think they're beginning to realize it. So these
days they seem to spend most of their time arguing among
themselves about what to do next. Debs and his friends think
politics is part of the answer, but men like 'Big Bill' Haywood
are still clinging to the original big-union idea. And as in any
losing game, you'll always find a few bright sparks who are
willing to up the stakes, especially when it's other people's
lives they're gambling with."

"Tiernan strikes me as that kind of man."

"Handle him with care, then. And watch out for yourself in
Paterson—trouble's more likely than not, and they don't mess
about in this country. Neither the owners nor the unions.
They'll both be out for blood."

"An area like this," McColl said, casting his eyes over one
colonnaded, graystone mansion, "and you can see why. If you
have a house like that, you're not going to give it up. And if
you don't have one, you hate the man who does."

＋   ＋   ＋

On Tuesday afternoon McColl accompanied Jed and Mac to Pier 59, where the White Star Line's *Olympic* was loading for departure. The ship looked much like her sister *Titanic*, but none of the boarding passengers seemed overly concerned that history might repeat itself. As Mac wryly noted, icebergs never struck twice in the same place.

Earlier that day they had all said good-bye to the bottle green Maia, which a Yale professor had driven away after drawing the lucky short straw. The other New York buyers would have a few months' wait while theirs were built and shipped.

"So what shall I tell Ma?" Jed asked his brother once Mac had ascended the gangplank. "About when you're coming home."

"Nothing," McColl told him. "I'll write to her tonight and tell her you're on your way. And that I'll be home soon."

"You will?"

"I will. I can't stay here forever, can I?"

"I suppose not. But for God's sake be careful while you are. After everything that's happened, it isn't that easy just leaving you here on your own."

"What, alone in the big city?"

"You know what I'm talking about."

"Of course I do. But I'm pretty sure that danger's passed." And he was. Keeping an eye out for trouble had become almost second nature, but since their arrival in New York he'd noticed nothing untoward and had never had the feeling of being watched or followed.

"I hope you're right," Jed was saying.

"So do I, but let's talk about something else. Are you heading straight back to Glasgow?"

"I have to. They're expecting me at the Prudential a week tomorrow. April Fools' Day," he added bitterly. "It's going to be so *boring* after all of this. I'm almost hoping for a war to liven things up."

"Don't say that," McColl said. "Not even in jest."

"Who was joking?"

McColl couldn't help laughing. A few minutes later, he watched his brother board, exchanged final waves, and walked off down the quay toward the city. The ship wouldn't leave for an hour or so, but it felt like they were already gone, and despite his earlier teasing of Jed he did feel alone without them. They had spent the best part of six months together, and he had grown accustomed to their silly jokes and ridiculous bravado.

Jed's comment that a war might save him from boredom came back to McColl. His younger brother was a fool in so many ways, but he loved him dearly. Caitlin's Colm was also a fool, and in ways that might prove much more damaging, but she would love her brother every bit as much.

Mill-Town Alley

♠

He had some business loose ends to tie up, but by Wednesday evening McColl was wholly a man of leisure, with no one else for company. Over the next couple of days, he did a lot of walking and made the most of the city's attractions, gazing out from skyscraper observation platforms, sitting in smoke-filled moving-picture houses, puzzling over the latest European paintings in the Metropolitan Museum of Art.

He was still staying at the expensive Aberdeen, having convinced Kensley that leaving his luxury hotel for a fleabag would dent his credentials as a successful businessman and thereby cast doubt on the story he had told the Hanleys, that business was the reason for prolonging his stay. According to Kensley's probably fanciful account, Cumming had huffed and puffed at first but then agreed to transfer the funds McColl needed to support this Reillyesque life.

Paterson, he knew, would be another world. On Saturday morning he took the Christopher Street Ferry across the Hudson and met Caitlin, Colm, and Seán Tiernan at the Hoboken terminal of the Delaware, Lackawanna and Western Railroad. She had already bought his ticket, and he was pleasantly surprised by the lack of overt hostility from her two young companions. Tiernan in particular seemed in a jovial mood, as if they were heading out on a picnic rather than visiting an industrial battlefield. Neither he nor Colm questioned McColl's presence on the jaunt, and Colm actually asked him about his time in South Africa. Caitlin had obviously begged him to be civil.

"So pretend I'm one of your less knowledgeable readers," McColl told her as the first factories and chimneys of the New Jersey shore flitted past their carriage window, "and explain what's been happening since last year's strike."

She did her best, but it was a complicated story. The 1913 strike had been defeated, but not as comprehensively as some had claimed. In the immediate aftermath, some owners had conceded a nine-hour day while others had increased the wages they paid. Some were now using the economic downturn to renege on these deals, and Sunday's rally was intended, among other things, to demonstrate the widespread opposition to such backsliding. But as always seemed to be the case, defeat had sown divisions among the various groups of workers and their political champions. The ribbon weavers had different priorities from the broad silk weavers, and the latter saw things differently from the dyers' helpers. The socialists and the IWW had blamed each other for the strike's failure, and now the former were concentrating on securing deals on a plant-by-plant basis, while the IWW remained committed to an all-or-nothing approach.

"Which is why this rally's important," Caitlin concluded. "All the silk workers have to agree on a few basic demands—like the nine-hour day—and then hold together until they're met."

"How many hours are they working now?" McColl asked.

"Ten hours five days a week and four on Saturday morning."

"For the princely sum of six dollars," Colm added. "But you're still fighting last year's strike, sis. A few basic demands, holding together—they did all that for six months, and they lost. Something has to change. We have to scare the bastards."

"How?" Caitlin asked. "The last time I heard, the IWW was still opposed to violence."

"It still is," Tiernan agreed, without turning his face from the window. "But the owners aren't, and when their tame sheriffs and hired hands use violence against us, then we have the right to defend ourselves in any way we can."

"With guns?" Caitlin asked.

"We must fight like with like," Tiernan said, finally turning to face her. "If they use sticks, then so do we. And if they use guns . . ." He shrugged.

"And this is IWW policy?"

"Not so you'd notice, not yet. But it will be."

"God, I hope not."

"There are a lot of us feel this way, sis," Colm said.

She shook her head. "You won't beat them that way. They have all the weapons, for God's sake."

"We don't need to beat them," Tiernan said calmly. "Every time they bring out the militia, your average American has to reach in his pocket. He won't stand for that, or not for long any-way—eventually he'll turn against the bosses. We don't have to win a war, just keep fighting battles."

"I think you're overestimating the influence of the average American."

"I'm a stranger here, so that's possible. But what I know from Dublin, and what surely to God you must know from all the doings in Paterson, is that the old ways don't work anymore. If there was a God looking down who was ready and willing to intervene, then maybe a worker could shame his boss into pay-ing a decent wage by striking and starving his family. But there isn't, and the boss has no reason to care. And until we give him one that he can't ignore, nothing will change."

On reaching Paterson, Colm and Tiernan headed off to the IWW local, where lodging had been organized for visiting activists. Caitlin, to McColl's delight, had decided to share his hotel room rather than stay with the family she'd gotten to know during the previous year. "They hardly have room for one another," she said, "and I have to sleep with the children. If someone's going to keep me awake for half of the night, I'd rather it were you."

They found a middling hotel on Main Street and registered as Mr. and Mrs. Wilson. She asked the clerk to have their bags taken up and told a disappointed McColl that she was going straight out. "I won't drag you around with me," she said as they reached the street, "but at least come and meet Ruthie. It's not far, and after that you can do what you want."

As they walked toward the river, downtown's seeming prosperity gave way to wretched tenements and the mills where their residents toiled. "I'll be spending the next few hours with wonderful people," Caitlin said, "and they're all going to be at the end of their tethers. I'll swan in and I'll swan out again, and their terrible lives will just go on. And I'll go back to New York and earn money from telling their story. Sometimes I hate what I'm doing."

"Journalists have to be paid," McColl said. "And if you tell their stories well enough, their lives might get a little less terrible."

"I know. But . . ."

Ruthie lived on the top floor of a three-story tenement building. There were two small rooms and an even smaller kitchen—the toilet was three flights down in the yard. Her three children shared the double bed that filled one room, she and her husband a pull-down bed in the room where everyone lived. This was uncluttered by possessions and very clean. As Ruthie poured coffee from that day's jug, her two girls and one boy sat watching their visitors in respectful silence.

McColl looked for a sense of relief when Caitlin announced that she wouldn't be staying, but Ruthie and the children seemed genuinely disappointed, and the latter were mollified only by the promise of another visit in the summer. When Caitlin got down to business, Ruthie told her that times were hard and that most people were still trying to pay off the debts they'd incurred during the previous year's strike. "And the feeling's still bad," she said. "People won't work with them who crossed picket lines. The bosses have had to fire a few of them—some reward for loyalty, eh? Well, they should have been loyal to their own people."

The workers at one mill had come out on strike the previous week, when the owner had demanded a speeding up of production. So far no other mills had come out in support, but there was a meeting at a nearby school that evening, which Caitlin could use to judge the local mood. Though she might find it depressing.

But not all the news was as bad. At the mill where Ruthie's husband worked, there had been some changes for the better. "The bosses brought in fire alarms and put safety guards on one machine where a woman lost her arm last year—too late for her, of course, but better late than never. And Manny says that the foremen don't shout as much as they used to." She shrugged. "A small thing maybe, but he appreciates it. Makes him feel more like a person, less like an animal at the carnival."

After agreeing to meet up at the rally next day, they walked down to the street and along past the school where that evening's meeting was due to be held. A children's choir was singing somewhere inside, but no smoke was rising from the boiler-house chimney despite the chill March air.

Gina's family home was smaller than Ruthie's, and she seemed less inclined to detect any silver linings in the overall situation. Her youngest was sick and looked it, but they already owed the doctor several weeks of her husband's pitiful wages.

Her bitterness was palpable, and so was that of her sister, who dropped in while they were there. Unlike Gina, who had greeted Caitlin like a long-lost friend, the sister had obvious difficulty keeping her hostility under wraps. She ignored McColl but stared at Caitlin with the weary air of someone thinking, How could anyone dressed like you are have any idea of what we're going through?

"I'll send her some money for the child," Caitlin said when she and McColl were back outside. "Anonymously. I tried to give her ten dollars last year, and she refused to take it."

"Where next?" McColl asked, peering down the street. There were several people on stoops, giving them curious looks.

"How would you feel about doing some work for me?" she asked.

"Like what?"

"Just listening, really. A few hours in cafés and bars shouldn't be too taxing. I'd like a better idea of what the men are thinking," she explained. "When they talk to each other, I mean. I can't ask them—I can't—they just see a strange woman and look at my breasts."

"Like Father Meagher," he murmured.

"I doubt you're immune," she said tartly. "What is wrong with men?"

He could think of no answer to that, but she kissed him anyway and promised to see him back at the hotel. He watched her walk away up the desolate street and turned back toward the downtown area, where he'd noticed a row of suitable establishments. It seemed early for lunch, but he felt surprisingly hungry, and a plate of corned beef hash filled the spot for a minimal outlay. The only other customers in the café were nursing cups of coffee at a shared table, staring out the window, and murmuring occasional observations he was too far away to understand. They were all at the young end of middle age and looked like they could take care of themselves. Not to mention anyone who got in their way.

A tawdry bar three doors down was doing better business, but a similar group of hard-faced men had occupied one of its tables and set up an obvious no-man's-land between themselves and the workingmen who made up the rest of the clientele. McColl took up residence in the latter's territory and used his English accent to disarm the suspicion his presence seemed to generate. He was an automobile salesman, he told the barman, loudly enough for others to hear, and he soon had several men straining to see the publicity shot of the Maia he carried in his wallet.

"You won't find much demand for fancy cars round here," one obviously Irish immigrant told him cheerfully.

"I think I will," McColl disagreed, offering his cigarettes. "What town doesn't have a handful of bastards with more money than sense?"

There was general agreement that Paterson had its share of rich bastards, and several meaningful glances at the table across no-man's-land.

"Who are they?" McColl asked one of his new friends in a quiet voice.

"They call themselves 'special deputies,'" the friend told him, "but they're really hired thugs," he added rather more loudly. "They say they work for the city, but Barlow pays their wages." Barlow, it seemed, was the millowner keen to have his workers work faster. And the general feeling on this side of the bar was that Paterson's silk workers were too weak to resist him.

McColl moved on to another establishment, and another after that. By dusk he had bought drinks in seven of them and left most of his glasses virtually full. The story was the same wherever he went, of angry workers hanging on to what little gains the previous strike had brought them, knowing they were still too weak to fight for something better. For the moment at least, the owners held most of the cards. Not all, or they wouldn't need to flood the town with imported thugs. But most.

Paterson felt like an occupied city by day and something worse once dusk had fallen. It was probably just his imagination, but the downtown streets seemed to empty too soon, their lights much fainter than they should be. The passage of a streetcar sounded preternaturally loud, and in the silence that followed, he could hear the distant roar of the town's famous falls.

Back in the warmth of the hotel lobby, he read the city's evening paper while waiting for Caitlin. There were reports of local society gatherings, an article on the restoration of a local church, and a preview of the forthcoming baseball season, but no mention whatever of trouble in the local mills.

He supposed there was little point in writing about such matters when those most concerned could not afford the newspaper.

Many more days in Paterson and he would end up a socialist.

Caitlin eventually appeared, looking more worn out that he'd ever seen her. "We have to get going," she insisted. "The meeting starts in fifteen minutes."

They walked through the dimly lit streets, swapping stories from the last few hours. She seemed drained by her interviews, but unalarmed by his news of the "deputies."

"The owners brought hundreds of them in during last year's strike," she said. "And mostly they just stood there looking mean. All the real violence came from the police."

They reached the school entrance. Just inside the door, a couple of men were controlling admission, and as Caitlin explained who she was, McColl noticed a long line of baseball bats leaned up against a wall. Journalists were not welcome, one man was saying in the tone of someone who had suffered at their hands, but the ensuing argument was cut short when a local woman insisted on vouching for Caitlin—"She was the only one who told the truth!"

Inside the auditorium the lines of chairs were mostly occupied. There were pictures of American presidents on the walls, and McColl wondered what Washington, Jefferson, and Lincoln were making of the IWW banner that stretched across the front of the stage.

Colm suddenly appeared, accompanied by Tiernan and a big man with dark, longish hair and a luxuriant mustache. He was wearing a workingman's cap and trousers and a long coat with leather lapels. "This is Aidan Brady," Colm told them.

"Caitlin Hanley," she said, shaking his hand.

"Pleased to meet you," he said, in what sounded to McColl like a midwestern accent.

"Brady's been in Oregon," Colm said as McColl shook hands. "He was in the logging wars."

"So what are you doing this far east?" Caitlin asked him.

Brady smiled. "Fighting the good fight," he said.

"For the IWW?"

"That's right. And this is a good turnout," he added, looking around. Someone on the platform was waving at him, and he raised a hand in acknowledgment. "I have to go," he apologized.

"He's going to say a few words on the situation in Detroit," Colm explained. "Things are going well there."

They weren't in Paterson, as the meeting made depressingly clear. Speaker after speaker from the strikebound Barlow Mill made impassioned pleas for others to follow their example, and speaker after speaker from those still in work explained why they couldn't, shouldn't, or wouldn't. It wasn't hard to sympathize with the opposing points of view, but that didn't stop the meeting from becoming increasingly impassioned, and often acrimonious. This town had suffered too much, McColl thought; there was nothing left to give.

When Brady started to deliver his report from Detroit, McColl was expecting him to use developments there to bolster the Paterson strikers' case. Up to a point he did, but there were no appeals to solidarity; he seemed more intent on stressing the importance of individuals and their actions—how they had furthered the Studebaker workers' struggle in Detroit and how they might do so here. He never actually argued for violence, but a faith in its efficacy seemed to lie just beneath the surface of everything he said. His audience applauded when he finished, but without any great conviction, as if they weren't quite sure what they'd heard.

More appeals and rejections followed, but a worried-looking man with a message proved the harbinger of renewed solidarity. The chair's announcement of "a couple of dozen deputies outside" had most of the men on their feet, several loudly proclaiming that if the bastards wanted a fight, then they could have one. Others countered by pointing out how many women were present, and a decision was taken to inquire what exactly the deputies had in mind. A volunteer was dispatched and arrived back a few minutes later with the answer: The deputies had come to keep the peace. The gale of hysterical laughter this provoked felt more like relief than humor.

After a short impromptu conference on the stage, several of the men involved walked back up the aisle, inviting others to join them. "The young men will hold the door, so to speak," the chair announced. "But stick together as much as you can. And don't do anything foolish."

McColl and Caitlin joined the exodus, straining their ears for any clue as to what was transpiring outside. Nothing was the answer, if two lines of silent, grim-faced men on either side of a barely lit street could be so described. The deputies were armed with nightsticks, the silk workers and IWW men with the baseball bats from the wall inside. As far as McColl could see, the only man smiling was Aidan Brady.

Colm and Tiernan were there, too, Colm looking young and nervous, but most of those attending the meeting were hurrying away, and the deputies seemed ready to call it a night. "Your brother will be okay," McColl assured Caitlin. "The deputies have made their point, and they're outnumbered two to one."

She hesitated, as if to check his arithmetic, then allowed him to lead her away. As neither of them had eaten, they stopped at a restaurant close to the hotel, but Caitlin just picked at her food and seemed more depressed than McColl had ever seen her. "What a terrible day," she said once they were in their room. "All those desperate women I talked to, and then that meeting."

McColl sat down beside her, wondering what he could say.

"What sort of world is it," she asked, "when a worker can feel that a foreman not shouting at him is some sort of progress?" She was crying now, and he put his arm around her. "You know what one woman said to me today?" she almost sobbed. "That you can't afford to cry in this world."

"My mother once told me that tears were the only sure sign that someone still had a heart."

She laughed through hers. "I think I'd like your mother."

The sky was clear on Sunday morning, but by the time they reached the riverside park, the clouds were swiftly gathering, the sun an intermittent presence. McColl reckoned there were more than two thousand people there, men outnumbering women by something like three to one. There was a scattering of youngsters, but most parents had opted for prudence and left their children at home.

The various organizations involved—unions, union branches, political parties—all had their beautifully embroidered banners on display, and there was no shortage of rough-and-ready placards demanding a nine-hour day. The overall mood seemed strangely muted to McColl, apprehensive rather than frightened, quietly defiant rather than angry.

Colm, Seán Tiernan, and their new friend Aidan Brady were there, awaiting a decision of the rally's organizing committee. "The socialists are insisting that we leave these behind," Colm explained, brandishing his baseball bat.

"I think they're right," Caitlin said bluntly. "The owners aren't going to attack an unarmed march with so many women. They'd never live it down."

"My sister the optimist."

"Well, if there's trouble and our people are carrying weapons, they'll be able to blame us for starting it."

"They'll do that anyway," Brady said with a smile.

He had a point, McColl thought. But so did Caitlin, and it was hers that eventually carried the day. The baseball bats were gathered up, loaded into a convenient cart, and driven back to where they were usually stored.

The unarmed march set off, snaking out of the park along Front Street and heading for the bridge across the river. Her brother and his friends were up near the head of the parade, along with most of the IWW contingent, but Caitlin hung back, hoping to find Ruthie. It was McColl who spotted her, carrying one of her children. The other two were also there, striding forward with resolute faces on either side of their mother.

Her husband, Manny, Ruthie told them, was somewhere up ahead. He had wanted her and the children to keep well back, just in case.

There was no sign of the enemy so far. The faces watching from the sidewalks as the march advanced along Front Street were full of curiosity and pity but lacking in hostility.

They crossed the wide bridge over the Passaic River. The famous falls were just out of sight downstream but well within earshot, and the clamor of the water seemed, paradoxically, to shroud the march in silence and lend it the air of an unaccompanied moving picture.

A sheet of gray cloud now covered the sun, and the street ahead was shadowed by the tall stone buildings of the downtown area. There was no traffic in evidence, as if the city were already under curfew.

Looking back as they turned in to Market Street, McColl noticed the line of uniformed policemen that had swung in behind the rear of the march. The faces on the sidewalk looked grimmer now, and small groups of deputies were keeping pace with the marchers on both sides of the street. He pointed them out to Caitlin and Ruthie, both of whom looked alarmed. "We should tell the people at the front," Caitlin decided.

"I know who to speak to," Ruthie said. "But can you . . . ?"

"We'll look after the children," Caitlin assured her.

Ruthie hurried forward with the baby, leaving Caitlin and McColl each to grab a worried child by the hand. "This is David," she said of the boy she had hold off. "And that's Carmen."

The little girl began to cry but managed to stop when her brother insisted she should.

They had almost reached the small open space in front of City Hall, where the march was due to climax in song, speech, and a general show of strength. But looking over the shoulders of the crowd ahead, McColl had the impression that the space was already occupied by men in uniform. And just as he reached this conclusion, the clatter of iron horseshoes became distressingly audible. A line of mounted police bearing nightsticks was emerging from a side street like bunting from a conjuror's sleeve.

A collective gasp went up from the crowd. Hundreds turned to retrace their steps, only to find Market Street blocked by the line of following police. Panic set in, and people were already running in all directions before the voice on the loudspeaker demanded, almost sadistically, that they disperse at once or face arrest.

And now the mounted police were charging down the center of the street with no regard for anyone in their path. Screeches of alarm rose above the rhythmic pounding of hooves; curses of fear and frustration followed as people crashed into one another in their haste to escape. As the horses approached, nostrils billowing breath in the cold air, McColl scooped Carmen up in his arms and barged his way toward the sidewalk, looking back only once he'd reached the relative safety of a store doorway. The last of the horsemen were cantering by, leaving fallen victims scattered behind them. He couldn't see Caitlin, and it took him several terrible seconds to verify that none of the prone bodies was hers. Where had she gone?

There was fighting up ahead now—he could see the night-sticks rising and falling, hear the cries of anger and pain. Carmen was repeating "I want my mama" like a Hindu mantra.

Two horse-drawn police wagons had pulled up at the rear of the march, and a man was being frog-marched toward one of them, a woman beating ineffectually on one of his tormentors' backs. If Caitlin had gone that way, McColl should be able to see her, but there was no sign of the familiar rose-colored hat.

He took a firm hold of Carmen and started working his way forward through the milling crowd, weaving around several clusters of flailing arms and legs, stepping over one fallen banner announcing the brotherhood of man. The hard-eyed men in plainclothes seemed intent on dragging certain men away—McColl even saw two on the sidewalk consulting a sheaf of photographs—but no one seemed interested in him. They were probably deterred by the child in his arms, but how long would that last? There was still no sign of Caitlin, and the fighting up ahead seemed even more intense. He couldn't risk carrying Carmen into that.

So where should he take her? Her home, if he remembered correctly, was on the far side of City Hall and the battle now raging in front of it. His hotel was a couple of blocks to the left and seemed a much better bet. He sidestepped a woman who lay moaning on the ground, blood pouring out of her forehead, and made for what looked like an alley. There were two policemen in the entrance, but he just ran between them, ignoring a shout to stop, not glancing back until he'd covered at least twenty yards. Seeing no one in pursuit, he slowed his pace to a walk and tried to reassure the whimpering child in his arms.

There was a maze of alleys and passageways between the street they'd left and the one in the distance, and they were close to its center when McColl heard the cantering horse and swiftly sought the shelter of some fire stairs. But the horse wasn't first into view—a man came racing around a corner from the City Hall direction, coat flapping at his knees.

It was Aidan Brady.

The mounted rider appeared a split second later, nightstick raised and ready to strike. Seeing that Brady had taken the wrong turn and was now standing still, the policeman slowed his horse, calmly dismounted, and walked toward his prey, rehearsing blows from the nightstick on the palm of his other glove.

McColl couldn't hear what was said and couldn't see Brady's face, but he did catch the sudden movement, the faint shimmer of the knife, and the way the policeman's mouth gaped open.

The man sank to his knees. Brady wiped his blade on his victim's back, toppled the body with the sole of his boot, and calmly looked around. Seeing no one, he strode swiftly away.

McColl put Carmen down. "Stay here," he told her. "I'll be back in a moment."

"Okay," she said, her voice quavering slightly.

He walked up to the body, half hoping that the man was beyond help, because providing it would complicate matters no end. His wish was granted—Brady had effectively gutted the policeman, emptying his life out onto the cobbles with a butcher's economy.

He went back to Carmen, who asked him if "the stick man" was dead.

"Yes," McColl said, picking the child up again. "But don't look," he insisted, as he carried her past the corpse. "You might get bad dreams."

When they entered his hotel a few blocks away, they could no longer hear the fighting, and as they sat waiting in the hotel lounge—he with a whiskey, Carmen a soda—it felt as though they'd been transported to another world. Until, that is, a horse-drawn wagon went by on the street outside, full of prisoners. The scene was archaic—if it hadn't been for the glint of steel handcuffs, the cart might have been heading for the Place de la Révolution and an appointment with Madame Guillotine.

They had been there about twenty minutes when Caitlin walked in with a short, dark-haired man who turned out to be

Carmen's father. She was relieved, he overjoyed, to find the girl safe and sound. Ruthie and the other children were already at home, and Manny insisted on taking her back to join them, despite the situation outside. "I know the back streets," he said. "We'll be fine."

"They're arresting anyone they know was there," Caitlin explained. "The rumor is a cop's been killed, but that's probably just an excuse—"

"One was," McColl said. "I saw it happen. And so did Carmen," he warned her father. "It wasn't pretty."

Manny was horrified. "Oh, God," he said, going down on one knee and looking his daughter straight in the eyes. "Are you all right?"

The girl burst into tears, which seemed a sane reaction.

Once father and daughter had left, Caitlin wanted details.

"It was Aidan Brady," he said.

Her eyes widened. "Why? What happened?"

He told her what he'd seen.

"So it was self-defense."

"I doubt a judge would think so."

"No, but . . ."

"The cop was certainly intent on hurting him." McColl didn't want to argue the point, not with her.

"Brady was alone?" she asked, a hope as much as a question.

"He was."

She sighed her relief. "Well, thank God for that."

"Have you seen Colm?"

"No, but someone saw him and Tiernan back at the local. He's all right. And anyway, I have to stop worrying about him—he's a grown man."

"Easier said than done," he told her, taking her in his arms.

"And I thought yesterday was a bad day," she said after a while. "But I'm glad we're staying here tonight—they'll be all over the railroad station, hoping to catch the IWW organizers who came out from New York. In fact, we'd better not go out at all. We can eat downstairs."

"All right . . ."

"And then I need to get the whole thing written down, for posting off first thing tomorrow. You can help."

It wasn't how he'd imagined their evening, but he had no complaints. If he closed his eyes, he could still hear the sound of splintering bones, still see the sudden jerk of Brady's shoulder as he thrust the blade home.

Staten Island Ferry

♠

Kensley was reading the *New York Times* in the Aberdeen lobby when McColl arrived back from Paterson. After dropping his bag off in his room, he reluctantly went back down to meet the Canadian—after the events of the weekend, he felt that Cumming and the British Empire could allow him a few days off.

There wasn't even a coffee to be had—the normally phlegmatic Kensley hustled him out the door and onto Thirty-Second Street as if their professional lives depended on it. "I was afraid you'd ended up in the Paterson city jail," he said as they began walking.

"I nearly did."

"And Seán Tiernan?"

"He wasn't arrested, as far as I know."

"So he's back here?"

"Probably. Why the panic?"

"Kell's people came through with information on him. He's only twenty-seven, but up until a year ago Tiernan was on the ruling council of the Irish Republican Brotherhood."

"But no longer?" Tiernan was obviously a bigger wheel than McColl had thought.

"We don't know. Have you heard of the ICA—the Irish Citizen Army?"

"Nope."

"It was set up last summer by Jim Larkin. A workers' militia to defend the strikers against the police during the lockout. The only weapons they had were hurling sticks and cricket bats, but they can be pretty effective in narrow streets."

"I know," McColl said wryly.

Kensley looked at him. "Was it that bad?"

"I can't say I expected American cops to treat women and children quite that viciously. Stupid of me really, especially after the way the British police have treated the suffragettes."

"They don't take many prisoners," Kensley agreed, with only the faintest hint of disapproval. "But getting back to Tiernan . . . He was an ICA commander. Second-in-command of the whole shooting match, according to one source, but he was never arrested. When the strike was defeated and the men went back to work, he and others kept the ICA going, and it's still very much in existence. But it seems there's been a split at the top, between those who see it the way Larkin originally did, as a workers' defense force in time of dispute, and those, like Tiernan, who see it as an embryonic revolutionary organization. Tiernan and his friends want to drive out the English, abolish capitalism, and set up an Irish socialist republic."

"Don't the IRB?"

"Not all of them. The IRB is a broad church—all kinds of socialists, old-fashioned liberals, Gaelic mystics, even traditional Catholics who think socialism is a Protestant trick. And most of them will dismiss the ICA as being far too radical. Some because they loathe the idea of socialism, others because they don't think such an extreme program has any chance of success."

"But Kell's people think they're dangerous?" McColl asked once they'd crossed Ninth Avenue.

"The jury's out on how effective they might prove, but they're considered reckless enough to make a splash. No one seems to think the people in this group would have any compunction about committing treason if the reward looked promising enough."

"Is there any indication that they've approached the Germans?"

"None. But that could be why Tiernan is here in New York."

"It could be. He met someone in Paterson, by the way. An IWW man named Aidan Brady. I don't know if Tiernan had met him before, or if Colm Hanley had, but they seemed pretty close. With a name like Brady, I'm assuming the man has Irish connections, but they might not matter to him. He *is* a murderous bastard—I watched him kill that policeman in Paterson, the one in the newspapers."

"Jesus!" Kensley almost shouted. "You witnessed it?!"

"I did. And for obvious reasons, I didn't go to the police."

"You did right," Kensley said after a few moments' reflection. "We don't want your name and face all over the papers. What made him do it?"

"The cop came at him with a nightstick."

"I take it the cop didn't see the knife."

"Not till it was too late."

"Jesus," Kensley said again, softer this time. "Do you know where he is now?"

"No idea. He came from Detroit, so maybe he's gone back there."

They were approaching the end of Thirty-Second Street, the last few buildings framing the view of New Jersey's chimneys and factories.

"I'll ask my BOI contact to see what they have on him," Kensley said. "But we'll concentrate on Rieber. Cumming has sent two men over from London, and he's even authorized the hiring of a couple of automobiles, which shows how seriously he's taking this business. So we'll be covering all Rieber's waking hours, one pair watching from seven to three, the other from three till eleven. Neither of these new boys has ever been to America before, so we'll each have to take one in hand. And since I know the city better than you do, you can have the daylight hours. Okay?"

"Okay. Though if I'm spending the night with Caitlin Hanley, I might have trouble explaining what I'm getting up so early for."

Kensley was unsympathetic. "I'm sure you'll think of something."

At six the next morning, a blond Englishman named Neil Crabtree picked McColl up at the corner of Fifth and Thirty-second in a rented Model T. He looked as sleep-starved as McColl felt and seemed lamentably short on driving experience. "I've only ever driven in the countryside," Crabtree cheerfully explained, "and until yesterday I had no idea that Americans drive on the wrong side of the road." When McColl told him to pull over, he managed to leave half the vehicle on the sidewalk.

They swapped seats, and McColl drove them north toward Rieber's address. It was still dark when they reached Forty-Fourth Street, but lights were already burning in the German's windows. McColl parked a hundred yards from the apartment building and reminded himself to make time for coffee the next day—the first cigarette didn't taste the same without it.

Crabtree didn't smoke and pointedly opened his window. His clothes were smarter than McColl's, a charcoal ensemble of suit, overcoat, and hat that had probably cost a fortune. The plummy accent added to the impression of inherited privilege, but he seemed friendly enough. As they sat waiting for Rieber to put in an appearance, he brought McColl up to date on all matters English and offered an enthusiast's preview of the upcoming cricket season.

McColl was on the verge of falling asleep when his companion suddenly interrupted himself. "Here comes our German!"

It was fully light by this time, and there was no mistaking Erich

Rieber as he descended the building's front steps, briefcase in hand. The German took a cursory look in their direction, and McColl was glad that theirs wasn't the only automobile on display. He let the man cross Tenth Avenue before starting the engine and easing forward in slow pursuit.

As expected, Rieber strode all the way to the Hudson before turning south on Twelfth, forcing McColl to advance down Forty-Fourth Street in stages, like a player in Creeping Up on Grandma. It was a two-mile walk to the Hoboken Ferry, but as Crabtree bitingly observed, the Germans did love their exercise.

Once certain that Rieber was headed for the ferry and work, McColl drove past him, parked by the terminal, and ordered Crabtree to beat the German aboard. He waited until they were both through the turnstile before leaving the automobile and following them onto the ship. According to Crabtree, Rieber had taken a seat up front, so the two of them stayed by the stern rail until the ferry docked on the New Jersey side and then followed their quarry at a very safe distance to his inevitable destination— his office on the Hamburg America pier. While Crabtree leaned against a convenient wall and kept watch on the shipping office's entrance, McColl scoured the immediate locality for suitable observation points. He found two cafés, which was better than nothing but not much. Sitting in these for hours on end was likely to attract notice or comment, and they certainly couldn't afford to loiter outside in view of Rieber's window. But there was no other choice.

McColl collected Crabtree and led him to the closer of the two. They ordered coffees and established a routine, one reading the *New York Times* that McColl went out and bought while the other kept both eyes on the distant entrance for Rieber's familiar figure. They were too far away to make out other faces, but Kensley had been sure that Rieber would keep his American contacts far from his place of work.

The newspaper was only slightly more interesting than the

surveillance. Smoking cigarettes, McColl discovered, decreased one's "power of initiative, of grasp, and of facility of execution"—the smoker thought his mind was working better, when it was actually 10 percent less efficient. On the political front, President Wilson was moving heaven and earth to reinstate one Miss Mattie Tyler as postmistress of Courtland, Virginia. After a "clique of Virginia politicians" had conspired to displace her, she had called on the president for help, and he had taken time off from national and international affairs to sort things out. Mattie was, after all, the granddaughter of a former president.

In France a more dramatic story was unfolding. A woman named Henriette Caillaux had walked into a national newspaper editor's office and emptied a pistol into his chest. Her reason: that the editor had published a leaked letter damaging to her government-minister husband's reputation. It looked an open-and-shut case, but the defense lawyers were calling it a crime of passion, as if that were grounds for acquittal. He wondered how Caitlin would see it.

After a couple of hours, he and Crabtree began to feel like they'd outstayed their welcome and moved to the second café. He could barely imagine a more boring job, and McColl soon found his attention beginning to wander. It was hard to keep your eyes focused on the one spot, particularly when you knew that the chance of anything happening was remote. The river was so much more interesting, the ferries weaving their way between tugs and other small craft, the occasional liner almost filling the view as it headed for a quay or the open sea.

At two o'clock Crabtree walked over to the passenger terminal and used one of the public telephones to tell Kensley where they were. He arrived to relieve them at three, along with a dark-haired boy of not much more than twenty. Peter Gladwell, as Crabtree told McColl on their ferry ride back to the automobile, was a decent enough sort but not the brightest star in the sky. He had been seasick for most of their Atlantic crossing and blushed whenever a woman came near him. His father was an admiral.

Crabtree, as McColl discovered the following day, had been to Winchester and Cambridge before spending a few years in the diplomatic corps. He had become friendly with one of Cumming's people while stationed in Cairo, and when a "misunderstanding" had forced his resignation from the corps, he had wangled his way into the Service. Serving one's country was what mattered, not how or where one did it. Crabtree was keen to see the world, and particularly its women. He had always heard that American women were "fast," but none had so far confirmed it.

These confidences were shared in the familiar cafés. Rieber showed no signs of changing his routine, and the only differences from the day before were an obstructed view—courtesy of the huge and newly docked *Europa*—and utterly miserable weather, with cold wind and rain sweeping across the puddle-strewn quays and turbulent river. And it was probably all for nothing, McColl thought. Rieber could be doing his clandestine business by telephone. Or mail.

Kensley and Gladwell arrived at three, looking like they'd swum across the Hudson. Rieber had gone straight home the previous evening and not gone out again before turning off his lights.

"Does he have a telephone at home?" McColl asked Kensley.

"Not anymore. I persuaded the BOI to disconnect him for a couple of weeks. He thinks there's a fault at the local exchange."

"He could be using the one in his office."

"He could, but I don't think he'd risk it. It's a German company line, after all. He'd be afraid the Americans were listening in, either for themselves or on our behalf."

Kensley looked at them all, like a teacher addressing his pupils. "I know this is really boring, but it'll pay off. Believe me."

It did, and sooner than McColl expected. Soon after noon on the Thursday, Rieber emerged from the shipping office, briefcase in hand, and set off in the usual direction. "Half day off?" Crabtree wondered out loud.

"We'll soon know. Why don't you get ahead of him?"

Crabtree did so, hurrying down the other side of the street toward the Hoboken terminal. McColl kept about fifty yards adrift of Rieber, collar up and hat pulled down lest the German decide to look back. Away to their left, a French liner was gliding majestically up the river.

As they approached the terminal, McColl closed the gap and was rewarded for his foresight. Rieber walked straight past the gate to the Twenty-Third Street Ferry and on through the one signed BARCLAY STREET. McColl joined the queue two places behind him and looked back in the hope of seeing Crabtree. Though he'd boarded the other ferry, his partner should have realized by now that Rieber had not.

McColl passed through the turnstile, walked aboard, and waited by the rail, hoping that Crabtree would appear. There was a dull clang as the gate shut, a blast on the ferry's horn, and a churning of water as the wheels began to turn. He was on his own.

The German was at the head of the disembarkation line as they approached the Barclay Street pier, consulting his pocket watch with the air of someone who had an appointment to keep. He ignored the queue of waiting cabs, though, and strode off down West Street at a remarkably brisk pace. There was no doubt about it—the man loved walking. He probably hiked around the Alps on his holidays.

There were a lot of people on the sidewalk, so it was easy for McColl to keep bodies between himself and Rieber. He tried to avoid looking at the man's back for more than a few seconds at a time, as experience had taught him that many people sensed another's stare.

The German crossed Battery Place and entered the park of the same name, McColl still fifty yards adrift. The trees were springing into bloom, the benches full of giggling secretaries enjoying the sunshine and devouring their packed lunches. Out in the bay, two Staten Island ferries were crossing, a sight that caused Rieber to consult his watch and lengthen his already impressive stride.

The German disappeared through the maw of the terminal building, and McColl slowed his own pace, confident that the incoming ferry was several minutes away from loading. He almost miscalculated; lacking the requisite change and having to procure it, he ended up being one of the last to beat the gate. Having done so, he walked aboard with his hat tipped even lower over his face. He might be mistaken for a criminal on the run, but at least Rieber wouldn't recognize him.

A cautious tour of the boat found the German close to the stern on the upper deck, alone and looking out across the sunlit bay at the smoke-raddled New Jersey shoreline. McColl worked his way up the other side toward the bow and found a spot on the crowded rail from which he could keep watch with only a minimal chance of being spotted. But no one approached the German, who seemed, for all of the twenty-minute journey, fully engaged by the panoramic view.

As they docked at the Staten Island terminal, Rieber made no move to disembark, and McColl took his eyes off the German for a few moments to scan the people who were streaming aboard below. And there was Seán Tiernan, lifting his head to survey the upper deck as McColl stepped hurriedly back out of sight. He thought he had moved quickly enough, but he couldn't be sure.

The ferry suddenly seemed a very small place. One of the toilets, he decided; he would lock himself away until Tiernan and Rieber had convened their conspirators' meeting. Because that was what it had to be. Anything else would be far too much of a coincidence.

The toilet stank, but he stuck it out for several minutes, until the ferry was under way once more and someone started hammering on the door. He first thought it must be Rieber or Tiernan but immediately realized he was being ridiculous—they were hardly likely to simply confront him, and if they wanted to kill him, they would choose a more private location.

It was a young boy, holding himself with panic-filled eyes. As the door slammed behind him, McColl hoped he'd made it.

Rieber and Tiernan were side by side on the upper-deck rail, deep in conversation. Neither man was casting glances over his shoulder, which surely must mean that McColl hadn't been seen. And there was no point in watching them further and risking one of them spotting him. He moved back out of sight and descended the stairs to the lower deck.

If Tiernan had seen him, it would have been a disaster in so many ways. Another group of Germans would be after his blood and might prove more successful than the last lot. In the fight to prevent whatever it was that Rieber and Tiernan were planning, the Service would lose Cumming's "knowing what they don't know you know" advantage. And most importantly to McColl, as he realized with no little shame, Caitlin would find out. Tiernan would tell Colm, and he would tell his sister. It would be over.

How had he gotten into this mess? A piece of worldly wisdom from an Englishman he'd met in India came back to him. "Some men follow their hearts," the drunken sage had told him, "and some go where their minds take them. Most of course just follow their cocks. Any one of the three can lead you to happiness, but only if you stick to that one alone."

He seemed to be following all three.

There was no point in agonizing about it. Across the bay the sun was shining on the Statue of Liberty, and McColl found himself seeing it through Tiernan's eyes. He didn't like the man but could understand his hunger for Irish independence and see the logic of seeking German help to achieve it. The notion of "joint action on enemy soil" might be treasonous in law, but no doubt Tiernan saw it as a patriot's duty. That wouldn't stop McColl from doing all he could to foil any such endeavor, but he felt no sense of outrage.

Was that was why von Schön had been opposed to his being killed? A belief that men pursuing their own country's interest in good faith should be thwarted rather than punished?

The whole business suddenly seemed unreal. A German, an Irishman, and an Englishman, playing deadly games in the middle of New York Bay, while ordinary American life went on all around them.

Real or not, he was one of the players. He hung back in the stern when the ferry docked, giving Rieber and Tiernan plenty of time to disembark and go their separate ways. It was almost three, so his colleagues would be waiting for him at the Twenty-Third Street terminal, the meeting place Kensley had chosen for such a contingency.

He took the elevated and then walked down to the river, feeling depressed by what he had to report. If Tiernan was involved, then so were the Hanleys, and any hope of McColl's disentangling his new work from his love life seemed to be receding. He was meeting her after work that evening.

His colleagues were sitting in one of the Model T's, with the roof thrown back. He climbed into the empty front seat beside Kensley. "Success," he announced. "He met up with Seán Tiernan on the Staten Island Ferry."

"Yes!" Kensley exclaimed, slapping both palms on the steering wheel. "What did they talk about?"

"God only knows. They both know me, for Christ's sake, and there was no way I could get close enough to hear anything without being seen."

Kensley raised both hands in mock surrender. "Fine. It doesn't matter. We have the connection. Now we just have to be patient and watch them hang each other." He turned to McColl. "But not you. Cumming has other plans for you," he added, reaching for the door handle. "Let's walk."

He led the way off the busy City Plaza and down the sidewalk by the end of the basin beside White Star's Pier 61. There was no liner at the quay, but enough rubbish in the water to keep the gulls happy. Kensley removed an envelope from his inside pocket, handed it over to McColl, and leaned up against the parapet with the apparent intention of studying the view. "It's been decrypted," he said as McColl opened up the message.

Cumming was ordering him to Mexico. Or, more precisely, to the Tampico oil fields, where German agents were using the chaos wrought by civil war to threaten the Royal Navy's newest ships' principal source of fuel. "I'm sure you can understand the seriousness of this threat," Cumming wrote, somewhat portentously, but McColl could see his point.

Von Schön, he suddenly remembered, had been on his way to Mexico.

"You do speak Spanish?" Kensley asked without turning around. "Cumming's lost his list of your languages."

"Yes," McColl muttered. He was expected to "assess the seriousness of the threat" and take "whatever steps deemed necessary to counter it." He would have access to Britain's diplomatic representatives in the area, but, regretfully, "no recourse to military assistance will be possible." A briefing paper covering both the wider Mexican situation and that pertaining to the oil fields was being prepared by the Foreign Office and would be forwarded as quickly as possible, along with the necessary funds.

Well, he supposed this was what he had asked for.

"Sorry to lose you," Kensley was saying, "but less sorry than I was an hour ago. Now that we know Tiernan's involved, you'd be no use to me here."

"You don't really trust me around the Hanleys, do you?"

"As much as you trust yourself. It's Rieber and Tiernan knowing you by sight that disqualifies you."

"And we don't know for certain that Colm is involved," McColl said, although both of them knew that he had to be. Suddenly the prospect of Mexico came as a relief, as a chance to put some distance between his work and her. She would never accept his working against her family—who could?—but at his most optimistic he could sometimes imagine her accepting his work for his country. "He doesn't say when he wants me to leave," he told Kensley.

"Yesterday, I expect, but let's say Monday. The money might be here by then—if not, I'll send it on."

"How do I get there?"

"Someone at the consulate is researching boats and trains, and they've also asked the embassy in Mexico City for advice— we don't want you pitching up in a war zone. The moment I get anything, I'll have it sent to your hotel."

"Okay."

"At least it'll be hot down there," Kensley told him. "Most likely in more ways than one."

McColl went back to his hotel and soaked in the bath for almost half an hour, pondering the sudden change in his situation. How was he going to explain an abrupt departure for Mexico? Business, he supposed, and once he thought about it, the fictional details came readily enough to mind. Sometimes he couldn't help wondering why Caitlin hadn't seen through him, but that, he knew, was only because he was so guiltily aware of the deception. She was focused on her own affairs, and he had given her no obvious reason to doubt him.

She arrived soon after six, her eyes shining with excitement. "I've got a new job," she burst out after they'd kissed and embraced. "On the *Times* no less. I'm the new editor for women's issues. The very first one, come to that."

"That's wonderful," he said, and kissed her again. He knew how much this meant to her. "When do you start?"

"Monday, eight A.M. Let's go out and celebrate!"

"Let's."

They walked to a swanky restaurant she knew a few blocks north on Fifth. After eating a ridiculously expensive meal and drinking far too much, they took a cab back to the hotel, negotiated the elevator with what felt like great aplomb, and somehow ended up making love on the floor of his room. It was only after room service had provided the coffee to sober them both that he felt able to broach the matter of his imminent departure.

She looked stunned. "But why Mexico?"

"Our rep there has been taken ill, and right in the middle of sewing up some deals. So Tim wants me to go down there and tie things up."

"To Mexico City?"

"Yep," McColl lied, thinking Tampico might sound suspicious.

"Will you be coming back here or going straight on to England?"

"I don't know that yet. But I'll be back here eventually. You haven't seen the last of me."

"No," she said, and put her head on his shoulder. "And there's no hurry, is there? For us, I mean."

"None at all."

"And we can have this weekend."

"Can you stay?"

She smiled but shook her head. "Not tonight. They're expecting me home, and I want to tell Aunt Orla about my job. She's waited a long time for something like this."

"Of course."

"But Saturday and Sunday—I'll make up some sort of story. Look," she said, putting him at arm's length and looking him straight in the face. "Come to Brooklyn in the morning—there are places I want to show you, places that mean a lot to me."

"I'd love to," he said. "I love *you*," he added, the words just slipping out, like light through carelessly drawn drapes.

"And I love you," she replied, with a smile that seemed almost sorrowful. "And that's usually the end of the story, isn't it? Not the beginning."

Next morning a package arrived from Kensley. The wad of dollars seemed more generous when McColl also found a railroad ticket to Galveston—the US government was apparently sending ships down to Tampico from the Texas port to pick up American citizens threatened by a rebel advance. It seemed less beneficent when he realized he still had the hotel bill to pay.

He was expected to travel under the name John Bradley. The vice-consul in Tampico knew that someone with that name was coming, and would brief him on the local situation when he arrived. If Tampico fell to the rebels—a possibility, McColl noticed, that Kensley had previously neglected to mention—communication would be through the embassy in Mexico City.

His journey would begin with a train to Washington, D.C., leaving from the New Jersey terminus of the Pennsylvania Railroad at ten on Monday morning.

After breakfast on Saturday, he took the subway down to City Hall and the el from Park Row across the Brooklyn Bridge to the other Fifth Avenue. She was waiting at the Sixteenth Street exit, looking as gorgeous as ever and drawing admiring glances from every male who passed her. After taking McColl's arm and steering him eastward, she told him how happy she'd made her aunt and how even her father had offered his congratulations. Neither had objected to her spending two nights in Manhattan with Eleanor, even though her fictional friend lacked a telephone. "My aunt might have her suspicions," Caitlin admitted, "but I think she's realized that either I'm still a virgin—in which case there's no need to worry—or I'm already far beyond saving. Either way . . ."

For the next couple of hours, they toured her childhood haunts—her first school, the family church, the store where she and Colm had bought their Saturday candy. They crossed Prospect Park, stopping to look at the menagerie—"I was crazy about animals when I was little"—and the swan boats on the lake in the Long Meadow, before riding the carousel with a host of noisy children. The last place on Caitlin's list was Green-Wood Cemetery, a Gothic-gated enclave of forested hills, ponds, and mausoleums in the heart of the city. She added flowers to those already adorning her mother's grave. "Finola comes every week," she explained. "She remembers our mother. I don't, not really. And sometimes I wonder how different my life would have been if she had lived. She wasn't a strong woman like Aunt Orla. So I expect my loss would have been Colm's gain." She looked down at the gravestone. "But she was my mother," she said after a few moments.

Neither said much on the train back to Manhattan. He'd felt touched that she wanted to show him her past, but the tour had served to emphasize the reality of their imminent separation. He couldn't stop counting hours now, imagining the world without her while she was still on his arm.

She seemed to feel it, too, and her insistence on visiting friends that evening seemed designed to distract them both. The gathering, when they reached it, was part party, part political meeting, with animated discussions under way in every nook and cranny of several smoke-filled rooms. McColl was able to put faces to several of the names Caitlin had mentioned: the anarchist Margaret Sanger, who was vigorously lecturing two much younger men on the political significance of birth control; the author Sinclair Lewis, holding court with a pair of younger women; the journalist Jack Reed, who moved from group to group, wineglass in one hand, cigarette in the other, dropping off ideas like an intellectual postman.

And there was also the famous Elizabeth Gurley Flynn, who, much to McColl's surprise, looked even younger than Caitlin. She had missed the rally in Paterson but had been there for much of the strike and seemed heartened and dismayed in equal measure by Caitlin's report on the wives and McColl's account of the mayhem on Market Street.

He could see that Caitlin was in her element and found himself wondering if he'd ever fit in. He had hoped Oxford would be something like this but had soon realized his mistake. The crushing burden of hierarchy and tradition, the breathtaking prejudice, the remarkable stupidity of so many fellow students, who were only there because Daddy had money or breeding—all combined to thwart any real adventures of the intellect. Perhaps he was being naïve and Harvard and Yale were every bit as bad, but in these rooms, in this city, America did feel like the land of the free. These people were using their brains, and they seemed to enjoy the process no end.

The party moved on soon after ten, when Reed announced he was keen to go dancing. Almost everyone came along, though some could barely keep to the sidewalk, let alone move to music. The dance hall around the corner was already full, the Negro orchestra louder than any that McColl had ever heard. He and Caitlin managed two dances before agreeing it must be bedtime.

Sunday was the third bright day in a row, ready-made for a walk around Central Park. They were sitting by the lake when Caitlin suddenly announced that Colm was going back to Ireland that summer.

"With Tiernan?" McColl asked.

"Yes, I'm afraid so."

"Are you worried about him?"

She laughed. "Of course. I spent most of my childhood looking after him. It's hard to lose the habit." She sighed. "But he's a grown man now, and I'm the last person who should object to anyone chasing after his own star."

"But?"

"I don't like Seán very much. He's one of those people with a deep sense of injustice but no sense of love."

"Yes," he agreed. She had described Tiernan perfectly. And his friend Brady.

That evening, lying in bed after making love, she asked him if he was tired of her.

"God, no. How can you ask?"

She took a moment before replying. "Do you remember me saying, on the ship, that one day we could part like friends, with no regrets?

McColl felt a literal pain in his heart. "Yes."

"In case you hadn't realized, I've changed my mind. So how about you? Do you think we have a future together?"

"I thought you were about to say that this is good-bye."

She reached out a hand to caress his cheek. "You haven't answered my question."

"There's nothing I want more."

"I have to take this job."

"I know."

"Will you think about coming to live here?"

"If you'll think about living in England. We have newspapers, too, you know."

She smiled. "All right. Anything's possible."

Monday morning he was awake before her, and lying there studying her sleeping face, he had a sudden, almost overwhelming urge to make a full confession. But after waking she went straight to the bathroom and on returning snuggled into his arms, scattering all semblance of resolve.

He had packed the previous evening, and after breakfasting downstairs they took a taxi together to the railroad ferry. One long last embrace and he was walking aboard, hardly able to credit the fact of their parting. As the ferry set off, his eyes sought and found her, standing by the open cab door, waving and blowing him a kiss. He waved back, and she stood there for what seemed a long time before finally turning and climbing inside. The cab pulled out behind a passing streetcar and was swallowed by the city.

Hotel México

♠

The ship's auxiliary tender moved up the wide Pánuco River in the tropical darkness, showing no lights and, so far, attracting no attention from whoever held possession of the two shores. It was still remarkably hot but not particularly humid, and over the last few minutes a welcome breeze had sprung up. That morning, according to the grizzled Texan named Doherty who commanded the tender, Tampico had still been in the hands of Huerta loyalists. It probably still was, but Pablo González's Constitutionalist troops had been probing the town's outer defenses for several days and sooner or later seemed bound to break through.

The tender had already passed abandoned oil-company wharves and storage installations on both sides of the torpid river, and it was hard to judge how far away the occasional bursts of gunfire were coming from. Several fires were burning out on the coastal plain to the north, but it was impossible to tell whether they were intentional burn-offs or consequences of war.

All in all, McColl had been to more welcoming places. Maybe by day it would look less threatening, but by night it reminded him of paintings by Hieronymus Bosch, and he wouldn't have been shocked to see men spread-eagle on fiery wheels lining the banks of the river.

A week had passed since his departure from New York City. It had taken him two days to reach Galveston and two more for Cumming to secure him a place on one of the relief ships heading south down the Gulf coastline. This rusty old freighter had a top speed of around eight knots and had been overtaken by every other ship heading their way. Many of those had been American warships, whose reason for rushing southward doubtless had something to do with the escalating squabble between the two countries. This had broken out while he was still twisting his thumbs in Galveston; as the city rag had explained it, some American sailors in Tampico—whose only crime had been to purchase some much-needed fuel for their boat—had been taken into custody by insolent Mexican soldiers. They had quickly been released with an apology, but the local American naval commander had deemed the latter insufficient. He had demanded a more formal obeisance, one that included a twenty-one-gun salute to his flag.

When McColl's freighter had finally arrived off the mouth of the Pánuco three days later, the sea had been thronged with warships. The Dutch, German, and British were all represented, but most of the ships were American. This threatening presence suggested that the latest Mexican response had been insufficiently obsequious, an impression verified by the locally based Doherty. And in the meantime another incident had taken place—an American army orderly had been arrested in Veracruz, farther down the coast. According to Doherty, Washington had reacted to this second misunderstanding with an equally childish lack of proportion. "Wilson wants to make a point," the Texan had concluded. He himself had voted for Roosevelt's Progressives.

Oh, good, McColl had thought—now he had the Americans to worry about as well as the Germans.

The tender was gliding past another silent oil jetty, but if the faintly glowing sky ahead was any guide, the city of Tampico was not yet in darkness. Ten minutes later, as the tender rounded a sharp bend in the river, he could see it for himself, a scattering of yellow lights along the northern shore. These were soon hidden from view by the warehouse stretching the length of the wharf, which seemed suspiciously deserted.

But no fusillade greeted their approach or interrupted their tying up and landing. McColl thanked Doherty for the lift and hung back while the representatives of government, navy and Big Oil who had shared his trip upriver started out, with evident trepidation, in the direction of the town.

It was closer than it looked. Beyond the long warehouse, a pedestrian footbridge carried arrivals over a fan of railway tracks and deposited them at the southern edge of the town's principal plaza. And here, McColl was pleased to see, life was still going on. There were uniforms on display but no drawn guns, and most of the walkers enjoying the evening air were couples, with or without obvious chaperones. Although the cantinas on the rim of the plaza were hardly doing a roaring business, none looked in any danger of going bankrupt.

A sudden ripple of gunfire sounded in the distance, but no one seemed to pay it any mind. Still, McColl thought, it might be wise to check how far away the front line actually was. In the morning, when it was light.

There were several hotels in the plaza, all looking much of a muchness. He had no idea whether von Schön was still in Mexico, let alone in this one small Gulf port, but if this was where trouble was brewing for the British, then McColl wouldn't be the slightest bit surprised to find him frequenting one of the hotel bars. According to the briefing from London that Kensley had sent on to Galveston, Mexico supplied over 90 percent of the oil that kept the Royal Navy at sea. It was hard to imagine a bigger prize for a German spy.

If McColl ran into von Schön, he supposed he would shake the German's hand. The man had probably saved his life, after all. And then each would try to thwart the other, in as civilized a manner as possible. Or something like that. But everything being equal, McColl decided, he would much rather that the German remain in ignorance of his arrival. Looking back over his relationship with von Schön, it was hard to escape the conclusion that his counterpart's experience in these matters was greater than this own.

He decided to eschew the plaza itself. On one of the streets leading off it, he found several other hotels, slightly more seedy perhaps, but less likely to have German guests. The young man at reception seemed slightly surprised to see a gringo, but business was clearly business, and at McColl's request he showed him a room overlooking the street. It was remarkably devoid of furniture, just a bed and a jug of water, side by side on the floor. The walls were splattered with squashed mosquitoes, but that didn't worry McColl overmuch—when it came to natural gifts, his unpopularity with that particular insect rivaled his linguistic aptitude.

On impulse he showed the young man the picture of von Schön leaving the Ghadar house in San Francisco. "Yes," the Mexican said. "I have seen him in the plaza. Two days ago maybe. A friend of yours?"

"A business acquaintance."

"Ah. You pay in advance, please."

After handing over the cost of an American coffee for a three-night stay, McColl was shown a cleaner-than-expected bathroom and toilet down the hall and advised to patronize a particular restaurant up the street, which was famous for its guachinango. Once the boy had retreated downstairs, McColl opened the door-length windows that led onto his balcony and stepped gingerly out onto the wrought-iron structure. He could give speeches from here, he thought.

It seemed too early for bed, so he walked back down to the plaza and its parade of local life. He found a seat outside a cantina in a convenient patch of shadow and sat with a beer for half an hour, pondering the task that Cumming had given him. The first step was to seek out any suspicious German travelers without alerting them to his own presence or purpose. And provided he didn't run into von Schön, that shouldn't be difficult. The next move would be to intercept any communications with embassy or homeland and get a better idea of what they were up to.

As he sat there in the semidarkness, watching insects orbit the lamp above the door and listening to the singer inside croon mournful melodies over a badly tuned guitar, it all seemed a bit unreal. He had never been to Mexico before, but he already felt fond of the place.

He got up and walked warily around one side of the square and back across the footbridge to the long wharf. A line of big birds was perched on the ridge of the warehouse roof—vultures or buzzards of some sort or other—but they showed no interest in him. He sat on an iron capstan at the edge of the slow-moving river, feeling the weight of the rolling water and wondering what Caitlin was doing in New York. He had not yet written to her, and when he did work out what he wanted to say, the letter would have to be sent via the British consulate in the capital.

Next morning he was coming back from the bathroom when he noticed a set of stairs heading upward. These brought him out onto a flat roof with panoramic views. The sun had risen above the American warships lying off the river mouth, some six miles to the east, and was already bathing the slopes of the mountains that bordered the plain to the west. There was a low rumbling of guns to the north, and smoke was rising in several places. A long black pall seemed to be hanging over the northwestern outskirts of the city, where Doherty had placed the front line.

He wondered what would happen if the Constitutionalists took the city. Life would presumably go on, at least for most of its Mexican inhabitants. As far as McColl knew, the Constitutionalist leader Carranza was popular with the American government, and he wouldn't want to alienate Wilson and his cronies by destroying oil installations or shooting the foreigners who ran them. And if the Americans remained persona grata, they would probably ensure that the British did, too.

The Mexicans weren't the problem. And wouldn't be, unless President Wilson or Prime Minister Asquith did something stupid enough to unite the warring factions against the United States and Britain. That *would* benefit Germany.

He walked back down to his room, finished dressing, and took to the street in search of breakfast. A café near the plaza provided eggs, refried beans, and a huge cup of coffee, as sweet as it was bitter. A boy of about six sold him a one-page newspaper, which publicized several local society gatherings but avoided any mention of the conflict raging in the city's outskirts.

The town didn't seem big enough to warrant a vice-consul, but the oil field clearly did, because the address of His Majesty's local fixer had been included in McColl's briefing notes. Following the café owner's directions, he walked two blocks west and took the next turn toward the river. And there, a few buildings down, was the sign he was looking for.

The vice-consulate occupied a couple of rooms over a local shipping office. There was a secretary's desk in the outer office but no sign of a secretary, unless he or she was part of the argument under way in the inner sanctum. McColl took the absent secretary's seat and listened to two male voices angrily expressing their lack of satisfaction with His Majesty's agent. They were oil engineers, working in the fields to the north of the city, and most of their personal possessions had been "confiscated" by marauding members of Pablo González's army. "We need protection," one kept saying, as if repeating the phrase would conjure up a gunboat.

The vice-consul was given little chance to respond, but McColl had the feeling he'd heard the man's voice before.

He had. Once the two engineers had blustered their way out, he walked in on a familiar face. They'd hardly known each other, let alone been friends, but Rodney Wethers had been in McColl's year at Oxford and even attended some of the same tutorials.

"I wondered if it was you when I got the message," Wethers said, standing up and offering a damp hand. He had put on a lot of weight since Oxford and doubled his number of chins. The heat had hardly begun to build outside, but he was already sweating profusely.

A couple of minutes proved sufficient to establish their lack of common acquaintances. "So," Wethers said, "you're looking for Germans. There's quite a few pass through, but they're mostly travelers or salesmen. Nothing suspicious as far as I know."

"How about this man?" McColl asked, sliding across his creased photograph of von Schön.

Wethers shook his head, dislodging several drops of sweat. "Is he a spy?"

"He is."

Wethers looked at the picture again. "But who would he spy on round here? What secrets could he unearth?"

"What about González?" McColl asked, changing tack. "Will he take the town?"

"Probably, sooner or later. But nothing much will change. I went to see him a couple of weeks ago, at his headquarters. He's a bit rough and ready, but he seemed reasonable enough. When I stressed the importance our government attaches to the local oil fields and how upset we would be if extraction or delivery were to be interrupted, he told me not to worry. We would have to pay what he called 'extra taxes' for operating in a war zone, but he offered his personal guarantee that the wells would keep pumping. And in the circumstances, that seems like quite a good bargain."

"Maybe," McColl conceded. "But what if the Germans offer him more to cut the supply?"

"I suppose they might try. But I think González knows which side his bread is buttered. Unlike us and the Americans, the Germans have only one ship in the area. They can't put any real pressure on him, whereas we, as a last resort, could occupy the oil fields."

"If we did that, wouldn't the Mexicans blow up the wells?"

"And destroy their main source of income? I don't think so."

"What if Huerta's army looked to be forcing them out again—then they'd have nothing to lose."

Wethers smiled. "That's all very hypothetical, old chap."

"Maybe it is. Tell me about this latest business, the arrests and Washington's response."

"Ah, the Tampico Incident." He made it sound like a dime novel. "It was nothing really . . ."

"The Americans don't seem to think so."

"They're very touchy at the moment. If they're not careful, they'll make Huerta's position untenable and find that they've landed us all with somebody worse."

"Are all the other leaders anti-American?"

"No, they're just more unreliable. Zapata and Villa aren't much better than bandits, and the others . . . I suppose Carranza might fit the bill—he's the one with the forked beard who looks like he's itching to part the Red Sea. Villa, Obregón, and González are all ostensibly loyal to him, but who knows? From our point of view, none of them would be an improvement on Huerta. Better the devil you know and all that."

"The Americans don't seem to think so."

"Most of them do. The American ambassador in Mexico City is Huerta's biggest supporter. The American oilmen around here think he's everyone's best bet. It's Wilson who can't wait to get rid of the man, and his reason, believe it or not, is that he thinks Huerta is a *bad* man. Forget American interests, which are much the same as ours. He'd rather be righteous."

"It's almost endearing," McColl muttered.

"It's madness."

McColl had to smile. "Will Huerta bend the knee?"

"I doubt it."

"So what will Wilson do then?"

Wethers shrugged. "I don't know, and I doubt if he does either. He's our number-one problem, not the German."

"Well, maybe they'll send me to Washington next," McColl said, getting up. "If any messages come for me, I'm staying at the Hotel del Centro."

"Where's that?"

"Just off the plaza on Calle Arista."

"Oh, yes, I think I remember it. You'll find better places on the plaza."

"And be more noticeable."

"Ah, yes, the cloak-and-dagger. I'm sure there're plenty of Oxford chaps in your line of work."

McColl shook the moist hand again and wiped it off on his trousers as he walked back down to the street. The temperature was rising steeply now, but the air was clear, humidity low. He needed a hat, he decided, and headed back toward the plaza, where'd he seen them for sale.

Where should he start? After what he had heard from Wethers, Cumming's fears seemed exaggerated, at least in the short run. But McColl was acutely aware of the gaps in his own knowledge. He had no idea how easy it was to sabotage an oil field or how long it would take to get the oil flowing again. He presumed the Royal Navy had stockpiles of the stuff, but that might be giving it too much credit.

He had to find out what von Schön was doing. He had to find von Schön.

The hotels were the logical place to start, and after buying a fetching straw hat, he worked his way around the plaza. The desk clerk in the third and plushest hotel recognized the photograph. After pocketing the proffered pesos, he said that Señor von Schön had checked out three days ago, and when McColl looked doubtful, he brought out the register to prove it. The clerk had no idea where the man had gone but would gladly look out for him, if sightings were to be rewarded.

McColl assured him they would be and continued around the plaza, on the off chance that the German had simply switched hotels. By noon he had visited every establishment he could find in the vicinity. Von Schön, it seemed, was gone.

After lunch he tried the station, where a train had reportedly left for the capital two or three days before, but either no one there had seen his man or all those he asked were too annoyed at having their siesta disturbed to admit it. Seeing their point, he went back to his room and dozed for a couple of hours.

That evening he worked his way around the hotels again, this time searching for von Schön's fellow countrymen. He eventually found a couple who claimed to be water-treatment specialists, just as von Schön had done in Tsingtau. These two, he decided after several minutes' conversation, really were what they claimed. And more to the point, they had met von Schön, the visiting botanist. He had gone into the interior—collecting specimens, they assumed, although they didn't know what or where—but they expected him back before long. A few days, he had said.

McColl was up at dawn and spent an hour on the roof writing two cables—a brief one to Cumming reporting his arrival, a longer one to Tim Athelbury, apologizing for his nonappearance, announcing his resignation from the firm, and suggesting that Mac be given his job.

After breakfasting at the same café, he called first at the vice-consulate. Wethers was pleased to see him and happy to pass on McColl's request that someone from the Mexico City embassy check the major hotels for von Schön. "They won't like it," Wethers said with something close to relish. "But they'll have to do it."

McColl moved on to the town's telegraph office. This, as he'd hoped, was a basic affair, with only one operator sending and receiving at any given time. The incumbent's name was Alberto Ruiz, and as McColl soon discovered, he ran the office with his brother, Diego. After paying for his two cables and saying how much he liked Mexico, he asked to meet Alberto and his brother after the office closed. "I have a business proposition for you," he said, "and I'll buy you both a beer while you think it over."

They met in the plaza at seven, and neither brother needed much convincing. Alberto stared hard at the photo of von Schön and repeated McColl's proposition out loud to confirm his understanding. "If this man sends a cable, you want a copy. And for each cable we copy, you pay us ten American dollars."

"*Sí.*"

"Okay." He passed the picture to his brother, who studied it for what seemed an age, then shyly nodded his acquiescence.

McColl walked back to his hotel feeling he'd done all he could. If von Schön had gone to the capital, the embassy should find him. And if he was out there making anti-British deals with González, then he'd surely wait until he got back to Tampico before reporting his success to Berlin.

Over the next three days, McColl's confidence slowly eroded. Von Schön did not check back in to his hotel, and

there was no word from either Mexico City or the brothers
Ruiz. It was possible that the embassy staff had been too busy
attending social functions to do the requested chore, possible
that Pablo and Diego had reconsidered their involvement in
international espionage. But he doubted it. As the days went
by, he became increasingly worried that the German was stirring up trouble somewhere else.

Waiting for word certainly lengthened the days. He
explored as much of the town as seemed safe, but there wasn't
much in the way of sights—a relatively new cathedral, a red-
brick customs house that looked far too British for its tropical
surroundings. The intricate wrought-iron balconies gave the
streets a touch of class and also came from Blighty, but being
an actual white man was obviously becoming something of
a liability. Not many minutes went by without a malevolently
whispered "*Gringo*" pursuing him up the street.

Down by the river, he watched small groups of foreigners
being evacuated, and more were doubtless leaving from the
various oil-company wharves, but despite the growing antipa-
thy toward outsiders, he never felt really under threat. Gunfire
was often audible, though it never seemed to come any nearer,
and one morning's unexpected shelling of the northern suburbs by federal gunboats was not repeated. As far as the rest of
the town was concerned, business went on as usual.

He devoted many hours to watching the plaza for von
Schön, nursing *cervezas* and improving his Spanish with a copy
of *Don Quixote* a fellow hotel guest had left behind. He wrote
several letters to Caitlin that he tore up, finally settling for
a simple statement of how much he missed her. How long
the missive would take to reach the Mexican capital, let alone
New York City, didn't bear thinking about.

The vice-consulate received daily news updates from the
embassy, so he dropped in at lunchtime each day to find
out what was happening in the wider world. On Wednesday,

Wethers informed him that Huerta had offered Wilson a compromise, on Thursday that Wilson had turned it down. On Friday the news came through that the Americans had delivered an ultimatum.

"Threatening what?" McColl wanted to know.

"It's not been made public," Wethers said, "but they're planning to blockade Veracruz."

"Why not Tampico?"

Wethers shrugged. "Too close to the fighting, perhaps. If Huerta's enemies take it, then a blockade won't do *him* any damage. And Veracruz is the country's biggest port."

As McColl walked back to the plaza, it crossed his mind that von Schön might have headed in that direction. But why? What interest did the Germans have in Veracruz?

How would he get there? McColl walked on down to the railway station and consulted the beautiful map of the national network that a local Michelangelo had painted on the booking hall's ceiling. Veracruz was only 250 miles down the coast from Tampico, but a rail passenger between the two would have thrice that distance to cover, taking in not only Mexico City but several towns farther north whose names he recognized from war reports. Not a trip to take lightly.

Lying in bed that night, he decided to give it another couple of days and then seek advice from Cumming. Next moment, or so it seemed, his shoulder was being shaken and a voice was urging him to stir himself. The person above smelled far less fragrant than Hsu Ch'ing-lan, and he recognized the clammy hand.

"I've had news from the embassy," Wethers told him. "There's a ship named the *Ypiranga* heading for Veracruz with a cargo of German arms for Huerta. It'll probably be there on Monday or Tuesday."

"The American blockade," McColl murmured, hoisting himself up on one shoulder.

"Precisely. And it might explain why your friend von Schön hasn't turned up. He's probably waiting for the ship in Veracruz."

McColl swung himself out of bed and went to pull back the sheet that served as a curtain. The sky above was blue, the street below still in shadow. "How the hell do I get there?" he asked. "I checked out the trains yesterday, and even if they're running, it would probably take a week."

"There's no other way that I know of."

"What about the roads?" he asked, although he knew the answer already.

"There aren't any. Not to the south, anyway. They're just cart tracks."

McColl nodded. In the unlikely event that an automobile was available, his chances of driving one that sort of distance over unsurfaced roads without a breakdown were negligible. He could probably hire a cart and horses, but the latter would need frequent rests or changing, not to mention food and water.

"I don't even know how you'd get across the river," Wethers was saying. "Last I heard, the ferry was out of service."

The mention of a ferry gave McColl an idea. There had been at least one Royal Navy ship among the flotilla standing guard at the mouth of the Pánuco. It was beyond cheeky, but what was the harm in asking? The ship had to be somewhere, and maybe his presence in Veracruz was worth the price of a run down the coast.

Wethers laughed at the suggestion but agreed to give it a try. He did caution McColl against expecting a swift response—it was already Saturday afternoon in London, so they could hardly expect a reply before Monday morning. McColl feared even that might be optimistic, but for once the empire was firing on all cylinders, and a breathless Wethers came rushing up to McColl's table in the plaza soon after noon on Sunday, inviting him to pack his duds and hurry on down to the dock.

He looked as surprised as McColl felt. They shook hands for the last time, and McColl ran back up to the Hotel del Centro, eliciting mutters of "*Loco*" from most of the Mexicans he passed. He rammed all his possessions into the suitcase, sat on it, and finally managed to fasten the buckle.

The river, when he reached it, looked depressingly empty, and he had a sudden mental picture of himself, the lonely British agent, hopelessly stranded in some steamy foreign back-water. He was still admiring this romantic portrait—"Far From the Country He Serves" seemed a splendid title—when a ten-der rounded the distant bend of the river and headed in toward the wharf. A sailor grabbed McColl's suitcase and helped him aboard, and soon they were gliding back downriver.

None of the crew seemed interested in conversation, but he did catch several curious looks. The empty banks and idle wharves looked even more desolate in daylight, and reach-ing the sparkling ocean was almost a relief. The light cruiser *Glasgow* was waiting about a mile offshore, but most of the ships he'd seen the week before had left, presumably for Veracruz.

The cruiser's retractable steps had been lowered for his embarkation. "A king for a day," he murmured to himself as he climbed toward the deck. The captain was waiting to wel-come him aboard, a tall man of around forty with bright blue eyes in a weather-beaten face. If his opening remarks about running a taxi service might have been mistaken for resent-ment, the boyish smile with which he delivered them ruled out any such implication.

"Sorry to make work for you," McColl replied in similar tone.

"Don't be," the captain said. "We're all bored stiff here and glad of the excuse. If the Yanks and Germans are planning a dustup in Veracruz, we'd love to be there to see it."

That said, as the afternoon slipped by, his ship didn't seem in much of a hurry. It was probably outspeeding the freighter from Galveston, but not by much, and a predicted arrival the following evening came as no great surprise.

Which was probably a blessing, McColl decided—after dark any movement from ship to shore would be that much more discreet.

The sun was dropping behind the distant mountains when the *Glasgow* edged her way into Veracruz's outer harbor and dropped anchor beside another, larger British warship. The scattered lights of the town were visible a mile or more to the southwest, beyond a large fleet of visiting vessels.

McColl was kept waiting while the captain visited the adjacent battleship, then called in to hear the news he returned with. The American ultimatum to Huerta had expired without a satisfactory response, but no punitive action had been taken as yet, either here or in Tampico, and no one knew when or if it would be. But everyone was preparing for the worst. That evening American and other foreign civilians resident in Veracruz had been invited aboard two of the American warships berthed in the inner harbor, and a loose column of several hundred people was now strung out across the port area. The Mexican authorities were conspicuous by their absence, however, and no one seemed to know why. There were a few nervous-looking naval cadets patrolling the docks, but the soldiers, customs officials, and police had vanished. They'd either gone home to wait out the crisis or retreated out of sight to organize resistance. "You could wait until daylight or until we have a better idea what the Yanks are planning," the captain said, "but if the balloon does go up, I doubt we'll be staying in harbor. So if you want to slip ashore, this would probably be the moment. It's a clear night, but at least there's no moon, and a small dinghy shouldn't attract any attention."

"Do you have a map?" McColl asked.

"A chart of the harbor. but I can't help you with the town. We'll row you into the inner harbor, and you can pick your spot to go ashore."

"Fair enough," McColl agreed. He offered the captain his hand. "And thanks."

Ten minutes later he was seated in a gently rocking dinghy watching his suitcase being lowered toward him. The four sailors at the oars looked about sixteen years old, the lieutenant in charge around twenty. The latter had a chart spread across his thighs, but McColl doubted there'd be light enough to read it.

They pulled away from the side of the *Glasgow*, the swish of the oars barely audible above the sound of the harbor swell. As the captain had said, the sky was clear, the mountains farther inland silhouetted against a field of stars. The air was warm, a slight breeze blowing in from the sea.

Warships were berthed on both sides of the main channel, sailors moving on the dimly lit decks, figures sometimes visible in the yellowish glow of a bridge. Up ahead, through the wide gateway leading to the inner harbor, McColl could see more ships, both civilian and military. And, beyond them, low white buildings beneath a barely discernible halo of light.

The fresh smell of the sea was now mingling with something much less attractive, an underlying reek of decay, faint at first but growing more acrid with each passing minute.

The seamen rowed on past the grim-looking fortress that commanded the entrance to the inner harbor. Two small American warships were anchored on the town side, one blazing with lights. Directly ahead of the dinghy, a pier lined with warehouses jutted out into the water, playing host to a couple of passenger steamers. "Behind that lot?" the lieutenant whispered in McColl's ear, extending a finger toward the pier.

"Looks a good bet," McColl agreed. The blend of nerves and excitement took him back to his childhood, walking out onto the pitch for an important game of soccer.

It was a good bet. There were no signs of life in the harbor's innermost reaches, and the only ship at the two small jetties beyond the main pier was sitting so low in the water it might have been touching the bottom. The lieutenant steered the dinghy along a quayside wall until they found a ladder of rungs, then handed McColl the end of the rope and quietly wished him luck.

After hauling himself up the rungs, McColl hoisted up his suitcase, untied the rope, and dropped it back down. Save for a trio of railway wagons, the jetty stretched dark and empty before him. He set off quickly but slowed his pace after wedging a foot in the inlaid track and almost twisting an ankle.

There were industrial buildings to his right, but the bulk of the town was off to his left, and he followed the tracks that curved in that direction. The large building in his path turned out to be the railway station; it had apparently closed for the day, but soldiers were visible at the far end of the platform, gathered beside one simmering locomotive. Walking across the empty concourse and out the other side, he found himself opposite the American consulate, its flag still flying, windows dark and shuttered. A few doors down, a large signboard announced the Hotel Alemán, which was presumably favored by Germans. There were lights in some of the windows, and McColl was tempted to visit reception and ask after Rainer von Schön.

Tomorrow would do.

Turning left, he walked down a wide avenue—INDEPENDENCIA, the sign proclaimed—until he reached the inevitable square at the heart of the town. The Plaza de la Constitución boasted two impressive structures: a government building with a domed roof and a Moorish arcade at the harbor end, a church with an ornate tower and steeple at the other. The space between them contained a bandstand, several lofty coconut palms, and many stone benches. Rather to McColl's surprise, the seats and pathways were full of people enjoying the balmy evening air—if the locals expected Yankee retribution, they didn't expect it till morning.

And there were still Americans in residence. At the tables outside the imposing Hotel Diligencias, one group was loudly discussing the inevitable occupation and wondering out loud how the locals would react. "They'll just put a higher price tag on their daughters," one said, eliciting a gale of drunken laughter.

This was obviously a hotel favored by foreigners, one of whom might be von Schön. McColl walked in and asked the desk clerk. "We do have some Germans," the man confessed, reaching for the register. But if von Schön was using that name, he wasn't one of them.

It was too late for scouring the town. McColl took a room for himself and hoped he wouldn't run into the German on his way to the bathroom. On the following day, he would have to establish whether or not his adversary was actually in Veracruz. He sincerely hoped he was—if not, he'd have to tell Cumming that he'd commandeered one of His Majesty's cruisers for a wild-goose chase.

The sky had clouded over when he got up next morning, and the gyrating fronds of the coconut palms suggested that a storm was on the way. But there was no sign of unusual activity in the square or the harbor—the people of Veracruz were going about their normal business, apparently oblivious to incoming arms shipments or associated American threats.

The Hotel Diligencias supplied hot water and a bountiful breakfast, and then he had a cable to encrypt announcing his arrival. It was past ten when he finally emerged and set off down Independencia toward the Hotel Alemán. At the hotel desk, an old man with rheumy eyes glanced at the photograph, shook his head, and reached out a hand for the pesos.

"Try with your spectacles," McColl suggested after noticing the pair on the desk. The old man was still fumbling with these when a youth with similar features came out of a room at the rear and examined the picture over the old man's shoulder. "He is here," he said. "Not at this moment—he went out an hour ago. But he is staying here. His name is Schneider."

The boy proved equally helpful when it came to finding the post office—the building was just around the corner, on the other side of the Terminal Plaza. It seemed unusually busy to McColl, but maybe Veracruzanos were overfond of writing letters. Or perhaps a harbor full of American warships was making people nervous.

His cable accepted, he went back outside. The plaza seemed full of hurrying people, all moving in different directions. As his eyes followed one group toward a gap between two warehouses, he noticed a small boat crammed with troops moving from right to left. As this craft disappeared behind a building, another came into view. They had to be heading for the large pier that he and his helpers had passed on the previous evening.

The Americans were coming ashore. And they were drawing a gamut of reactions from the townsfolk of Veracruz. Some were heading for the metaphorical hills, others for the water's edge to get a better view.

McColl joined the latter, as least as far as the end of the northernmost warehouse. From there he could see the troops flooding up the harbor steps and forming into units on the quay. The ones in pointed hats and khaki fatigues were marines; those in white, their bell-bottoms gathered in canvas leggings, were sailors. They all seemed heavily laden, carrying bulky knapsacks or haversacks and shouldering Springfield rifles.

There was no sign of Mexican troops in the streets behind him, and the local civilians seemed more curious than angry. There was even a small group of American visitors among the latter, and if the two nationalities were exhibiting any hostility toward each other, it was more in the manner of sporting rivals than citizens of countries at war.

All of which boded well, McColl thought. A quick and peaceful demonstration of American power and righteousness, a long-suffering "What can you expect from such people?" Mexican response, and things would soon return to normal. The Germans would be left with nothing to work with.

The troops were on the move, heading straight toward him. He backed away across the Terminal Plaza and took up position on the first street back from the waterfront. As the marines disappeared from view behind the Hotel Terminal and railway station, two columns of sailors started toward the town center, advancing along either side of the warehouses that stood between McColl and the harbor.

He decided to keep ahead of their advance rather than risk being stranded behind it and was almost at the next street corner when a shot rang out somewhere above his head. He hardly had time to look up before a fusillade of fire broke out all around him. Looking back, he saw one of the American sailors drop to the ground, a splash of red on his virginal trousers. As two comrades stooped to pick him back up, others either dashed for cover or sprawled themselves out on the pavement, rifles searching for targets.

More firing was audible in the distance, much more, as if a thousand Mexicans had been waiting for that single shot to start their war.

As if on cue, a thin rivulet of cold sweat ran down McColl's back.

A bullet bit into stone above his head, showering him with chips. He stood where he was for a second, stupidly looking around, then set off in a crouching run for the corner of the building. He had only ten yards to cover but ample time to imagine as many bullets thudding into his back.

He rounded the corner without thought of what lay beyond,

but luck was with him—no Mexican soldiers were advancing up the narrow street to do battle with the Americans. He soon realized that most of the would-be resisters had taken to the rooftops and upper stories. He could see guns protruding from several windows and hear the sputter of their fire on the sailors below. As he watched, one Mexican came tumbling out of a second-floor window, his head striking the cobblestones with a sickening crack.

"Discretion, et cetera," he muttered to himself. He jogged away from the battle zone, keeping as close to the walls as he could and frequently glancing back over his shoulder. His best guess put the Plaza de la Constitución a block to his left, and the next street up should bring him back to his hotel, which seemed the obvious sanctuary.

He was halfway to the relevant corner when a group of Mexicans came around it. They weren't wearing uniforms but all were brandishing weapons of one sort or another. And if the expression on their faces was anything to go by, they were more than a little eager to use them. As if to confirm that fact, one man raised a pistol, loosely pointed it in McColl's direction, and casually pulled the trigger.

The bullet sang harmlessly wide, and he didn't wait for another. Ducking between two buildings, he sprinted down the passage and into a courtyard, startling a woman who was hanging her washing and grabbing the attention of two huge dogs. The woman screamed, dropped her basket, and ran for the nearest door, but the dogs were less intimidated, inching toward him with slavering mouths and ominous growls. McColl felt like screaming himself but managed not to. Frantically looking around, he spied one fence that looked vaguely jumpable and headed straight for it, dogs in pursuit. He couldn't remember vaulting anything since army training, but he just about cleared the top, and falling to earth in a damp pile of ill-smelling refuse only partly diminished his sense of achievement. As he got to his feet, the dogs began barking fit to burst, but not, it seemed, at him. Through a crack in the still-quivering fence, he saw two young Mexicans backing away, their shining machetes thrust out to ward off the dripping fangs.

McColl beat a hasty retreat in the opposite direction, tracing a path through the maze of alleys until he reached a restaurant kitchen's door. The staff looked askance and wrinkled their noses at him but gestured him on through to the front door, which, much to his relief, opened onto the empty plaza. Away to his left, toward the harbor, a machine gun was adding its familiar rattle to the single shots of rifles. At the bottom of the square, occasional puffs of smoke offered evidence of gunmen on the Hotel Oriente's roof. The fighting hadn't yet reached the northern end, but it was only a matter of time. As McColl watched, half a dozen men with rifles disappeared through the open door of the Parochial Church, presumably intent on manning its tower.

More surprisingly, several white guests were sitting at the tables outside the Hotel Diligencias, reading their papers and drinking aperitifs with a sangfroid that verged on the ludicrous. Every now and then, one man or other would glance toward the bottom of the square, reassure himself that nothing untoward was actually heading his way, and go back to what he was doing.

It was quite insane, but also strangely calming. Breathing a little easier, McColl worked his way around the edge of the square to the hotel entrance.

Ten minutes later he was soaking in the bath, having rigged a sheet across the window to catch any flying glass. His head was still vulnerable to the strayest of bullets, but if fate proved that malign, he would probably never know it.

He wondered whether the Americans had expected a fight and supposed that they probably hadn't. In one way they'd been right—McColl had seen no sign that the Mexican army was offering official resistance. But even he could have told Washington that ordinary Mexicans would put up a struggle if they could. Why did Americans always feel that they'd cornered the market in patriotism?

Von Schön would certainly be pleased—the Americans were doing his work for him. If the Yanks killed enough Mexicans, there would be nothing the British—or McColl himself—could do to prevent an alliance between Huerta and the Germans, an alliance that would deprive the navy of its oil.

Huerta might lose the civil war, but if the Americans did enough damage, even that wouldn't matter. By then all Mexicans would be united in their loathing of Washington and its British ally, and any new leader would have to embrace the wretched Kaiser.

It was a mess all right, and not one that McColl could clear up. He dried himself, moved his mattress onto the floor, and spent the rest of the daylight hours reading, dozing, and stealing glances around the edge of his window. By four o'clock the firing was dying down, but the Mexican irregulars were still holding most of their original positions, and no American soldiers had arrived in the plaza below.

When darkness fell, he went downstairs, introduced himself to the other guests as a freelance journalist, and set himself to listen. The consensus among the foreign visitors and Mexican staff had the Americans in control of the railway station, yards, and central port area, which included the post office, customs houses, and the old Juárez Lighthouse. The municipal palace and the Hotel Oriente, whose silhouettes could be seen at the foot of the square, were still in local hands.

The composition of the Mexican resistance had become clearer over the last few hours. It was now known that the official army had retreated up the railway line, along with all but one locomotive, and set up camp some ten miles outside the city. Before leaving, its commander—or someone else in authority—had seen fit to free the city's prisoners, both political and criminal, after offering them reprieves in exchange for their taking up arms against the foreign invader. It was several hundred of these *rayados* along with a similar number of ordinary citizens and a small force of naval cadets, who had taken the fight to the Americans.

There was much debate as to what would happen next, but as far as McColl could see, there was only one real possibility. The Americans could hardly retreat with their tails between their legs, and they certainly couldn't stay where they were, so they had to take the city. The only real question was whether they had enough men to do it straightaway or would need to wait for reinforcements. After joining several curious journalists in a cautious reconnaissance of the Mexican-held portion of the city center, McColl found himself hoping it would be the former. Most of the fighters busily building barricades seemed happy to talk to gringo journalists, but the frequent screams of invisible women and the sound of gunfire far from the known front line suggested that more than a few *rayados* were making up for time lost in prison.

Back in his hotel room, McColl pondered his own course of action. With the Hotel Alemán now behind American lines, he had no way of monitoring von Schön and his activities. All he could do was sit tight until the fighting was over, and the Diligencias at least offered safety in numbers.

He went to bed with the curtains drawn, but every now and then a ship's searchlight would sweep across the window, like a monster in a child's dream, trying to force its way in.

He was woken by the sound of his window shattering. The curtains had caught the splintered glass, but the bullet had buried itself deep in the plaster of the opposite wall, a few feet to his left.

He had slept later than he meant to, and it was fully light outside. Knowing that it was foolish but utterly unable to resist the temptation, he slowly edged an eye around the window frame for a look at the plaza. Several uniformed figures were running along the inside of the municipal palace's arcade while puffs of smoke erupted on the roof. There was no sign of movement in the square itself.

As he pulled back his head, he heard people running past his door. The footsteps receded, and by the time he cracked open the door, the corridor was empty. But now he heard movement above—whoever they were, they were on the hotel roof. Mexican fighters, most likely, lying in wait for the Americans. If so, his wake-up bullet had been the first of many.

He dressed hurriedly, keeping well away from the window. Downstairs, he found that foreign guests had occupied the kitchen and were cooking their own breakfasts. Most of the Mexican staff had obviously decided that this was an excellent day to take off, and McColl found the mood reminiscent of a children's party abandoned by parents. It was only when one of the large front windows of the restaurant exploded inward that hysteria turned to panic and everyone tumbled down the stairs to the basement.

They could still hear the rattle of gunfire down there, and a few minutes later there were several louder booms, which one old American gentleman identified as naval guns. "They're shelling the city," he announced, with an enthusiasm few of his fellow residents seemed to share.

One thunderous explosion nearby caused a shower of plaster from the basement ceiling, but the big guns soon fell silent and all they could hear in the basement was the clatter of machine guns and rifle fire. They had been there about an hour when an American sailor in coffee-stained whites appeared at the top of the steps and told them that the building was almost secure. "We're just mopping up on the roof."

After twenty minutes they were given permission to go back upstairs but were warned against leaving the hotel. Purely out of curiosity, McColl tagged along with a couple of real journalists intent on visiting the roof, and he almost wished he hadn't. Around twenty Mexican corpses were spread across the wide expanse, most missing sizable chunks of their heads. There were almost as many wounded, and two American women were doing what they could to help, tearing up sheets for bandages and offering a few words of comfort.

"We tried to surrender," one man was saying in his native Spanish. "We threw down our rifles, but first they shouted and then they shot us."

The woman didn't understand what the man was saying, but one of the journalists did. "What did they shout?" he asked.

"I don't know," the man said. "They shout in English."

It was probably "Put up your hands," McColl thought. And when they didn't—bang.

In the plaza the fighting seemed over, but gunfire was still echoing across the city. There was one battle going on in the streets behind the hotel, another in the opposite direction, out toward the harbor. The Americans were clearly advancing, but far from having it all their own way.

As one of the women pointed out, the rising heat made it necessary to move both wounded and dead. The corpses would soon start to smell, and the audience of *zopilotes* would swell still further. As the only refuse collectors the city possessed, Veracruz's vultures were protected by law and seemed well aware of that fact. Several flew over to perch on the parapet and were driven away only by a concerted flailing of arms.

Once sufficient volunteers had been gathered, the wounded were carried down to the restaurant and laid out in lines to await a doctor. The corpses were wrapped up in sheets, brought down, and left in a pile in the plaza until a cart could be found to take them away. It was a rotten job, and once they had finished, McColl joined several of his fellow bearers in sharing a bottle of the hotel's brandy.

With nothing better to do, he went back up to the roof alone, thinking to follow the course of the battle. The machine guns had fallen silent, leaving only the occasional crack of a rifle—a Mexican sniper perhaps, or an angry American avenging a comrade. Veracruz was an occupied city.

In the plaza below, an incredible sight met his eyes—a posse of marines bearing musical instruments were setting themselves up in the central bandstand. A few minutes more and "The Stars and Stripes Forever" was rolling out across the plaza. McColl listened for a few moments, shook his head in wonder, and zigzagged his way to the steps leading down between the pools of congealing blood.

There was a de facto curfew that Wednesday evening, but by Thursday morning the occupiers were eagerly encouraging the resumption of normal life. McColl took to the streets somewhat gingerly, the pistol from San Francisco wedged in the small of his back. But the sporadic gunfire seemed far away, and most shops and cantinas were lifting their shutters, albeit with some trepidation.

The Hotel Alemán was open for business, a third family member behind the desk. The son and father of the two he had met, McColl guessed, as the man examined the usual photograph. "The bird lover," he finally said in Spanish. "Señor Schneider. He checked out an hour ago."

"Do you know where he's going?"

The man shook his head. "But he asked about boats to Guatemala. A paradise for birds, he said."

A likely story, McColl thought, handing over some pesos. Outside on the pavement, he stopped to consider his next move. Where had the German really gone?

One bit of news had reached the hotel the previous

evening—the *Ypiranga* had arrived that afternoon with Huerta's arms shipment, but the Americans had refused to allow its unloading. As far as McColl knew, the German freighter was still at anchor in the outer harbor—might von Schön be on board?

It would have been difficult to reach the *Ypiranga* when the harbor was swarming with American boats. It would be hard to get anywhere, come to that. There were no passenger ships leaving Veracruz, no trains. The Americans would be watching the roads out of town, and there was nowhere the German could walk to.

No, McColl decided—von Schön was still in Veracruz. He would have to conduct another search, starting with the other hotels.

He walked across to the Hotel Terminal and immediately struck gold. Señor Tubach had checked in only that morning. A journalist, of course, all the way from Vienna.

McColl went back to the Diligencias, where several foreign patrons were sitting outside lamenting their lukewarm drinks. Strenuous efforts had been made to repair the shell-inflicted damage to the hotel's ice plant, but all to no avail—replacement parts would have to be ordered from the makers in Chicago.

The suffering some people had to endure!

The waiter on duty was the one McColl wanted to see. A youth of around sixteen, Ernesto had been one of the hotel's few employees to turn up for work on the previous day—he couldn't afford to lose a day's wages. During their confinement in the basement, he and McColl had talked for a while, and the boy's natural intelligence and fervent ambition had been only too evident. Now McColl asked Ernesto if he knew of anyone who might like to earn some extra pesos keeping an eye on a rival reporter. "Someone with a brain," he insisted. "Someone as clever as you are."

A couple of hours later, Ernesto brought his cousin Hugo

up to McColl's room. He looked about fourteen, with floppy black hair and impish eyes, and it didn't take McColl long to work out that the boy was sharp enough for the job at hand. After showing him von Schön's photograph and telling him where the German was staying, he outlined the task: "I want to know where he goes, what he does, who he meets. But he must not realize that he's being followed."

Hugo nodded sagely, and after several minutes' bargaining the two fees were agreed upon—one for him, one for his agent, Ernesto.

After lunch at the hotel, McColl joined a group of journalists keen to examine the destruction wrought on the naval academy. The damage done by the five-inch guns of the *Chester* and the *San Francisco* seemed almost slight from the outside—cornices chipped away, several windows blown in—but once one was inside, the full force of the onslaught became apparent. The bodies of the young cadets had been removed, but there were bloodstains everywhere and what looked like pieces of flesh stuck to the upper walls. The cadets' possessions, bedding, and furniture were strewn over the floor in broken profusion, like so much bloody confetti. Every now and then, a recognizable object would meet the eye—a hairbrush, a glove, the page of a letter. In almost every room, a sign had been posted forbidding the taking of photographs, and it wasn't hard to see why.

Back in the Diligencias bar, he sat with a beer and listened to the journalists swap tales of "overzealous action" by the occupying forces. Resistance had not been expected, and the shock of losses had led many to lash out blindly at the first available Mexican. Women and children had died in their parlors because snipers had perched on their roofs.

Not surprisingly, the local Mexican politicians had refused that morning's American offer to resume control of civic affairs. The national constitution forbade them from serving invaders, they had told the American commander. Which might be true but was only half the story—they knew very well that their people would never forgive them.

Had reports of American excesses filtered beyond the city? No one seemed to know. The mere fact of the American occupation had convulsed opinion in Mexico City, where the embassy was besieged by demonstrators, and white foreigners with even an ounce of sense were keeping to their hotels. Huerta, however, was willing to let them leave, and a first trainload of Americans, Britons, and Germans had reportedly departed the capital that morning. The American authorities in Veracruz were sending a train out to meet them, at the point six miles from town where the Mexican army had torn up the rails.

Next morning McColl took to the town on his own. The night before had been significantly quieter, and now an hour would often pass without someone somewhere firing a gun, but he still felt safer knowing he had one in his belt and kept a vigilant eye on the roofs and windows above.

On the far side of the battered Hotel Oriente, he came upon a group of off-duty marines teaching Mexican children how to play baseball. Marines and children were all smiles, which was more than could be said for the watching Mexican adults, who were tight-lipped to a man. McColl found it hard to blame them—as he walked through the streets, the ravages of one day's fighting were everywhere. Only a handful of buildings had been destroyed, but hundreds had been damaged, and very few walls had escaped being scarred by bullets. Several bore the slogan MUERAN LOS GRINGOS.

There were funeral processions that morning. He watched one from a respectful—and safe—distance, was moved by the dignity of the mourners and the melancholy song of a trumpet, and then arrived back at the plaza just as the marine band began stomping its way through another slice of patriotic bombast. He would have murdered them all if he could, so it wasn't hard to imagine what the Mexicans were thinking.

Up in his room a few minutes later, he was looking out through the star-shaped hole in his window when he spotted a familiar figure crossing the plaza below. Von Schön was wearing a white tropical suit and hat, with a small pouch on a strap strung like a bandolier across one shoulder. What was in it—binoculars?

The German had company, a portly Mexican in high-heeled boots who was jabbing the air with his fingers as if dispensing an explanation.

And there was young Hugo, ambling along behind them at a very sensible distance, gazing from side to side like a peon new to the city.

The three of them walked on past the bandstand and into the street at the bottom that ran past the Hotel México.

Hugo was only a few minutes late for their six-o'clock appointment. He had followed Señor Tubach when he went out the previous afternoon, stood guard outside his hotel once he'd retired for the evening, and followed him again today.

"I saw you cross the plaza around one o'clock," McColl told the boy. "Who was the other man?"

"His name's Rivera. He's well known in Veracruz. Some people call him a man of the people, but others just think he's a troublemaker."

"And what was he doing with Señor Tubach?"

"Acting as his guide, I think. They went to lots of places together."

"What sorts of places?"

Hugo shrugged. "Places to do with death. They went to the naval academy yesterday, and then to a field near the power plant where bodies were being burned. This morning it was the fiscal wharf. The Americans have dug a big grave there, and they're bringing bodies from all over the city."

"And what did Señor Tubach do at these places?" McColl asked, already knowing the answer.

"He took photographs, but not when the Americans were watching. He has a type of camera that I've never seen before— it's really small."

"Which he keeps in the pouch around his neck?" Now that he thought about it, McColl remembered reading that one German camera company had been trying to manufacture a pocket-size instrument.

Hugo confirmed as much.

"And this afternoon?"

"After the fiscal wharf, they visited a house on Cinco de Mayo—I don't know why, but the number was seventy-five— and then they went to the whorehouse on Calle Morelos. But they didn't stay long enough to enjoy themselves. They came back out with one of the whores and brought her to the Hotel México. I have a friend who works there, and he says they took her to the room at the top where three men died on Tuesday. When they came out, she was counting pesos. Rivera walked off with her, and Señor Tubach went back to the Hotel Terminal."

McColl smiled, told him he'd done well, and added a bonus to the agreed sum.

"Tomorrow?" Hugo asked hopefully, pocketing the bills.

"I don't think so," McColl decided after a moment's thought. "But I do want to know when he checks out. Do you have any friends at the Terminal?"

"I can buy one," the boy said, tapping his pocket.

McColl let him out, then wandered across to the window. The eastern sky was almost dark, the harbor lights rippling in the water.

So that was it, he thought—a propaganda coup. Though could you call it propaganda if it was actually true? The photograph taken at the Hotel México would have been staged, but who would question it among so many genuine images? It wasn't hard to imagine how von Schön had used the prostitute—a ravaged, half-naked Mexican heroine, lying in pools of patriots' blood.

How was he going to stop the man? He had to get hold of the camera and any other damning evidence of American bad behavior, real or faked. One obvious solution was to take the whole matter to the American authorities, who would presumably ensure that the photographs never saw the light of day.

But would they? Englishmen tended to assume that Americans preferred them to Germans and thought of the latter as their common enemy, but the facts suggested otherwise. There were many Americans who heartily loathed their British cousins, and, like any other nationality, they had their share of idiot officials. The last thing he needed was an American too prejudiced or stupid to appreciate the international ramifications of these pictures being published.

He'd be better off dealing with the business himself, and the best way of doing so looked like the simplest—he would pay von Schön a visit, take the camera away at gunpoint, and throw it into the sea. Unless he shot the German and threw him in, too, von Schön would be free to take his revenge, but what did that matter? The pictures would be gone.

It would be risky. Von Schön would have a gun of his own, and McColl would need to surprise him. He would wait until one in the morning and trust that his last American dollars would be sufficient to tempt the night clerk.

There were still people in the bar when he slipped out of the hotel, but the moonlit plaza was empty. He kept to the shadows as he made his way down Independencia, but the only other thing moving was a sad-looking dog, which padded after him for a couple of blocks before running out of interest or energy. There was no sign of an American patrol, which suited him fine. If his meeting with von Schön went badly wrong, he wanted no witnesses to his being out.

A single yellow lamp was burning over the entrance to the Hotel Terminal. He looked around, half expecting to see Hugo lurking in the shadows, but if von Schön had returned for the night, then the boy would have gone home to bed.

He walked in, expecting to find the night clerk asleep, but the young man concerned had a girl in his lap. From the sound of the panting, it seemed safe to assume that at least their tongues were entwined, and he felt almost cruel interrupting.

McColl said "*Buenas noches*," quietly, and the heads leaped apart. "I am a friend of Señor Tubach—"

"He is no longer here," the young man said automatically. The girl just looked stunned.

"When did he leave?" McColl asked disbelievingly.

"One hour ago."

"Where was he going?"

"He did not say. Now . . ."

The girl turned her face to McColl, adding her own appeal for privacy. She had a beautiful face.

He wished them both a good night and walked back out. Where the hell had von Schön gone? There was no way he could wander around town checking out all the other hotels, not with a curfew in force.

It suddenly occurred to McColl that Hugo might have followed the German to his new hotel before he called it a day. But he had never asked for the boy's address. A mistake, no doubt about it. Now he would have to wait, and probably till morning.

But could he afford to? As he worked his way back up

Independencia, he tried to put himself in von Schön's shoes. Even if the American authorities would let him, there was no point in publishing the pictures in Veracruz, because the town was effectively cut off from the rest of Mexico. The capital was where they would do the most damage, but how could he get them there? He wouldn't risk the mail, not with the Americans in charge at the post office. Someone would have to take them, and McColl couldn't imagine von Schön trusting anyone else with the job.

The only way there was by train. One had left early on Thursday morning, steamed the six miles to the rail break, and returned with three hundred foreigners from Mexico City. It had been scheduled to collect another batch that morning, and he had no reason for thinking it hadn't. But were the trains from the capital waiting for passengers traveling back? Who would be? Not foreigners, and he doubted that the Americans were allowing any locals to leave.

The two journalists still propping up the Diligencias bar agreed that this was unlikely, which eased his mind a little. The news that the last two trains had left long before daybreak had the opposite effect, and he'd more or less resolved to head for the station when a breathless Hugo rushed in from the plaza. "Señor Tubach has gone to the train, and I think it is leaving in a few minutes."

As McColl ran the four blocks, slowing only once in a vain attempt to placate the stitch in his side, he cursed himself for not searching the station earlier. He'd passed it twice on his way to and from the Hotel Terminal, but nothing he'd seen or heard had suggested that anyone was inside, let alone preparing a train for departure.

The reason, as he now found out, was depressingly simple. The train—a locomotive and several coaches—was standing out beyond the platforms, another few hundred yards away. He forced himself into motion once more, stumbling across loose stones until he reached the flattened ground between the tracks. As if eager to thwart him, the loco released a huge plume of steam, which hung in the moonlit air until further, more purposeful blasts scattered it.

The train was beginning to move, and it was several despairing seconds before McColl realized, with a surge of hope, just how slowly it was actually traveling. He was still gaining, and as long as his legs held out, he could catch it.

It was a close thing. He must have run another quarter mile before his reaching fingers grasped the rail of the rear vestibule steps. After hauling himself aboard, he just stood there for a couple of minutes, gasping for breath as the tracks receded beneath him.

He told himself there was no hurry—at this speed the train would take the best part of an hour to travel six miles.

Once he had his breath back, he pulled out his pistol and opened the door to the rear carriage. There were no seats inside, just a couple of crates, on which two British sailors were sitting. The British, McColl remembered someone saying, had taken charge of at least one of the trains to the rail break.

The sailors were shocked to see him—or his pistol at least—and looked more than relieved when he put it away. "I work for a special department of the Admiralty," he told them, more or less truthfully. "Who's in charge of the train?"

"That's a bone of contention," one of them said. "The Yanks agreed to us having it tonight, but then they found out their ambassador is on the one we're meeting, so then they wanted it back. Couldn't bear the thought of him being met by the wrong flag."

"So who's in charge?" McColl asked again, with as much patience as he could muster.

"Captain Hogg-Smythe is our man, and theirs is a major, I think. We're flying both flags, if they're still stuck on. We had a devil of a job fixing them to the front of the engine."

"Okay," McColl said. "Could one of you go and fetch the captain for me? I need to talk to him, without any of the passengers seeing me."

"There's only one. The German bird-watcher, and he looks harmless enough."

"Just do it," McColl suggested.

"Okay, okay. Keep your hair on."

The sailor was back in a couple of minutes with a tall, fair-haired young Englishman in a shining white uniform. He smiled at McColl, shook his hand, and asked him what the blazes he wanted.

McColl shepherded him down to the end of the car and explained the situation as briefly as he could. Rather to his surprise, Hogg-Smythe got it straightaway—he was clearly not as dumb as he looked. "So let's go and get them," he proposed.

"What about your American counterpart?"

"I can't see he'll have any objection. Quite the reverse. He'll probably want to arrest the blighter. But let's go and ask him—he's two cars up. The bird-watcher fellow has a carriage to himself at the front."

They walked forward and found the American major—his name was Matheson—dozing in his seat. He was also quick on the uptake and equally willing to confront von Schön. He'd been lucky with these two, McColl told himself as they walked on up to the front car. Through the windows the Mexican countryside looked flat and uninspiring, but as they crossed between cars, the moonlit mountains in the distance looked decidedly inviting.

Von Schön was sitting with his back to them and didn't bother turning his head at the sound of approaching footsteps. The surprise in his eyes when McColl appeared in his line of sight quickly gave way to the wryest of smiles.

"Hello," McColl said, sitting down in the opposite seat.

"Herr McColl. How unexpected."

"Herr von Schön. If that's your real name."

"It is. We met on German soil, remember? No need for an alias there."

"Of course. Well, we need to search your suitcase, I'm afraid. And to confiscate your camera."

Von Schön nodded, as if expecting nothing less.

The camera was in the suitcase, the smallest camera McColl had ever seen. He put it in his pocket and went through the rest of the contents. There was one printed photograph, showing a small group of American soldiers, arms held triumphantly high, boots firmly planted on the backs of Mexican corpses.

"And your wallet," McColl remembered in time.

The German handed it over.

There was nothing in it but Mexican money and the picture of von Schön's wife and daughter that he'd produced in Tsingtau. The former could be used for bribes, but there seemed no point in confiscating the latter, so McColl returned it.

Von Schön glanced at the woman and child and handed the photograph back. "An actress and her niece," he confessed. "I can't even remember their names."

The American major was growing impatient. "You'll be coming back to Veracruz," he told the German.

"You're arresting me?" Von Schön asked. "For taking a few photographs?"

"Espionage is espionage," Major Matheson insisted. "If my superiors think otherwise, you can catch tomorrow's train."

McColl turned to the American. "Could I have a private word?" he asked. "If the captain will look after our friend here."

The two men went out onto the vestibule platform. "I think we should let him go," McColl said without preamble. "Hear me out," he added as the major began to protest. "You don't want an open conflict with the Germans, not with the situation in Tampico the way that it is. And you don't want to make a martyr of this particular German. If the Mexicans find out why he's been arrested, you might as well publish the photographs—it'll look like you're punishing a German for siding with your victims."

Matheson was not stupid. "I take your point," he said after a few moments' thought. "So what'll we do with him?"

"Just let him go on to the capital. He can't do much harm without the pictures."

"I hope you're right."

"So do I. Let me go and talk to him." McColl walked back in and asked Hogg-Smythe to join the major.

Von Schön was not exactly grateful for the offer. "And what if I prefer American custody?" he asked.

"That's no longer on the table," McColl lied. "I managed to convince the major that arresting a German would be embarrassing after Tampico, so he's given you to us. If you come back to Veracruz, you'll be traveling home with me on a British warship."

Von Schön gave him a look, uncertainty warring with disbelief.

"But I'd rather you didn't," McColl went on. "Not after you saved my life in San Francisco."

"I'm beginning to regret that," the German said, smiling as he did so. "But not really," he added more seriously. "Dying for one's country in war is one thing. Dying for one's country in peace seems . . . I don't know—disproportionate?"

"So you'll take the train on?"

"I suppose I must. But I expect we'll meet again."

McColl offered his hand. "In happier times, perhaps."

Von Schön took it and gave him a sad smile. "I doubt that."

Ten minutes later McColl watched the German stride off past the hissing locomotive and up the empty track bed. It was a two-kilometer hike across the cactus-studded plain to where the rails resumed, but a beautiful night for a stroll. If McColl had known how to work the confiscated camera, he'd have taken a picture. As it was, he just raised a clenched fist to the starry heavens. He was, he had to admit, feeling pleased with himself.

He took the train again the next day and this time walked the gap himself. The Mexicans on the other side had refused to allow any Americans up the line, so the British had volunteered an officer named Tweedie to retrieve those foreigners still trapped in the capital, and McColl was along for the ride. The trip was punctuated by arguments with Mexican officers, but Tweedie, in true imperial style, had persuaded the first of these to lend him a train and all the others to let it through. Mexico City proved remarkably fraught, the locals far from friendly, but while Tweedie saw to business, gathering a horde of would-be refugees for the return trip, McColl warned the embassy to keep a watch on von Schön. On impulse he also dropped in at the central post office. Expecting a cold shoulder at best, and demands for his arrest at worst, he was pleasantly surprised to be handed a letter from Caitlin. He read it in a nearby park, surrounded by birdsong and pantomime whispers of "*Gringo.*"

She had written the letter not long after he left, but he was still astonished to receive it—civil wars were clearly less obstructive than he'd thought. Her new job was going well, but she missed him. She was glad he was in the capital and warned him against venturing anywhere near the Gulf Coast—"I fear my government is about to do something stupid in that neck of the woods." She asked him to write back.

He did so, bookending a glibly concocted false history of the last few weeks with honest protestations of his feelings for her. It felt wrong, but what else could he do? He took the finished article back to the post office and was almost comforted by the look on the clerk's face, which suggested that it would never reach her anyway.

The return journey proved equally eventful, with several hundred semihysterical refugees adding to the excitement. White people weren't used to being hungry, scared, and in fear of their lives, McColl realized, particularly in a brown people's country. It didn't bring out the best in them.

But they all reached the safety of occupied Veracruz, where boats were waiting to carry them forward to mother- or fatherland. There was certainly no room for them in the occupied city, which seemed fuller than ever now that the US Navy had decanted another few thousand marines. The final snipers had been mopped up, but off-duty troops brimming with tequila were posing a new threat to life, limb, and a woman's right to say no.

Three days after his return from Mexico City, a young Royal Naval officer arrived at McColl's hotel-room door with fresh instructions from Cumming. He was to stay in Veracruz for the time being, keep an eye on the local Germans, and, if the Americans insisted on shooting themselves in the foot, try to limit the damage. Another visit to Tampico might be in order, but Cumming left that to McColl's own discretion.

As far as he could tell from the bits and pieces of news that reached him, the battle for Tampico was coming to a climax, and before he ventured north, he thought he would wait until one side or the other was in undisputed control. Over the next couple of weeks, he did as Cumming had asked, but as far as he could tell, all the Germans still in Veracruz were genuine businessmen of one sort or another. More to the point, perhaps, the wider situation was growing less congenial for anyone intent on stirring up trouble. President Wilson was certainly responsible for the initial blunder of occupying Veracruz, but so far he had avoided making matters worse by sanctioning the march his generals wanted on the Mexican capital. Chile, Argentina, and Brazil had also soothed the relationship between the two nations by offering to mediate, and talks were under way at Niagara Falls between the Americans and Mexicans from both sides of the civil war. The war itself was clearly going against Huerta, so any German hope of using him against Washington seemed to be fading.

All in all, McColl felt his job was done, and there were only so many ways of filling an idle hour in an increasingly steamy Veracruz.

Toward the end of May, boredom got the better of him and he begged a ride up the coast on an American refugee ship. Tampico had fallen to the anti-Huerta forces almost a fortnight earlier, and the town, though sadly scarred by the fighting, was already settling back into its habitual torpor. McColl found no trace of German plots—in fact, over the past few weeks the German sailors and diplomats had worked closely with their British counterparts on behalf of all the white foreigners, and the hotel bars were full of Fritzes and Cecils toasting each other's countries and wives. The oil was still flowing, albeit in slightly reduced volume, but even that didn't matter any longer. According to a British oilman McColl met, their government had just asserted its control over several privately owned fields in the Persian Gulf. Mexico, it seemed, could safely be left to the Mexicans.

The very next day, a cable arrived from Cumming, summoning him back to London. A homebound warship would be stopping to collect him in a couple of days at the mouth of the Pánuco. If he could arrange his own trip downriver, it would be most appreciated.

Oakley Street

♠

After Tampico and almost three weeks of ocean horizons, London seemed to whir with activity. Automobiles had been few and far between in Mexico, but as he stood on the pavement outside Embankment Station, it seemed clear to McColl that they were well on their way to inheriting the earth. The horse-drawn hansoms still jostling for space already looked out of place.

During his nine-month absence, the pace of innovation had shown no signs of slowing. On the train up from Portsmouth, a buffet attendant had told him that tea was now sold in small porous bags, for dipping in individual cups, and only a few minutes earlier he had been brought up from the new Hampstead Railway platforms on a moving metal staircase.

He walked under the South Eastern & Chatham Railway bridge and turned away from the sparkling river. The Service's HQ had moved into 2 Whitehall Court in 1911, gaining more space and easier access to the nearby Admiralty. The building's entrance was on the corner with Horse Guards Parade, the actual offices in Flat 54, up under the roof. McColl took the lift, reported in, and was shown straight through to Cumming's spacious office, where nothing seemed to have changed. The large desk was covered in papers, the various shelves and side tables crammed with maps and charts; models of airplanes, submarines, and automobiles filled all the space that was left. The painting on the wall—of a Prussian firing squad executing French villagers in the War of 1870—had survived the move from the old HQ on Vauxhall Bridge Road.

Cumming seemed his usual self—friendly but brusque, or was it the other way round? His gray hair showed no sign of thinning, gray eyes no sign of dimming, and if he'd put on weight, no one could tell.

His first questions were also typical. How had the Maia behaved in tropical climes? Was a new model under development? What did McColl think of the new De Dion–Bouton, with its electric ignition and water-cooled engine?

McColl answered the first question but regretfully pleaded ignorance regarding the other two. He had been away a long time, he reminded Cumming, and obviously had a lot of catching up to do.

The Service chief did his best to help, and McColl tried to look more interested than he actually felt. The two of them had met at a motor rally, and McColl suspected that his knowledge of automobiles ranked above linguistic skills in Cumming's estimation of his talents.

They eventually got around to Mexico and the job McColl had done there. No actual praise was forthcoming, but his boss seemed satisfied. He had news of "that character von Schön," who had last been sighted heading back across the Pacific. "I doubt we'll see him for a while," he announced, with the air of someone watching a foe limp off into the distance. "But I didn't call you back to hand out plaudits," he went on. "Kell's people can't seem to find your Irishman."

McColl tried not to show how little he liked that news. "Tiernan?" he asked. "Didn't he come back to Dublin?"

"They think so, but they've only got hearsay to go on. Either the picture they have is poor or he's changed his appearance somehow, but no one has actually recognized the man. So Kell would like to borrow you for a few weeks."

"In Dublin?"

"In Dublin's fair city, as the song has it."

"How long do they think Tiernan's been back? What happened in New York after I left?"

"Not a great deal, I'm afraid. As far as we know, Tiernan and Rieber had no further contact before Tiernan took ship at the end of April. Rieber's still in New York, so if Tiernan's still plotting with the Germans, he must have a new contact."

"What about Aidan Brady? And Colm Hanley?"

"Brady left New York with a ticket to Chicago, but he wasn't on the train when it got there. We've no idea why, or where he went, but as Kensley said, at least he was headed in the right direction— away from us. Colm Hanley, on the other hand, left New York two weeks after Tiernan, jumped ship at Queenstown, and promptly disappeared. He's presumably with Tiernan."

Oh, shit, McColl thought.

"And we still have no idea what the 'action on enemy soil' might be," Cumming continued. "Or even which 'enemy soil' we're talking about. Kell's people think it might be Belfast, the enemy being Ulster."

"No," McColl said flatly. "Tiernan's after bigger fish than that."

"Well, I guess we'll find out the hard way if we don't find Tiernan first. Can you leave tomorrow?"

"I'm visiting my family this weekend," McColl said firmly. "I haven't seen them in a very long time. But I can take the boat from Glasgow."

"That should do," Cumming conceded.

"And my expenses?"

"Ah. I took the liberty of opening a bank account for you. My secretary has all the details. You'll find that your salary for the last three months has already been deposited, and any further expenses . . . well, you'll just have to claim for them in the usual way."

It was better than nothing, McColl thought. The three months' salary might even cover his debts. "What about the wider situation?"

he asked. "We and the Germans were getting on like a house on fire in Tampico, and I read in the paper that the government's just reached an agreement with them on the Berlin-to-Baghdad railway. It sounded promising . . ."

Cumming shook his head. "Don't get your hopes up," he said. "The Germans have just finished widening the Kiel Canal to accommodate their biggest ships, and last week the chief of their General Staff met with his Austrian counterpart. He told him—and I quote—'any adjournment will have the effect of diminishing our chances of success.'"

"Oh. But surely they'll need an excuse."

"They'll find one."

The night sleeper from Euston didn't leave until ten, which gave him time to meet Mac for a homecoming drink on Eversholt Street. The pub Mac had chosen was full and noisy, so they joined the overflow out on the pavement and stood with their beers watching the sun slide down through the smoke suspended above the station.

Mac was in good spirits. He said their former boss was trying his best to be furious with McColl—"First he abandons my sister, then he abandons my business"—but couldn't quite get there. "If he was really angry with you, he wouldn't have taken your advice and given me your job."

"How is business?" McColl asked.

"Booming, but I think it's the beautiful summer. In this sort of weather, the rich all want to drive themselves down to their country piles for the weekend. *And* have the best-looking automobile in the park."

"Is it still the best?"

"One of them. Have you been in New York all this time?"

"No, I left soon after you did. I've been in Mexico, trying to save the navy's oil."

"And now?"

"First Glasgow, then Dublin. Have you heard from Jed lately?"

Mac sighed. "Yes. He's not happy. He says he hates his job, and he probably does, but, you know, a trip like the one we did—it can either cure your itchy feet or make them itch all the more."

"And you?"

"Oh, I've seen enough of the world to keep me happy for a while. I'm enjoying London."

"What's her name?"

"Ethel, if you must know."

"So tell me about her."

"She's lovely. She likes me. Her father's an office manager at St. Katharine Docks."

"Hair color?"

"Auburn."

"Nice."

Mac smiled reflectively, as if he were picturing her. "What happened to the American girl?" he asked.

"We're still in touch. She was taken on by one of the big New York papers."

"Ah."

"And there's a favor I'd like to ask you. If I sent you letters for her, could you mail them on from here?"

"Of course I will. I take it you don't want her to know you're in Ireland."

It was McColl's turn to sigh. "It's not the simplest of romances."

Which was something of an understatement, he thought an hour or so later, as the sleeper rattled out of Euston and chugged its way up Camden Bank. Two such different lives could be spliced together only by one person utterly subsuming the other. That was not going to happen to him and Caitlin, and he didn't want it to. The things he admired about her were the things that made that impossible. The woman he loved would never settle for less than equality.

In the night bar, he composed the last letter he could send

himself, telling her he was back in England and on his way north
to visit his parents. Two cigarettes and a whiskey later, he walked
back to his compartment half expecting a sleepless night. The next
thing he knew, a steward was shaking his shoulder with a ten-minute warning of their arrival. He had slept like a stone.

He'd sent a telegram the evening before, and Jed was waiting at
the ticket barrier in a smart blue suit and tie. "I have to work this
morning," he said, "but I thought I'd meet you for a cup of tea."

They sat in the buffet for twenty minutes, bringing each other
up to date. According to Jed, things at home were much the same,
which McColl supposed was better than worse. "Have you told
them anything about my working for the government?" he asked
his younger brother.

"A little," Jed admitted. "Just that, I think. That you work for the
government abroad. I might have mentioned the Foreign Office."

He left McColl at the tram stop and walked briskly off down
Hope Street. He seemed older, McColl thought, and, beneath the
welcome, more subdued.

Twenty minutes later he was staring at the familiar house on
Oakley Street and catching a glimpse of his mother at the window.
She had the door opened before he reached it and stood there
looking at him, tears running down her cheeks. Breakfast and his
father were waiting in the back parlor, the one still warming on the
stove, the other cold as ever. His father complimented him on his
tan and somehow managed to make it sound like an accusation.
He was home.

He talked to his mother for most of the morning, about the
round-the-world trip and his brother, about neighbors and relations he hadn't seen for years. Jed had told her about Caitlin, but his
mother didn't press when she realized his reluctance to discuss her.
His father sat there listening for a while, interjecting the odd barbed
joke, but then tired of the sport and took refuge in his garden shed.

Jed came home for lunch, and they contrived to act like a normal family for the time it took to eat it. After washing and drying,

the boys and their mother listened to the new gramophone Jed had bought her with his earnings, and then the brothers went out for a walk around the old neighborhood, which seemed even more depressing than McColl remembered. The weather played a part—the gray skies hanging over Glasgow were enough to make anyone yearn for Mexico.

Their father went down to his local soon after tea, and their mother insisted on their doing likewise and "giving her some peace." They decided to brave the city center and joined a sizable crowd at the local tram stop.

"I don't know how long I can stand living here," Jed confessed as they waited.

"Get a room," McColl suggested. "I'll lend you some money if you need it."

"No. I don't mean with them. I mean Glasgow. Everyone's so damn narrow-minded."

"That's true of most places."

"Not London."

"Not so much maybe. Is the job not going well?"

Jed shrugged. "I could do it in my sleep. Some days I do. It's boring."

It was hard for McColl to argue—fifteen years earlier he'd felt much the same. "Just don't run away to join the army," he warned. "They wrote the book on narrow-minded."

Jed smiled. "You survived it."

"Only just."

The tram arrived, and everyone squeezed aboard. They ended up in a pub on Sauchiehall Street, reminiscing about their long trip and taking bets with each other on which of the male patrons would throw the first punch. In the end it was a middle-aged woman, who swung her handbag like a medieval mace and knocked a hapless youth to his knees.

"You're not seeing anyone?" McColl asked.

"No one special. I don't want more reasons to stay here."

Their mother was drinking cocoa when they got back, and the two of them followed her upstairs rather than wait for their father. McColl lay awake in the dark listening for the sound of a key in the lock, remembering all those nights in the past when the sound of a curse or a stumble would tell him how drunk his father was. Tonight, though, the feet on the stairs were steady and the murmured conversation carried no hint of threat.

How did his father live with himself? How did he, come to that? Selling cars to the rich wouldn't get him to heaven, and neither, he suspected, would working for Cumming. So far he had thrown one Chinese girl to the German wolves, helped keep Britain's boot on India's jugular, and prevented evidence of American atrocities in Mexico from seeing the light of day. All could be justified as preserving the British advantage in competition with the Kaiser's Germany, an aim that seemed defensible, though some way short of meriting sainthood. But when it came down to it, the only enemies who didn't leave him feeling conflicted were the Irish extremists and their nasty German friends. If only Colm Hanley hadn't been one of them.

On Sunday morning he escorted his mother to church, then went to the pub with his father and brother while she stayed home to cook lunch. His father was on his best behavior, radiating unspoken pride in his two boys. It would have been hard for anyone present to imagine a cross word passing between them, let alone realize that the man's sons couldn't wait to get away from him.

While the brothers cleared up after lunch, both parents fell asleep in their armchairs, and eventually McColl found himself standing in the parlor doorway, staring at his mother and thinking how old she looked. She was pleased to see him, pleased to have Jed back, but there was an underlying sense of resignation that he hadn't noticed before. Her husband might not beat her anymore—there were no bruises these days, and Jed would probably kill the old man if he did—but over the years he had slowly beaten her down. If Jed left Glasgow, she wouldn't have much to live for.

As she saw him off at the door, fighting back the tears, McColl felt like a heel, felt like running. He and Jed took the tram to Central and sat, mostly in silence, with their cups of tea until his train was finally announced. "It was easier for you," Jed said as they walked to the ticket barrier. "You knew I would still be there."

An hour later the train pulled in to Ardrossan Harbour station. Boarding was already in progress, but it seemed hours before the ship pulled away from the jetty and out into the Firth of Clyde. He managed a few hours of fitful sleep, then took to the deck to enjoy the early sunrise, thinking that most of his life these days was spent on boats and trains. When the counter finally opened inside, the bacon rolls proved worth the wait.

It was almost six when the ship entered Belfast Lough, the sun-lit green fields sloping up from the southern shore, the scattered white houses of Carrickfergus nestling beneath the hills to the north. Most of the city was still asleep when the ship docked, but a few of the old-style cabbies were waiting with their horses. As he listened to the iron-shod hooves clip-clopping across the cobbles, a heretical thought crept into McColl's mind: that this mode of transport was something he would miss.

He bought a newspaper from the boy at the station entrance and glanced at the front page as he waited in line for his Dublin ticket. The writer of the lead article was spitting venom at all those responsible, no matter how obliquely, for the apocalypse known as Home Rule—the reckless Liberal government, their spineless Tory opponents, Redmond and his hated Nationalists, the Pope and all his works. If Ulster had to fight them all, then Ulster damn well would.

Elsewhere, as the adjacent article made clear, blood had already been shed. On the previous morning, the heir to the Austro-Hungarian throne had been riding through the Bosnian town of Sarajevo with his wife when a lone gunman had shot and killed them both. It was not yet known who the gunman was or what, if any, his motives had been.

Killoran's Tavern

♠

Arriving in Dublin late in the morning, McColl parked his suitcase at a modest-looking hotel close by Tara Street station and used the telephone in the lobby to call the number he'd been given in London. An Irish voice took his name, left him hanging for almost a minute, then returned with a name, a time, and a place. "You'll be meeting Mr. Dunwood on the corner of Henry and Sackville streets—that's by the general post office. At one o'clock. He'll be carrying a red book."

The hotel desk clerk had a map of the city for visitors to consult, and McColl spent some time familiarizing himself with the basic layout. The specified meeting place was on the other side of the river, only a ten-minute walk. He wandered down to the Liffey and worked his way eastward along the quay until he found an open bar. Someone had left a wooden chair outside, so he took his beer out into the sunshine and watched the people walking past on both sides of the river. It probably wasn't the cleverest place to put himself, but the chances that Seán Tiernan or Colm Hanley might happen by seemed negligible.

He realized he should probably make some attempt to disguise himself. His hair was slightly longer than it had been in

New York, but letting it grow like a Sikh's would only attract attention. He supposed he could grow a mustache or a beard, but the prospect was unappealing. Perhaps a pair of glasses, he thought. But how could he ask for a pair with plain lenses without raising suspicions?

The trials and tribulations of the secret agent.

He drained his glass and refrained, with some misgivings, from ordering another. Dublin felt like a friendly town, but few places on earth housed more of the empire's bitterest enemies. He needed to keep his wits about him.

Sackville Street was the city's finest, a wide boulevard lined with impressive stone buildings. A local version of Nelson's Column stood between the tram lines at the junction with Henry Street, and as he approached the corner, McColl wondered how long the monument would survive an Irish republic. The man with the red book was already there, puffing on a pipe and looking around with obvious impatience. "Dunwood!" McColl said effusively, as if they'd known each other for years. The contact was a man of similar height to himself but considerably stouter, with a reddish face and sharp, almost cruel blue eyes. Ex-army, was McColl's first thought.

At the other man's instigation, they walked on up Sackville Street, crossed another wide road, and entered a well-tended square surrounded by Georgian buildings. "This'll do," Dunwood said. He had a southern Irish accent, McColl realized, and wondered why this was surprising. Most of Kell's men in Dublin would be locals—Englishmen would be far too obvious for undercover work.

Having found an empty bench, Dunwood plunked himself down, re-lit his pipe, and asked McColl where he was staying. "That won't do at all," he said when supplied with the answer. "You'll have to live rougher than that."

"Okay," McColl said equably. "Suggestions?"

"It's all in the book," Dunwood said, placing it between them.

"We've created a false identity for you, and all the details are there. I assume you can you manage an Australian accent?"

"Australian?"

"You're visiting the old country after a spot of bother Down Under. Remember 'Black Friday in Queensland'?"

"Vaguely."

"Well, it was two years ago. You spent a year in prison for your part in it, and when you came out, you were on a blacklist. So now you're back in your father's country and angry as any damn republican."

"What am I living on?" McColl wanted to know.

"You sold all your worldly goods before you left Australia, and you worked your passage. But the money won't last forever, and you're looking for a job. Really looking, I mean. There's none to be had, but the real Paul O'Neill would keep on looking."

"That's my name, is it?"

"It is."

"Right. So just to be clear, my one and only task is to find Seán Tiernan?"

"As of this moment."

"And if I do?"

"Just lead us to him."

"You don't sound convinced he's here in Dublin."

"I'm not. We've looked everyplace we could think of." He shrugged. "And not a trace."

"Where *have* you looked?"

"All the hotels and guesthouses. The pubs and clubs we know the republicans use. We've had men in the audience at all the likely public meetings, and we have a lot of informers out there. A lot," he repeated. "And they're hearing stuff—there's no end of talk about arms arriving for the Volunteers. But not a word on Tiernan. The people running the guns have heard of him, but they haven't seen him for months."

It didn't sound promising, McColl thought. When it came

down to it, Tiernan might be in England by now, preparing his "action on enemy soil." Or the man could be in Germany, doing deals with England's enemies.

But he would have to give Dublin a try, starting, he supposed, with Dunwood's republican haunts.

"There's a list with the briefing," Dunwood told him. "I included anything I thought was relevant, but if you need anything else—or if by some miracle you actually find him—call the same number. Whoever answers will know where to find me."

McColl spent the afternoon buying a new wardrobe from sundry pawnshops. There was no lack of choice following the lockout and its hardships; in some shops it seemed as if half the city's population had brought in their coats once the cold weather ended. He begged a spare sack to carry his purchases in and, once he was back in his room, swapped his new wardrobe for the one he'd brought with him. Later that evening, when the streets were dark, he dropped the sack off the nearest bridge and watched it float away downriver.

Next morning he threw out his razor and took lodgings at one of the places Dunwood had listed. He paid extra for a room on his own, claiming with a laugh that his snoring might get him killed and that while he still had some money he might as well live high on the hog. His landlady, who looked like she hadn't enjoyed anything since childhood, took his coins, placed them in a worn purse, and left him to appreciate the cupboard-size space, lumpy mattress, and gray sheets.

The only thing she asked him, in the four weeks he was there, was whether kangaroos really hopped.

It was not the most pleasant month of his life.

According to Dunwood's false history, Paul O'Neill had been a tram driver in Brisbane, so it seemed sensible for him to seek similar work. Thankfully, there were no vacancies at the city depot, and he didn't have to make up some story about Australian trams having different controls. Over the next couple of weeks, he did the rounds of the factories and big stores, but none were hiring drivers. The only real possibility, had he actually wanted a job, was chauffeuring one of the local rich, who often advertised in the press for men "of good standing, able to drive and service a modern automobile." If push came to shove, he would say that he'd been hired by some lord or other but dismissed the same day for inadvertently disclosing that he'd spent time in a Queensland cell.

Most of his waking hours were spent looking for Seán Tiernan and Colm Hanley. He attended every political meeting he saw publicized. There were Nationalist meetings at which old men were heckled by young republican firebrands for daring to say that Home Rule was enough, republican meetings at which old men were heckled by younger versions of themselves for daring to believe that independence was enough. There were cultural gatherings at which men insisted, in English, that Gaelic was the only language worth speaking and that Ireland had only truly been itself on some long-vanished misty morning, centuries before. He even attended two meetings of the local Protestants, who were bitterly divided over the issue of Home Rule now that their Ulster brethren seemed set on abandoning them to the Catholics.

Most of the pubs, clubs, and cafés on Dunwood's list were in the poorer quarters. McColl spent many an hour nursing cups of tea or glasses of beer, playing skittles or dominoes or cards, talking with those he was with, eavesdropping on those he wasn't. A simmering rage and despair over last year's lockout never seemed far from the surface, and hatred of the bosses and their English protectors seemed more or less universal, but only a few seemed worried by the details of Home Rule or what happened in far-off Ulster. Most wanted jobs and a decent place to live, and if a revolution provided one, then they would thank the revolutionaries. Their Ireland was the tenement they lived in, not some emerald Eden or republican utopia.

He found no trace of Tiernan or Caitlin's brother. And the reason, he decided, was simple—he was looking in the wrong places or, more precisely, among the wrong people. A few of the people he met would have worried Kell—those who hoped for guns, who wanted to bring Ulster to heel, who would even take help from the Germans if the opportunity arose—but none of them looked beyond Ireland. People like Tiernan and his friend Aidan Brady—they did. They might persuade themselves that they were fighting for a wider humanity, but they weren't interested in ordinary people or mass movements. They were conspirators, outsiders. They barely trusted each other, and they used everyone else. Ireland to them was a vehicle.

Or, McColl thought, recalling Cumming's phrase, an excuse.

But where else could he look? If Tiernan was trying to start a war, was Dublin the place to choose?

He decided he was approaching things from the wrong end and spent the third week of July scouring the city's hotels and guesthouses for Germans. He found thirteen, eleven of them men, five of whom seemed, for various reasons, unlikely to be agents. But when he contacted Dunwood and asked that the remaining six be watched or taken in for questioning, he met with refusal. There were not that many men available for surveillance, and with the situation in Europe as tense as it was, the government had no intention of arresting a slew of innocent Germans on the off chance one was a spy.

Through the weeks of searching, McColl did his best to keep in touch with the world beyond Dublin's tenements. In London the Irish Home Rule Bill passed in May was subjected to an amending bill, which further limited the original's application to the northern counties. As this was still too much for Ulstermen to bear, yet not enough to satisfy the Nationalists, the process was essentially deadlocked.

In far-off Mexico, Huerta resigned and traveled into Spanish exile on a German ship. McColl's old acquaintance Mohandas Gandhi was also on the move, returning to India after more than twenty years in South Africa. He had to be almost fifty, McColl thought—time to go home and leave the stress of politics behind.

Europe, meanwhile, was still waiting for an Austrian response to the murder of the emperor's heir. And with every day that passed, hope grew that the men in Vienna had lost their nerve.

In vain, as it turned out. On July 24 the British prime minister announced two unwelcome pieces of news: Talks held at Buckingham Palace to resolve the Irish deadlock had ended in utter failure, and the Austrian government had delivered an ultimatum to Belgrade, an ultimatum—as the newspapers made abundantly clear—that no self-respecting nation would dream of accepting. And the Serbs, as everyone knew, were almost overendowed with self-respect.

On Sunday the twenty-sixth, the day the Serbs were supposed to reply, McColl took a tram out to Howth. This small fishing port on the northeastern lip of Dublin Bay was the latest destination of the route marches that the Irish Volunteers had been undertaking on a weekly basis since mid-June, and he planned to scan the faces for the ones he was seeking. This march, though, turned out to be different—a small boat, the *Asgard*, was waiting for the marchers, heavily loaded with illicit rifles. The Volunteer leaders had been clever, McColl thought; he found himself wondering whether all the month's marches had been designed with this one in mind. The first one had attracted a significant police and military presence, but over the weeks familiarity had turned to complacency, and there were not nearly enough police in Howth to prevent the *Asgard*'s unloading.

He watched from the cobbled quayside as hundreds of guns and several boxes of ammunition were loaded into taxis and driven away. The remaining rifles were shouldered by some of the marchers, and the Volunteers set off on their return journey with a noticeable spring in their steps. If the Ulstermen could arm themselves, then so could they!

McColl joined in, drawn more by curiosity and the crowd's good mood than by any lingering hope of running into Tiernan or Colm. It was almost ten miles back to Dublin, but the exercise would do him good.

Everything was fine until the marchers reached the village of Clontarf, where a large posse of policemen and a detachment of the King's Own Scottish Borderers were deployed across the road. McColl, in the middle of the march, could see talks going on up ahead and guessed that the police were demanding the surrender of the smuggled rifles. As if to confirm that fact, those bearing the illicit arms started slipping off across the fields that bordered the road. The authorities had no answer to this, other than to seize what weapons they could from those near the front and let everyone else go home. The remaining Volunteers dispersed, and the police headed back into Dublin with their paltry cache of guns, leaving only the soldiers and a crowd of hostile onlookers.

Eventually the troops set off, a jeering crowd in close attendance. As the procession entered the outskirts of Dublin, some of the soldiers made mock lunges with their bayonets to keep their tormentors at bay, and the latter were steadily reinforced by fellow citizens. By the time the procession reached Sackville Street, there were several hundred people shouting insults at the troops, and as they turned onto Bachelor's Walk, the abuse turned to bottles and stones.

On more than one occasion in the last half hour, McColl had reached the conclusion that slipping away was the sensible option, but simple curiosity had kept him with the crowd. Now, as the last few ranks of the soldiers wheeled and raised their rifles, he realized his mistake. A uniformed arm went up, a single shot gave way to a brief but shocking fusillade, and people were falling, screaming, crying for help. The dense crowd of bodies between him and the soldiers seemed to melt away, and he found himself looking at a row of frightened young boys.

Someone screamed "Cease fire!" and there, at the edge of his vision, was Aidan Brady, disappearing around a corner.

For a few seconds, McColl stood rooted to the spot in surprise, staring at the space where Brady had been. And then he was in motion, leaping across one prone body and sidestepping another man on his knees. As he reached the corner that Brady had turned, he forced himself to slow and take it at walking pace. Several people were hurrying away down this particular street, Brady the tallest, bringing up the rear some fifty yards away. The American glanced over his shoulder only the once and clearly found no cause for concern in the ragged figure behind him.

McColl made sure to keep his distance. He didn't want to lose Brady, but he was more afraid of tipping him off. Now that he knew the man was here, he could always find him again; tip him off and he'd go to ground along with the others.

He also had a vivid memory of what had happened to the cop in Paterson.

The gunfire by the river had brought a lot of curious people out of their homes, and the crowded pavements, along with the darkening evening sky, provided some welcome cover. Brady turned right, crossed Sackville Street, and followed a winding route to the small square in front of Amiens Street station. There was a line of cheap hotels across from the station entrance, and the American disappeared through the door of the third. The name—or misname—on the barely readable sign was THE DUBLIN CONTINENTAL.

McColl went into the station and was relieved to find a pair of public telephones in the booking hall. In Dunwood's absence a message was taken, and McColl settled down to wait, keeping an eye on the illuminated hotel entrance through a convenient window.

It had been dark for an hour when Dunwood arrived. He listened to McColl's story but had little help to offer. "I can maybe spare you a man in the morning," he eventually conceded, "but not tonight. Half the city's in an uproar, and every man we have is out on the street."

McColl tried, without success, to change his mind.

"It's not even Tiernan," Dunwood insisted, "just some American who knows him. And now that Tiernan's got his guns, he'll be out celebrating."

"He wasn't at the pickup," McColl pointed out.

"The ones who matter never are," the Irishman said wryly.

"All right. I'll hold the fort this evening. But tomorrow . . ."

"I'll try to have someone here by eight, but you'll have to point the American out."

"I'll be here," McColl said tiredly. He'd walked a long way that day and not had much to eat. As Dunwood disappeared around a corner, he realized he should have asked the man to fetch him something.

At any rate there was no time to dwell on his empty stomach. Only ten minutes had passed when Brady reappeared, this time wearing a cap and carrying a large carpetbag. He headed south toward the river, and McColl went after him, inwardly thanking the Dublin authorities for the inadequacy of their street lighting. Tonight there was no moon to help—the sky was overcast, with more than a hint of moisture hanging in the air.

Brady crossed the swing bridge over the Liffey, strode past the elevated Tara Street station, and turned left under the railway bridge. McColl reached the corner just in time to see the American walk in through the entrance of another hotel. It was, he knew, the Emerald Palace. One of the thirteen Germans had been registered there, a man named Suhr whom McColl had previously discounted.

He stood there, staring at the entrance. Should he risk going in and walking into Brady or risk staying outside and missing a chance to eavesdrop? He still hadn't made up his mind when Brady reappeared with the German, whose cadaverous face looked almost frightening under the yellow streetlight. Suhr had been staying at the hotel with his wife, which was why McColl had ruled him out.

Maybe he'd brought her along for just that purpose, or maybe she'd wanted to see Ireland. Maybe she wasn't his wife.

McColl hung back, ready to retreat if they came his way. But the two men set off in the other direction, zigzagging south to a wide and busy road, which they followed toward the bay. Given the hour and the rain now falling, most of those out would be hurrying home—if Dunwood's uproar had ever existed, it was now the dampest of squibs.

Ships' masts were visible over the roofs—they were approaching the docks. Brady and the German turned right down a narrow, cobbled street, and McColl reached the corner just in time to see them disappear through the entrance of the seedy-looking Killoran's Tavern. Piano music and cigarette smoke were drifting out of the only open window.

McColl gave them a minute, then sidled up to take a look within. The ground floor was divided by a wood-and-glass partition, with both rooms having access to each other and the semicircular bar. A young man was seated at the piano in the near room and seemed to be playing more for himself than the half dozen drinkers at the widely spaced tables. Brady and Suhr had joined a single large group in the farther room—McColl could see the American's cap above the partition.

If he wanted to hear anything, he had to go in. He could buy a beer, sit by the partition, and hope that no one he knew came into his half of the bar. If anyone did, he would just have to keep his head down and pray that whoever it was would be taken in by the new beard and old clothes. The risk seemed enormous, but so did the potential rewards, and what other choice did he have? If he waited outside until the group emerged, he'd have to pick one man to follow. He'd still have no clue as to what was intended, or who they all were, or where all the others were going.

He patted the gun in his pocket for luck and carefully opened the door. Nodding a cursory greeting to the faces turned toward him, he walked up to the bar and asked the middle-aged man behind it for a bottle of porter. Behind him the pianist seemed unable to decide which tune he wanted to play, starting several before settling for one McColl didn't recognize.

"New in Dublin?" the bartender asked in response to his Australian accent.

"I am," McColl told him with a smile. "From Down Under," he added before carrying his bottle and glass over to a table beside the partition. On impulse he sat facing away from the bar—and from anyone rounding the end of the partition. Not being seen felt more important than seeing.

On the other side, a voice was asking why it wouldn't be simpler to take the ferry.

McColl heard no reply, only silence and the shifting of chairs. Then feet sounded behind him, and it took all he had not to turn around.

Something hard jammed into his side. A gun.

"Keep your hands on the table," the familiar American voice ordered.

He did as he was told. "What the fuck do you want?" McColl protested angrily, emphasizing the Australian accent. "And who the fuck are you?" An innocent man, he realized, would do what he couldn't risk doing—look his assailant in the eye.

Brady seemed to sense as much. He placed the barrel of his pistol under McColl's chin and, almost gently, used it to lever his head around. Curiosity gave way to surprise, and that to amusement. "Mr. McColl," he drawled. "Stand up."

McColl did as he was told, wondering how the rest of the room was reacting to events. The pianist had stopped playing.

"Let's move to the other room," the American suggested, adding a jerk of the gun in support.

As he walked in the required direction, McColl allowed himself a glance around the room. There were bleak stares aplenty and no hint of sympathy. The barman looked pleased with himself, presumably for supplying the tip-off.

In the other room, one of those waiting was Colm Hanley. "It's your sister's boyfriend," Brady told him with a laugh. "Donal," he said to the nearest man. "Check his pockets."

The gun was taken and laid on the table. "Now sit," Brady said, prodding McColl toward an upright chair by the wall.

"Who is this man?" Suhr asked.

"His name's Jack McColl," a familiar voice answered. Seán Tiernan's.

"McColl!" the German expostulated, half rising to his feet.

"You know him?" Brady asked. The pianist was at work again, playing, if anything, a little louder.

"He is an Englander agent. Two times already he escapes from us."

"Third time lucky, then," Brady said with a grin, sending a shiver of fear through McColl. The tune the pianist was playing was "After the Ball is Over."

"Are there any more questions?" Tiernan asked, glancing around at his comrades. McColl mechanically noted their number—there were nine including the German, and all but Suhr were still in their twenties.

"Just him," one man said, gesturing toward McColl.

"Leave him to me," Brady said shortly, drawing momentary looks of relief from one or two faces.

Everyone got up to leave, and McColl noticed for the first time that each of them had brought a bag or suitcase. As if they were all going off on vacation together. But presumably not to the seaside.

Some looked at him on their way out and some didn't, but there was no pity in any of their eyes. Colm had been staring at him ever since his appearance, and when he stopped in front of McColl, there was still surprise in his. "How could my sister have been such a fool?" he asked, shaking his head in stupefaction.

"She was never that," McColl said quietly.

Colm shook his head again, offered a withering look, and walked out.

The bartender, meanwhile, was whispering something in Tiernan's ear. "Not here," were the two words that McColl recognized.

Brady soon confirmed as much: "We're going for a walk. A short one." He handed his gun to Tiernan, put on the long coat that McColl remembered from Paterson, and took the weapon back. "This way," Brady said, inviting him through an open door at the side of a bar and into the passage beyond. McColl walked slowly down it, supremely aware of the gun in his back, trying to steel himself. If he did nothing, he was a dead man—he had no doubts on that score. Doing something would probably end the same way, but there was always a chance. And it was better to die fighting back than just let the bastard gun him down.

Which was all very well in theory. He felt almost frozen by fear and oh, so eager to heed those voices advising him to wait for the perfect opportunity.

"Stop," Brady told him as they reached a door to the outside world. "You'd better take a look," he told Tiernan, increasing the pressure of the barrel in McColl's back as the Irishman squeezed by.

The door opened, and rain blew in. Cursing, Tiernan stepped out into what looked like an alley between buildings. "All clear!" he shouted back after glancing both ways.

"Out," Brady ordered.

Now, McColl thought. It wasn't much of a chance, but it had to be better than none at all. He stepped away from the gun faster than Brady expected and levered himself around the jamb with one hand. Tiernan was momentarily in the way, but the force of McColl's onslaught knocked the Irishman down, and the dark, rainswept alley lay open before him. Twenty feet to run, he told himself, and not in a straight line. Who was he kidding?

He heard Brady's first shot scrape along a wall a split second ahead of the booming gun. He felt the force of the second, was aware of his sprint turning into a stagger as he passed through the mouth of the alley. He didn't know where he'd been hit, but it took every ounce of will to keep his legs moving across the cobbled quay, toward the only possible place of safety. It seemed to get no nearer, and his body was almost at the point of giving up on him when another blow in the back provided the propulsion he couldn't provide for himself, throwing him over the edge of the quay and into the side of the ship that was berthed alongside, to drop through the dark well between them.

Even in July the water was cold enough to jerk him back from unconsciousness. He experienced one brief moment of panic as he bumped into the harbor bottom, but growing up beside the sea had cured any fear of water, and he had the presence of mind to seek out the faintest strip of light above and rise painfully up between ship and dock. He knew he'd been hit at least twice, but it was difficult to tell how serious the wounds were, and for the moment it hardly seemed to matter—if those shots hadn't killed him, his enemies still might.

They would be looking down, he thought, but they wouldn't be able to see him. And the rain on the water would mask any sounds.

He was right, but the next few moments were still terrifying. When his head broke surface, it took forever to clear his eyes, and the night sky above seemed so much brighter than he'd expected. And there were two silhouetted heads up above, leaning over the lip of the dock. He waited for gunfire, but none came. They couldn't see him.

He edged closer in among the pilings in search of something to grab. When he found it, the pain of seizing hold almost made him cry out, and he had to use the other arm. He wondered how long it would be before he lost consciousness—he had to be losing blood, and he still wasn't sure where he was wounded. The second bullet had hit him in the shoulder, uncomfortably close to the neck, but the first was lower down, and the only organ he was sure it had missed was his heart.

He heard a voice above—Brady's, he thought, but he couldn't make out what the American had said.

"He must be dead," Tiernan said, loudly enough for him to hear. "You put two bullets in him."

The American said something McColl couldn't catch.

"And we have a boat that's waiting," Tiernan reminded him.

If Brady replied, McColl didn't hear it. For the next five minutes, all he heard was the rain and the water lapping against the pilings. He was feeling weaker with each passing second. He had to do something.

Leaning out, he could see no other heads up above. He felt sure they were gone, but if they weren't, they weren't. He couldn't stay where he was.

Half swimming, half clinging, he worked his way down the quayside wall until he found a ladder of rusted iron rings. He had no idea how long it took to pull himself up, but the last thing he remembered was slumping forward onto the cobbles, straining to roll himself free of the edge, and lying stretched out on his back with raindrops tap-tap-tapping on his face.

For the second time that year, he woke up in a hospital ward. According to the blue-eyed nurse on duty, he'd been discovered by a passing constable and brought into the hospital on a collier's cart. Her smile as she tucked in his sheet reminded him a little of Caitlin, and he felt his heart tighten. Now that Colm knew, so would she.

A passing sense of relief, which he ascribed to the end of pretense, quickly gave way to a much more lasting sense of loss. It was over; it had to be.

His body felt strangely unimpaired until he tried to move. Then pain kicked in with a vengeance, as if he were being stabbed in several different places. After a few minutes, he was sufficiently recovered to call the nurse, who told him a doctor would soon be around to explain his condition.

But it was Dunwood who arrived first. McColl told him all he could, which wasn't much—there were nine of them, including one German and at least two Americans, and most if not all had been about to take ship. "You might still be able to intercept them," he added, noticing for the first time that it was still dark outside.

Dunwood shook his head. "Too good a start," he said.

The penny dropped. "What day is this?"

"It's Tuesday evening. You've been out for nearly forty-eight hours—they're in England by now."

"Shit."

"Which probably means you're safe enough here," Dunwood continued as he got up to leave. "But just in case, there's an armed constable outside the door."

An hour or so later, the doctor turned up. McColl had lost a great deal of blood from the two wounds, and for a while on the Sunday they'd been "a trifle concerned." But now it was only a matter of time and healing. The wound in his shoulder wasn't serious, but he wouldn't be able to do much with his left arm for a couple of weeks. Hold a cigarette perhaps, but not much more. The other bullet had passed between his right lung and his liver, narrowly missing both but creating "a bit of a mess." That, too, would need time to heal, and he could expect a fair amount of stiffness and pain.

"How long before I'm out of here?"

"Ten days if you're lucky, but then you'll need some convalescence."

It wasn't a rosy prospect, given how fast things seemed to be moving in the world outside. When she came to empty his bedpan next morning, the staff nurse was full of the news that Madame Caillaux had been acquitted in the sensational French murder trial, but she was less up to date on Balkan affairs. It was only when he got hold of a newspaper that McColl discovered Serbia's less fortunate fate. The Austrians had declared war the previous day, and fighting had already begun.

Over the following days, he lay there in the crowded ward with nothing to do but watch and listen to the other patients, pick at the dreadful food, and stare at the bare gray walls. In truth, he didn't have much to be proud of. In the unlikely event he would ever get to offer one, he rehearsed a defense of his conduct toward Caitlin and found it far from convincing. When he caught himself hoping that Colm wouldn't live to tell her, the sense of self-disgust was almost overwhelming.

He wondered where Colm and his comrades-in-arms were now and what they were doing. Each day he scanned the papers the nurses brought him for news of an outrage in London or some other city, but thus far in vain. If they'd been caught, Dunwood would have told him, so they had to be out there somewhere, waiting for their chosen moment to strike.

By Friday he was able to walk to the toilet and to sit at other bedsides and talk to his fellow patients. Ever since the Austrian declaration, the main topic of conversation was the possibility of British involvement if the conflict started to spread. The consensus was no—why should Britain involve itself in a Continental squabble over a murdered archduke? No one even knew where Bosnia was, and the whole business seemed like a comic opera.

Dunwood, when he came again on the Saturday evening, offered rather a different slant. Germany had just declared war on Russia, he told McColl in a whisper, as he plunked some grapes on the bedside table. Which meant that Germany would also declare war on France in the next couple of days.

"Why?" McColl wanted to know.

"Because they have only one strategic plan, and that involves defeating France before Russia has time to mobilize."

McColl could hardly believe it. "They've been that stupid?"

"It looks like it. And attacking France will bring us in."

"Definitely?"

"I think so. The French moved their whole fleet to the Mediterranean because we promised to cover the Channel, so we can hardly abandon them now."

"Will people really accept that as a reason for war?"

"Who knows? The government are hoping the Germans invade Belgium and let them off the hook."

"And will they?"

Dunwood shrugged and helped himself to a grape. "Everything we know suggests they will. They've given themselves only six weeks to beat France, and their plan involves swinging round the left end of the French line and enveloping them from the rear. The wider the swing, the better, and the more likely they'll go through Belgium."

"But if we know this, so must the French."

Dunwood smiled. "According to our people in France, it doesn't fit in with the French generals' plans, so they've decided not to believe it."

"You're kidding me." The older McColl got, the more stupid those in authority seemed.

"The worst thing is—guess who'll be taking up position on the French army's left, plumb in front of the German charge?"

"Us."

"Exactly. According to the plans our generals have drawn up with the French, the British Expeditionary Force is supposed to set sail four days after war is declared and take its place in the line eight days after that. The way it looks at the moment, they'll arrive in northern France about the same time as the Germans."

McColl clutched at a straw. "But someone could still stick a spoke in a wheel and stop the whole damn thing in its tracks."

"It's too late," Dunwood said. "Nothing'll stop it now."

He was right. Two days later the German army moved into Belgium. McColl was discharged the next day, but not to a place of convalescence. Despite the best efforts of Cumming, Kell, and the regular police, Tiernan and his team were still at large, and McColl was wanted back in London. Only he had clapped eyes on the nine wanted men.

The Arun Bridge

♠

It was only after his ship docked at Holyhead that McColl discovered his country was now at war. His gloomy reaction to this news was not shared by his fellow passengers on the London express, most of whom seemed unreasonably excited by the prospect. He sat there listening to two young men exchanging heroic fantasies and knew that Jed would embrace the same delusions. What better excuse to leave Glasgow?

"Express" proved something of a misnomer. The journey across North Wales seemed to last forever, and every stop-start offered painful reminders of the damage Brady's gun had inflicted. There were no obvious reasons for the delays, and he could only surmise that the needs of the military were already beginning to gum up the system. The platforms at Crewe were certainly crowded with uniforms, and joining the main line did little to improve their timekeeping—it was midafternoon by the time the train reached Euston.

The terminus was crowded, the atmosphere more febrile than usual. He thought about going straight to Cumming, but his flat was more or less on the way—a quick bath and fresh clothes might raise him from the dead. The taxi ride to Windmill Street took a couple of minutes, and he managed the several flights of stairs with rather more ease than he expected. Among the small pile of mail waiting on the carpet were two ominous letters, one from his mother and one from Caitlin. Which, he wondered, would be the unhappier read?

Before reading them, he picked up the telephone. There was no reason it shouldn't be working, but he still felt slightly surprised that it was. He rang Cumming's office, ascertained from the secretary that the man himself was there, and arranged to see him in an hour or so.

His mother's letter had been posted on Saturday evening, which confirmed his worst suspicions. He sliced the envelope open with the paper knife and extracted the single sheet of paper. Jed had taken the train to London so that he and Mac could enlist together. The letter, he knew, was a plea for help, but she hadn't managed to put that in words. Asking things of others wasn't something she did anymore.

Caitlin's letter could hardly have been more different. She was coming to England to see him, after stopping off in Ireland to tell Colm "a few home truths." Her brother's letters home were worrying them all, and she felt she had to spare the time. But she wouldn't stay long in Dublin and was really looking forward to seeing him in London. Her letter was dated July 15; he had, he now remembered, assured her he would be back in England by the end of that month.

Maybe the war had changed her plans, he thought. Maybe she was already in London. She would probably have reached Dublin before her brother left; if so, she now knew who McColl worked for and might even think he was dead. If she turned up here, it would only be to shoot him.

He placed her letter on top of his mother's and stood there for several moments, hands on the table, head bowed down. "No time for regrets," he eventually murmured, and went to run a bath. Half an hour later, his suit smelling faintly of mothballs, he was hailing a taxi on Tottenham Court Road.

Cumming was waiting in his aerie, where a space had been made for a camp bed—the Service had gone to war. "You look exhausted," were his first words, which he might equally well have applied to himself. "But I take it you're sufficiently recovered to lend a hand." It was a statement, not a query.

McColl had nothing to add to what he'd told Dunwood about the fateful evening, and Cumming had no fresh news of the week-old manhunt. "Special Branch have turned all the Irish neighborhoods upside down, and big rewards have been posted, but not a glimmer."

"If they have any sense, they'll avoid the Irish neighborhoods," McColl thought out loud.

"Perhaps," Cumming conceded, "but won't they be conspicuous anywhere else? There *are* eight of them."

"Eight?" McColl asked.

"The German turned up at their embassy a week ago—he's on his way home, with all the other diplomats. He was identified from the pictures Kell's man took—his real name's von Busch, and he's a major in the German army. An explosives expert."

"That makes sense."

"And it's not the worst of it. A huge amount of dynamite was stolen from a quarry in Surrey four nights ago. The night watchman had his throat cut."

"Oh, Jesus. So what do you want me to do?"

"Get a good night's sleep. Then tomorrow morning start going over the same ground again. You're the only one who's seen them all, and you *might* see a face you recognize. I know it's a long shot, but there's nothing else. Bar the waiting. I'll send an automobile to pick you up—the police have loaned us half a dozen."

McColl took another taxi home and summoned up the energy to call Tim Athelbury. It was Evelyn who answered.

"So you're back at last," she drawled, friendly in her usual cold way. She showed no interest in where he had been, simply called her brother to the phone.

As Mac had suggested, Tim Athelbury felt no real resentment at being left in the lurch, by either McColl or his chosen replacement. "Mac quit this morning," he said. "He and your brother went down to the enlisting office together."

They talked for a few minutes more, but McColl was hardly listening, and his first port of call after hanging up was a dust-covered bottle of whiskey. He poured himself a generous shot, stared at it awhile, then carefully poured it back. In the bedroom he tore the blankets off the bed, gingerly undressed, and stretched himself out on the sheet. Tomorrow was another day, and it could hardly be worse than the one he'd just had.

Next morning he had just finished shaving and dressing when someone knocked on the door. Cumming's lift, he assumed, but the face that confronted him was hers. She looked lovely as ever, but the frozen expression told him she knew.

"Jack," she said coldly, and walked past him into the flat. "Once upon a time, I was looking forward to seeing this."

He could think of no response.

She continued on into his living room, then turned to face him, anger glittering in her green eyes. "When I got to Dublin, there was a letter waiting for me. From Colm. He said you're a British agent and that you used me to infiltrate my family. Are you? Did you?"

"I do work for the British government."

"As a spy."

"Other countries have spies—we have agents."

The joke fell predictably flat. "And you used me?"

"Yes, but . . ." He fell silent. The buts had felt real at the time, but now they seemed utterly spurious.

"Is that all you've got to say?"

He shook his head. "I fell in love with you long before that." He hesitated. How much could he tell her? Why not everything? "In China I was spying on the Germans. In San Francisco I was investigating the links between the Germans and their Indian revolutionary friends when I found out that both had links to the local Irish republicans. It was pure coincidence that your chaperone turned out to be one of the couriers they use, but once I'd found a letter in his suitcase containing details of an Irish-German plot . . . well, my boss already knew that I was involved with you"—McColl couldn't bring himself to admit that he had asked London to check up on her—"and once he found out who your father was . . ."

"He asked you to spy on me and my family."

"More or less. I didn't think I'd discover anything incriminating, and I wanted to keep my job. And then I met Tiernan and discovered he was involved. After that they sent me to Mexico."

"But not to sell automobiles," she said acidly.

She was standing only four feet away, but it could have been four thousand miles. It was utterly hopeless, but he kept on talking because he knew if he stopped, she would leave. "I was sent to prevent the Germans stealing our navy's oil. And when that was done, they brought me home. Tiernan was supposedly in Dublin, but they couldn't track him down, and I was the only one who'd actually met him. You thought there was something wrong with him," he added, and realized how pathetic it sounded.

She gave him a long look, and there was no love in it. "I can't believe what a fool I've been," she said, unconsciously echoing Colm.

"You haven't," he said quietly. "You thought I loved you, and I did. I still do."

"No," she said vehemently. "You haven't behaved like a person in love behaves."

Excuses came to mind—several of them—but she was right. "Is there anything I can say or do to make you forgive me?"

She almost laughed. "No," she repeated. "But if you're feeling guilty—and by God you should be—there's one thing you can do by way of atonement, and that's to help me save my brother."

"How?" he asked, feeling a ridiculous surge of hope.

"Help me find him. I don't know my way around this city."

"At this moment half the police in London are looking for him and his friends." And if they found them, he thought, then some would probably die.

For the first time, there was something in her face besides anger. "Then you do know he's here?"

"We're pretty certain. A large amount of dynamite was stolen a few days ago. The night watchman was killed."

"But Colm couldn't . . ."

Her brother obviously hadn't told her that he'd left McColl to be executed. She was, he realized, still thinking of Colm as the boy she'd helped bring up.

"If he's caught," she was saying, sounding uncertain for the first time, "will you let me know? Will you do what you can for him?"

"Yes, for your sake. But you must realize—he's put himself in a very dangerous position. I know he's young, but now there's a war, no one will want to take chances."

"I understand," she said.

He had never seen her so close to tears. "Tell me where you're staying."

She gave him the name of her hotel. "It won't change my mind about us," she warned him. "Apart from anything else, I could never trust you again."

"I know."

She looked him straight in the eye, as if determined to prove her resolve. "I shall go now."

"Caitlin . . ."

"No, we're finished here."

He opened the door and watched her walk out, listened as the sound of her feet on the stairs slowly gave way to silence, heard the distant click of the street door closing. She was gone.

It might have been ten minutes later when Cumming's

policeman arrived; it might have been an hour. McColl's brain registered the news that the Irish gang's hideout had finally been found, but he spent the drive across London staring dumbly out at the hurrying crowds, replaying his conversation with her, obsessing over all the things he should and shouldn't have said. It was only when they drew up outside the house in Lambeth that he managed to shake himself free and bring himself back to the job in hand.

The three-story house was brimming with police. There were constables on every floor, pulling out drawers and lifting up carpets, searching through wardrobes and bedding. One was even tapping the walls, presumably in hopes of finding a secret passage, while out in the small backyard two men were staring at the flagstones, presumably with an eye to lifting a few.

The evidence that mattered, as the inspector in charge informed him, had already been discovered. The remains of several unmarked crates had been dumped in the coal bunker outside, along with a fair quantity of the packing material used for wrapping sticks of dynamite. And one of the neighbors had confirmed that a group of Irish laborers had been staying in the house for over a week. She'd spoken to one man across the back fence, and he'd told her they'd all come over from Dublin to work on one of the new Tube extensions—she couldn't remember which. But she had seen four of them that morning, walking down the street in the direction of the river, all carrying large canvas bags.

The inspector was just admitting that their search of the house had proved fruitless when a smug-looking constable emerged from the front room and presented him with a small piece of cardboard. "It was down the back of the settee."

It was a railway ticket, a return from London Victoria to Ford, dated July 29.

"Where the hell is Ford?" the inspector asked, handing it over.

McColl had no idea, but even a week-old ticket might provide some sort of clue to where the eight had gone. And there didn't seem to be anything else.

He talked to the neighbor and asked her about the four men she'd seen that morning. One description fit Brady, but none matched Tiernan or Colm.

When he reached Whitehall, the first thing he asked was how they'd found the house.

"Ah, that was my brain wave," Cumming admitted. "After you'd gone yesterday, I realized that we'd neglected the German end of business, and I got the police to run a check on all the London properties that German nationals had bought in the last couple of years. There were more than thirty of them, and they didn't get round to the Lambeth house until a couple of hours ago. Too late, I'm afraid. Of course, all the obvious places are being watched, but these people can make the headlines without blowing up Buckingham Palace or Nelson's Column—a department store would do, or even a couple of crowded pubs."

McColl wasn't convinced. "I don't think so," he said. "They're ruthless enough, but they're not idiots. Killing a lot of innocent bystanders won't win them many supporters, and it certainly won't help the Germans. The only enemy they actually have in common is the British army."

"Which is mostly on trains, en route to France."

McColl rummaged in his pocket for the railway ticket. "This was found in the house," he said, passing it across the desk. "Do you know where Ford is?"

"I seem to remember passing through it. On the line that runs along the south coast, I think. Let's have a look," he said, reaching for his atlas.

It was McColl who found it, just south of Arundel, a station without so much as a village.

"There's nothing there," Cumming complained.

"Yes there is," McColl pointed out. "There's a river, and that means a bridge. Which ports are the troops leaving from?"

"Portsmouth and Southampton."

"Well, take out that bridge and you've cut the coastline and one of the major routes from London."

"My God, I hope not." Cumming stared at the map. "But look, there's lots of other lines. They couldn't cut them all."

"There can't be that many," McColl countered, "and they don't need to cut them all. Cut the main ones and you'll be left with a few minor routes, single-track most likely. We'd still get the soldiers to port, but how much longer would it take? And that's what they're after—delays. The longer it takes our army to get across, the better chance the Germans have of knocking out the French."

Cumming sat back in his chair and released an explosive breath. "Go to Victoria," he said; "the railway police office. I'll ring ahead and tell them you're coming. They'll know who to ask if any of this makes sense."

McColl was halfway through the door when Cumming called him back.

"You'd better have this," he said, taking a gun from one of his drawers.

It was a Webley revolver, which McColl tucked into the back of his belt, taking care not to stretch his wounded shoulder.

His automobile was still outside, and the drive to Victoria took only a couple of minutes. Both the forecourt and the London, Brighton & South Coast Railway concourse were crowded with uniforms, and he was taken back to the day, almost fifteen years earlier, when he'd caught a troop train from Platform 12, bound for Portsmouth, the sea, and South Africa. It had all felt like a great adventure, and most of these soldiers seemed equally deluded—laughing, joking, and teasing one another, looking for all the world like they couldn't wait to engage the enemy.

At the railway police office, a middle-aged commander was waiting to escort him back across the concourse and up an iron staircase to the room overlooking the Brighton line platforms where the engineering department had its headquarters. Once he had outlined his theory, maps were spread out on a table and all the lines to the ports in question duly noted and described. As he had guessed, cutting them all would be a very tall order, but just severing the four main lines would greatly reduce the chances of getting the army to sea on time.

But where would they cut them? The bridge at Ford was one of many that might have been chosen on that particular line, and the same would be true of the others, none of which belonged to the LB&SCR. He would have to talk to their London and South Western Railway colleagues at Waterloo.

He rang Cumming with the bad news.

"Check with the ticket office there," the Service chief told him. "See if anyone remembers Irishmen or Americans buying tickets to Ford this morning. I'll get onto Waterloo and ring you back. You'd better give me that number."

McColl did so, told the chief engineer he'd be back shortly, and took his railway police helper down to the ticket office. None of the clerks remembered selling a Ford ticket to anyone that morning, let alone to a foreigner. "I think I sold one to an American last week," one man said. "It might have been Ford. You know," he added, screwing up his face in concentration, "I think it was. A young man with curly brown hair. He seemed nervous."

Colm Hanley.

Back in the engineering office, McColl sat and watched as troops boarded one of the trains below, good-naturedly jostling one another as they funneled through the doors. He knew he wouldn't be seeing Jed or Mac—they'd be given several weeks' training before being shipped to the front. Some of these he was watching now would be dying long before that.

The telephone eventually rang. "It seems that Irishmen and Americans have been buying tickets to everywhere," Cumming complained. "Guildford, Godalming, Southampton—you name it. The railway people are drawing up a list of obvious targets, and the order's gone out to check every bridge on the lines in question, but there are hundreds of the damn things. We can only hope that they've been predictable and chosen the longest bridges on the busiest lines."

McColl told him about the tickets for Ford, those that had been bought and those that seemingly hadn't.

Cumming thought for a moment. "It's still the only location we have any evidence for. You'd better get down there. I'll put the local police in the picture and get them to meet you."

Despite the heavy military traffic, regular trains were still running, and a Portsmouth-via-Horsham was allegedly leaving in twenty minutes. McColl bought a newspaper and some food for the journey, prevailed on his railway police helper to authorize free passage with the guard, and settled into a first-class seat. Much to his surprise, the train left on time and was soon steaming out through Battersea's tangle of bridges and lines.

Working his way through the newspaper, he realized that wishful thinking was already taking over from truth. The words in the headlines—"airships," "mine laying," "Belgium"—told their own story, but a long piece on how hard the British had worked for peace seemed pathetically self-righteous. Another article claimed that Americans were as supportive of the British cause as were Canadians. Some of them might be, McColl conceded, but he knew whose victory the Shamrock Saloon would be toasting.

There were twenty thousand Americans said to be stranded in London and another sixty thousand spread across Europe, and arrangements were being made for their repatriation. She would go back to New York, he thought.

Should he have put in a word for Colm Hanley? Some sort of plea for mercy—that was what she wanted. But how could he have justified it to someone like Cumming? On the grounds that it might persuade his former lover to give him another chance?

Who was he kidding?

He tried to focus on the business at hand. Four lines and four bridges were his best bet. Two men to each, all trained by the German explosives expert at some secluded location in the Irish countryside. Which was why no one had seen Tiernan or Colm through June and most of July.

Why were they doing it? That wasn't hard to guess. They were doing the Germans an enormous favor and proving in the process that they could be taken seriously. Success would increase their chances of having the favor returned, in the form of German military support for their wars against England and Ulster.

He couldn't fault the strategy or argue with their goal of Ireland for the Irish, minus an alien crown. Even Brady and Tiernan's fondness for violence was largely irrelevant—there were enough men on his own side of the fence who suffered from that disease.

But job or not, by God he wanted to stop them. The bridges might blow with no one on them or go down with a crowded train—the latter would no doubt prove more disruptive. Those lives were worth saving, and so was Europe from German rule. There was no doubt who had started this war; the Austrians might have pulled the trigger, but only once Berlin had primed the gun. Belgium's neutrality was irrelevant—it wasn't the Germans' strategy he objected to but their reason for going to war. Which was national aggrandizement, pure and simple. They were not defending themselves, not seeking to spread civilization or democracy. It was only a ruler's restless greed and an officer corps with something to prove. At everyone's else's expense.

An Irish republic might be a laudable goal, but not if the price were a German Europe.

They were beyond Croydon now and leaving London behind. It was another beautiful summer's day, the parched meadows bearing testimony to weeks of sunshine. A day for picnics, not marching to war. He knew why Jed had done it, but that didn't make it any easier to accept. He wondered if he'd ever see his brother again. Or, her.

He spent most of the rest of the journey going over their conversation that morning, hearing the awful coldness in her voice, the phrases echoing in his head, like lines from some ghastly music-hall piece. Nothing lasted forever, he told himself, but some things felt as if they were meant to.

The first sight of Arundel Castle, on a slope overlooking the valley, seemed positively medieval, and it was only a few seconds later, when the town beyond came into view, that the modern world reasserted itself. When the train stopped in Arundel station, he leaned out the window, half expecting that the passengers would all be ordered off. But the green flag fluttered, and the engine chuffed into motion once more. Clearly the Arun Bridge was still standing.

They were probably waiting for darkness. Which might explain the lack of tickets sold to Ford, he realized. There was nowhere there to wait unobserved, so they had bought their tickets to the station before or after and were planning to walk to their target once the sun had gone down.

A sound theory, but he still felt a pang of apprehension as the train rounded the curve to join the Brighton line and rumbled across the bridge. Rather to his surprise, there was no sign of anyone guarding the structure.

Alighting at Ford, he found a waiting deputation of six, comprising one middle-aged police sergeant, three young constables, and two young soldiers. The sergeant was carrying what looked like a Crimean War pistol in a service holster; the two soldiers—both of whom looked about sixteen—had Lee-Enfield rifles. The constables—one of whom looked even younger—had only truncheons.

The welcome was less than inspiring, as was the news that the bridge was untended. The six had been gathered and told to wait for "a government man from London," but no one had thought to tell them why.

McColl took the sergeant aside and explained the situation

as simply as he could. "So we must occupy the bridge," he concluded, "and wait for the enemy there."

"Germans, is it?" the sergeant asked.

"Irish," McColl told him. It didn't seem worth complicating the story by introducing an American element.

The sergeant was not surprised. "Never did like them," he said gruffly.

One happy family, the British, McColl thought as he led the party down the side of the tracks. Away to the north, Arundel Castle stood above the town; behind them as they walked, a red sun was sinking toward the horizon. It would be fully dark in an hour.

It was only a five-minute walk to the end of the bridge, but two trains passed by in that time, one thundering north around the curve toward Arundel, the other chugging slowly in the opposite direction, with the obvious intention of stopping at Ford. The central span of the bridge was retractable, but there was no sign of any shipping or of anyone there to do the retracting. A relic of the past, McColl decided, when cargo ships were small enough to use the river.

There was a signal box on the far side, which presumably controlled the junction, and some empty skiffs tied up a hundred yards downstream. McColl drew the sergeant aside again and suggested that he lead one soldier and one of his constables across the bridge, checking as they went for any sign of explosives. He should tell the signalman what was up before taking up position with the other two on that side of the river. "I'm going to ask your other two constables to get into one of those skiffs and have a look under the bridge," he added.

The sergeant accepted his suggestions without objection and led his two charges out onto the structure. McColl thought it unlikely that the saboteurs would approach from the far side—there seemed nothing but open meadows beyond—but he couldn't afford to leave it unguarded. He wondered if he should have cautioned the others against opening fire with explosives in the vicinity and decided not. Dynamite would only do real damage if properly placed and fixed—unless, of course, they had a truly prodigious amount. He should have asked.

His constables were rowing their way toward the bridge against the sluggish current. When they reached it, one used his oars to keep them in place while the other stared up into the web of girders. After a minute or so, he turned to McColl and shook his head. Nothing untoward was attached.

By the time the two men got back, the sun was below the horizon. One crossed the tracks to join McColl while his younger partner remained with the soldier on the opposite side. As the minutes lengthened and the sky darkened, McColl could hear the young constable enthusing about the war and asking the soldier which service he most recommended. The answer, though inaudible, sounded less than enthusiastic, but whatever it was, it failed to deter. The young policeman burbled on, sounding louder and louder as the darkness deepened, until McColl told him to keep it down. McColl was dying for a cigarette but couldn't take the risk of betraying their presence.

A couple of trains rattled by in quick succession, their lighted windows reflecting on the water. As McColl watched the second one pass through the illuminated station, two figures walked across the tracks and promptly disappeared from view. Half a minute later, he picked them up again, passing in front of a lighted cottage. They were just walking down the road.

Turning back to the river, he saw a small boat appear around the bend. It was about two hundred yards away, and there seemed to be two people in it. He had been right about their getting off at another station, but the thought of their stealing a boat and approaching the bridge by river had never crossed his mind. How dense could he be?

He pointed the boat out to the constable beside him, who breathed in sharply and gave him a nervous glance. "Don't move," McColl told him, a message he repeated after slipping down the bank and walking across beneath the girders. "Just keep quiet," he whispered. "And whatever you do," he added to the soldier, "don't open fire until I give the order." The soldier gave him a *Who the hell do you think you are?* look but didn't argue.

McColl went back under the bridge and slithered painfully back up the bank to avoid being seen. The boat was now about a hundred yards away. Would the two men come ashore or fix their charges to the piers of the bridge? If the latter, they'd have to be offered the choice of surrender and shot out of the boat if they refused. If the former, the twosome would be at their mercy.

Over the next minute, it became apparent that they were indeed coming ashore, and on his side of the river. McColl couldn't see why, but then he knew no more about bridge demolition than did the average automobile salesman.

The boat inched into the shore below them, some ten yards short of the bridge. McColl recognized Colm in the bow and was fairly sure that the other was Tiernan. He had hoped for Brady, but life was rarely that neat.

Colm stepped out into the shallow water, slipped a rope around the nearest piling, and stepped up onto the bank. Tiernan followed suit, and for a moment both men stood looking up at the bridge, as if picturing its ruin. As far as McColl could see, neither had a gun.

He rose to his feet, shouting "Stay where you are!" as he did so.

Both men seemed to cower for a second and might have surrendered if left to think things through. But they weren't. The young constable on the far side of the tracks was charging down the bank toward them, as if only seconds remained to stake a claim on glory.

McColl didn't see Tiernan reach for a gun, but he saw the flash from the barrel, saw the constable stagger on and topple into the water. He heard the crack of the rifle, saw Tiernan thrown backward against the pilings.

Colm just stood there for a second, desperately looking this way and that, as if inviting a similar fate.

As McColl walked down, he noticed that the boat had drifted out into the river, still holding one of the canvas bags. For a single dreadful moment, he thought it might hit one of the piers and blow the bridge up anyway, but it just sailed through the gap and on toward the distant sea.

Colm was staring straight at him, calmer now, as if he'd come to some sort of decision.

"It's over," McColl told him, not that there was any doubt. Tiernan was dead, half his head blown away, and so was the young constable. Up above, he could hear the other three running across the bridge.

"I thought you were dead," Colm said, almost plaintively.

McColl thought quickly and by the time his group was gathered had a passable plan worked out. "You get to the station," he told the sergeant, "and let someone know that there's a boat full of dynamite heading downriver."

"Who?" the sergeant asked stupidly.

"Your superiors, the army, someone. Use your initiative. And hurry."

The sergeant labored up the bank and hastened off along the tracks.

"Right," McColl told the two soldiers. "One of you should go back across and tell the signalman that the emergency's over. And then both of you can carry him"—he indicated Tiernan—"back to the station. You two can carry your colleague," he told the pair of constables. "I'll take charge of the prisoner."

He hustled Colm up the bank and urged him into motion. The sergeant was at least two hundred yards ahead, the constables still fully engaged in heaving the dead boy up the bank. How was he going to explain it? McColl wondered. A lucky blow to one of his wounds? Cumming would see through the charade, but he realized he didn't care.

"Okay," he told Colm. "This is your chance. Disappear."

"What?"

"Go."

"So you can shoot me in the back?"

"Why would I do that, when I can deliver you up to the hang-man?"

"Then why?"

"Because your sister asked me to."

Colm looked like he'd been slapped in the face. "When?" he demanded.

"This morning. Now go."

Colm just stood there, staring at him.

Caitlin's little brother, McColl thought. He felt pity and anger in equal measure. "They *will* hang you, you know."

"'Rise up, O dead of Ireland! / And rouse our living men,'" Colm quoted, in an almost singsong voice.

"Oh, for God's sake!" McColl exploded. "You're not even Irish!"

It was the wrong thing to say.

Colm just stood there, eyes brimming with hatred, limbs locked in obstinacy, like a five-year-old boy.

McColl sighed. If the boy chose martyrdom over freedom, there was nothing he could do.

The last he saw of Caitlin's brother, he was being bundled into a guard's compartment, on his way to the cells at Chichester. He was sharing the ride with Tiernan's corpse, but not the body of the young policeman, which was still in the station office, wait-ing for transport to Arundel.

McColl took the train back to London, two hours of darkness in more ways than one. It was almost midnight when he reached Whitehall Court, but Cumming was still awake at his desk, both hands cradling a glass of port.

He already knew what had happened at Ford and gave McColl the rest of the evening's story along with a glass of the ruby nectar. The bridges across the Wey at Godalming and the Itchen north of Eastleigh had both been saved, the latter without loss, the former at the cost of three lives. One of the saboteurs—the American named Brady from all accounts—had shot two constables dead before escaping into the night. His partner had been killed by police fire.

A bridge over the Test outside Romsey had been brought down and would probably take weeks to repair. "But if we had to lose one, that was the one to lose," Cumming said. "And both men were caught an hour or so later."

"But not Brady." It wasn't really a question.

"Not so far. Look, I'm sure I don't need to tell you this, but the quieter we keep this business, the better. The newspapers won't be allowed to print anything, of course, but let's try to keep the rumors to a minimum. Losing a bridge in Hampshire doesn't reflect too well on the state of our defenses, and I have the feeling morale will be under enough strain as it is. And neither," he added, almost as an aside, "do we want an anti-Irish witch-hunt, not when Irishmen are enlisting in droves."

McColl shook his head, as much in wonder as in agreement.

"Another?" Cumming asked, offering the bottle.

"No, I think I'll be off," McColl decided. He got wearily to his feet, shook Cumming's hand, and headed for the lift.

His automobile was still waiting, but on impulse he told the driver to call it a day and walked slowly down to the Thames. The Embankment was empty of traffic, a tug leading a line of barges along the center of the stream. Away to his right, Big Ben was silhouetted against the clear night sky.

Leaning his head and shoulders over the parapet to stare at the water below, he remembered the night in Dublin and how lucky he had been to survive.

And thanks to that good fortune, he had helped to . . . to what?

To save the empire? It remained in peril. The Germans might still win the war, and it would all have been for nothing. Or they might have lost it anyway, in which case the same applied. Or maybe, just maybe, saving three bridges would make all the difference in France.

There was no way to know, now or ever.

He turned away from the river and started for home. There were lights still burning on Whitehall and more policemen than usual loitering in the shadows of the gray-stone monoliths. Trafalgar Square was occupied by a small group of drunken soldiers, one gaily pissing off the back of a lion. They were probably leaving for France in the morning, across the bridges he had helped to preserve.

He walked on up Charing Cross Road, passing the theater where he and Evelyn had agreed to divorce between acts of *Major Barbara*. There was a phrenology booth outside—closed, of course, but plastered with diagrams of well-measured skulls and descriptions of what each configuration implied.

Closer to Cambridge Circus, a faint tinkling of ragtime piano suddenly grew louder as doors parted to expel two young revelers. The man was in tails and holding a red balloon, the woman wearing a shining silver dress; they stopped in mid-pavement to share a lingering kiss. As McColl swerved around them, they offered apologetic glances, as if well aware of how unbearably happy they seemed.

He strode on toward Tottenham Court Road, wanting to weep, wanting to scream. Whatever he'd done for his country and career, there was no disputing the cost. His gut and shoulder were aching, but not half as much as his heart. He had lost the woman he loved.